LOVE I

"I don't even know ...

"We're both nervous and unsure of how to act, but we shouldn't be. We've been friends for years."

"You're nervous, too?"

He laughed. "As a schoolboy."

The anxiety coiled in Juli's stomach released itself. She took a deep breath and smiled. "Thank you."

"For what?"

"You could tell I was nervous, so you said that to calm me down."

"And did it?"

She laughed easily. "Yes."

"I'm glad. But the truth is, Juli, I *am* nervous. I came out here because you meant something to me. I came to find a wise, independent, honest older woman who would help me set my life back in order. And what do I find?"

Juli swallowed hard and blinked owlishly at him. "What?"

"A beautiful young woman who could have my heart with the snap of her fingers."

—From "Liar's Moon"
by Kristin Hannah

Harvest Hearts

KRISTIN HANNAH
REBECCA PAISLEY
JO ANNE CASSITY
SHARON HARLOW

J
JOVE BOOKS, NEW YORK

HARVEST HEARTS

A Jove Book / published by arrangement with
the authors

PRINTING HISTORY
Jove edition / November 1993

ISBN: 0-515-11233-X

A JOVE BOOK®
Jove Books are published by The Berkley Publishing Group,
200 Madison Avenue, New York, New York 10016.
JOVE and the "J" design
are trademarks belonging to Jove Publications, Inc.

PRINTED IN THE UNITED STATES OF AMERICA

10 9 8 7 6 5 4 3 2 1

CONTENTS

Harvest Hearts

LIAR'S MOON

Kristin Hannah

Dear Reader,

As I sit at my computer, putting the finishing touches on "Liar's Moon," evidence of the harvest season is all around me. Outside my window the world is awash in reddish gold, bright yellow, and burgundy. Crinkly brown leaves litter the dying grass. On my kitchen counter, amid a pile of old newspapers and dried ornamental corn, a pumpkin awaits. My son, who has diligently designed the jack-o'-lantern's face, is looking forward to tonight when he and his daddy will sit on the deck and carve it.

Yesterday was my son's first preschool Halloween party. Four Batmans (or is it Batmen?), a cowboy, a witch, a Ninja Turtle, and a fairy princess bobbed for apples, decorated pumpkins, and sang "ghosty" songs. It was like every Halloween party everywhere, and it brought back a rush of unexpected memories. Haunted houses in the high-school gymnasium, homecoming games in the pouring rain, and Halloween parties at my parents' house. It's a great time of year no matter how old you are.

"Liar's Moon" grew out of my memories of small-town life of the small, Pacific Northwest farming community in which I grew up. There, the harvest season was a special time. After a long, hot season of field and crop work, autumn was a time for laughter, relaxation, and camaraderie. A time of parades, parties, and princesses.

In my story I created a town much like the one I remember.

It's a quirky, quiet, humble little place where dreams are possible. And where magic exists beneath a harvest moon.

I hope you enjoy it.

> Best wishes,
> *Kristin Hannah*

CHAPTER
1

Julianna Sparks nudged the wobbly spectacles higher on her nose and stared at the letter in her lap. The envelope was a stark, pristine white against the graying cotton of her ragged, patched apron.

She ran her finger along the expensive, textured paper and felt a rush of anticipation. Sweet anticipation. Her hands trembled with it, but she didn't give in. Not yet. A letter from Nicholas was something to be savored. Each one transported her to a magical place; a world unlike her own, where poverty didn't exist and dreams were always possible.

She couldn't stand the suspense any longer. She eased the envelope open and gently pulled out the letter. With bated breath, she began to read.

Miss Sparks:

It is with great pleasure that I inform you of my upcoming trip to Russetville . . .

Juli paled. Her fingers tightened on the paper. She hadn't read it right, surely she'd only imagined the words . . .

She glanced down at the paper again, but the words were still there, bold and black and undeniable: *My upcoming trip to Russetville.*

She clutched the settee's threadbare arm. "Oh my God . . ."

5

Her grandmother, Gladys, looked up from her sewing and grinned expectantly. "That fella finally propose marriage?"

Juli opened her mouth to speak, but nothing came out except a tiny squeak of dismay.

The bright smile on her grandmother's face slowly faded. She set her sewing aside and called for Juli's mother. "Mildred, get out here."

Mildred pushed open the kitchen door and peeked out. "What's the—" She took one look at Juli and shoved the door fully aside. Wiping her floury hands on her apron, she hurried to the settee and sat down beside her daughter. "Honey, what's the matter?"

The letter slipped from Juli's numb fingers and fluttered to the floor. "He's coming to see me, Mama."

"*He?* Nicholas?"

Juli bit her lower lip to keep it from trembling. Even the word "yes" was beyond her.

"What is it, Julianna?" her mother asked softly. "You've been writing to this man for years. I thought—we all thought—you were waiting for this day."

Juli thought back on all the letters she'd written and received throughout the years. Her stomach twisted into a sick knot. All the lies she'd told. She plopped her elbows on her knees and buried her face in her hands.

Mildred stroked Juli's hair. "What is it, honey?"

Gladys scooted her chair closer.

Juli brought her head up slowly. Her mother was perched birdlike on the edge of the sofa, her faded, flour-sack gown drawn tightly across her bent knees.

Juli felt a rush of guilt. Unable to meet her mother's steady gaze, she looked away. "You remember when I first met Nicholas?"

Mildred smiled. "How could we forget? It was when you went to that society thing in San Francisco."

"That was the best damn newspaper column you ever wrote," Gladys said. "Even better'n the time I put a sack on your grandad's head at the festival dance, and you called it a masquerade ball. I still got it in my scrap book."

Juli swallowed thickly. "Well, things didn't go quite as smoothly as I said."

Mildred frowned. "What do you mean?"

Juli squeezed her eyes shut, fighting a sudden tide of painful memories. The night in San Francisco had been so horrifying and humiliating. All her life she'd known she was poor, but until that night she'd never been ashamed.

God, she wished she didn't have to tell her mother and grandmother the truth, wished there was nothing *to* tell.

But there was. She inhaled deeply and looked at the two women who loved her most in the world.

"It was an awful night," she said quietly. "Everyone was in silk and satin and diamonds. I looked like exactly what I am— a dirt-poor potato farmer's daughter. I . . . I had to lie to you. You were all so proud that I went . . ." Her voice faded away as the memories came back.

The Seattle newspaper had been heralding the charity auction for months, promising the most glittering array of society's stars ever assembled in one place. From the first mention of it, Juli had ached to go. All of her dreams of traveling, of seeing the world, seemed destined to come true on that one night in San Francisco.

For months she'd scrimped and saved for the train fare, and when it was obvious she wouldn't have enough, the whole town had kicked in the difference. There'd been no money left over to buy gowns or shoes or those fancy silver-trimmed handbags all the other women had, but she hadn't worried about that. She was going to San Francisco; nothing else had seemed important.

On the night of the big ball, she had dressed in her best muslin gown and proudly signed in as society columnist for the Russetville Gazette.

She walked slowly across the marble-floored foyer, her mouth agape at the grandeur of the mansion. For a split second, it was magical, her dream come true. Then reality came crashing in.

Veiled glances assaulted her, hushed snickering nipped at her heels. She was studiously ignored by the radiant, well-dressed people clustered throughout the rooms.

She'd tried to ignore them. She'd held her head high and sipped the exorbitantly expensive champagne, but the magic of the night had gone for her. Instead of wonder, all she felt was alone and lonely. And ashamed.

Then she saw him, standing amidst a crowd of people, a head taller and twice as handsome as any of the men around him. She almost forgot her misery. She'd wanted desperately to push through the crowd and meet him, to know—just for a moment—what it would feel like to be the center of his attention.

She hadn't moved, of course, and he'd never even looked her way.

After the pageantry of the ball, the charity auction the next morning had been a subdued, quiet affair. Each participant, chosen for impeccable family name and inestimable wealth, had brought one item to be sold. That's when Juli had seen him again and learned his name. *Nicholas Sinclair.* And that's when she'd seen his paintings.

His work had touched her deeply, revealing a vulnerability that seemed wholly inconsistent with the Adonis-like man standing on the stage at the charity auction, surrounded by people who were everything Juli wasn't. In his art, she'd seen the same restless longing that marked her own life, the same emptiness that caused a thousand tiny, nameless aches in the middle of a cold dark night.

She forced her thoughts back to the present, to her mother's sympathetic eyes.

"Oh, baby . . ." Tears welled in the older woman's eyes, "I'm sorry . . ."

Juli sighed. "I didn't meet Nicholas in San Francisco. I never had the courage to actually walk up to him, but after I wrote my column that month, I sent him a copy. I couldn't believe it when he wrote back." She smiled, remembering the exhilaration she'd felt when that first letter had arrived. "He said my comments on his paintings had gratified and, well . . . touched him. One letter led to another, then another. Before I knew it, we were corresponding regularly."

Mildred covered Juli's hand with her own. "Obviously he likes you, honey. So, what's the problem? Are you afraid he won't find you attractive?"

"I wish it were that simple, Mama. I . . . lied to him."

"About what?"

Juli bit down on her lower lip to keep it from trembling. "I was . . . ashamed of my life. Of myself. Oh, Mama, I'm sorry. It's just that when I got that first letter I looked around this house, at the shabby, ripped furniture, and the dirt beneath my fingernails, and . . . I just wanted to make it all go away. I wanted to be the kind of woman who would have *belonged* at that party. I wanted Nicholas to respect me." Her voice fell to a throaty whisper. "Who would respect someone like me?"

"What did you tell him?"

"I wanted my opinions to mean something to him; so I created a woman he could admire and respect. A wealthy, educated, adventurous journalist." Juli saw the pain in her mother's eyes, and it hit her like a physical blow. "I didn't think anyone would be hurt, Mama. I never believed we'd meet."

"Oh," her mother said in a quiet, saddened voice.

"I'm sorry, Mama. I *never* meant to hurt you."

"Oh, for God's sake, you two, quit yer snifflin'," Gladys interrupted loudly. "It ain't like she shot the President. She lied to a fella. Who hasn't?"

Mildred looked at Gladys. "Mom, she—"

"She's just a girl, Millie. Barely past twenty." She shot Juli a wink. "Now, I got an idea 'bout how to fix this mess. You know the Hanafords are out of town on family business? They're usually gone for at least a month." She turned to Juli. "How long is Nicholas plannin' to stay?"

Juli scanned the rest of the letter quickly. "He's arriving late Saturday afternoon and leaving first thing Monday morning. Why?"

"Perfect!" Gladys beamed. "He'll be here for the Otatop festival."

Juli shook her head. "I can't see him, Grandma. He'll know I've been lying all this time. I've got to make an excuse for being out of town."

"Not necessarily. I'm sure the Hanafords wouldn't mind if we . . . borrowed their house. If we get the whole town together, we can show Nick exactly the Julianna Sparks you created."

Juli felt the beginning of a smile. "You mean *pretend* to be rich and educated?"

"Why not?"

Juli's heart was thumping so loudly it was hard to think. Her dreams tumbled back to her, one after another. *Time with Nicholas*. It had been her every wish, her every prayer.

She'd give anything to make it come true.

Still, it wasn't right . . .

"I don't know, Grandma. It means more lying."

"Lying-shmying," Gladys said with an airy wave of her plump hand. "It's magic. One measly little weekend with the man of your dreams. What could it hurt?" She leaned close, pressed a warm palm to Juli's face. "You deserve this tiny bit o' happiness, honey. Take it."

"I want to," Juli whispered.

"Think about it carefully," her mother warned. "Things ain't usually so simple—especially not when it comes to lying."

Juli turned to her mother. She understood her mama's concerns, and if there were any other way, she wouldn't pretend or lie. But there was no other way; this was her one and only chance to meet Nicholas. "I just want what every girl wants, Mama: a chance to be Cinderella. Even if it's only for a few days. It can't hurt anyone, and I'll remember it all my life. When it's over, Nick and I can go back to our letters, and I'll have the memory of our time together. It's more than I ever expected."

"I only want you to be happy."

"I know that, Mama, and I love you for it."

"Okay, you two," Gladys cut in. "Before you get all weepy again, we got plans to make. Work to do."

"Work?" Juli and Mildred said at once.

Gladys gave them a crooked grin. "Course. It's Cinderella, ain't it? We got to turn a few potato farmers into footmen."

Nicholas Sinclair settled deeper into the plush velvet of his seat and stretched his long legs out in front of him. The sideways swaying of the Pullman car and the hushed clackety-clack of the train's wheels grated irritatingly on his already taut nerves.

He stared down at the Waterford glass in his hand, noting with almost scientist-like detachment the length of his fingers and the perfection of his manicure. Disgust thinned his lips.

There was no paint on his hands, no dirt beneath his nails, no darkening of his flesh by the sun. His were hands that did little more than lift a fork or pour a drink. Useless hands.

In an angry gesture, he tossed back the last of the drink and slammed the glass down on the table beside him.

"Are you all right, sir?"

Nick didn't spare a glance at the aging, snobby valet whose very presence was a reminder of Nick's "station."

"You can tell my father I'm fine." Turning, he glanced out the window. Dust caked the outside of the glass, obscuring all but the image of his own face. Narrowed, resentful blue eyes stared back at him. They were the eyes of a man who'd let himself be caged by other people's expectations and dulled by too much money.

But no more. He was taking his life back. It didn't matter what his father or grandfather thought, or what anybody thought. Nick was sick and tired of being unhappy.

In the past few months, the boring, useless pattern of his days had blurred into the senseless, alcohol-drenched cycle of his nights. He'd evolved into the one thing he'd always despised above all else: a playboy. A wastrel. He lived fast, talked a lot, drank too much. He no longer had any respect for himself.

Strangely enough, that's why he was on this train, hurtling through the countryside toward a town whose name he couldn't remember and a middle-aged woman he'd never met. In the past years, Julianna Sparks had come to mean something to him, something settling and lasting. With her, he could be himself. He could talk about his art, his dreams, his restless longings. Through the impersonal medium of their correspondence, he had found a kindred spirit, someone who expected more of him than good grooming and a thick wallet. And right now, Nick needed someone who expected something from him. It had been too long since he'd expected anything from himself.

He hoped that maybe some of her goodness, her honesty and integrity, would rub off on him. She was a woman who stood up to the world and did as she pleased. Julianna Sparks would never find herself trapped by someone else's expectations. She was a reporter, a woman who lived on the edge and made her own rules, and lived the truth.

God, how he envied her.

CHAPTER
2

Juli stood at the bedroom window, staring down at the sleepy little town that had been her home for twenty years. It lay shrouded in darkness, with only the barest hint of red-gold along the horizon to mark the coming dawn. Soon, the last remnants of nighttime would be shattered by the rising sun, and the new day would truly begin.

The new day.

Anticipation shivered through her. Today was the day she would meet Nicholas.

She shifted her weight from one foot to the other, too excited to stand still. Thoughts and hopes and expectations cascaded through her mind. She was pretty sure she was ready to meet him. She'd spent the last few days reading from sunup to sundown—everything from the stock market averages to etiquette rules were crammed in her brain. She'd prepared something witty to say on any of a hundred topics.

She was ready.

Turning away from the window, she looked around, awed once again by the bedroom's opulence. A huge canopied bed, swathed in emerald green moire silk, dominated the center of the room. On either side stood intricately carved mahogany tables, their mirror-polished surfaces cluttered with all manner of gold and silver knickknacks. A beautiful painting of a woman on a thoroughbred horse graced the far wall, its vibrant colors a sharp contrast to the muted, elegant peach and ivory striped wallpaper behind it.

Even now, after hours spent in this room, she couldn't believe she was really here. It was the most breathtakingly beautiful place she'd ever seen. Standing here, she could almost make herself believe she belonged . . .

The secret she'd withheld from Mildred and Gladys surged to the forefront of her mind, bringing with it a bittersweet smile. She loved Nick; she had from the first moment she'd seen him, and every letter over the last few years had solidified her feelings until they were as strong and secure as a rock. As much a part of her as breathing.

She knew he didn't love her and she accepted that fact. She might be poor, uneducated, unsophisticated, but she wasn't stupid and she wasn't crazy. She and Nick could never be together. Besides, whatever his feelings might be, they weren't really for her. She was practical enough to know that.

He was a perfectly cut diamond that deserved—and demanded—a setting of only the finest quality gold. A dirt poor farmer's daughter would never do.

That's why his upcoming visit was so very precious. For the next few days, Juli could dress up in satin and jewels and make believe the world was different. That *she* was different.

For one bright, shining moment, she could pretend she belonged to the man she loved.

The train pulled, clattering and wheezing, into Russetville. As the locomotive came to a complete stop, Nick glanced back at his valet, who was fast asleep in his window seat.

Perfect. He picked up his expensive leather portmanteau and the large wooden box that held his gift to Juli. Juggling the heavy items, he tiptoed down the aisle of his private car. At the door, he paused and hazarded a glance backward. His valet was still sound asleep, his pinched, pasty-white face smashed against the glass, his thin-lipped mouth hanging open.

Nick set his black fur fedora at a jaunty angle and disembarked from the train. He stepped down onto the platform just as the whistle blew. Turning to face the window, he rapped sharply on the thick, clouded glass.

His valet came awake with a start. Blinking rapidly, the old man looked around. As he spied his employer standing outside on the platform, the color washed from his cheeks.

"Mr. Sinclair—!" he mouthed, shaking his head in denial.

Nick waved as the train pulled away from the depot.

He sucked in a deep, cleansing breath of country air. For the first time in years, he felt free. There would be no narrowed eyes watching his every move, no tales being told behind his back. He could do whatever he wanted here, *be* whatever he wanted. He could paint.

Grinning broadly, he turned around and saw Russetville for the first time.

His smile faded. The station, a low, rickety wooden building badly in need of new paint, sat huddled alongside the platform. Two dirty windows parenthesized a cracked, half-open door.

The heavy wooden box slid from Nick's grip and landed on the platform with a *thunk*. Frowning, he glanced at the "town." Two-story brick buildings lined a muddy, pockmarked street. No people walked along the makeshift boardwalk, no horses stood at the hitching posts. It looked like a ghost town.

The sign told him he hadn't gotten off at the wrong stop. Yet, certainly, a well respected journalist like Julianna Sparks didn't live in this tumbledown town . . .

With a disappointed sigh, he bent to retrieve his box. As he straightened, he heard the creaking clip-clop of a horse and buggy coming toward him.

"Whoa, Gladiola," said a scratchy male voice.

Nick looked up and saw an unkempt man seated on a dilapidated wooden wagon. The dark-haired, thin-faced man was middle-aged, with skin that bespoke years of hard work beneath a hot sun. He leaned over the side of the wagon and spat a brown stream onto the road, then glanced at Nick. "You Sinclair?"

Nick nodded.

"I figgered so." He tilted his battered felt hat back and gave Nicholas a tobaccoey grin. "I'm George. Juli sent me ta fetch you." A frown furrowed the sun-darkened flesh of his brow. "No, that ain't right. What I mean to say is, Miss Julianna Sparks sent me round ta . . . convey you to your hotel."

"I'd . . . be much obliged."

"I figgered so."

Nick waited patiently for the driver to get down. When he didn't move, Nick glanced pointedly at his bag and box.

"Best get a move on." George tilted back his hat and spat another thick stream onto the street. It landed with a resounding *thwack* in a mud puddle. "And don't forget that bag. Looks expensive."

Nick glanced into the back end of the wagon. Mud, straw and fallen grain littered the slatted bed. A low layer of steam clung to a pile of fresh manure in one corner.

He winced. Hardly the ideal location for a $37.00 custommade portmanteau. Holding his luggage firmly in hand, he eased the box over the edge of the platform and let it plunk to the street below, then he jumped down after it. The minute he hit the ground, he sank up to his ankles in oozing mud.

"Watch that mud there, it'll suck up a small goat."

Nick slogged through the mud to the wagon and climbed aboard. He'd barely gotten his things situated in the back when George snapped the reins hard.

The plow horse bolted forward.

Nick flew backward and slammed into the wooden-planked seat. His portmanteau slid into the pile of manure and stuck fast.

They were off.

George cast a sideways glance at Nick, but didn't say a word.

Nick shifted in his seat, discomfited by the man's scrutiny. He tried to think of something to say that would break the awkward silence. "Gladiola's an . . . odd name for a horse," he said for lack of anything better.

George drew back on the reins. The big gray plow horse came to a grudging halt in front of a two-story brick building. "Named her after my mother-in-law, Gladys. The two sorta have the same butt. Here we are," he said with a grin. "Spud House. They're waitin' for you."

Nick nodded. "Don't bother moving, George. I'll help myself down."

George gave him a sharp look. "Was I s'posed ta help you before? Nobody told me."

Nick sighed and shook his head. "No, you did a fine job, George. Perfect."

His tanned face broke in a bright smile. "Thanks. I'll see you tomorrow tonight at the Otatop festival."

Nick tried to figure out what the hell an otatop was and why it would warrant a festival. "I can hardly wait."

"Yep, it's a humdinger, that's for sure."

Nick got down from the wagon and retrieved his belongings. Bag and box in hand, he went to the hotel's front door. As he reached for the knob, he thought he heard a rustle of activity and a harshly whispered "He's comin'."

Frowning, he turned the handle and went inside. The lobby was unusually dark.

"Goshdarnit! We forgot the lights." There was a flurry of footsteps from somewhere in front of Nick, and then a candle sputtered to life in the darkness. In the trembling halo of light, Nick made out half of a pudgy, smiling face.

"You Sinclair?"

Nick nodded, squinting for a better look. "I am. Do you have a reservation for me?"

The man laughed. "Yeah. Sure." He lit the other candles on his candelabra and then waddled to the center of the room to light a large brass lamp. Gradually the room became visible. It was a large, plank-floored place with a single settee that faced a dirty picture window. Two ragged chairs flanked the threadbare settee and a low-slung, crudely carved table stretched between them.

The man turned quickly and shoved a damp, fleshy hand at Nick. "Welcome to the Spud House. I'm Jemmy Wilson, the owner."

Nick shook the man's hand. "Call me Nick."

Jemmy bobbed his head and grinned.

The two men stared at each other in the half light. Nick waited for Jemmy to call for a man to take the bags. Who knew what Jemmy waited for.

Somewhere, someone cleared his throat.

At the sound, Jemmy perked up. "Oh, right. I'll show you to your room."

Nick grinned. "Good plan, Jemmy." He held his bag out to the man.

"Nice bag," he said. "Looks expensive." Then he turned and headed for the stairs, talking over his shoulder. "Miss Julianna Sparks has invited you for a late supper. Her da—her *driver* will pick you up in about an hour."

Nick barely heard Jemmy's words. Slowly, he drew the portmanteau back and re-settled the unwieldy box beneath his arm. He had obviously spent too much time in hotels like the St. Francis and restaurants like Delmonico's. He'd lost touch with how real people treated each other.

This was good, he told himself. So what if it wasn't what he expected. He'd wanted to break out of his staid, luxury-steeped life.

He just wished the box wasn't so damn heavy.

Nick felt considerably better after a bath and a shave. The town wasn't as odd as he'd first thought—it couldn't be. The people weren't exactly . . . pictures of big-city comportment, but they didn't expect anything of him, either. And that was a relief.

There was a knock at the door. "Mr. Sinclair? Your carriage is here."

Nick stifled a smile at the characterization of George's wagon. "Thanks. I'll be right down."

"Good." There was a long pause, then Jemmy added as an obvious afterthought, "Sir."

Nick grabbed his hat and coat and headed for the door. Yanking it open, he strode out.

Jemmy was standing in the hallway, grinning. "Hi."

Nick skidded to a stop just in time. "Oh. Hello, Jemmy."

"I figured on leading you down."

Nick glanced sideways quickly, noticing there was no third floor. The stairs led only one way—down. "Th-thanks."

"You bet." He nodded again, still grinning. "I just want to be the perfect host on this special day."

"An admirable goal," Nick said.

Jemmy lumbered down the stairs, crossed the empty lobby, and opened the door for Nick. "You'll like Miss Juli. Everybody does. She's pretty as a picture."

Nick paused. "Pretty?"

Jemmy nodded. "Prettiest gal in town."

Nick eyed the big man suspiciously. "You aren't related to her by any chance?"

"Nope, can't say as I am."

"Oh. Well, thanks, Jemmy. I'll be back after supper."

"No hurry. I won't wait up. Martha and me'll be decorating the wagon for the festival tomorrow night." Jemmy leaned close, giving Nick a proud smile. "The Princess rides in my wagon."

"Really?" Nick banked a smile. "That's . . . outstanding. Goodnight, Jemmy."

" 'Night, Mr. Sinclair."

Turning, Nick walked across the boardwalk and climbed onto George's rickety old wagon. Bracing himself this time, he sat steadily as Gladiola bolted forward.

As the horse settled into a slow, plodding gait, Nick's death grip on the wooden side eased. He leaned against the loose seat back and closed his eyes, listening to the sounds of the country: the slurping smack of the horse's shod hooves on the muddy road, the whining turn of rusted wheels, the creak of the wooden seat. In the distance, he heard the lowing of hungry cows and the whooshing current of a river. The sounds relaxed him, reminded him with every turn of the wagon wheels that he was here, in Russetville, and he was finally going to meet his best friend.

Pretty.

It was strange, but in all the times he'd pictured—or tried to picture—Miss Sparks, he'd never once thought of her as anything other than a thirty-five-year-old spinster with prematurely graying hair and spectacles.

Pretty.

He smiled. Somehow that single word changed everything.

Juli gazed at herself in the mirror, unable to believe the transformation. Her ordinary brown hair was a crown of curls and ringlets interwoven with tiny sapphire-hued bows. Beneath the dark mass, her skin looked almost translucent.

A soft, wistful smile shaped her mouth. Her grandmother had done it. She'd waved her magic wand and sprinkled fairy dust across Russetville and Juli. Tonight, for the whole town—but especially for herself—she was going to be Cinderella. And she was going to meet her prince.

Tonight.

She threw a nervous glance at the mantel clock. It was 6:49. He'd be here any minute.

She fought the urge to wring her hands together. (She was pretty sure it wasn't something a lady would do.) So, what did *ladies* do with enough nervous energy to heat a small room?

In a quick movement, Juli spun away from the mirror. Pacing back and forth across the plush carpet, she said a prayer over and over again. It was, like all her prayers, short and sweet and to-the-point.

Please God, don't let me screw up.

Nick rapped on the door. Again.

From behind the door came the sound of shuffling feet, and then a curious stillness.

Nick tried again.

This time the door was wrenched open so hard it banged against the wall. Inside, stood a stoop-shouldered old man in an ill-fitting servant's uniform. The man's eyes narrowed, sweeping Nick from head to foot in a single, judgmental glance. "You Sinclair?"

It was obviously the only greeting he was going to receive in Russetville. Sort of the country version of "Hello, how are you?"

"I am." Stepping forward, Nick pulled the hat from his head and handed it to the doorman.

The servant looked at the hat as if it were a live snake. "Sorta . . . furry, don't ya think?"

"Psst!" said a feminine voice from somewhere inside the house. "Take the damn hat."

The man yanked the expensive fur hat from Nick's hands. "I'll take that."

Nick stared at his hat, smashed against the man's concave chest, and wondered if it would ever fit his head again. "Is Miss Sparks home?"

"I hope to hell she is after all this trouble."

There was a loud gasp from the hallway. "Je-sus Christ, Jonas." Suddenly a stocky, gray-haired woman in a dangerously tight black and white uniform barreled out of the kitchen and hurried toward them, her utilitarian heels clicking matter-of-factly on the marble floor. The moment she saw Nick, her fleshy face broke into a bright, yellow-toothed grin. "Holy mother o' God, you're good lookin'."

Nick felt an unfamiliar heat crawl up his throat. He cleared his throat and wished fervently that Miss Sparks wouldn't keep him waiting long. This was the oddest set of servants he'd ever met.

The heavyset woman walked over to the doorman and elbowed him. Hard. "Idiot," she hissed, before turning a charming smile on Nick. "C'n . . . I mean, *may* I take your coat?"

Nick shrugged out of his elegant caped black Mackintosh and handed it to the woman. She gazed down at the thick black wool, running her work-roughened fingers over it as if she'd never seen anything so fine.

Then she looked up. "I'm Gladys." She cocked her head at the man beside her. "This here's my husband, Jonas. We're the—"

"Poor slobs who—"

Gladys nudged her elbow in his gut. Jonas's breath expelled in a tobacco-scented rush. She didn't miss a beat. "Servants."

Jonas glared at Nick. "No good comes from puttin' on airs. That's what I always say."

"The only thing you *always* say, you crotchety old man, is 'where's supper?' "

Nick was having a hell of a time not smiling.

Gladys turned her attention away from Jonas and focused her gray eyes on Nick. "You're even better'n we expected."

This time he couldn't help smiling. It was such a damn *odd* thing for a servant to say. Before he could say "thank you," Gladys threw his coat toward the upholstered settee against the wall. It hit with a hushed *thwack* and slithered to the floor.

"What were you aimin' for? The potted plant? Even *I* know you're supposed to hang it up, dear," Jonas said.

Gladys shrugged easily and looped her arm through Nick's, offering him a charming smile. "Come on."

She headed toward the foyer in a stride that would have made Stonewall Jackson proud. Nick bit back a grin and kept up.

At the edge of the sitting room, she stopped dead and turned so quickly, Nick felt light-headed.

"There she is."

Nick followed her gaze. At the top of the stairs stood a vision in jewel-toned blue. His breath caught, a tingling heat crawled through his blood.

Jemmy had been wrong. Dead wrong.

Julianna Sparks was a long way from pretty. She was stop-in-your-tracks gorgeous.

CHAPTER
3

"He's looking at you," Mildred whispered.

Juli clung to her mother's arm for support. She wished desperately that she'd mentioned her poor eyesight in the letters to Nick. But *no,* she'd had to write that she was a sharpshooter on top of everything else. So, now her spectacles were tucked in the nightstand and she was as blind as a bat. Unless Nick was standing more than fifty feet away, she wouldn't be able to tell him from a tree.

Suddenly Juli was afraid. She thought of all the mistakes she could make, the possible pitfalls. She was no lady. She turned to her mother. "Oh, Mama—"

"Ssh now. It's your Cinderella night. Have fun."

Juli forced herself to turn away from the safety of her mother's arm. Carefully she lifted her skirt—just the right amount to show an elegant shoe and no stocking—and took her first step toward the man of her dreams.

Unfortunately, without her spectacles, she misjudged the distance. Her tiny French heel came down on the edge of the step. In one split second, she realized she was going to fall. She flung her hands out for balance, but found none. With a shriek, she tumbled down the carpeted steps and landed with a *thunk* on the expensive oriental rug at the bottom of the stairs.

Nick surged toward her and kneeled. "Are you all right?"

His face swam in and out of focus. She caught sight of piercing blue eyes and a smear of jet black hair, and the colors sparked a dozen treasured memories. She'd had her spectacles on at the ball in San Francisco, and his every feature was seared into her brain. She didn't need her spectacles now to see his face. It was firmly set in her heart.

"Nicholas," she whispered, aching to reach up and touch his face, to feel the warmth of his skin against hers. She fisted her hand and bolted it to her side, afraid she'd embarrass herself even further by pawing him.

"That's our Juli," Gladys said. "She knows how to make an entrance."

Juli smiled up at Nick. "I've been practicing that fall for weeks. It's for a . . . circus act I've been writing a book about. Mr. Ringling has asked me to join. What do you think?"

Nick laughed. It was a rich, rumbling sound that seemed to wrap Juli in layers of warmth. "I must admit, I thought it was real. Here, may I help you up?"

"Yes, thank you." Juli wiggled to a sitting position and offered him her hand. When his fingers curled around hers, squeezing ever so slightly, she momentarily lost the ability to breathe. She wished fervently that she wasn't wearing gloves, that she could actually feel the warmth of his touch. But, of course, gloves were the one necessity in the little charade.

A society columnist wouldn't have a potato picker's hands.

But that was something she didn't want to think about now. She got awkwardly to her feet and smoothed the thick blue satin of her gown.

"Juli?"

The rich timbre of his voice sent tingles down her back. Slowly she looked up. Their faces were close, inches apart. She felt the whisper-soft movement of his breath against her parted lips.

"It's good to finally meet you," he said.

Juli swallowed a lump of emotion and nodded. "It's nice to meet you, too, Nicholas. I've . . . waited a long time."

"I must admit, you're not how I pictured a wealthy, intrepid journalist."

"I'm not?"

He stepped even closer. Juli felt the brush of his sleeve

against her bare arm. "You're so young and beautiful."

"Beautiful?" Juli bit her lower lip to keep it from trembling. No one but her mother or grandmother had ever called her beautiful before. Even her daddy just said she was pixie-cute. She felt a blush seeping across her cheeks and she looked away. "I don't know what to say . . ."

He leaned close—so close she could feel the warmth of his breath along her cheek. "How about thank you?"

She met his gaze. "Y-yes, that's it. Thank you."

Nick grinned and offered her his arm. "Shall we sit down?"

She looped her arm through his. "Certainly. The parlor is just through those doors."

Juli squinted hard, trying to see as she moved along beside Nick. She hoped she'd pointed at the right doors, but she couldn't be absolutely sure. The house was a blur of dark brown wood and clear glass and sparkling light. She gave a sigh of relief as they came to a stop in the sitting room.

Nick stood there, apparently staring at her as he withdrew the comforting support of his arm. He appeared to be waiting for something. For what? she wondered. What was she supposed to do?

Sit down, you ninny.

That was it. The lady sat down first. Smiling, Juli plucked up her skirts and started to sit.

"Aah!" Nick grabbed her hand and yanked her back to a stand.

Juli winced. *Damnation.* What in the world had she been about to sit down on—the fireplace tools? *Probably the poker.*

"H-here," he said. "Why don't you sit here?"

Mortified, Juli stumbled along beside him and sat down on the tufted burgundy velvet settee. He sat in the chair to the right of her. She brought her hands into her lap and twisted them into a nervous ball. *Sit straight. Don't fidget—a lady never fidgets. Smile politely and speak when spoken to.*

The rules turned through her head until she was half dizzy. The hardest one was not fidgeting. It was something that came quite naturally when she was nervous. And right now, she was as nervous as she'd ever been.

"I don't even know where to begin," Nick said. He propped his elbows on his bent knees and leaned toward her. "We're both nervous and unsure of how to act, but we shouldn't be. We've been friends for years."

"You're nervous, too?"

He laughed. "As a schoolboy."

The anxiety coiled in Juli's stomach released itself. She took a deep breath and smiled. "Thank you."

"For what?"

"You said that to calm me down."

"And did it?"

She laughed easily. "Yes."

"I'm glad. But the truth is, Juli, I *am* nervous. I came out here because you meant something to me. I came to find a wise, independent, honest older woman who would help me set my life back in order. And what do I find?"

Juli swallowed hard. "What?"

"A beautiful young woman who could have my heart with the snap of her fingers."

Juli let out her breath in a dreamy sigh. She leaned forward. He did the same. Their gazes locked.

Suddenly the door banged open. Jonas stood in the doorway. Juli couldn't see her grandad's face, but she was pretty sure he was frowning.

"Supper's ready," he growled.

Juli popped back into her seat, settling a respectable distance away from Nick. "No, it's not, Gran—Jonas."

"It ain't? Your cook said it was."

Juli realized her error instantly. "It's only just seven o'clock, Jonas."

"You said supper was at seven."

"Seven means around eight or eight-thirty," she explained.

"Well that's the dog-damndest thing I ever heard." He leaned against the doorjamb, and even through her blurry vision, Juli could see that he had no intention of going anywhere.

Nick saved the situation. "Perhaps you could get us some tea and biscuits to sustain us until supper?"

"Sustain you?" Jonas snorted. "Well, if that don't beat all. Supper's ready right now—all hot and good-smellin'—and you two wanna wait 'til eight-thirty to eat it, but you want a snack to *sustain* you. Missy, your *cook* ain't gonna be happy about this."

Nick got to his feet and offered a hand to Juli. "Maybe we should eat now?"

Juli gave him a relieved smile. "Perhaps that would be best."

Jonas nodded. "Well, I hope to shout it is. Damn rich-folks rules." He turned and headed toward the dining room.

As they followed Jonas, Nick leaned down to Juli and whispered, "They've been in your family a while, haven't they?"

Juli laughed. "You could say that."

Nick settled deeper into the plush chair at the head of the long table and stared down the polished wooden surface at Juli. She was staring at him intently. At least, he *thought* she was staring at him. All he could see was the top of her head and her blue, blue eyes focusing on him from above the ridiculously huge floral centerpiece.

Silence stretched the length of the table. Juli leaned side-ways and peered past the flowers. She smiled, then frowned and squinted at him.

"Nick?" Her tone of voice was odd. Almost hesitant. As if she thought perhaps he'd left the table.

"I'm right here," he answered. *Just west of New Jersey.*

"It's certainly a long table," she offered.

"It certainly is. Do you think—"

Jonas barged into the room. The elegant windowed doors cracked against the wall and rattled ominously. "You want some wine?" he asked.

Nick stared at the old man, wondering what he had against guests. "That would be fine."

Jonas cocked his graying head toward Juli. "*She* don't get none."

Juli gasped. "Jonas!"

He spun on her with amazing speed for one so old. "Remember your allergy, miss. How just a whiff o' spirits makes you puke?"

Juli's face turned flamingly red. "*Puke?*"

Jonas tugged at his white collar, as if it were suddenly overtight. He shot a nervous glance at Nick. "Er . . . throw up?"

Juli forced a smile. "Fine. I'd forgotten about my . . . allergy. I appreciate your reminding me. I'll not have a glass of wine, thank you, Jonas."

A satisfied smile stretched through the old man's wrinkled cheeks. "I din't think so, miss. Very good." Turning, he hurried from the room and returned a few moments later with a dusty green bottle.

He stopped directly beside Nick. "This 'ere one looked the oldest, and that's what Juli tole me ta get." He lifted the bottle and blew hard on the label.

Dust flew at Nick's face in a cloudy puff.

Jonas seemed unaware that he'd blinded his guest. "It's somethin' called port. Is that good enough fer the likes o' you?"

Nick tried to open his eyes and couldn't. He nodded instead. "That'll be fine, Jonas."

"Good." Jonas poured a ridiculous amount of the after-dinner drink in Nick's glass, then set the bottle down with a resounding clunk. "I'll be back."

Nick watched him leave through a painful blur.

Juli peered around the flowers again. "Is something wrong?"

Nick blinked hard, feeling gritty tears pool in the corners of his eyes. Pulling out his handkerchief, he wiped his eyes and shook his head. "Everything's fine."

She immediately smiled. "Good."

They lapsed into another long silence. Finally Nick couldn't stand it any more. "Do you think we could get rid of the flowers?"

She looked momentarily confused. "Flowers?"

He pointed toward the centerpiece.

"Oh! The flowers. Certainly." She got to her feet and felt her way along the table. Taking the crystal vase in her hands, she very carefully—inordinately carefully, Nick thought—moved the arrangement onto the sideboard. Then, with an almost triumphant smile, she returned to her seat. He got the odd, but rather distinct impression that she'd been afraid of missing the sideboard.

"Did you know that this year the United States is producing more pig iron than Great Britain?" she said suddenly.

Nick was so surprised by her choice of topic, he could only stare at her. "Really?"

She blushed. "I remembered you telling me once that your family had an interest in iron, so I knew you'd be interested. Why, just the other day I was reading about . . ."

Nick couldn't believe it. She'd done research to find a topic of conversation that would interest him. At the realization, a thread of warmth curled around his insides. Of course, she couldn't know that the family "interest" in iron extended to stock ownership alone, and that Nick himself cared nothing whatsoever about any metal—including gold.

But that was unimportant. What mattered was the fact that for the first time in his life, Nick felt special. This young woman, whom he'd never even met before, had given him the one thing his parents had never even attempted: attention. For whatever period of time she'd spent reading about pig iron, Nicholas Sinclair had been important to her.

He felt a slow smile start. Her words rambled together in his mind, becoming a swirling, confusing mass. But it didn't matter because he wasn't listening to her. He was memorizing her. Everything about her; the way her blue eyes sparkled with happiness over his feigned interest, the way her perfect, rose-colored lips moved as she spoke, the almost absentminded way she tossed a wayward lock of hair from her eyes.

"You're beautiful," he whispered, surprised to realize he'd spoken aloud.

Juli sputtered something about the care required in handling molten metal and looked up at him. Their gazes locked across the table and for an instant—a split second, really—it was as if they were alone in the world.

The spell was broken by Gladys as she pushed a heavily laden, clanking tea cart into the room.

Disappointment flashed through Nick. He eased back into his chair.

"It smells delicious, Gladys," Juli said.

Gladys's wrinkled brow crinkled even more. "Yeah. I hope so. The damn—er, darn glass is sorta small. I don't know . . ."

Nick glanced down at the cart and almost burst out laughing. He covered his near-miss with an extended bout of coughing.

Gladys slapped him on the back. Hard. "You okay, sonny?"

He swallowed the last of his laughter and nodded.

The maid looked at him, then at her two plates of food. "Somethin's wrong, ain't it?"

Nick chewed on his lower lip. "Pheasant under glass?" he guessed.

"Chicken, actually. We couldn't find no pheasants."

Nick eyed the food. "What are those things on top of the birds—pickle bowls?"

"Yep. They're glass, sure as sugar beets, but they don't quite fit, do they?"

Nick's lips twitched traitorously. "Not quite."

She turned to him. "It doesn't matter, does it?"

The uncertainty in her voice touched Nick, reminded him that she was offering her best. And that was more important than perfect preparation of pheasant under glass. "No, Gladys, it doesn't matter a bit. But, you know what does matter?"

"What?"

He crooked his finger. "Come closer."

She shuffled sideways and bent toward him. "What?"

"There's a beautiful woman at the other end of the table, but she's so damn far away I can barely see her."

Gladys grinned. "Yep, I can see where that's a bit of a problem."

"What are you two whispering about down there?" Juli demanded.

"Come on down here, girl," Gladys said with a wave of her hand, "this here gentleman wants to see you better."

"Oh." Juli got to her feet and made her slow, hesitant way down the length of the table. Near the chair, Gladys grabbed her by the arm and maneuvered her into her seat.

"That's much better," Nick said.

Juli blinked owlishly at him. "It certainly is."

Without another word, Gladys served the meal of chicken-under-glass-pickle-bowls, fresh green peas swimming in butter, mashed potatoes, piping hot biscuits, and applesauce. Then she turned to leave.

Nick got a clear picture of her . . . healthy backside. He bit back a smile at the sight. "Gladys, you aren't by any chance George's mother-in-law, are you?"

Gladys spun around and drilled Nick with her eyes. "You comparin' my butt to that damn horse's?"

Nick almost spit up his port. "Uh . . . no."

Gladys burst out laughing. "I'll take you to task for that someday, sonny."

Nick grinned up at her, relieved by her easy laughter. "I don't doubt that in the least, Gladys."

Chuckling, she left the room. Nick and Juli stared at each other for a long, awkward moment, then both began to eat.

"So," Nick said between bites, "tell me about Rome."

"Ed Roam? The butcher? How do you—"

Nick laughed. "Rome, Italy. You just got back from there. How did you like it?"

Her smile seemed to freeze in place. "Of course, I don't know what I was thinking. Rome was . . . fabulous. That statue of David—"

"Florence."

"No, David. Michelangelo's statue."

Nick frowned at her. "That's in Florence."

Juli dropped her fork. A blush crawled across her cheeks. "Oh, right. Well, the trip was such a dizzying blur, the cities sort of blend. You know how it is." She glanced at him sharply. "Don't you?"

"Of course." He took a sip of the port.

She pushed her plate aside. Propping an elbow on the table, she rested her cheek in her gloved hand and gazed up at him. "Tell me about your painting."

Nick's response to the innocently uttered question was lightning fast. Pleasure seeped through his body like the port had, leaving in his blood a swirling, heated wake. God, he'd waited so long for someone to ask about his painting, for someone to *care* about what he cared about.

For years, he'd told himself it didn't matter what other people thought, but now, in this darkened dining room with Juli at his side, he saw the truth. It did matter; it mattered a lot.

"That article you wrote about my paintings," he said softly, finding his voice embarrassingly husky, "it meant . . . a lot to me."

More than a lot. Even now, years later, the memory of that simple article had the power to warm the dark, lonely spots in Nick's soul.

"You're so talented, Nick. Every time I read about an art exhibit, I expect you to be listed as a participating artist, but you never are. Why is that?"

Nick picked up a fork and pushed the food around on his plate. "You're the only person who thinks I'm any good, Juli."

"What about you, Nick? Don't *you* think you're good?"

Nick sighed. It was a question he asked himself all the time—every time his father ranted and raved and called him a "no-talent."

"I don't know . . ."

Juli leaned toward him. Their eyes met. "Yes, you do."

Her blue eyes beseeched him silently to be honest, with her and with himself. He thought about her life, her integrity and her honesty. Julianna Sparks wouldn't run from the truth. He'd traveled a thousand miles to draw upon her strength, and by God, he wouldn't walk away now.

Her presence, her quiet assurance and acceptance, gave Nick a courage he'd never found before. He looked deep within himself, deeper than ever before, and there, buried beneath a lifetime's worth of doubt, was a grain of certainty. "I could be good," he said quietly, half afraid she'd laugh. When she didn't, he added, "All I need is training. A year or two in Paris, and who knows?"

"Paris." The word slipped from her mouth in a wistful sigh. "It must be so beautiful there."

"Have you ever been there?"

She drew in a sharp breath. "Have I?"

He frowned. "I just meant, you've never written to me about Paris . . ."

She smiled suddenly. "Of course, I haven't. I've never been there. But I've read everything there is to read about it." Her eyes lit up. "Can you imagine the Louvre? Seeing the Venus de Milo and Winged Victory and the Mona Lisa . . ." She blushed again and looked away. "I'm sorry, I must be boring you."

Impulsively he touched her cheek in a featherstroke-soft caress. "Never."

Nervously she wet her lower lip. But she didn't look away. "You're being polite. Ladies don't go on about museums. We're supposed to talk about needlework and charity balls."

"I've never cared much about ladies, and less about needlework. I care about people, about how they think and feel about life, about art. I care . . . about you."

Her gaze dropped to her plate. "You don't even know me."

"Are you joking? We've been writing to each other for years. I know you as well as I know myself. There's been many a time in my life when I found myself asking *what would Julianna Sparks do in this instance?* Truly, your honesty and integrity and fearlessness have been my light in a dark world."

"My . . . honesty." Juli squeezed her eyes shut for a moment, surprised by the swift stab of pain his words brought. Beneath the concealing ledge of the table, her gloved hands curled into fists.

Don't think about it. If you do, you'll go mad.

She took a deep breath and forced herself to look at him. "It means a lot to me that you like my letters." Her voice was soft, with only the barest hint of a tremble in it.

"I can't imagine life without them."

Juli tried to smile. "Neither can I."

Indeed, it was her biggest fear that someday Nick would marry and their special correspondence would end. He was *her* light in a cold, dark, poverty-stricken world, and she couldn't imagine the emptiness of her life without his letters.

Nick put down his fork and took another sip of port. "Tell me something about you, Juli. Something special."

"I want to go to cooking school in Paris. I know it sounds silly, but cooking is something I do well. I love it."

"So, we both have dreams of going to Paris," he said softly, smiling enigmatically above the rim of his wineglass.

The observation jolted Juli. It seemed so . . . intimate. A thread of warmth slid through her, bringing a smile to her lips.

Their conversation spun out from there, gliding from topic to topic with the ease of long-time friends. They sat at the table for hours, Nick drinking port and Juli sipping tea. They talked of many things, important and unimportant, deadly serious and hilariously funny.

The evening was everything Juli hoped it would be. Oh, deep inside her, there was still an ache—a longing for that which she could never have—but it spoke to her in a small, weak childish voice that was easily ignored. Especially on so magical a night.

CHAPTER
4

Nicholas was wakened by the sound of someone pounding on his door. Bleary-eyed, he pushed to his elbows amid the mass of pillows. The battered Bee Nickel clock beside his bed came slowly into focus. Seven o'clock. A.M.

He swore softly. No wonder people moved into cities. The hours were better.

"Who is it?"

"It's me, Juli. I've brought you breakfast."

Nick's heart did a strange little flip at the sound of her voice. "I'll be right out."

"Dress warmly."

He tossed back the thick eiderdown coverlet and got out of bed. After quickly brushing his teeth at the crockery washbasin and running a comb through his unruly black hair, he donned a charcoal-colored wool cutaway suit and hurried to the door.

Juli was standing on the landing, waiting for him. The sight of her was like a breath of fresh air. He smiled.

She backed up, her hands twisting together at the movement. "I-I hope I'm not unfashionably early . . ."

Her shyness sparked a surge of protectiveness in Nick. For all her strength and grit, she looked incredibly vulnerable right now, almost afraid.

She needs me. The thought surprised him. It went against everything he'd ever believed of Julianna Elizabeth Sparks,

35

and yet, somehow he knew it was true, knew that deep down, she was as lost and lonely as he.

And you need her. The second the words sped through his mind, he expected to combat them with cold, rational arguments about how little he needed anyone.

But none came to mind.

Nick smiled at her. "I couldn't wait to see you, either."

A hesitant hope filled her eyes. For a moment he felt as if he were tumbling head-first into those fathomless blue pools. He gave himself a mental shake and moved toward her, his arm outstretched. "Where are we going, mademoiselle?"

Looping her arm through his, she smiled up at him. "Paris, monsignor."

He laughed with an ease that was completely foreign. "I think you mean *monsieur*."

She missed a step, then paused, looking up at him with a worried frown. "Really?"

He laughed again, and damn, it felt good. "Really."

She gave a small shrug and took a hesitant step downward, her gaze pinned on the dark wood beneath her feet. When they reached the bottom, she let out a sigh of relief. "We're here."

"You sound as if it's unexpected. Did you expect to get lost?"

She laughed. "It would not have surprised me. Now," she said, pulling a length of fabric from her pocket. "I'm going to blindfold you."

"What?"

She pressed up on her tiptoes and tied a soft flannel strip across his eyes. The sudden darkness made his other senses come alive. He felt the feather-softness of her breath against his lips, sensed the warm outline of her body pressed so closely to his. The jasmine-scent of her hair filled his nostrils.

"There. How's that?"

"Fine. But what—"

She pressed a warm finger against his parted lips. Then, slipping her hand around his waist, she called out. "We're ready."

The hotel door creaked open. Footsteps shuffled across the wooden floor.

Nick smiled. "You need help to lead me to the door, Juli?"

"Only if I want to find it," was her enigmatic reply.

Nick allowed Juli and the mystery man to lead him across the hotel lobby and outside onto the boardwalk. It was surprising how much he enjoyed the game. He couldn't remember the last time he'd done something so wistful and childish. It was fun.

Suddenly Juli stopped. "We're in front of a wagon, Nick. I'll help you up."

She guided him into the wagon's manure-pungent bed. They sat side-by-side on a rough woolen blanket, their backs tilted against two rickety wooden slats.

There was a harsh *whkk* sound, then a splatter.

Nick grinned. "Hi, George."

A man's throaty chuckle floated in the air. "Hiya, Mr. Sinclair. You ain't no dunderhead, are you?"

"Darn it, George, I asked you not to spit," Juli said.

"I know, missy, and I'm sorry. But sometimes a man jest has to. Ain't that right, Mr. Sinclair?"

Nick kept a straight face by sheer force of will. "Either that or bust, George."

Juli gave a delicate snort. "Well, if either one of you feels the busting urge to spit, I hope you'll point your mouth downwind."

George laughed quietly. Nick heard the creaking sounds of the older man turning forward in his seat, then the snapping *crack* of the reins. There was a momentary lull before the wagon lurched forward.

They bumped along deeply rutted country roads for about an hour. All the while Juli and Nick spoke quietly, their heads bent together.

Finally, George reined Gladiola to a halt.

Nick breathed deeply of the clean, fresh air. He heard the telltale creak of George turning around in his seat.

"Here we are, pumpkin. Paree."

"George," Juli answered with a laugh, "a good *driver* doesn't call his employer 'pumpkin.' "

"Course he don't," George answered.

Nick reached up to remove his blindfold. "May I take this off now?"

Juli stayed his hand. "Not yet. George, help Nick down, would you? I've got a few things to do." She rustled around for a few moments, then got to her feet and made her creaking, thumping way from the wagon.

"What's she carrying?" Nick asked, hearing the wheezing sound of her breath and the occasional *thud* of something heavy hitting the wooden boards. "A cannon?"

George's spit hit the ground with an unmistakable *thwack*. "Ain't none o' my bizness. Come on, young fella. Let me help you down."

Nick allowed George to guide him down from the wagon. The older man led the way across a rolling field, toward the sound of rushing water.

"By the way, George, I met your mother-in-law."

"Course you did. Was I right about the butt?"

"I think I'd best decline to answer that."

George laughed. "No wonder you're a millionaire. Yeah, she has a butt on her, that Gladys, but her heart's pure gold." He came to a stop. "Here he is, Julianna."

Nick heard footsteps coming toward him, and his heart picked up its pace. A foolish grin spread across his face. He was acting like a callow youth on his first date, and he couldn't have cared less. It felt good to care about something again. To be happy.

"Thanks, George," Juli said. "You'll be back in . . . an hour?"

There was a sputtering sound of disbelief from the old man. "I ain't goin' nowhere, missy. It wunt be proper."

"George, we all agreed—"

"I din't agree to leave my baby gi—"

"*George*—"

He cleared his throat. "I mean, I din't agree to leave my *young* employer stranded up here with a fella I don't know nothin' about. Oh, no, missy. I did *not* agree to that."

Nick struggled with a smile. It was really touching the way everyone in town watched out for Juli. "George is right, Juli. It wouldn't be proper for us to be unchaperoned."

Juli let out an irritated sigh. "Fine. George, you go sit in the wagon." She waited a beat, then added firmly, "Quietly. And no spitting."

"Good nuf."

Nick listened to George's footsteps as he made his way back to the wagon.

Juli came up beside Nick. She was muttering something quietly, but he couldn't make out the words. She reached up behind him and untied the blindfold.

The flannel slipped away from his eyes. He blinked hard at the unexpected brightness. It took him a minute to focus on his surroundings, but when he did finally get a good glimpse of the world around him, his breath caught. "Good God . . ."

"It's beautiful, isn't it?"

He looked around. The field was a rich, lush green dotted with red-gold maple leaves. A frothy white waterfall spewed past a barricade of granite blocks and tumbled downward, melting into a swirling, pewter-hued pool. Behind it all was a craggy, snowcapped peak that obliterated all but the hardiest rays of the sun. Cool gray clouds scudded overhead, leaving a series of dancing shadow-like shapes on the surface of the water.

Slowly, he turned to look down at her. She was looking up at him through eyes that held nothing back. In the clear blue depths, he saw a longing that mirrored his own.

She smiled and pointed over to his right. "Look."

He turned. There, in the center of the field was a wooden easel with a large academy board on it. An inexpensive box of oil paints and brushes lay in the grass beside it.

"It's from my grandparents," she said quietly.

A warming sense of wonder crept through Nick. He looked down at Juli and felt a surge of longing so sharp and strong his knees almost buckled from the force of it. Emotion filled his throat and kept words at bay.

She was offering him so much more than she knew. It wasn't just a piece of paper and a few paints. It was acceptance, an unconditional belief in him and his talent.

Such a little thing, he thought. And so damn big. For the first time in his life, he felt as if he mattered to someone. Self-confidence surged through his blood, and its sudden presence was like a bright light, reminding him how long he had lived in the darkness, alone and lonely. Now, with her standing beside him, he felt as if he could do anything.

"What will you paint?" she asked. "The waterfall, the sky . . . what?"

He shook his head. "I'll paint the most beautiful thing here."

"What's that?"

He touched her face. "You."

"There's a bug on my lip."

"Don't move." Nick frowned. The arch of her eyebrow wasn't quite right.

"I think it's a bee."

He added a dab of brown paint. Much better. "Is it buzzing?"

"No. I think it's getting ready to sting."

Nick laughed and looked up from his painting. Juli was sitting on a bright red blanket atop the grass. Fallen leaves in a dozen autumn hues lay scattered around her. She was frozen in the position in which he'd placed her. And there was a horsefly on her lower lip.

"Don't move," he commanded. Setting down his paintbrush, he walked across the pasture and kneeled beside her. Moisture from the dewy grass seeped through his pantleg and chilled his skin. He barely noticed.

At the movement, the horsefly disappeared.

She flashed him a bright smile. "Can I see it yet?"

"The horsefly?"

She laughed. The sound filled the clearing and knocked at Nick's tired heart. "No, silly. The painting."

As he stared at her, a painful sense of longing seeped through him. Never in his life had he wanted to kiss a woman more. She looked incredibly lovely right now, with her hair let down and her lips curved in a smile. And her eyes, sweet God, her eyes . . .

It wasn't just that they were big and blue and fringed by thick black lashes. Beautiful women were commonplace in San Francisco society. It was what he saw *in* her eyes that made her so extraordinarily attractive. Caring, compassion, humor. All the things he'd searched for in his own life and so rarely found.

He'd never felt as free as he did with her.

"Nick?" she said. "Can . . . I mean, *may* I see the painting yet?"

He pushed to his feet and offered her a hand. "Of course. But don't expect much."

She brushed the leaves from her skirt and placed her gloved hand in his. Together they walked toward the easel.

With each step, Nick felt his gut knot up tighter. Nerves twisted his stomach and dampened his palms.

At the last moment, he stopped. He couldn't do it, couldn't reveal himself so completely. Not even to her.

Juli looked up at him. "What is it, Nick? Don't you want me to see it?"

I want you to like it. The ridiculous thought made him feel weak and stupid. "Yes," he said quietly. The small word eased the burden from his shoulders. Once he'd said it he felt stronger, more in control.

"Are you sure?"

He looked down at her, and knew he'd never been more sure of anything in his life. "I'm sure."

Juli stepped around Nick and looked at the painting. A small gasp escaped her. She clasped a pale, shaking hand to her throat. "Oh, my Lord."

"What?" he asked sharply.

She looked up at him through huge, earnest eyes. "It's magnificent."

Nick was so relieved he laughed out loud. "Thanks."

"Is . . . is that how you see me?"

He looked at the painting, then at Juli, wondering what error she found in his work. "Isn't it how you see yourself?"

She laughed, but it was a small, self-deprecating sound that inexplicably tugged at his heart. "Only in my dreams."

Nick frowned. There it was again: that unexpected vulnerability. He moved toward her. Taking her face in his hands, he forced her to meet his steady gaze. "You're much more beautiful than my painting."

"What if I weren't in this expensive gown?"

With the question came an instant image. Nick almost said *I wish,* but then he noticed the earnestness in her eyes and he paused. For some strange reason, this absurd question was important to her. "What do you mean?"

"I mean, what if I were wearing a worn, patched flour-sack skirt and had dirt under my fingernails?"

Nick smiled, relieved that it was nothing serious. "After all my letters, surely you know the answer to that question."

She seemed to deflate before his eyes. Her shoulders sagged. "Yes, Nick. I do know the answer."

He slipped an arm around her waist and drew her close. "Good. Now, what do you say we delve into that picnic basket I see?"

She nodded, but didn't look up at him. "Certainly, Nick. That sounds wonderful."

Sunset drizzled across the pasture in hazy streaks of red and gold as the wagon headed for home.

Juli sat beside Nick, her legs drawn casually up to her chin, her arms wrapped around her ankles. There was a wistful, faraway look in her eyes that roused his curiosity.

"I want to know everything about you, Julianna Sparks," he whispered.

She flinched and cast him a guilty look. "Y-you do."

Nick laughed quietly. "I was joking. I know a lady has to have her secrets."

He sidled closer to Juli, feeling the heat of her body against his. He turned his head, slightly, slowly, trying to see her better in the quickly fading light. She was close; close enough to kiss. Her perfect profile was like an ivory cameo against the darkening sky beyond.

God, how he wanted to kiss her right now, *ached* to kiss her. And yet, for the first time in his life, he was nervous.

This wasn't like the other times; Juli wasn't like the other women. She was different. As fresh and important as the first day of spring is to the last cold night of winter. He didn't want to frighten her away.

She turned to him. Their eyes met, and in the sapphire depths he saw a restless longing that mirrored his own.

"Nicholas . . ." His name was but a whisper of promise, a question unasked. Her breath grazed his cheek, left a trail of warmth. "Kiss me."

He couldn't believe it. A groan slipped up his throat. He moved closer. His lips brushed hers in a hesitant sweep, lingering barely long enough to savor her sweetness. "Come with me to Paris," he whispered against her lips.

She pulled away. "Don't say that, Nick." There was an odd, desperate tone to her voice.

Nick worked to calm the erratic racing of his heart. The taste of her lips, like wildflowers and light, remained on his mouth, the jasmine scent of her filled his nostrils. He thought fleetingly of all the women he'd kissed, all the women he'd courted and sat beside in a gilded scrolled carriage, all the women he'd slept with. And now, just like with all the others, he felt a heady sense of sexual attraction, a building heat in his groin.

And yet, he felt something more. Something so tentative and frightening it filled him with awe. Never in his life had he felt this compelling sense of well-being, of peace and relaxation. Of coming home.

Smiling, he curled an arm around Juli and drew her close. She melted against him. Together they leaned back against the wagon and stared at the falling darkness.

The memory of the kiss was so consuming, it took Nick a few minutes to remember what he'd asked of her. What she'd denied him.

"Why can't I ask you to come to Paris with me?"

She laughed, but it sounded forced, almost bitter. "I'm not that kind of woman."

Nick frowned. It was a pat answer. Not really an answer at all.

An evasion, he realized. Not at all the sort of thing he would have expected from Julianna Sparks.

CHAPTER
5

Juli stood at the Hanafords' bedroom window, staring down at Front Street. The town was abuzz with activity. Floats were being decorated for the upcoming parade, people were running around for last-minute costume adjustments.

Normally the scene would have made her smile. But tonight was a long way from normal.

She hugged herself tightly, fighting a sudden chill from within. Today with Nick had almost broken her heart. It was beginning to hurt just to look at him.

Come with me to Paris.

She never thought she'd hear those words from him. They should have filled her with happiness; instead they brought an almost crushing sense of regret and pain.

She'd been wrong to lie. Terribly, desperately wrong. She saw that now. The lies were an invisible wall between her and Nick, every deception a brick that kept them a-part.

When she'd started this charade, all she'd wanted was a few nights of make-believe, a chance to be Cinderella. She'd thought there was no risk. She and Nick would spend a couple of fun-filled, bittersweet days and then go their separate ways—it had made such perfect, exciting sense to her.

Now, however, she saw that she'd been wrong. Everything was at risk. If Nick found out about her lies, it would all come crashing down around her, burying her in the rubble of her own deceit.

The letters—the friendship—would stop.

The thought filled her with horror. Nick and his letters were all she had. All she cared about . . .

"Oh, God," she whispered. Her breath clouded the pane, obscured the outside world.

She couldn't tell him the truth now, not even if she wanted to. If she did, she'd lose it all.

She had to keep her head up, keep smiling. Keep pretending.

"It's only another day," she said aloud. "You can do it."

But even as she said the words, she wondered if they were true.

Today had been absolutely perfect. Nick couldn't remember when he'd had a better time.

He smiled, thinking about the day, about Juli's carefree laughter, her beauty, her caring. After the picnic, he'd returned to his painting, and when he finished, they sat beside the pool, talking and laughing. They hadn't talked about anything earth-shattering or world-altering; just things.

They'd been together for hours, and yet now, as he sat in the sitting room of Spud House, waiting for George to pick him up, he couldn't wait to see her again.

"Hi, Mr. Sinclair." Jemmy Wilson's voice broke into Nick's thoughts.

Nick looked up. Surprise rendered him momentarily speechless. There was a tall, fat green thing looking down at him through ragged eye holes.

Nick tried unsuccessfully not to smile. "Jemmy?"

The green woolen sack with a thorny crown nodded. "Do I look like a zucchini?" he asked in a worried tone. "Last year's costume was too tight, so I had to make another one. I think it looks a bit too . . . pepper-like."

"A zucchini was my first impression."

"Phew. Well, I gotta go. The vegetables are first."

Nick nodded solemnly. "They would be."

"Yeah, but sometimes the fruits get tricky—and the tomatoes always try to lead." He tried to wave. The movement was a ripple of the green sack. "See yah at the festival."

"I'll certainly be able to find you," Nick said, watching Jemmy waddle away.

As the door closed behind Jemmy, Nick finally let himself grin. He shook his head. What the hell kind of man appeared in a zucchini costume with no stammering excuses?

The answer came easily: A man happy to be a zucchini.

Nick's grin flattened. Suddenly it wasn't funny. It was . . . humbling. He crossed to the big window and stared outside at the slow-moving Snohomish River and the endless green and yellow fields beyond. This was such a quiet little town: a place where people lived as they wanted and dressed as they cared to.

Jemmy didn't care what Nick—or anyone—thought. He wanted to be a vegetable in the legendary Otatop festival, and damn it, he wore the ridiculous suit with pride.

It was exactly that kind of ease and self-confidence Nick had sought all his life. And Jemmy Wilson, innkeeper-cum-zucchini, had Nick beat to hell on that one.

No, Nick thought. There was nothing to grin about.

Behind him, the door creaked open. An early evening breeze wafted into the room, bringing with it the rustling flutter of autumn leaves and the fecund scent of moist earth.

Nick grabbed his coat and turned around. George was standing in the door in a dull orange sack with slitted eye holes.

"Hiya, Mr. Sinclair. You ready?"

"I am." Nick grinned suddenly. "Get it? I *yam*."

George laughed. "Let's go. The vegetables are first."

Juli stared at the exquisite gown draped across the bed. The rich moiré fabric shone like a sheet of polished copper against the bed's deep green coverlet.

She should start getting dressed. Nick would be here any moment.

But she couldn't move. She could only stand there, her hands twisted together, her gaze pinned to the expensive walking suit. Anxiety was a freezing cold knot in her stomach.

She couldn't pull off the charade tonight. If Nick touched her, or kissed her, or asked her to come with him to Paris again, she'd burst out crying and ruin everything.

She'd never felt so miserable in her life. Now she truly

understood why lying was a sin. In the past, her little fabrications had never seemed like lying. The whole town loved it; Juli took the ordinary facts of their dull, hard-working existence and transformed them into a fictionalized fantasy.

Society Maven Gladys Fipperpot Hosts Tea for Town Officials
Elegant Masquerade Ball Held by George and Mildred Sparks
Postmaster Jim Butterman Overwhelmingly Re-elected to Third Term

Headlines like these had fueled the town's imagination for more than four years. Juli loved the challenge of taking the mundane and making it seem extraordinary. And her readers cherished her every word.

But now, looking back, it didn't seem like fiction as much as it seemed like lying. She'd been lying to herself, and everyone, for as long as she could remember.

Now that she realized that, realized the cost of lying, she didn't have the strength to continue. She couldn't see Nick tonight . . .

There was a knock at the door.

She sighed tiredly. "Come in."

Her mother came into the room and carefully picked up the heavy gown. "You'd best get dressed, honey. Your young man will be here any minute."

Juli groaned. "He's not my young man. That's the problem." Her voice cracked a little. She turned to her mother, seeing her through a blur of hot tears. "I love him so much . . ."

"I know you do, sweetie."

She ran a shaking hand through her unbound hair. "Oh, Mama . . . it's such a mess. I don't want Nicholas for one Cinderella night. I want him for my whole life. I want to wake up with him beside me, and hold our babies in my arms. I want to sit for hours and watch him paint. I want—" She spun away. "Oh, damnation, who cares what I want? I'm not going to get it. Not now."

"Why not?"

"I've lied to him about everything. He'll never respect me."

"Does he respect you now?"

"I . . . I think so."

"Does he love you?"

Hot tears stung Juli's eyes again. She bit her lower lip and nodded slowly. "I think he might."

Mildred pressed a warm hand to Juli's cheek. "Then everything's fine. You've lied about *things*. That's not what's important to two people who love each other. So, you told him you were a journalist instead of a farmer's daughter. So what? Have you lied about what's in your heart?"

Her answer was a quiet "No."

"Then you still have a chance with him. Don't let it slip away. Love doesn't come along that often."

A chance. Juli clasped her cold hands together and bit down on her trembling lower lip. That's all she wanted—just one measly chance.

Maybe her mother was right. *Please God, let her be right.*

"I . . . I never lied about what I believed in, or how I felt about something."

Her mother smiled. "You see? Your words showed him the real Juli Sparks and that's who he fell in love with. A few trimmin's like gowns and houses don't matter a whole lot when you know what's inside a person's heart."

Hope spilled through Juli at her mother's simple words. Then came a wave of doubt. "But if I tell Nick the truth, he'll hate me for lying to him." She turned to her mother. "He could stop writing to me."

Mildred nodded sadly. "That's the risk, Julianna. I never said it would be easy. You'll have to decide: Do you want to keep your love a secret and pretend to be someone you're not? Or do you want to put yourself on the line and risk your heart for love?"

Juli let out her breath in a tired sigh. Put that way, there was only one thing she *could* do. "I don't want to spend my whole life wondering 'what if.' I love Nick. I'll just have to risk . . . everything and tell him the truth."

"When will you do it?"

Juli shrugged. "Tonight, I guess. After the festival." Apprehension scudded through her at the thought. *Please God,* she thought, *don't let him turn away in disgust. Please . . .*

"It'll be all right," Mildred said. "You'll see."

Juli turned and looked at her mother. "Will it, Mama? Will it really?"

A sad, nervous frown plucked at her mother's lips. "I don't know, honey. I hope so."

Juli bit down on her lower lip to keep it from quivering. "Yeah, Mama. Me, too."

But deep inside, in that tiny place reserved for intuition, Juli knew the truth. It wouldn't be all right. It would be the end of everything.

Nick and Juli strolled arm-in-arm along the river. On either side of them was magic. The wide, slow-moving river was a swath of pewter liquid edged in ever-darkening green. At even intervals along the banks were lanterns set atop metal poles. Light cascaded onto the water, creating shifting, dancing circlets of gold.

To their left was a huge cow pasture that, tonight, had been transformed by light and laughter into another world. Children streaked back and forth from the food to the "potato-tivities" like sack races, pie-eating contests, and pumpkin carving. At one end of the field was a makeshift dance floor ringed by bales of hay and strung with candlelight. The whiny, high-pitched squeal of a fiddle filled the cool night air.

"I-it probably seems pretty . . . providential to you," Juli said quietly.

Nick smiled softly. "You mean provincial. And no, it doesn't. It seems magical." He turned and looked down at her. "Like you."

Guilt washed through her. "Nick . . ."

He stopped, turned her toward him. "Last week, I would have seen this place as a desperate attempt to make poor lives seem rich for a single night. But now . . ."

"Now what?"

"I see it differently. These people"—he indicated the laughing, loving, gesturing people milling through the pasture, running three-legged sack races, and chasing after greased pigs— "are so much richer than I've ever been." He leaned down to Juli, until their lips were almost touching but not quite. "Thank you."

"F-for what?"

"You've changed how I see the world."

Juli tried to smile, but couldn't. Her heart felt heavy and aching inside her chest. The lies stood between them like a living, breathing presence, keeping them apart. It wasn't fair, not to either one of them. Her mother was right. Juli had to risk it all for love, and pray that everything would work out.

She pointed to a small wooden bench up ahead. "Let's sit down, shall we? This dress is incredibly heavy."

Nick laughed. Tightening his hold on her arm, he led her to the bench. They sat side by side, silent, staring down at the river.

The silence between them stretched out, thickened.

Juli searched her soul for the right words—just the right words. They eluded her. A tiny, cajoling voice whispered in her ear: *Let it go. Be happy with what you have. The letters are enough. Don't risk it all . . .*

She gave herself a mental shake and glanced heavenward. A huge, red-gold harvest moon hung suspended in the charcoal-hued sky, its color muted by a nearly transparent pewter-gray cloud.

"Liar's Moon." The words slipped from her mouth.

"What?" Nick asked.

Juli pointed at the sky. "My grandad calls that a Liar's Moon."

"It's beautiful."

Juli took a deep breath and turned to him. "What do you think of lying?"

He grinned. "I'm against it."

Juli forced a smile. "I . . . I mean, what if you found out someone had lied to you about something important? Could you forgive them?"

A cold implacability came to Nick's eyes. "That's a question I've thought a lot about."

Juli frowned. "Why?"

He tried to give a casual shrug, but the movement appeared stiff and forced. "My father is a liar."

"Have you . . . forgiven him?"

"No. I never will."

Juli's pent-up breath released in a sharp gust. If he wouldn't forgive his father for lying, he certainly wouldn't forgive a woman he barely knew.

Sadness was a wrenching pain in Juli's heart. What little hope her mother's words had given her evaporated. Tears flooded her eyes and she looked away.

Hope had always been something she could rely on, the bedrock of her personality. Even in her poverty, she had always had hope in the future. Now, without it, she felt cold and lonely and more than a little afraid.

He would leave her.

A tiny, miserable moan escaped her.

"Juli!" someone shouted her name.

Juli brought her head up and saw Jonas running toward them. Her grandfather came to a wheezing stop directly in front of them. "It's time fer the parade. Juli, you best run along to Chester's store." He cocked a head toward Nick. "I'll stay with the nabob."

"All right." She gave Nick a last, trembling smile and got to her feet. "See you in a few minutes."

He stood. "But—"

Turning, she hiked up her skirts and ran into the darkness.

Nick and Jonas exchanged sly sideways glances. Neither said a word. The noises of the night seemed to fade away, leaving only the old man's harsh, labored breathing and the gentle lapping of the river against its grassy bank. Far away a child laughed, but the sound was transient, lost almost immediately in the quiet stirring of the breeze.

Nick frowned. A strange sense of apprehension scurried down his neck.

"Let's go," Jonas said suddenly.

Nick followed Jonas across the rolling green field, past the makeshift dance floor, to a rutted dirt road on the edge of the field. There they stopped.

People buzzed like excited bees all along the road. Carefully placed lanterns cast the field in pockets of shimmering light, their glowing centers dollops of concentrated gold amidst the darkening night. Old folks whispered, young ones laughed. Anticipation was a throbbing, tangible presence in the air.

Somewhere in the distance a bell tinkled, then another and

another. The sound swelled and grew and rode the breeze. A fiddle joined in.

"Look!" someone yelled.

Almost as one, the crowd turned. Far down the road, where the light ended and the charcoal-hued shadows began, there was a subtle shifting of movement.

Nick found himself caught up in the excitement of the moment. He leaned forward, craning his neck to see.

Gladiola the plow horse surged into the light. The whining creak of rusted wagon wheels accompanied her every step.

As the wagon came more fully into the light, Nick grinned. The bed of the wagon had been transformed by huge bent willow circlets into a pretend platter. On the huge oval sat a profusion of harvest foods.

The vegetables were first.

After the wagonload of harvest vegetables came a carefully constructed "basket" full of summertime fruits, then a wagon filled with children dressed as Pilgrims sharing the first Thanksgiving.

Wagon after wagon rumbled past, each one filled with a different part of Russetville's past, present, or future. Mothers along the parade route smiled and waved, shouting encouraging remarks to their vegetable-husbands and Pilgrim-children.

At the last wagon, a rousing cheer swept the crowd.

Nick turned to leave, but Jonas grabbed his sleeve. "It ain't over yet."

Nick glanced down the road. "There's nothing coming."

"Wait."

"For what?"

"The Otatop princess."

"I keep hearing that word, Otatop. What is it, Indian?"

Jonas laughed. "No, we ain't too big on fer'n languages."

"What then?"

"College boy like you shoulda figured it out. It's potato spelled backward. It's our biggest crop, don't ya know."

Nick could help himself. He chuckled. "You actually have a potato princess?"

"Here she comes!" someone yelled.

"Ssh," Jonas whispered harshly.

Grinning, Nick turned his attention back to the dusty road.

A pure white horse stepped out of the darkness. Behind it, a wagon had been magically transformed into a huge orange pumpkin that seemed to sparkle with fallen gold dust. On top of the pumpkin sat a woman, waving.

Nick's grin faded as he looked at the princess. It was Juli, and she was so beautiful she took his breath away. A longing ache settled around his heart and squeezed.

He watched, spellbound, as she came closer.

As she passed him, their eyes met and held across the crowd. In that moment, time seemed to stand still for Nick. He felt as if they were the only two people in the world. The crowd melted away, became a distant blur of color and sound.

She smiled down at him. Long brown hair haloed her face and fell down her back like a velvet curtain. A crown of wildflowers circled her head. Her gown had been transformed into an almost magical thing of beauty by invisible netting and colorful maple leaves. Her eyes glittered so brightly they seemed filled with tears.

The wagon moved on.

Nick snapped out of his reverie. All around him the crowd was cheering and clapping and laughing. Slowly, the people disbursed, and Nick and Jonas were finally left standing alone.

"You really care about her, don't you?" Jonas said softly.

Strangely, Nick wasn't surprised by the question. "Yes, I do."

Jonas turned to him. "Remember that."

Nick frowned. "Why would I forget?"

The old man's gaze moved pointedly to the moon. "Just don't." And with that odd statement, he walked away.

Nick was about to follow him, when he heard Juli calling his name.

"Nick!" She waved at him and started to run.

Nick saw where she was headed and his heart stopped dead. "Juli, stop!"

She ran right into a tree.

He raced to her side and kneeled beside her. Obviously dazed, she blinked up at him. "Nick?"

"Are you all right?"

She gave him a wobbly smile. "I'm fine."

Nick's heart was thudding so hard it took him a moment to catch his breath. "You scared me."

She touched his face, gazed steadily into his eyes. "Nick, I . . ." Her voice trailed off. The edges of her mouth quavered and turned down, but she didn't look away. "I love you, Nick. I want you to know that. No matter what happens later, or what you think of me, I want you to know I love you."

The simple declaration breathed new life into Nick's lonely heart. "Juli." He said her name quietly, almost reverently. She was so unlike any other woman he'd ever known. So straightforward and direct. She cared and she told him so. No games, no coy eyelash fluttering, no trembling fan. Just a plain, simple "I love you."

"And I love—"

She pressed a finger to his lips, silencing him. "Not yet, Nick," she said in a throaty voice. "*Please,* not yet. First we have to talk."

He helped her to her feet. Together they stood beneath the huge willow tree. The night-black branches formed a shadowy bower around them. A strand of moonlight slithered through the leaves and cast Juli's upturned face in blue-white light. He gazed down into her face and saw the sadness in her eyes. She looked young suddenly: young and afraid and vulnerable.

He brushed a finger along the velvet-softness of her cheek. "What is it?"

She shook her head. "Not here. Let's go back to the . . . house."

Nick was confused. This ought to be the greatest moment in his life. For the first time ever, he'd been ready to say "I love you."

But Juli had stopped him. Why?

He looked down at her, standing so quietly beside him. Something was wrong. Desperately wrong. And he couldn't figure out what the hell it could be. She appeared to be on the verge of tears.

"Let's go," she said quietly.

He nodded. Silently, together and yet somehow achingly separate, they started the long walk back to town.

CHAPTER
6

He'd been about to say "I love you."

Juli clung to his arm and stared straight ahead, battling a tidal wave of regret. Her heart felt as if it were being torn in half.

It's what you deserve.

But it's not what he deserves . . .

It was that thought, more than any other, that almost brought Juli to her knees. Her pain was one thing; she'd brought it on herself with her lies and her exaggerations. But not Nick. He was the innocent in all of this.

Now it would end. They would make their slow, silent way back to the house, and then Juli would force herself to look in his eyes and tell him the horrible truth. The tiny thread of hope she'd had only moments before was now completely gone. The Liar's Moon had shown her the naive folly of her girlish dreams.

If only she'd been strong enough—proud enough—to stand up at the beginning and say "I lied." If she'd said that last night before supper, even after supper, they might have had that chance she wanted so desperately. Or if she'd met him at the depot in her own clothing. If she'd done anything but add lie to lie to lie.

Juli squeezed her eyes shut and stumbled along beside Nick. Pain and regret and shame merged into a huge, throbbing knot in her throat.

That was the cruelest irony of all. She'd misjudged Nick. If she'd bitten the bullet and told Nick the truth then, he probably would have accepted her. Maybe even fallen in love with her anyway.

But not now. He might have forgiven her letters' unimportant fabrications. What he wouldn't forgive was the past two days. She hadn't trusted either him or herself, and that he wouldn't be able to forgive. The lies stood between them like a thick brick wall. Insurmountable and unbreakable.

God knew she didn't want to crack that wall. She wanted to simply pretend for another day, then wave good-bye to the man she loved and go back to the way things were.

She could do that if she didn't love him so much. She thought she'd loved him before they'd even met, but that emotion was a pale shadow of the way she felt about him now. He was part of her, twined through her soul so deeply she couldn't imagine living without him.

She loved him enough to do the right thing. She had to tell him the truth. Because he deserved it.

"Hey, Juli!" yelled a familiar voice.

Juli caught her breath. *Don't stop us, Daddy,* she thought desperately. *I've got to tell the truth. If you stop me now, I might never find the courage again to try . . .*

George came running up beside them. Panting loudly, he unbuttoned his yam costume and yanked it from his face. "It's time fer the games, Julianna. You don't want to miss that."

She shook her head. "George, I don't—"

"No, you don't, missy. We have you all set up for blind man's bluff." He winked knowingly at her. "Get it? You're *all set up.*"

Juli's stomach sank. She'd forgotten that this night wasn't hers alone. It belonged to the whole town, and they were waiting with bated breath to see her and Nick together. They'd worked so hard, all of them, to give her this incredible, magical night. How could they know that magic and deception were incompatible?

She cast her gaze downward and nodded dully. "Certainly, George."

Her father led them to the makeshift dance floor, where Gladys was standing with a blindfold.

At their entrance, a crowd appeared as if by magic. Within a matter of seconds, the area filled with laughing, talking people. Her mother and father stood together in the corner.

"Let Juli go first," someone yelled.

"Yeah, she don't need the blindfold," answered another.

Gladys bustled up to Nick and Juli. "I'm glad you two could make it." Without a word to Juli, she commandeered Nick and led him to a bale of hay. "Sit here."

Smiling, Nick did as he was told.

Gladys hurried back to Juli and dragged her to the center of the dance floor. Loudly enough for all to hear, she said, "I'm gonna blindfold Juli here, twirl her around, and set her to find . . ." She brought a pudgy finger to her lips and appeared to think a minute. "That package over there."

Every head turned to the large, gaily wrapped and beribboned package beside Nick.

Gladys slipped the blindfold over Juli's eyes and tied it tightly. "All right, honey," she whispered. "Here goes." She spun Juli around and around, then stopped her dead and gave her a hard shove.

Juli stumbled forward. She knew exactly where she was headed, whom her grandmother had pushed her toward. Fighting tears, she played along.

All around her, people were laughing and talking and calling out directions.

She moved cautiously forward, step by step.

Something warm and solid touched her leg, kept her from moving to the right. She leaned down and touched it. Soft, expensive wool brushed her skin, told her immediately whose leg it was.

She started to move to the left, but another leg came up and boxed her in.

The crowd gasped and twittered.

Juli's heartbeat increased. She drew in a shaky breath. The proper thing to do would be to back away. A *lady* would never be so bold as to stand between a man's legs in public.

But you're no lady, Juli Sparks. God knows there's proof enough of that.

She should back away and remove her blindfold. But she

couldn't move. Her breath came in shallow, almost painful spurts.

This was her last chance. After she told him the truth she'd never be this close to him again.

She took a deep, trembling breath and boldly leaned toward him. Her hands searched for and found his shoulders, moving along the hard ledge, and up the fine column of his neck to his face.

The crowd whooped and hollered with approval.

Juli barely heard them. She breezed a fingertip across his lip. He shuddered, exhaled heavily.

Desire coursed through Juli at his response. For the first time in her life, she felt sexy. Her own breathing quickened. Swallowing hard, she leaned forward. Close. Closer.

She felt his every breath against her face, and still she inched forward until their lips were almost touching. Her costume crinkled with every breath.

"Juli . . ." Her name slipped past his lips. It was a quiet plea, a promise of magic.

Juli froze. *Back away now, while you still own a piece of your heart.*

The sound advice shot through Juli's mind, and she knew it was the smart thing to do. She knew, too, that it was too late to be smart with Nick. Far too late. And this might be her last opportunity to kiss him.

If she pulled back now, she'd be left with nothing. Not even the most wonderful of memories.

She touched her lips to his. The kiss was soft and short and filled with all the yearning in her soul. A gasp rippled through the crowd, the sound underscored the erratic beating of Juli's pulse.

The beauty of the kiss, its very perfection cut through Juli's heart like a jagged blade. She didn't deserve this moment. It was as wrong as anything she'd ever done—and after this weekend, that was a sizeable list.

With a pain-filled gasp, she stumbled backwards. Distance, she thought. *Dear God, I need some distance between us.* Her heart was beating so hard she felt dizzy. Self-loathing and regret was a tangible, acrid lump in her throat.

"Juli?" Gladys came up beside her.

Juli forced a laugh. "I guess I'm not so good at this," she said, removing the strip of cloth from her eyes.

Disappointment moved through the crowd in a buzzing mumble. The people got to their feet and stared at Juli. No one moved.

Her mother pushed her way to the center of the room, dragging her father behind her. "All right, everyone, the show's over. It's time for the pumpkin carving contest." Then she turned to Julie and lowered her voice. "What do you want us to do?"

Juli glanced at Nick. At the sight of him, so handsome and out of place in the musty, makeshift dance floor, she felt an almost sickening wave of shame. Regret tugged at the corners of her mouth. "Bring the wagon around, Daddy."

Mildred gave her a worried frown. "Are you going to tell him?"

"Yeah, Mama," she answered tonelessly.

"He loves *you*," Mildred said. "Not some rich hoity-toity writer."

Before Juli could answer, Nick walked up beside them. He looked pale and more than a little shaken.

Juli blushed. "I'm sorry about that. I didn't mean to—"

"I could tell," he said quietly. "I wish you had."

Juli turned away before he could see the tears glazing her eyes. He reached for her arm, but she lurched sideways and hurried over to the box by the bale of hay. "Here," she said, forcing a lightness in her voice that wasn't in her heart. "This present is for you."

A smile softened his face. "You didn't have to do that."

"I . . . wanted to."

"I've got a surprise for you in George's wagon. What do you say we open them at your house?"

It took every scrap of Juli's courage to keep her gaze on his. "All right, Nick. Let's go."

For the first time in his life, Nick was excited about the future, about the possibilities spread out before him. The world was his now. With Juli beside him, he could be anything, *do* anything. The burden of his name and the strictures of his society-conscious parents meant nothing, less than nothing.

He was an artist, by God, and whether he made a living at it or not, he wasn't going to deny his heart any longer. He was going to go after what he wanted. From this day forward, he lived his life the way he wanted to. As long as he made Juli happy, he'd answer to no other.

Juli.

Her name filled him with the most intoxicating sense of peace he'd ever known. He understood finally, with a longing that was almost an ache in his soul, what it meant to be in love.

He glanced at Juli. She was sitting beside him, staring straight ahead. She had that vulnerable look again, as if she were battling with some weighty inner question. There was the barest downturn to her full mouth, and an almost undetectable trembling in her hands.

He scooted closer to her and slipped an arm around her shoulders. "Cold?"

She stiffened, swallowed hard. He thought he saw a glittering of moisture in her eyes. "No." There was a wistful, almost frightened edge to her voice.

A cold breeze seemed to curl around Nick's heart. There was something wrong. He wanted to touch her chin and force her to look at him. To ask her what was on her mind. But he couldn't do it here, with George less than three feet away and the night as silent as a tomb.

Finally, they came to a stop in front of the house. Nick grabbed both wrapped boxes and jumped down from the wagon. Carefully placing the gifts on the porch, he returned for Juli.

When she slipped her small, gloved hand in his, he felt the shaking of her fingers. He curled his hand more tightly around hers, a silent offer of support and warmth.

She stepped down from the wagon and followed Nick up the front steps. Together they waved good-bye to George.

Then they were alone. The darkness of the porch enfolded them. Wind crept up the steps, tugging at Juli's hair. Behind them, a rocker creaked. Crickets chirped somewhere in the night.

Nick had to shake off an eerie sense of impending doom.

Juli leaned down and dragged the wrapped box toward Nick. "Here," she said. "Why don't you open it?"

"Let's take them inside."

Juli's eyes widened. "I don't want to go inside."

She looked . . . frightened. Nick breezed a finger along her cheek, felt the coldness of her skin. "You're freezing." He cocked his head toward the door. "Come on. I'll make a fire."

She looked away. "All right."

Nick picked up both boxes and carried them in the house. He set them down in the parlor, then turned around and waited for Juli.

She seemed to have difficulty crossing the threshold. Her hands were curled into a tight wad at her midsection, her gaze was pinned to the floor. There was a tremble in her lower lip.

He was beside her in a few steps. "Juli? Is something the matter?"

She looked up at him through wide, sad eyes. "No, Nick, nothing's wrong." Her voice was as insubstantial as a whisper.

Nick was at a loss. He could tell that something *was* wrong, but he had no idea how to get her to talk about it. He was a loner; he had been all his life. His experience in talking with women consisted largely of bedroom banter and dance floor flirting.

Maybe opening her gift would cheer her up. He slipped a hand around her waist and led her to the parlor. Side by side, they sat down.

He moved the present closer to her. "Here," he whispered, leaning near her, "open it."

She brought shaking hands to the big red bow. She hesitated for a heartbeat, then eased the ribbon away. Setting it on the table beside her, she carefully unwrapped the gift and pulled the painting from its box.

"Oh, Nick . . ." Her voice cracked with emotion. She moved her fingers across the canvas, feeling the paint as if she were blind. "It's beautiful."

Warmth spilled through him at her simple words. "It's Paris, in the springtime. At least, that's how I imagine it would look."

She turned to him, her eyes filled with tears. "I've never had anything as magnificent. Thank you."

Smiling, Nick opened his gift from Juli. As he pulled it

from the narrow wooden crate, his smile fell. It was the most beautiful picture frame he'd ever seen. His fingertips grazed the intricately carved mahogany. The wood was as smooth as silk. "Juli, this is . . . incredible."

"My father made it for you."

"Your father?" Nick turned to her. "Does he live here in town? I'd like to meet him. I have an important question to ask him."

Juli let go of the painting and lurched to her feet. Whirling away from the settee, she began to pace.

Nick frowned. Her movements were jerky, nervous. She marched from the room, her gaze pinned to her feet. She missed hitting the doorway by the barest of margins.

Nick followed her out to the foyer. "Juli?"

She turned toward his voice.

He walked up to her and took her hands in his. They stood closely, holding hands, their gazes locked, in the middle of the huge, marble-floored room. Above their heads, a gaslight chandelier sparkled and hissed, sending a dozen dancing, multi-hued lights across them.

"Juli," he said her name softly, on a sigh of wonder. He still couldn't believe he'd found her. Couldn't believe how much he loved her. "Marry me, Juli."

She paled. "Oh, God . . ."

"I hope you're crying because you're happy."

She took a deep, quavering breath and shook her head. "I'm not happy, Nick. I . . . I have something to tell you."

Cold fear slid through Nick. He pulled her into his arms, hugged her with sudden desperation, as if by holding her close he could keep her close. Before she could say a word, he leaned down and kissed her.

The kiss was nothing like the others; it was hard and hungry and filled with longing.

"Nick . . ." she whispered, drawing back.

He brought his hands to her face, his fingers burrowed in her hair. He covered her face with dark, desperate kisses. "Don't leave me, Juli," he murmured.

She made a soft, whimpering sound. "Oh, Nick. I'd never leave you. I love you."

Nick pulled back and looked down at her. Relief spiraled

through him. "Marry me," he said again.

Before Juli could answer, there was a sound from the front door. A key turned in the lock; the metallic twisting sound seemed obscenely loud in the silent foyer. The crystal knob turned slowly and the door opened.

A well-dressed older couple stood in the door.

Juli gasped and started to shake.

The woman, a gray-haired, grandmotherly-type frowned. "Julianna Sparks, is that you, dear?"

Juli made a strangled sound of assent.

"Whatever are you doing in our house?" She brought a monocle up to her eye. "And in my daughter's dress?"

Nick looked at Juli. "What does she mean?"

Juli looked up at him through wide, frightened eyes. "I was trying to tell you, Nick . . ."

"Tell me what?"

She lowered her voice. "Let's go outside to talk—"

"No, damn it. Let's talk here. What the hell's going on?"

She swallowed hard. "Nick, have you ever been so desperate for something, you'd have done anything to have it close to you. Even for a minute—"

He sighed impatiently. "Juli, what are you talking about?"

"I love you so much, Nick. So much." Tears filled her eyes. "I couldn't believe you'd ever love me."

Her vulnerability touched his heart. "Oh, Juli . . ."

She took a deep breath. "This isn't my home, Nick. I'm not who you think I am."

Fear settled in Nick's gut as a cold, hard knot. He frowned, pulled away from her. "What do you mean?"

"I . . . I live about ten miles out of town in a cabin with newspaper on the walls and hard-packed dirt for a floor. My family is dirt poor and I never made it past the sixth grade. I'm no journalist."

Disbelief swept through Nick. "You lied to me?"

She nodded dismally.

He tried to make sense of it. "All of it . . . all these years . . . lies?"

"I'm sorry, Nick."

"*Sorry?*" For a moment Nick couldn't breathe. A stinging, red-hot sense of betrayal suffocated him. Then he got mad.

"You give me the woman of my dreams, make me fall head-over-heels in love with her, then tell me it's all a lie, and you're *sorry*?"

She reached for him. "Nick—"

He wrenched away. "Don't touch me."

She bit down hard on her lower lip and fisted her hands at her sides. "I didn't mean to hurt you."

He laughed. It was a short, bitter sound as brittle as broken glass. "I loved you, Juli."

Juli heard the ache in his words and felt as if she were being slowly drawn into a cold, dark hole. She wanted to say something—anything—but there was nothing to say. Her lies had said it all.

Finally he brought his gaze back to her face. His eyes were narrowed, angry. "Poverty?" he spat the word as if it were offensive. "How could you think it would matter?"

She shook her head. Tears slipped past her lashes and streaked down her cheeks, but she didn't bother wiping them away. "You can't know what it's like, Nick. I just wanted . . ." She squeezed her eyes shut in shame. "I just wanted you to respect me."

"I *respect* people who tell the truth."

Pain almost brought Juli to her knees. She took a deep breath and banished it. She deserved this pain, this and more.

Nick pivoted suddenly and strode into the parlor. Wrenching up his overcoat, he started to leave. Then, slowly, he turned back around and touched the frame. "Did your father really make this?" he said in a husky voice.

"Yes." Juli pushed the word up her too-tight throat.

He wedged the frame beneath his arm and headed for the door. The Hanafords, wide-eyed and gape-mouthed, stared at him. He nodded curtly and reached for the doorknob.

"Nick, wait. Please—"

He tried to ignore her, but couldn't. Cursing his own weakness, he turned. Juli was standing in the center of the room, barely breathing, her skin as pale as moonlight. She looked young and vulnerable and afraid. Her cheeks were slick with tears.

Sweet Christ, how he wanted to take her in his arms and kiss her right now.

He had to get out of here. *Now.* He was about ten seconds away from crumbling like old clay. His insides felt dry and lifeless and gone.

She swallowed hard. "I . . . I never lied about anything important, Nick. Not about my feelings. I love you."

Her words drove through his heart like a stake. He bit back a groan of anguish. "Good-bye, Juli." He opened the door and paused. Without turning back around, he added, "Or whoever you are. And don't write to me again."

Trembling, breathing hard, he walked away from her and shut the door behind him.

CHAPTER
7

The train rolled out of Russetville and hurtled through the stark, autumn-draped landscape. Field after field sped past the window in a golden blur. Nick settled deeper in his chair and stretched his legs out.

He closed his eyes, tried to force himself to relax.

It was impossible. The scene last night kept churning through his mind. Juli's words matched the whirring clackety-clack of the train wheels and thundered through his brain.

I didn't lie about the important things, Nick. I love you, love you, love you, love—

"Enough!" Nick sat upright in his chair.

He had to let go of this obsession, had to forget about Juli. Last night he'd tossed and turned in his lonely hotel bed. Aching for the respite of sleep, oblivion, he'd found that slumber was irritatingly beyond his grasp. Every time he closed his eyes, he thought about her. About the smile that came so easily to her mouth, the softness of her lips, the gentleness of her touch. About the way her eyes lit up when she saw his painting.

A lie, he thought for the thousandth time. It was all a lie.

He rubbed the bridge of his nose and sighed raggedly. He felt drained, as if the life had been sucked from his veins and left him stranded in a dead, useless shell of a body.

How could she think so little of him? That was the question that haunted him most. He'd offered her everything that he was and everything he could be. His past, present, and future. He'd never allowed himself to be so vulnerable with a woman—with anyone. He'd bared his very soul.

She'd taken it, curled her little fingers around it, and offered him nothing but meaningless words and gilt-tongued lies in return.

Sweet Jesus, it hurt . . .

He felt so damned empty inside.

"Get used to it, Sinclair," he said bitterly. "You're going back to your old life."

Juli nudged the wobbly, wire-rimmed spectacles higher on her nose and re-read the words she'd just written. A small frown tugged at her mouth. Her heart just wasn't in it any longer.

"You settled on a story?" her grandmother asked quietly.

Juli shook her head. "I can't seem to do it anymore."

Mildred set down her cup of coffee and moved over to the settee. She sat down beside Juli. "Last time we all got together in the middle of the day your headline was: *Society Maven Gladys Fipperpot Hosts Elegant Tea for Town Officials.* How about something like that?"

"I don't think so, Mama."

Mildred cast a worried glance at Gladys, who only shrugged.

"I saw that," Juli said. "I'm depressed, not blind."

Gladys put down her knitting. "I shoulda wired Kate Hanaford about our plan. She was sick to death about ruinin' your special time."

"It wasn't Mrs. Hanaford who caused the problems, Grandma," Juli said softly.

Gladys frowned. "I didn't figure on him leavin' like that."

"Me neither," Mildred agreed. "I thought he'd at least stick around long enough for an explanation."

Juli appreciated the effort her mother and grandmother were making, but it didn't matter anymore. Nick was gone. He'd left on the early train, and he wasn't coming back. Tears scalded her eyes; she held them back by sheer force of will. She was sick to death of crying. She'd done nothing else all night.

"What explanation was there?" she said. "I lied."

Gladys snorted. "Hell's bells, so what? If he really loved you, he'd have stuck around."

Juli's head snapped up. The tears she'd been holding back squeezed past her lashes and streaked down her cheeks. She threw down her pen and raced for the quiet sanctity of her bedroom, slamming her door shut behind her.

"Good job, Mom," Mildred said.

Gladys sighed. "Aw, hell."

Nick glanced out the window, searching for something—anything, damn it—to take his mind off the pain of her betrayal.

The countryside was a golden-green blur with a steel gray edge of clouds and sky. As he stared, unseeing, into the fields, the train began to slow. It huffed and clanged into a tiny, ramshackle town that could have been Russetville.

A dirty, pockmarked road unfurled along a silver-bright stream. Whitewashed wooden buildings squatted along the street like mismatched building blocks.

Nick's gaze cut across the river, where a farmhouse lay shrouded in early morning mist. A small, unkempt clapboard house sat naked amidst a rutted, brown-earthed field. There were no shutters on the windows, and the door hung at a cockeyed angle from a single hinge.

Nick sat up straighter. A small frown worked its way across his brow. The horse—there was only one—stood huddled alongside a thin-trunked maple tree, his big black hindquarters backed against the wind. Gaping holes mottled the barn, providing little or no shelter from the elements.

But it was the house that held Nick's attention. It was small, smaller than Nick's bedroom at home. Moss furred the slanted wooden roof.

He didn't need to go inside to know that newspaper lined the walls and dirt made up the floor. What must it be like to live in such a place?

He began slowly to understand, and it made him feel sick inside. It wasn't that Juli underestimated him. It was more simple than that, more basic. She was ashamed.

I couldn't believe you'd ever love someone like me, Nick . . .
Her words came back to him, wrenching in their shame and anguish.

He banged his head against the window and closed his eyes, feeling ashamed of himself. What an idiot he'd been. What a goddamn, thick-headed, egocentric idiot. All he'd thought about was *his* pain, *his* anger.

He glanced at the letter lying in the seat beside him. George had given it to him this morning, when he'd driven Nick to the train station. But Nick hadn't bothered to read it. He'd been too steeped, too mired, in his own self righteous pain.

He picked it up, running his fingertips atop the bumpy, porous paper. Then he took a quick breath, broke the seal, and began to read.

My dear Nicholas:
I can only say again how sorry I am for hurting you. It is yet another shame I must bear. You are, even now, the most precious part of my life, and I would rather die than hurt you. But, of course, words are cheap, and mine most of all. I won't bother you with my remorse and regret.
The purpose of this last letter is to tell you to keep painting. You said once that you came to Julianna Sparks for advice. Allow me to give this final bit to you: You have a great talent, a rare gift. Do not squander it.
With the love in my heart,
Julianna Elizabeth Sparks

Nick squeezed his eyes shut. Even now, in the midst of her own obvious pain and shame, she was worried about Nick.

He slowly opened his eyes. And saw the frame she'd given him.

It was still flawlessly beautiful. But now it was something else, something that twisted Nick's heart. *Empty.* Without a painting to lend it color and vitality, it was a lifeless, useless piece of carved wood.

Like Nick without Juli in his life.

Outside, a storm raged. Wind pounded at the thin-paned glass and howled through the rafters overhead, but inside the Sparks' home, it was warm and cozy.

Mildred bustled from the hot kitchen, carrying a platter of squash. The sweet, brown-sugary scent filled the small, dark room. She set it down on the dining table alongside a perfectly cooked turkey. "Light a few lamps, will you, George?"

George lit the hanging brass lantern in the living room and the one suspended above the dinner table. Then he lit a couple of candles and set them on the cracked piecrust table by the settee.

"You gonna cut the damn bird, or set the house on fire?" Jonas grumbled.

Gladys elbowed her husband. "Shut up you mean-spirited old man. We're tryin' to make the place festive for Juli."

Jonas sighed and propped a wrinkled cheek in his palm. An unfamiliar sadness settled on his wizened face. "How is she?"

Gladys shook her head. "Not good. She's been holed up in that room o' hers all day."

All four of them cast worried glances at Juli's bedroom door.

"Go get her," Mildred mouthed to her husband, taking her seat across from Jonas.

George gave his wife a hesitant look and glanced at the closed door. Then, slowly, he crossed the room and knocked. "It's time for supper, honey."

"I'm not hungry, Daddy."

He leaned closer to the door. "Your mother and grandmother worked really hard on this meal. Please, come out."

After a seemingly endless moment, the doorknob turned.

At the dinner table, Gladys, Jonas, and Mildred drew in a collective breath.

Juli opened the door and came out. "Hi, Daddy."

George smiled, though his heart felt as if it were breaking. "Hi, pumpkin."

She glanced over at the rest of her family at the table. "Sure smells good." It was a feeble attempt at normalcy, but no one cared.

Gladys touched the chair beside her. "Come on, honey."

Juli went to the table and sat down. Her back was to the front door, with Gladys and Jonas on one side of the table, and Daddy and Mama on the other. The family joined hands for prayer time, then George stood to carve the bird.

Before his knife even touched the turkey, there was a rattling burst of thunder. Wind whipped the front door open and extinguished the lanterns and candles. Darkness swallowed the room.

Gladys lurched to her feet and re-lit the lantern above the table. A movement caught her eye and she turned toward the now open door.

"Oh, my God!" she screeched. Her fork clattered to the table.

Jonas followed her gaze and got slowly to his feet. "Well, I'll be damned."

George grinned. "I told them to cook extra."

Mildred started to cry.

Juli glanced at the faces around her. "What in the world is going on?"

"Turn around, Juli."

Juli froze. The soft, rich voice wrapped her in warmth and longing. "Nick?" His name slipped from her lips, alone, with nothing to follow it.

Slowly, shaking, she got to her feet and turned around. He was standing in the doorway, hat in hand.

Juli was too stunned to move. She just stood there, gape-mouthed, afraid to believe it was really him.

He grinned at her. "Being poor was the secret, right? I mean, you aren't hiding something else, are you?"

She shook her head and self-consciously removed her spectacles.

"Put them back on," he said.

"But, I look—"

"Beautiful. Now put them on. I want you to see my face when I say I love you."

Juli gasped.

His features softened. "I love you, Juli. Marry me."

Juli's spell snapped. With a strangled cry of joy, she ran to Nick and threw herself in his arms. He held her tightly and there, in the midst of a dark, shabby room with the scent of turkey and trimmings thick in the air and her family looking on, he kissed her.

It was a kiss that lasted all the way to Paris.

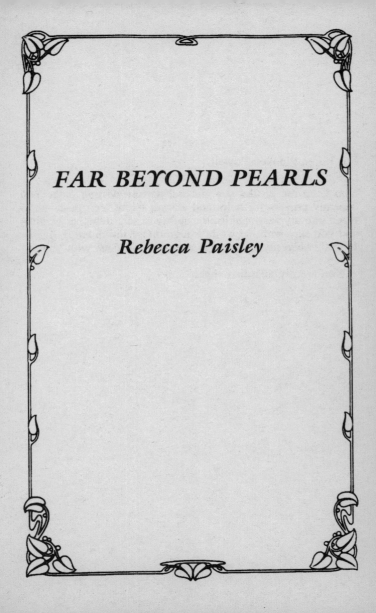

FAR BEYOND PEARLS

Rebecca Paisley

For Karen Plunkett-Powell

You keep me on the straight and narrow writing path. You hear my prayers for help, and answer them. You push me to reach into my very soul for the ability to soar to higher heights, and you stay with me while I begin those intimidating flights. Indeed, when my own wings tire, you carry me with yours.

You are my guardian angel.

Dearest Reader,

When my editor asked me to write a "Dear Reader" letter that described what I liked about autumn, I thought of pumpkins. There are pretty pumpkins, and there are ugly ones. At the pumpkin patch, the ugly ones are always pushed away from the mountain of pretty ones.

There are very few people in the world who can actually feel sorry for an ugly pumpkin.

We do.

So, my kids and I pick out the most pitiful one, the one no one on earth would want to buy. It's the misfit, the one that won't stand upright, but rolls to its side. It also has big brown dry patches all over it, and its stem has cracked off. We bring it home to carve. For as long as I have been carving pumpkins, I have never been able to cut out the eyes right. I always get them too close together, whereupon the section that divides them breaks. As a result, our pumpkins have one huge oval eye, rather than two round ones. In essence, we have Cyclops pumpkins.

In keeping with the compassion I feel for outcast pumpkins, "Far Beyond Pearls" is about four misfit people rejected by society. I hope you enjoy reading it as much as I liked writing it for you.

May the fall season bring you cool autumn breezes, beautiful red and yellow leaves, lots of Halloween candy, a succulent Thanksgiving turkey, and of course, sympathy for ugly pumpkins.

> Love,
> *Rebecca Paisley*

CHAPTER
1

"Maisie!" Dilly called out when he saw his older sister emerge from the shelter of the thick pine forest and head to the road. "They catched a real live wild *Indian* from the west! Hurry!"

Maisie Applejack stopped; her worn boots crunched into the brittle pine straw that edged the dirt road, and her heavy egg basket swung from the crook of her elbow. She didn't understand a word of Dilly's ranting, but when she looked beyond him, she realized something was happening at the mercantile. It seemed like every one of Snickle's Corner's ninety-eight citizens was standing in front of the general store. Some were pointing. Others were murmuring. All were staring.

At what? Confused, Maisie watched her two younger brothers, Dilly and Dally, leave the excited throng of people and dash across the muddy town square.

Dally leaped over a horse trough. "He's the *scalpin'* kind, Maisie!"

"And he's in a *cage*!" Dilly yelled.

Heaving with exertion, Dally approached a pile of wooden crates and prepared to jump it. Dilly reached it at the same moment. In midair the boys collided, then smashed into the crates. Tangled in a tight ball of flailing limbs, they rolled directly into a horse paddock, which caused the wild stallion inside to rear and buck. The boys were barely out of the paddock before the vicious steed came racing toward them. The huge horse came to an abrupt halt at the fence, snorting and pawing the ground.

Maisie gave a deep sigh. "Lord," she whispered, "Y'know I love my brothers nearly to death, but they're two o' the clumsiest youngsters You ever blew breath into."

"Maisie!" the boys chorused, both intent on being the first to tell her the thrilling story.

"A Indian!" Dally scrambled off the ground. "He—"

"The Snickles catched him and brung him into town!" Dilly added hysterically. "Dammit to hell, Dally, git off my hand!"

Dally hopped off his brother's hand and sped toward Maisie. "Mr. Snickle's fixin' to take off the cloth that's coverin' up the Indian's cage!"

Maisie had no time to dodge out of the way before Dally plowed into her. He wrapped his arms around her waist, his grubby fingers closing around the blond curls that streamed down her back. "Dally!" she scolded, holding her basket high above her head. "I cain't sell these eggs if y'break 'em! Stop—"

"He ain't one o' them peaceful, farmin' kind o' Indians neither, Maisie!" Dally let go of her waist and started tugging at her tattered skirts. "He's the *fightin'* kind! He's—"

"He's the kind that has them weird names like Snake-Go-a-Slitherin', and . . . and Real-Riled-River!" Not to be outdone by his brother, Dilly already had his fingers between the waistband of Maisie's skirt, and he, too, began to pull.

Maisie had no choice but to follow them to the mercantile. When they arrived, she attempted a friendly smile, hoping just this once someone in the cluster of townspeople might return it.

Naomi Potter and Eula Birch sniffed in disgust. Jed Nolly spat at her feet, and his two children, Abigail and Timmy, stuck their tongues out at her. The rest of the people in the crowd quickly turned their backs. Used to being ostracized, Maisie tried to squelch the hurt that rose within her. But it wasn't easy. Everyone save Reverend Jenkins rejected the Applejack family.

Maisie didn't like to recall the reasons why.

"Maisie, here comes Mr. Snickle," Dally whispered, squeezing her hand.

She watched the fat and pompous man strut out of the store and pat the thick white tufts of hair at his temples. His youngest boys, Wade and Rudy, walked beside him. Following were his two older sons, Cooper and Newton, who leered at her.

She cringed and looked away. For the very reasons everyone else shunned her, Cooper and Newton vied for her company. Shame still stained her cheeks as she gave her full attention to their father.

"Citizens of Snickle's Corner!" Burt Snickle shouted, holding up his pudgy right hand in a plea for silence. "As you all know, there has been a rash of bank robberies around here, all staged by that murderous thief, Smokey Joe, the same man who shot and killed that young girl over in Squirrel River last month. You are also aware that my boys and I left town a week ago to hunt the vicious criminal down. We'd vowed to catch Smokey Joe before he had the chance to sneak into Snickle's Corner!"

"What's that got to do with the Indian, Burt?" Les Winkler hollered. "And when are we going to get a good look at him?"

Irritated that Les had interrupted his oration, Burt stomped off the porch. In a dramatic gesture, he swept his arm toward the cage. "You've all read in the paper about how the Indians out west are being rounded up, stuffed into trains, and being sent to various reservations. About two weeks ago an Apache-laden train on its way to a Florida camp made a short stop, and one of the warriors escaped. A whole regiment of soldiers has been searching for that Indian, but it was Cooper, Newton, and I who finally captured him. Even after traveling some two hundred miles on foot, the warrior fought like something straight out of hell, but my brave sons and I succeeded in subduing him."

He paused briefly to revel in the murmurs of admiration. "Now, I must warn the ladies present that what you are about to see might shock some of you. The devil's half-naked." He reached for a corner of the cloth that covered the cage, and with one strong tug, he pulled it off.

Loud gasps and muffled shrieks filled the air. The men in the crowd pressed forward for a closer look; the women shrank back.

Maisie did neither. Instantly nausea assailed her, but she was unable to tear her eyes away from the appalling sight.

The warrior sat as still and tall as the cramped space and his numerous injuries would allow. A long gash on his arm oozed with blood that trickled down to his hand, seeped through his fingers, and stained the buckskin garment he wore around his loins. His coal-black hair fell to his waist, a few waves sticking to the cuts that marred his bare chest.

Maisie knew from the crisscross pattern of those wounds that he'd been whipped with a lash. She couldn't fathom the pain he must have suffered . . .

. . . until she looked into his eyes.

Within those unblinking ebony orbs, she saw an agony deeper than any physical injury could ever cause.

Misery stemmed straight from his soul, and the moment that truth hit her, Maisie forgot he was of a race she was supposed to fear and hate. All she saw was a man who clung to his last shred of pride, who had not a friend to his name or a hope in his heart.

And she understood exactly how he felt.

"Oh, Maisie," Dilly whispered, peering up into her vivid blue eyes. "He's bleedin'."

"Is . . . is he gonna die?" Dally asked shakily.

Hissing between her gritted teeth, Maisie handed Dally her egg basket and shoved people aside as she weaved her way toward the cage. "You meaner'n a bee-stinged *dog*!" she yelled at Burt Snickle. "For God's sake, let him go!"

"For *God's* sake?" Burt repeated and chuckled. "Miss Apple-jack, the good Lord probably rues the day He ever thought to create Indians. It's up to God-fearing people like us to help Him mend His error!" Still snickering, he motioned for his four sons to join him by the cage. "Go on, boys. Show everyone how dangerous this warrior really is."

Little Wade and Rudy began pitching sharp stones at the prisoner, giggling each time one of the rocks bit into his flesh.

The warrior remained motionless, his eyes focused on the endless sky.

Cooper brushed his younger brothers away. Sneering, he rammed the barrel of his rifle between the bars of the cage and into the Indian's shoulders, chest, and stomach.

Horrified, Maisie waited to hear the warrior's scream.

He didn't utter a sound.

Several men in the crowd laughed. "*That's* the man who fought like something out of hell?" Jed Nolly called out. "I've seen butterflies more dangerous than your Apache, Burt!"

"Get out of the way, Cooper," Newton ordered his brother. "*I'll* get him to fight." He pulled a cigar from his shirt pocket and lit it. After sucking on it until the tip glowed a bright orange red, he held it out for the crowd to see.

When Maisie realized his cruel intentions, she lunged toward him, but Cooper caught her by the waist and held her snugly to his frame. Tears sprang to her eyes as she watched Newton press the smoldering cigar into the Indian's bare thigh.

The crowd stilled and quieted. The only sound was a sickening sizzle as the cigar slowly, steadily burned into the warrior's skin.

And yet his sole reaction was the ominous glitter within his black eyes.

Determined to prove the Indian's fierceness, Burt snatched a long skinning knife from his belt. "Step aside, sons."

As Cooper moved to make room for his father, Maisie seized the chance to break away. She succeeded, and once free, she quickly retrieved her basket from Dally and withdrew two eggs.

The first splattered on the back of Burt's head; the next broke over the blade of his knife. Before he had time to understand what was happening, a third cracked on his cheekbone.

Quickly Maisie grabbed more, and hit Cooper on his temple and Newton on the bridge of his nose.

Dilly and Dally joined their sister's battle. They, too, snatched ammunition from Maisie's full basket, and with the greatest of pleasure but the worst of aims, they hurled eggs toward Wade and Rudy, causing many people in the crowd to shield their own faces and move aside.

"Get her!" Burt shouted, wiping yellow slime out of his eyes. "Dammit, get hold of her!"

As Cooper and Newton seized Maisie a loud and angry voice rose above the din of the crowd. "What is the meaning of this?" Reverend Jenkins demanded, pushing his way through the multitude of people. "Release Miss Applejack immediately!"

Cooper and Newton loosened their hold.

Before Maisie could utter a word, Burt stepped forward. "Reverend, I mean no disrespect, but this has nothing to do with you. Miss Applejack attacked my sons and me, and we—"

He cursed loudly as another of Maisie's eggs exploded in the center of his forehead.

"Maisie!" the reverend chided.

"Burt Snickle's got snake blood in his veins!" she hollered. "Y'see that knife he's holdin'? Well, he was fixin' to slice into—"

"You've been told time and time again that you aren't welcome in my town!" Burt shouted at her. "We don't want your kind here, so go on back to Applejack Shack! And take those two barbaric brothers of yours with you!"

Maisie saw fire. "Burt, you spread more manure with that nasty mouth o' yours than all the cats in Georgia could cover up!" She drew back her hand to pitch another egg.

Reverend Jenkins plucked the egg from her grip and placed it back into her basket. "Maisie . . ."

She whirled on him, her muddy skirts brushing his legs. "But just look what Burt done to that man!" She pointed to the Indian.

At his first glimpse of the warrior, Reverend Jenkins gasped. "Dear God, Burt! What—"

"He put up a struggle when we caught him," Burt said. "We had to—"

"In the name of all that's holy, let him go! The man needs a doctor!"

Burt spat a blob of egg white and threw back his shoulders. "I'm sorry, but I can't do that. The Indian is wanted by the U.S. Army. If you force me to let him go, you'll be committing a crime. It's my duty as a citizen of this country to—"

"To torture him? For the love of God, he's not some wild animal like that feral stallion of yours, but a human being!"

"He's not human, Reverend. He's a bloodthirsty savage. As such, he deserves no mercy. None at all."

Reverend Jenkins closed his eyes for a moment before turning back toward the assembled crowd. "Go home, and think about your sinful actions of this day."

"But we didn't do anything!" Naomi Potter cried.

The reverend shook his head. "You stood here and watched this poor man being tormented. Christians, all of you, and yet you did nothing to stop the outrage. You should be ashamed!"

When the crowd skulked away, Reverend Jenkins faced Burt again. "In just two months it will be Thanksgiving, a time for peace, gratitude, and brotherly love. And you, Burt, are mocking everything the season represents. Stop this violence and promise me that you will inflict no further harm upon this man."

Burt glanced at the Indian and saw that the warrior's eyes were closed. "Oh, all right, for the time being, I promise to leave him alone." With that, he stormed back into the mercantile, his four sons following.

"Is Mr. Snickle gonna leave that poor Patchy alone now, Maisie?" Dilly asked.

"Apache," she corrected him.

"He ain't gonna hurt him no more, is he, Maisie?" Dally queried.

"God only knows," Maisie replied. "That man's so mean, he'd make dice out o' his maw's knucklebones."

Reverend Jenkins placed his hand on her shoulder. "Don't hate him, Maisie. Pray for him."

"I don't hate him. But I feel powerful sorry for him. A man like him must be all eat up inside. Meanness does that to folks, y'know."

He smiled into her beautiful blue eyes, noting their flash of righteous anger. Maisie Applejack's spirit and sensitivity had impressed him for years, but never more than on this day. Cupping her chin, he prayed she would one day meet a man who recognized her true worth. For beneath Maisie's rags and beyond the stained reputation she bore through no fault of her own, there lay a pearl of inestimable value.

He tweaked her nose. "You were right to defend the Indian, Maisie, but unfortunately Burt and his sons don't agree. You and your brothers go on home now, where you'll be safe. In the meantime I'll keep a close watch on the warrior, and maybe I'll think of a way to help him."

She nodded. But before leaving, she neared the cage again. The Indian's eyes were still closed. "They didn't have nary a right to do this to you," she whispered to him. "But they—well, dumb's what they are. They treat me and my little brothers like this, too. Y'ain't gotta burn, beat, or bloody up somebody to torture 'em, y'know. There's all kinds o' torments, and ever' kind hurts."

She pushed her shawl between the bars of the cage. "The wind's stirrin' cool. When y'wake up, y'can wrap up in this here shawl." Unsure how to comfort an Apache warrior, she patted his knee and was startled by how white her fingers looked next to his dark skin.

"Maisie," Reverend Jenkins said, "he can't hear you. And even if he were awake, he probably wouldn't understand you. Go on home now, dear."

Maisie cast one last look of tender pity upon the Indian before taking Dilly and Dally's hands and starting toward the woods. . . .

Only then did the warrior move.

He opened his eyes. His black gaze missing nothing, he sought and found the beautiful yellow-haired woman who'd defended him.

The memory of her courage blazed in his mind. The image of her beautiful face flamed in his heart.

He watched her until she disappeared within the shadows of the forest.

CHAPTER
2

Soft, cozy light filled the tiny cabin as Maisie turned up the old, battered lamp. Outside, dusk had settled over the woodsy land and with it had come the shrill songs of the crickets. Ordinarily nature's music soothed Maisie, but tonight nothing could erase the haunting image of the Indian captive from her mind or the sympathy from her heart.

A sudden crash on the porch sent her thoughts scattering as she listened to the scrambling of booted feet just outside the door. Dilly and Dally had no doubt fallen again as each had tried to be the first one inside. "You boys raise more dust than Noah's flood could settle! Now come on in and eat!"

When they entered the cabin and took their seats at the rickety table, Maisie set a loaf of fresh bread next to the vase of dried straw flowers and filled the plates.

At her nod, Dilly folded his hands and bowed his head. "Boiled squarshes and onions make me gag, God, but I reckon I gotta thank You for 'em anyway. And do Y'think that maybe sometime when You're not too busy, Y'could let a deer wander into our yard and die? Maisie says we cain't eat our egg-layin' chickens, and I want me some meat."

Maisie rolled her eyes, then nodded at Dally.

"Thanks for the food, God," Dally said. "And please let us do real good in the Thanksgivin' Day competitions this year. Please let us beat the hell out o' them Snickle boys. Please—"

"Dally, y'shouldn't cuss at God," Maisie scolded.

Dally shrugged. "God's who maked hell, Maisie. Maked it right after He maked heaven. Since it's one o' His own inventions, I cain't see why He'd mind me talkin' about it."

Ignoring his twisted reasoning, Maisie closed her eyes. "Keep a close watch on my brothers, Lord. Most o' the time You're the only One who knows where they are and what they're doin'. And . . . whatever Y'might have to do to take care o' that Indian warrior, please do it. Amen."

"Amen," the boys whispered almost inaudibly.

Maisie noted the quick change of their moods and realized that her mention of the Indian captive had upset them. They might be hellions, she mused, but they were compassionate ones.

"Do we have to be Pilgrims again this year, Maisie?" Dilly asked after a period of thoughtful silence.

She smiled. The boys enjoyed watching and participating in the autumn competitions, but they detested dressing for their roles in the annual recreation of the first Thanksgiving feast. "Dilly, it's tradition in Snickle's Corner."

"It's a dumb tradition. I hate them costumes."

Maisie cut more bread. "Y'ought to be thankful that we even get invited. If it weren't for Reverend Jenkins, we'd never get to go. Now, what did the two o' y'all do this afternoon?"

"We been practicin' for the Thanksgivin' contests," Dilly replied. He lifted his slice of warm bread to his mouth and thrust his tongue through the middle. "Right after we got back from town, we throwed sticks at a post. Y'reckon we might win the shootin' contest this year if we can get us a gun? We ain't never got to shoot, Maisie."

She smiled sadly. "Dilly, y'know I ain't got the money to buy no gun."

Dally blew a brown curl away from his eye and pushed his squash around with his fork. "Dilly, even if we had us a gun, we wouldn't win. We don't never win nothin'."

Silently Maisie agreed with Dally. Neither one of her brothers stood much chance in the competitions. Not only didn't they possess weapons with which to compete, but they didn't possess any skills, either.

And as for the footrace . . . Well, they certainly possessed their own feet, and both boys could run fast. The problem was that they weren't sufficiently disciplined to finish the race. Once they were tired and thirsty, they simply gave up.

"When y'gonna get a man, Maisie?" Dilly asked. "Y'said when y'got one he'd learn us all the things that other kids' paws and big brothers learn 'em. Y'said if we had us a man around the house, he'd—"

"I know what I said, Dilly," she murmured, casting her gaze down to the faded blue-and-white-checkered tablecloth.

Upon noticing Maisie's dismay, Dally stood up and yanked Dilly's curly red hair. "Now look what y'done, Dilly! Y'hurt her feelin's! Y'think she don't *try* to get a man? She tries, you churnhead, but she just cain't do it! It ain't Maisie's fault that no man likes her!"

Maisie didn't know whether to laugh over Dally's awkward attempts to defend her or cry over the fact that he spoke the truth. Instead she rose and headed for the door. "Y'all finish up and go to bed. I'll be outside."

The boys smiled and nodded. Maisie was going for her nightly walk, they knew, and her absence would give them the chance to throw away their squash.

"And if y'throw out your squashes, I'll put somethin' on you that no kind o' soap'll take off," Maisie warned. "You two boys are so skinny, y'ain't nothin' but breath and britches, so y'better eat that supper, hear?"

Once outside, she strolled through the yard, grateful for the spill of bright moonlight that illuminated the path that led to the garden. There, she snapped off a hollow beanstalk and began walking down the rows of autumn squash, collard plants, and pumpkins. She'd already harvested and preserved most of the vegetables she'd planted in the spring, and the meager crops still growing were all that were left.

Her boots sank into the soft soil while a cool, pine-scented breeze ruffled her hair and teased her patched skirts. Just as she did every night, she waited for the bit of tranquillity she found in her garden.

Lord knew she had just about more than she could handle, what with trying to raise her little brothers and keep up with all the chores. There was the dilemma with money, too. The egg money dwindled to nothing in less time than it took the chickens to lay more eggs and, she remembered with a sigh, she hadn't made a cent on the eggs she'd taken into town today.

There was no choice; soon she would be forced to withdraw from the bank the two dollars she'd worked so hard to save.

When y'gonna get a man, Maisie?

Dilly's question swept into her troubled mind, intensifying her despair. She plopped down beside a large pumpkin. A man would sure make things easier for her and the boys. When *was* she going to get one? she wondered, slipping the dried beanstalk through her long blond curls. For that matter, *how* could she?

She couldn't. Not here in Snickle's Corner. Her mother's sins hadn't been forgotten by any of the townspeople. And she couldn't pack up and move, either. It wasn't only her lack of funds that deterred her, but also the fact that her tiny cabin and small plot of land were all she owned in the world, all she had to give to Dilly and Dally.

Stretching her legs out between the two bushy collard plants that grew across from where she sat, Maisie leaned against the pumpkin and searched for the biggest, brightest star in the sky. "If there's just one man in this world who wouldn't hold my . . . my *tainted* beginnin's against me," she murmured to the star, "I wish I could find him."

As she closed her eyes to ponder her wish, she felt a movement beside her foot. Thinking it a garden lizard or some other harmless thing, she tossed the beanstalk in the creature's general direction.

Just as the stalk left her hand something warm and strong . . . something desperate grabbed her ankle.

Cold horror took hold of her. For a moment she couldn't move, couldn't scream, couldn't think. Nor could she see over the plants that hid whatever it was that had seized her foot. Panicked, she grabbed the back of her knee and pulled at her leg.

But she'd hardly begun to fight when she realized she stood no chance of winning. Her captor was no garden creature, but a man, and whoever he was, his extraordinary strength defied her puny attempts to escape.

Fighting back tears of fear, Maisie twisted in the dirt and snatched at a medium-sized pumpkin. When the stem snapped, she lifted the pumpkin off the ground and hurled it over the collard plants.

A muffled groan filled the air.

In the next instant Maisie felt the man let go of her foot. Her terror climbing, she gathered all the pumpkins and hard gourds she could hold, and prepared to batter the man to death with vegetables.

But at her first sight of him she dropped her armload of ammunition. The gourds and pumpkins landed directly atop his bare chest, eliciting another low moan from him.

Maisie's mouth dropped wide open. There he lay. In the dirt. Wearing nothing but moonlight and a bit of buckskin.

The warrior.

Apprehension squeezed off her breath. Unsure of what he might do, she took several steps away from him.

He raised his hand toward her.

She glanced at his palm, then gazed deeply into his sable eyes. There was something in them. . . . A light. A kind of shine she hadn't seen when he'd been in the cage.

It was the glimmer of hope. And the moment she recognized the glow for what it was, compassion whispered through her fear. Warily she lifted her hand toward his, ready to pull away if he made any sudden movement.

He didn't. Slowly Maisie laid the whole of her hand upon his, a tremor coursing through her when he curled his long dark fingers around hers. Sweetly surprised by his gentleness, she stared at him with wide, curious eyes.

"Lordy," she murmured, and drew in a deep breath. "You're a handsome feller, anybody ever tell you that? And all that hair . . . I ain't never seed a man with such long, purty hair. . . ."

Her voice trailed away as she studied his hair more closely. It cloaked his bronzed torso like a midnight shadow. She wondered what he would do if she reached out and touched its dark length. Helpless to resist the temptation, she leaned down and extended her other hand toward the thick ebony waves that lay spread over his broad shoulder.

But she'd barely touched them when the sudden sound of cantering horses and loud voices forced her to spin toward the darkened thicket that surrounded her cabin.

Her fear returned; not fear for herself, but for the warrior. "Sweet Lord in heaven, somebody's comin'! What the hell am I s'posed to do with you, warrior-man? Them men—"

"Maisie!" one of the men shouted.

She snapped her head toward the forest again and saw Cooper and Newton riding toward her. "Dammit! Oh, damn, damneder, and damnedest!"

She had no time to hide the Indian in a truly obscure spot. Her mind whirling, she grabbed up the hollow beanstalk and stuck one end in his mouth. Frantically, she began shoving dirt over him, careful not to push any into the beanstalk. When he allowed her her odd task, she thanked all of heaven that he apparently understood what she was trying to do.

Once he was completely covered, she scattered the mound with dried leaves, pebbles, and a few of the gourds and pumpkins she'd picked. "We've got our tits caught in the wringer, warrior-man, and that means we're in a powerful heap o' trouble. If you've got a speck o' sense, you'll stay still as a frozen snake."

She'd only just gotten to her feet and brushed off her skirts when Cooper came riding into her garden, Newton close behind. A multitude of other mounted townsmen waited at the edge of the woods. Dear God, she thought, an entire army!

"What are you doing out here, Maisie?" Cooper asked.

Praying her voice wouldn't shake the way her body was, she glared at him. "Not that my doin's is any o' your damn business, Cooper Snickle, but I'm weedin' my garden." Nonchalantly she took a few steps to the right, thus casting her own shadow over the buried warrior. "Now get off my land. I ain't never welcomed good in y'all's paw's town, and y'all ain't welcome on my property."

Newton took off his hat and raked his fingers through his sweat-dampened brown hair. "You're gardening? But it's nighttime."

"Well, slap the dog and spit in the fire, Newton, really?" she yelled. "Look, I can pull weeds any damn time I got the itch to do it, hear? 'Sides that, I ain't never got no time durin' the day, what with all the other chores to tend to," she added, realizing that pulling weeds by moonlight *was* rather strange.

Cooper urged his horse forward and bent to finger one of her long, golden curls. "You shouldn't be tending the garden at night, Maisie. A pretty girl like you should be in bed. Flat on her back with a man between her legs."

She smacked his hand away. "And I s'pose you're volunteerin' to be that man, huh, Cooper? Ha! If I fried you for a fool, I'd be wastin' the fat."

"Come on now, Maisie," he said through his lewd grin. "There's got to be a bit of your mother in you. Newt and I have been waiting for a long time for your heritage to come out." He caressed her hair again.

Shame filled her entire being, but she'd be damned if she'd let either man know. "Get your hand away from me, Cooper, or I'll pinch your head off and tell God you died."

At her threat, Cooper chuckled. "All right, Maisie. You win for now. I'm too busy to dally with you tonight, anyway. The warrior escaped. You wouldn't happen to know anything about that, would you?"

Seeing the suspicion in Cooper's eyes, Maisie chose her words as carefully as the man was waiting to hear them. "Well," she said on a long, exaggerated sigh, "since you pro'bly already done figgered it out, I might as well confess. I came across him right out here in my garden patch, Cooper, and I buried him betwixt the collards and the pumpkins so's y'wouldn't find him. As soon as y'all are gone, I'm gonna fix his wounds, feed him good, and send him on his way back out west. Hell, them Apache'll pro'bly make me a honorary member o' their tribe once they learn what I done for that warrior."

"Funny, Maisie," Cooper snapped. "Real funny." He jerked on the reins and turned his horse around.

She struggled to keep her relief concealed. "How'd the Indian get away?"

Newton slipped his hat back on. "As best we can tell, the wily devil sharpened those rocks that Wade and Rudy threw at him this afternoon and used them to carve through the wooden slats on the bottom of the cage. He must have sawed at them all day. We figure he escaped right after nightfall."

"Well, good Lord," Maisie murmured. "He's smarter'n a tree full o' owls."

"He'll be dead soon," Newton growled. "Paw's so mad, he's going to hang the savage as soon as we find him." With that, he turned his horse and urged the steed out of the garden.

For the next few moments Maisie pretended to pull weeds. When the rustle of the pine boughs and the chirps of crickets were the only sounds she could detect in the crisp autumn breeze, she knelt beside the mound. Thrusting her hand into the soft dirt, she felt for the warrior's hand.

She found his upper thigh. The feel of his naked flesh and the solid muscle beneath sent unfamiliar sensations spiralling through her body.

But she had no time to ponder those feelings. The Indian rose to a sitting position, causing her to snatch her hand away from him. Embarrassed that she had touched him in such an intimate place and wondering what his reaction was to her behavior, she glanced at him warily.

Even through the darkness she could see he was watching her, his stare bold, black, and steady. She felt captured and taken into him, as though he'd seized her very soul and now held it in his keeping.

He lifted his arm. Thinking he was asking her to help him off the ground, and glad for the opportunity to escape the mysterious force of his eyes, she took his hand and began to rise.

But he was on his feet before she'd even managed to get off her knees, and *he* assisted *her* up. Once she was standing, he bent and retrieved the shawl she'd given him that afternoon.

As he draped the faded wrap over her shoulders, something warm and tender shimmered through her.

He was a dangerous savage, she reminded herself. He was tall; he was broad-shouldered; his lean frame bulged with sleek muscle, and from him radiated raw and ruthless power.

But she knew in her heart this man would do her no harm.

"Come," she whispered. Her pale fingers intertwining with his dark ones, she led him toward the cabin. Not until she'd reached the porch did the full significance of her actions slam into her.

This man . . . she was going to take him into her house. It didn't matter that her involvement with him was based on the most innocent of reasons; if the townspeople found out, they'd interpret her behavior in the same way they had her mother's. And worse was the fact that he wasn't even a white man, but an *Indian*!

God, how could she let that happen?

Her shoulders sagging, she turned to face the warrior. "What am I gonna do with you?" she asked him again.

The small, trusting smile he gave her rocked her, flooding her with shame.

She stood to lose the remote chance she had of ever being accepted and liked.

He stood to lose his very life.

She opened the cabin door and ushered him inside.

CHAPTER
3

Their backs to the door, Dilly and Dally were in the process of scraping the contents of their plates into the fireplace when Maisie entered the cabin. Her arrival startled them so badly, they dropped their plates, and then slid and slipped through the spilled squash as they tried to remove themselves from the scene of their crimes. Dilly fell first, and Dally landed on top of him.

"I weren't gonna throw my squarshes away, Maisie!" Dilly screeched, his face smashed into the wooden floor. "Dally *maked* me do it!"

"Did not neither, y'damn liar!" Dally countered, wiping wet squash seeds away from his eyes. "Maisie, I was eatin' my squarshes real good when Dilly come and snatched my plate away! I begged him to let me finish eatin' them delicious squarshes, but he—"

Dilly punched Dally in the nose. Snarling like two rabid dogs, the boys began to fight in earnest, rolling around and finally crashing into Maisie's pie safe.

"Boys!" Maisie moved toward them and attempted to pull them apart. Her efforts were rewarded by an accidental kick in the shin from Dally and an unintentional slap on the cheek from Dilly. "I swear," she hissed, still bent over the boys, "that when I get the two o' you heathens untangled, I'm gonna . . ."

Her threat died in her throat when she saw a tall shadow fall over her brothers. Without making a sound, the Indian was behind her. Accustomed as she was to Dilly and Dally's loud and frenzied comings and goings, the warrior's stealth unnerved her.

She straightened just as the Indian crouched. Her eyes widened when he took hold of the backs of Dilly and Dally's shirts. Utterly astonished, she watched him lift both boys off the floor as if they weighed no more than handfuls of whispers. How was it possible for him still to possess such strength?

But amazed as she was, she couldn't help smiling. He held Dilly and Dally out to his sides and level with his shoulders, as though they were two undesirable objects he planned to dispose of. She had half a mind to tell him to go ahead and follow his plans.

Simultaneously the boys twisted to see who owned the powerful arms that kept them swaying above the floor. Stern black eyes glared back at them, eyes so full of disapproval that Dilly and Dally shuddered visibly.

Maisie's smile broadened. "Looks to me that this here warrior's a mite riled at the two o' you boys. Throwin' away good food's pro'bly a real serious crime in Indian land. I bet if I put squashes in front o' *him,* he'd eat ever' bit of 'em."

"I—I th-thought he was caged up," Dally stammered.

"He ain't no more," Dilly responded, gulping fear.

Dally sent Maisie a pleading look. "We—we'll eat the squarshes off the fl-floor if he'll just put us down, M-Maisie."

Laughing, Maisie motioned for the warrior to release her brothers. When he complied, she sat the awestruck boys at the table and explained how she'd come to find the Indian. After she finished, the boys' apprehension turned into uncontrollable excitement.

"We won't tell nobody he's here," Dilly swore. He scrambled away from the table and hurried toward the warrior. "Can we keep him?"

"We'll take good care of him," Dally promised, following Dilly.

"And will y'give him a bone to gnaw on ever'day, too?" Maisie teased. "Good Lord, boys, he ain't no stray dog." Her gaze met the warrior's, and she thought she saw the sparkle of amusement in his obsidian eyes. The look vanished instantly, however, leaving her to wonder if she'd seen it at all.

"Y'reckon he's nekkid underneath that buckskin thing he's wearin' around his hips?" Dally asked, staring at the warrior's breechcloth.

Dilly rolled his eyes. " 'Course he's nekkid, sawdust brain. That there buckskin thing's his underwear. But what I wanna know is how he keeps his ding-a-ling from swingin' out for ever'body to see."

"Dilly!" Blushing, Maisie quickly busied herself by gathering clean clothes, hot water, a flask of witch hazel, and a small pot of salve. When her medical supplies lay on the table, she gestured for the warrior to approach her.

The man did nothing but put one bare foot in front of the other, but his walk across the room shattered her fragile grasp on composure. Awe stole over her as she watched the play of supple muscle in his thick thighs and broad chest, evidence of barely restrained might. And his smooth, fluid stride . . . Sweet Lord above, he wore gracefulness the way other men wore clothes.

Her hands shook as she dipped a cloth into the hot water. "Sit down." She indicated the chair.

"Indians don't got no chairs, Maisie," Dilly said as he arrived at the table. "They sit on rocks."

Dally shoved his brother aside. "If he can sit on a rock, he can sit in a chair, Dilly. Sittin's sittin' no matter where you do it. Any mush-mind can figger that out."

Dilly snorted in outrage. "Who y'callin' mush-mind, you . . . y'damn *nose picker*!" He balled his fist and swung hard.

But a large dark palm caught his punch before it neared Dally's face.

"Warrior-man?" Maisie said. Noticing the shadow of pain that passed over his chiseled features, she stepped closer to him and touched his thick upper arm. "You all right?"

He stared at her, then glanced back down at the boy's small, pale fist. The memory of other hands, small like the one he held, but dark as his own, slammed through his mind.

His nephews. He'd had three, all young, all mischievous, all loved.

All dead.

He closed his eyes against the horrible memory. But even in the darkness, he could still see the day the soldiers had come. Dawn had barely pinkened the sky.

The women and children had run. Most were caught. Some were killed, some were taken prisoner. He remembered watching his youngest nephew being thrown into a cookfire.

Crazed with rage, he'd fought with the other warriors, including his father, his two brothers, and his sister's husband. But there were so many soldiers and no end to their ammunition. His brothers died first, together. His sister's husband was next, and then his father.

He couldn't find his sister. But he found his mother. She bled to death in his arms. Later, as the soldiers prepared to lead him and the rest of his tribe to the white man's fort, he spotted his other two nephews. They lay beneath the large tree where they'd been slain. And their mother, his sister, lay with them. She'd died holding them.

His entire family . . . gone. In this life, he would never see any of them again.

A wave of deep sorrow swept over him. He opened his eyes and looked at the small, pale fist again before lifting his gaze and examining the cabin. It was nothing at all like the wickiup he was used to living in.

But the home was filled with a familiar sense of family. These people who lived here laughed in this cabin. They ate together, and they slept together. They shared their problems and their joys, and they cared for each other.

He wondered if he would ever know the beauty of belonging to a family again.

"Maisie," Dilly whispered, his eyes wide with trepidation as he studied the intense expression on the Indian's face. "He looks like he's gonna smack me."

Maisie knew full well that the Indian wouldn't hurt a hair on Dilly's head, but she did wonder what had caused the profound yearning in his eyes. "Warrior-man?" she asked again, closing her fingers around the muscle in his arm.

His gaze pinned to the boy whose fist he held, the warrior emitted a sound that was part impatience, part anger, and all authority. He then released the small hand, and his dark

eyes flashing, he pointed to the spilled squash in front of the
fireplace.

Maisie watched in disbelief as her two unruly and disor-
derly brothers left to obey the warrior's unspoken command.
Without a word of protest or even one look of irritation, they
began to clean up the mess they'd made.

Deeply impressed, she reached out to the Indian and moved
his hair off his shoulders. The silken feel of it sent a warm
gush of emotion flowing through her. Struggling to tame the
odd feelings, she gently smoothed the wet cloth over the lash
wounds on his chest, the gash on his arm, and the burn on
his thigh. She rinsed the cloth and repeated her ministrations
numerous times until his injuries were free of all blood and
grime.

"That ain't the way Indians get cured, Maisie," Dilly
informed her, he and Dally having finished cleaning up
the spilled squash. "Out there in Indian land they got these
medicine-man doctors who do jigs around the sick people and
sing real strange songs."

When the boys began dancing and chanting a nonsensical
singsong, Maisie was glad for the distraction. The warm feelings possessing her had not abated, rather increased each time
she felt the warrior's gaze upon her.

Endeavoring to pretend aloofness, she finished tending his
injuries, dabbing witch hazel and salve to them and finally
wrapping them with strips of clean white cloth. She thought
she'd done very well with her attempts at indifference until
she looked up and saw the lazy curve of the Indian's lips.

It was a knowing smile, she realized. Whatever mysterious
thing was causing her melting emotions, the warrior had
already sensed and identified it.

Flustered, she put her doctoring supplies away and set the
table with his supper. "Y'all go on to bed now, boys," she
ordered her brothers.

They stomped their feet, but one look at the harsh expression on the warrior's face induced them to leave quietly for
their room.

Maisie's admiration rose. "I bet Indian young'uns don't like
to go to bed neither, huh? Y'know, I reckon folks is folks, no
matter what color they are. It's a damn shame the citizens o'

Snickle's Corner don't understand that." Smiling shyly, she sat down, hoping he would follow her lead.

He stared at his chair for a long moment before lowering his massive frame to sit. Once seated, he drained his cup of apple cider, then began to eat the loaf of bread.

Maisie refilled his cup and laid his napkin across his thigh. When he took the frayed cloth off and dropped it back on the table, she frowned. "You're s'posed to put your napkin in your lap. *Lap.*"

He gulped down his second cup of cider and wiped his mouth with the back of his hand.

She gave him more cider, ignoring the napkin issue. There were more important things to think about than table manners. Instead she wondered once again what she was going to do with him. "I'd talk to Reverend Jenkins," she said, more to herself than to him, "but I'd hate for that sweet man to be involved if trouble comes along. 'Course, y'can stay here for a spell, but y'cain't stay forever. Them Snickles'll catch you for sure. I reckon y'cain't go back out west, neither, what with the army roundin' all y'all up. And I don't believe for one minute that y'want to go to that reservation in Florida. Lord o' mercy, what *am* I gonna do with you?"

In response, he offered her a bite of bread.

She shook her head. "Eat your squashes, warrior-man." She tapped the side of his plate. "Eat this."

He proceeded to devour the dried peaches.

"I'm Maisie," she said, touching her chest. "*Maisie.* What's *your* name?" She pointed to him, but received no answer. "I reckon y'don't understand nothin' I'm sayin'. But y'know? Maybe it ain't important. Maybe the sound of a friendly voice is just what you need."

Convinced her speculation was right, she gave him a brilliant smile. "You eat them squashes, and I'll talk. We're the Applejacks. I'm Maisie like I done told you, and Dilly and Dally's my brothers. Their real names is Seth and Caleb, but I been callin' 'em Dilly and Dally for s'long, I reckon they cain't even remember what their real names are. When it comes to chores? Well, them boys is like blisters. Don't never show up till the work's done. Dillyin' and dallyin' all day long, and that's the truth of it. Eat your squashes."

He looked at the food she pointed to and shook his head.

"Don't like it, huh? Lord, if Dilly and Dally knew that, I'd never be able to get 'em to eat squashes again. There's only eleven months difference betwixt Dilly and Dally, y'know," she continued. "Maw said that as soon as she got Dilly out, Dally come right up behind him to take his place. Maw . . . she . . . well . . ."

A soft sigh escaping her, she bent her head and picked up one of her flaxen curls. Sweet Lord in heaven, why had she brought up the subject of her mother? It was hard enough to *think* about, much less *talk* about.

Through lowered lashes, she glanced at the warrior and saw him watching her once again. She couldn't decipher the expression in his dark eyes, but the longer she studied him, the more it began to resemble concern. Whether he felt tenderness toward her or not, didn't matter. She wanted to see compassion in his gaze, and so she did.

She pondered what it might feel like to voice all the heartache she carried inside. She'd never discussed her troubles, not even with Reverend Jenkins. "I reckon I could bare my soul to you, huh, warrior-man? Y'wouldn't judge me because y'wouldn't understand me."

He dropped a peach into her hand.

She drew the fragrant fruit across her lower lip, dwelling on memories she rarely allowed to surface. "Maw died o' some fever when I was only fifteen. Dilly was two, and Dally was one."

She laid the peach on the table and absently ran her finger over the fruit's wrinkled surface. "She was a real purty lady, Maw was, and men liked her. She liked 'em right back, and folks called her a whore. But don't real whores earn money? I know for a fact that them men didn't give Maw none. If they had've, we wouldn't't've been s'poor all the time. What them men give her, y'see . . . was me, Dilly, and Dally."

She rose and began to amble around the room, her emotions intensifying with each step she took. "We're them— them *trashy Applejacks*," she spat, stopping by the window and peering out at the moonlit yard. "Briar-patch young'uns some folks call us. Woods colts and bantlin's. But all them names mean one and the same. Bastards. And if that ain't bad enough, me, Dilly, and Dally was fathered by three different men."

Folding her arms across her breasts, she turned from the window and leaned against the sill. "Bein' born out o' wedlock . . . It's like me and my brothers got some kind o' catchin' disease that nobody wants to be exposed to. That's why we're shunned by the townsfolk. It's why I ain't never been able to get me a decent job."

Her eyes began to sting. "And—and it's why no men want to keep proper comp'ny with me. Cooper and Newton's the only men who ever pay me a smidgen of attention, but all's they want from me's the same thing Maw used to give out. Both of 'em's just as worthless as a puddle o' spit, but that don't make it no easier to put up with 'em."

One warm tear slipped down her cheek. Lest the warrior witness her loss of control, she turned back to the window and picked up a small blue bottle from the corner of the sill. "Ain't fair," she squeaked, watching as her tear splashed to the bottle she held. "Me and my brothers ain't done nothin' but get borned. How can Maw's doin's be our fault? And what do I gotta do to show the townfolk that I ain't like her? I try to be as friendly as I know how to be, but they hate me more ever' time they see me."

Her warm sigh made a foggy circle on the windowpane. "And then there's Dilly and Dally. I worry somethin' fierce over 'em. We're out here in these woods all alone. If somebody ever tried to get 'em . . . or hurt 'em . . . Lord knows, I'd die before I'd ever let anything happen to 'em, but I'm just one woman, and the only weapon I've got is my kitchen knife. And what with that Smokey Joe varmint on the loose . . ."

She felt more tears fill her eyes. "Dilly," she whispered. "And Dally. 'Sides each other, they ain't got no friends a'tall. And there ain't no man around to learn 'em manly things that little boys need to learn. 'Cept for two dollars I got saved up in the town bank, I ain't got a cent to my name, and Dilly and Dally's all the time havin' to do without. Hell, I cain't even get 'em the meat they're always askin' for. Them sweet little rascals is my whole life, and it near about rips my heart to shreds to think on all the things they need that I—that I cain't never give'em!"

As the last of her story escaped her so did the tears she'd held back for too many years. They spilled forth on a violent shudder that shot through her entire body.

But her wave of anguish became a sudden jolt of surprise when she felt two strong hands clasp her waist. Too stunned to think clearly, she didn't resist when those same forceful hands turned her around.

She found herself pressed against the warrior's warm, hard body. His long, thick hair fell over her arms. His hips cradled hers; his thighs seemed melded to hers. Her breasts were flattened against his broad chest; she could feel his heartbeat. Its slow, steady rhythm calmed the erratic cadence of her own.

And when he smiled down at her, the pain of grief inside her gave way to a vibrant yearning. Security stole over Maisie, a gentle comfort she couldn't remember ever having felt.

How odd that this man she barely knew could make her feel so safe. "Warrior-man," she whispered.

He raised his right hand and gently dried her tears with his thumb. "Nubarrón."

It was the first time he'd spoken. The sound of his voice reminded her of the rumble of distant thunder, soft and lulling, yet hinting at the promise of awesome power, a force she instinctively knew he wanted to share with her now.

She closed her eyes, allowing comfort to seep into her. Like a sultry stream meandering down a slow-winding course, his strength spread through her, lending courage to her flagging spirit, and inciting nameless pleasures in the deepest parts of her. "Sweet Lord above," she murmured, savoring the beautiful peace he'd wrapped around her. "I wish I could stay in these wonderful arms o' yours for the rest o' my life, warrior-man."

He tightened his hold on her and curled his free hand around the back of her slender neck. "I am not warrior-man," he said, his words heavily accented. "I am Nubarrón. Storm Cloud. That is how I am called, woman with eyes of sky and hair of sun."

Her eyes flew open. She dropped the bottle and heard glass shatter on the floor. "Eng-English! You speaked *English*!"

He moved a silken gold curl away from her eye. His fingers grazed her flushed cheek, and he kept them upon her soft, smooth skin. "Many of my people speak the white man's tongue."

Her mind whirled with the recollections of all the things she'd told him. Not only did he know her darkest secrets and deepest feelings . . . he knew what she thought about *him*! Why, she'd actually told him she wanted to stay in his arms forever!

Mortified, she jerked out of his embrace. Shards of the broken bottle crunched beneath her boots. "Why didn't you *tell* me you could talk English? Them things I told you weren't none o' your business!"

"You are wrong." He moved his fingers to the delicate hollow of her throat. When she tried to slap his hand away, he caught both her wrists and gave her no quarter as she tried to squirm away. "I owe much to you, woman. You defended me when I was helpless against my enemies. You have hidden me. You tended my wounds and fed me. Do you believe I will turn away from your troubles? I will carry them as if they were mine. It will take many moons for me to repay you, but until my debt is paid, I will not leave you."

"*What?*" Thoughts of the townspeople filled Maisie's mind. It was one thing for her to hide Storm Cloud for the short time he would need to fully regain his health; that she would do gladly. But to allow him to live with her for any longer than that? And he was an *Indian,* for God's sake!

Panic pumped through her. "Look, y'don't owe me nothin', hear? Y'ain't gotta stay here for all them moons. You—I— ain't y'got no kin nowhere who might be worried about you? Don't y'think y'ought to go see if y'can find any o' your family—"

"I have no family. The soldiers killed them all."

At the whisper of grief she heard in his deep voice, Maisie stilled immediately. "I—I'm sorry."

He released her wrists. Scowling down at her, he folded his arms across his chest. "I stay."

The glitter in his black eyes echoed his adamant declaration. Maisie could think of no argument powerful enough to conquer his stubborness.

She raced to her room and slammed the door behind her. "Merciful Lord in heaven," she whispered raggedly, "what the hell have I got myself into?"

CHAPTER
4

Maisie had just fastened the last button on her blouse when Dilly and Dally burst into her room the next morning.

"He's *gone*!" Dilly cried.

Dally nodded wildly. "We got up at dawn and looked all over for him, but he weren't *nowhere*! Do y'think them Snickles come in the middle of the night and taked him away? Do y'think they already done killed him? Do y'think—"

"No, I don't think none o' them things." Worry nagging at her, Maisie swept into the front room and looked around. The uneaten plate of squash on the table and the garden dirt on the floor were the only evidence that Storm Cloud had even been in the cabin.

"Maybe he leaved because he didn't like us," Dally suggested, shuffling his feet on the braided rug in front of the fireplace. "Nobody else likes us. Why should he?"

Dilly gave a deep sigh. "Or maybe he thought we wanted him to go away. White folks is s'posed to hate Indians. Maybe he thought that about us."

Dilly's statements hit Maisie like a blast of frigid air. Cold shame skated through her. She'd told Storm Cloud he couldn't stay. He'd argued, but in the end perhaps he'd believed she wanted nothing to do with him.

"His name was Storm Cloud," she whispered. "And he called me woman with eyes o' sky and hair o' sun." And he'd held her, she recalled. He'd dried her tears, smiled at her, and offered to take on her troubles as though they were his own. Truly he'd tried to be her friend.

And now he was gone. Wandering and unwanted.

"You all right, Maisie?" Dally asked, taking her hand.

Utter misery settled over her. "I—I need to sweep this dirty floor."

"Storm Cloud's gone, and you're gonna sweep the floor?" Dally queried.

She didn't expect the boys to understand her emptiness or the need to fill the void with some mindless activity. She barely understood, either. Tears blurring her vision, she crossed to a small closet and reached inside for the broom. It was gone. Puzzled, but too distraught to hunt for it, she grabbed a loaf of bread from a basket nailed to the wall. "I'll make your breakfast," she mumbled incoherently.

She began to look for her knife. After a moment of futile searching, she realized she must have misplaced the blade as well as the broom.

A deep, painful sense of loss came over her. Not for the broom, nor for the knife.

For Storm Cloud.

Late-afternoon sunshine poured into the stream as Maisie plunged the last soiled garment into the cold water. Washing clothes was a dreaded, all-day chore, but she'd welcomed the task today in the hope that the exhausting work would keep her from dwelling on Storm Cloud.

It hadn't. And the fact that Dilly and Dally had gone into town and learned that he had not been recaptured by the Snickles did little to ease her worry. He had to be *somewhere,* and wherever that place was, he was there alone.

As if squeezing the guilt from her mind, she wrung the shirt so hard, her body shook with the effort. Water wet her blouse; a brisk breeze rustled past her, making her shiver.

And then the air stilled, replaced by a chilling silence. Maisie dropped the shirt. An eerie sensation rippled her skin into gooseflesh.

She wasn't alone.

Peering into the dim thicket that surrounded the stream, she saw nothing to alarm her, but the feeling that someone was watching her intensified.

"Smokey Joe," she whispered. Like so many vicious wasps, fear stung each part of her.

"Woman," a deep voice rumbled through the silence. "Woman with eyes of sky and hair of sun, do not be afraid."

"Storm Cloud!" Rising, she searched the area once more, but saw no sign of him until he stepped out of the thicket.

Her pulse quickened. Lord, she thought, if the man were any more handsome, it'd be a sin to look at him. With his copper skin, long black hair, and tawny breechcloth, he resembled some wild and beautiful animal, blending in with the untamed environment as well as any forest creature. No wonder she hadn't seen him. Maybe hiding him wouldn't be difficult after all.

He carried a deer over his powerful shoulders. In his right hand he held a crude spear, which she recognized to be her broom handle and her knife. "Y'been huntin'."

He joined her by the stream and laid the deer at her feet. Straightening, he allowed his gaze to roam over her face and down her body. Instantly his own body responded. Never had he seen such beauty in any woman.

"Storm Cloud?"

"I have brought meat for your brothers."

Such poignant emotions welled within her, she almost wept.

"You are sad that I brought the meat?"

"What? I . . . no." Taking a moment to get hold of herself, she stared at his bare chest and frowned. "Why'd y'take your bandages off? Them wounds is—"

"A hunter must wear the colors of the forest. I could not stalk the deer with the white cloth tied around me. And I could not eat the meal you prepared last night. It was filled with onions that the deer can smell."

His explanation deepened the security she gained by his nearness. "I . . . I thought you'd left for good."

He picked up her hand and stroked her wrist. "You did not have faith in my words, woman. I said I would stay."

Though he caressed her, his tone of voice told her he was displeased. "I'm sorry, but I—"

"An apology of words weighs nothing. If you are sorry, you must show me."

She was confused until he tossed down the spear and opened his arms. Knowing she would find comfort in his embrace, she longed to allow him to hold her.

Instead she shook her head. "Storm Cloud, I'm real glad you come back, but we cain't keep huggin' and carryin' on like we done last evenin'. I thought on it near about all night, and I . . . well, it just ain't fittin', y'see. I wouldn't never let no man touch me if he weren't my husband. I ain't . . . I ain't like Maw."

He moved swiftly, sweeping her off the ground and into his arms. "Woman," he whispered, "what you tell me I already know. The moment my eyes first met yours, your heart and your soul spoke to mine, and I knew you."

As he wrapped his warm strength around her the serenity Maisie so treasured enveloped her. An involuntary mewl of contentment escaped her parted lips.

The sensual sound drifting through his senses, Storm Cloud buried his face in the soft cloud of her hair and breathed deeply of her scent. "You smell of water and fire. Wind and earth and sun. You smell as a woman should."

His compliment, the first she'd ever received, touched a place so deep inside her she couldn't understand where that place was. Barely cognizant of her own actions, she laid her hand on his chest and trailed her fingers across his sun-warmed skin.

Storm Cloud groaned, desire setting his every nerve ablaze. "Look at me, woman," he demanded huskily, raising his head. "Look into my eyes and see what I feel for you."

Puzzled, she lifted her gaze to his. What she saw caused her breath to catch. His black eyes smoldered with what could only be flames of passion.

A twinge of dismay pricked at her. Was Storm Cloud just like the Snickles? "Storm—"

"I see you understand. And now you must also understand that I will never give you a reason to fear me. Believe what I tell you, woman."

How could she not believe him? she wondered. The truth of his words was so tangible, she felt she could reach out and hold his promise. He would control his feelings.

But how on earth was she going to control her own? Storm Cloud sired a powerful longing within her, and she knew instinctively that he could satisfy it.

God. Maybe she *was* just like her mother.

Instantly she squirmed her way out of Storm Cloud's arms and backed away from him.

He read her every thought in her huge, expressive eyes and sought to relieve her anxiety by giving her something else to think about. "My belly is empty. Prepare my meal, but take care with each part of the deer. I need weapons and clothing, and I will use all that this animal provides." He retrieved the spear and deftly removed the knife from the broom handle.

When he held out the blade, she stared blankly. "You 'spect *me* to cut up this deer all by myself?"

"That is a woman's work. I killed the deer; you make it ready to eat." He thrust the hilt of the knife into her hand. "I am the man; you are the woman. You do as I say. It is not a hard thing to understand."

In one fleeting moment Maisie's emotions went from confusion to incredulity and finally to anger. "You're the uppitiest man I ever come across in all my born days! Got your nose so high up in the air that you'd drown in a rainstorm! I'll cook this here deer, but if you think I'm butcherin' it all by myself, then your head's emptier'n last year's bird nest. And let me tell *you* somethin' that ain't hard to understand. Y'know all them many moons you was talkin' about last night? Well, while they're passin' I ain't takin' no orders off you!"

"You are finished shouting now, woman?"

His cool smugness intensified her anger. "My name ain't *woman*! It's *Maisie*!"

He bit back a smile, thoroughly amused by her wrath. She was full of passion, and this pleased him. "I will call you *woman*. It is the Apache way. Only when there is deep meaning in the moment will an Apache speak a name. To use a person's name without special feeling is wrong."

"Yeah? Well, I *ain't* no Apache, and I *ain't* skinnin' that deer!"

"Do you refuse to prepare the deer because you do not know how?"

His question silenced and embarrassed her. "Well, I . . ."

"I will show you how it is done, but only once. I am a warrior, not a woman, and I will not do this again." He took the knife from her and knelt beside the deer.

His arrogance irritated her anew. Her first impulse was to disappear into the cabin and leave him to do the work alone. But as she dwelled on what he'd told her, her emotions softened.

I am a warrior.

Yes, he was a warrior, but he no longer had a tribe. His customs and beliefs . . . his entire way of life was vanishing. She could hardly imagine how it would feel if someone destroyed her own world.

But she knew exactly how she would feel if someone tried to give back a small piece of that lost world.

She realized then that bending to this noble warrior's will would not diminish her. Rather her compliance would nourish the only thing Storm Cloud had left.

His pride.

"Storm Cloud," she murmured, holding out her hand for the knife. "Let me."

For the next two hours she wielded the blade according to his instructions. The task was a messy one and her stomach pitched several times, but she persevered.

And when she was finished, she knew by the warm glow in Storm Cloud's eyes that all the years of trying to win respect had finally come to an end.

She'd won Storm Cloud's.

As the days passed, Storm Cloud revealed to Maisie the full measure of his skills. Under his gentle and patient tutelage, she learned the techniques of tanning the hides of the game he continued to provide. When the skins were smooth and pliable, she sewed them into clothing for him, which she then enjoyed decorating with feathers, strips of fur, and the paints Storm Cloud made from assorted plants, nutshells, and clays.

He taught her how to create watertight baskets, cozy blankets, sharp needles, strong rope, soft, warm shoes, and many of the other necessities she was usually forced to buy at Snickle's

Mercantile. He even demonstrated the art of fashioning weapons, but made it clear to her that that particular job belonged to a man and that she was never to handle his bow and arrows.

While practicing the things he showed her, Maisie realized that in keeping his vow to take care of her, Storm Cloud had also taught her to rely on nature rather than money to provide for her needs. It was a lesson she knew would see her through many possible hardships in the future, and one that deepened her understanding and admiration for Storm Cloud and the culture that had molded him.

In Maisie's eyes, he was nothing less than magnificent.

And she soon began to dread the day when he would leave her.

Concealed within a dense thicket of pines and scrub oaks, Storm Cloud watched as Dilly and Dally tumbled down the tall, rocky hill he'd had them climb. Their moans and muttered cursing came to him on the breath of the cool afternoon wind.

He smiled. The boys tested his patience at every turn, never letting an opportunity pass to try to escape his stern supervision and ever-watchful eye. He'd been hard on them, and they often resented him. But they needed him.

Their need, as well as Maisie's, had begun to heal and fill the painful emptiness inside him.

As the boys reached the bottom of the hill, he raised his hand and pointed to the top.

Panting and sweating, bruised and crabby, Dilly and Dally glowered at him. Although they held him in high esteem, strenuous activities such as the one he'd had them doing this afternoon sparked their tempers.

"But we done climbed that mountain three times today already, Storm Cloud," Dilly whined, and kicked at a stray twig. "Why do we gotta climb the damn thing again?"

"Because you are lazy and weak." He pointed to the peak of the hill once more.

They knew by the adamant tone in his voice that there was no escaping. For the fourth time the weary boys scaled the steep hill. When they descended, they entertained high hopes of escape. The cabin was a three-mile walk away, but at least food, water, and soft beds would be waiting when they arrived.

"We will return to your sister now," Storm Cloud announced, suppressing a grin at the boys' relieved expressions. "But first you will each find a small stone to put in your mouth."

Both boys frowned. They knew him well enough now to realize he was about to give them another important Indian lesson, but they were too tired and irritable to learn it. "I ain't suckin' on no rock," Dilly declared. "Maisie says if we put dirty stuff in our mouths, we'll get worms."

"Yeah," Dally agreed. "And if we get worms, she'll pour turpentine, honey, and castor oil down our throats, and I'd rather have the worms."

Again Storm Cloud squelched his amusement. "Do you believe I would have you do something that would harm you? A rock will not give you worms. You will find a stone now and put it in your mouth. Then you will return to the cabin."

Properly chastised, the boys obeyed. Small pebbles in their mouths, they began the long walk home.

"You will run," Storm Cloud demanded, following them as closely and silently as their shadows. "You will avoid leaves, sticks, and other things that will make noise. Keep your step light, as if running on a cloud. You will run quickly, and you will not stop until you arrive."

They gaped at him. "But we ain't never been able to run so far!" Dally exclaimed, his words slurred by the rock in his mouth. "We get too tired!"

"You will become tired," Storm Cloud agreed, "but your mind is stronger than your body, and so you will not think about the pain in your muscles."

Dilly moved his rock to the side of his mouth. "But—but we'll be thirsty! Cain't nobody run that far without dyin' o' thirst!"

The boys' rising hysteria further amused Storm Cloud; he was barely able to keep laughter at bay. "Thirst will not be a problem for you. The stones you suck will keep your mouths moist."

"That's the dumbest thing I ever did hear!" Dilly blasted.

Storm Cloud's eyes glittered.

Instantly Dilly and Dally began to run.

An hour later they staggered into the yard, exhausted. Pain shot through their entire bodies. They'd run the entire way without stopping.

But they were not thirsty.

They were proud of what they'd accomplished.

And so was Storm Cloud.

CHAPTER
5

Maisie sat near the fire, letting out the hems in the black pants the boys would wear to the Thanksgiving feast. As she worked she listened to them tell the story of the first Thanksgiving to Storm Cloud, who was busy tending to his weapons, a task on which he spent many long hours.

But he was not so occupied that he could not find moments to slide frequent glances in her direction. Every time his black eyes settled upon her, she felt his touch and lifted her own eyes to meet his.

No words were uttered. None were needed. The warm and sensual messages in their gazes spoke far more eloquently. Before long, Maisie blushed and squirmed in her chair, her body afire with the yearning Storm Cloud's silent seduction evoked within her.

In response to her shyness, he grinned broadly, thoroughly pleased by her vulnerability to his bold, yet soundless courtship.

"Storm Cloud, ain't y'listenin' to nothin' we're tellin' you?" Dilly demanded. "We said the Pilgrims come to America from England. They sailed in a ship called the *Mayflower,* and when they got to America, they settled in a place they called Plymouth."

"It was winter then, and they didn't have hardly no food," Dally added. He picked up one of the thin pieces of flint Storm Cloud would use to fashion an arrowhead, and began scratching his name into the surface of the wooden table. One dark look from Storm Cloud induced him to drop the flint and continue with his story. "Lots o' them Pilgrims died before spring come. The ones that stayed alive was real worried, though, on account o' they didn't know too much about plantin' the corn seeds they'd finded."

Dilly nodded. "But the Indian come, Storm Cloud. Maybe you're kin to 'em. First come one called Samoset. Then one called Squanto, and finally, Massasoit, the chief. They was real nice to the Pilgrims and even showed 'em how to plant the corn seeds with a dead fish so's the corn would grow better."

"The Pilgrims had 'em a good harvest," Dally continued, watching carefully as Storm Cloud placed the final touches on one sharpened arrowhead. "So they decided to have a special day to thank God for all the stuff He'd give 'em. They had a feast, and—"

"And they invited their Indians friends," Dally interrupted. "Massasoit come with ninety members of his tribe. And they didn't come empty-handed, neither. They brung meat to share. Ever'body sat down at long tables under the trees, and they was peaceful and thankful and happy and hungry. So they ate all the food, and we been carryin' on that tradition ever since. It's why me and Dilly have to be Pilgrims and put on them stupid costumes ever' year."

Dally cast a disgusted glance at the black clothing Maisie was sewing. "We have competitions, too, Storm Cloud. Footraces and shootin' contests. Me and Dilly don't never win nothin', though."

"We ain't got no guns," Dilly explained. "And even if we had us some, we wouldn't know how to shoot 'em. Wade and Rudy Snickle always win the contest on account o' they got their paw and brothers to learn 'em how to shoot good."

Storm Cloud didn't utter a word of response. His features blank, he calmly continued to sharpen his arrowheads.

A few days later Maisie discovered that Storm Cloud had taken her brothers' problem straight to heart.

"It is time for you to have your own weapons," he announced to the boys one morning after breakfast. Ignoring his napkin—which Maisie had placed in his lap the way she always did—

he wiped his mouth with his hand and rose from his seat at the table.

In their excitement, the boys almost fell out of their chairs. "Y'got us some guns, Storm Cloud?" Dally yelled.

"Can we go huntin' with you?" Dilly screamed.

Maisie cringed as their shouts battered her ears. "Lord in heaven, y'all are loud enough to jar pecans off the trees."

After giving the boys a long, hot glare, Storm Cloud retrieved the large leather bag that lay near his sleeping pallet across the room. When he opened the pouch and withdrew its contents, Dilly and Dally watched in speechless wonder as he placed one bow, one quiver, and five arrows in front of each of them. The weapons were much smaller than the ones Storm Cloud had made for himself, but equal in beauty and craftsmanship.

Maisie regarded the awed expressions on her brothers' faces and witnessed the reverence with which they handled their weapons. With misty eyes, she peered up at the handsome Apache warrior who'd made such a difference in the boys' lives. Her heart stirred with tenderness.

But it also throbbed with anxiety. Each morning, when the first timid rays of dawn crept into her bedroom, she wondered if the new day would end with Storm Cloud's leaving. Deep down she knew he couldn't stay. He was an Indian, loathsome in the sight of her race. If he remained with her, he'd surely be caught and hanged.

Tears wet her lashes. She lowered her head and blinked the tears away, determined not to dwell on her apprehension. When she lifted her face again, she saw Storm Cloud watching her, deep concern in his fathomless black eyes. Quickly she flashed him her brightest grin, but knew her attempt to pacify his worry had failed. The man had seen straight into her soul the very night she'd found him, and he'd not looked away once.

"Can we go now?" Dally tugged on the long fringe that hung from the sleeves of Storm Cloud's buckskin shirt.

Storm Cloud contemplated Maisie's troubled expression for one last moment, then removed his shirt and picked up his own weapons.

"It's cold outside, Storm Cloud," Dilly warned.

"I allow only the wind between me and my aim."

Within seconds Dilly and Dally were as bare-chested as Storm Cloud. Maisie was just before demanding they put their shirts back on when Storm Cloud gave her a negative shake of his head.

He advanced toward the door, the boys following.

"Can I go, too?" Maisie asked, determined to spend as much time with Storm Cloud as possible before he . . .

She tore the thought from her mind. "I—I mean if it ain't one o' them man things that women cain't see, can I go?"

He raked his dark gaze down the length of her slender body before he centered it on her face. Though her features remained touched by a hint of tension, her beauty rivaled that of every woman he'd ever known, and he had to fight the urge to take her into his arms.

But he kept his need tightly leashed. He had not forgotten her sad confession about her mother's reputation, and had sworn not to shatter her growing trust.

"You will stay silent while your brothers shoot, woman?"

She bristled. Apparently he still didn't consider her special enough to call her Maisie. "I'll be as quiet as a mouse pissin' on a cotton boll," she promised softly.

He smiled, her silly vow reminding him that desire was not the only emotion this beautiful woman caused him to feel. She amused him. He respected her strength, determination, and capabilities, but even so, something about her roused in him the instinct to protect her as if she were a small and precious child.

She was working her way into his heart.

And for the first time since he'd arrived at her cabin, Storm Cloud wondered how he would be able to leave her.

Knowing if the boys shot at a hard surface they would break all their arrows in only minutes, Storm Cloud fashioned a thick, round bale of grass and pine straw and hung it from a branch of a tree that grew in the middle of a large clearing. In the center of the soft target, he attached a vivid yellow leaf.

"You will aim for the leaf," he told the boys as he joined them some twenty feet away from the target.

"I'll go first," Dilly said, sliding an arrow from his quiver.

"Your brother will go first," Storm Cloud announced, "because he did not show selfishness by wanting to be first."

At Storm Cloud's effective discipline, Maisie smiled and settled herself more comfortably in a nearby bed of pine straw to watch the lesson unfold.

Dally prepared to shoot. But though he tried desperately to remember all the things Storm Cloud had explained, he embedded his arrow in a mass of thorny brush several yards away. Tears of humiliation dripped down his cheeks.

"Will your tears help you to shoot?" Storm Cloud queried sternly. "Dry them and try again."

"But it's *my* turn now!" Dilly wailed. "Dally done shooted!"

Storm Cloud took hold of Dilly's chin. "Do you know why it is not your turn?"

Dilly gulped. "Be-because you say so?"

Satisfied with Dilly's answer, Storm Cloud released his chin and continued to assist Dally. When Dally spent all his arrows, Dilly finally got his turn, but shot no better than his brother.

While the boys continued to practice, Storm Cloud turned toward Maisie. "Their skills will improve," he promised her. "You will believe me?"

She tossed him a bright grin. "Storm Cloud, if you was to tell me a flea could pull a plow, I'd hitch one right up. Y'ain't never give me nary a reason to doubt what y'say."

Storm Cloud was still trying to understand what a flea had to do with his promise when a sudden wave of foreboding passed through him. He saw nothing; he heard nothing. But every instinct he possessed told him he was in danger.

Seconds later Maisie detected a crunching sound coming from within the woods that edged the clearing. Before she could scramble to her feet, Cooper and Newton emerged from the thicket, rifles propped on their shoulders. All color draining from her face, she spun toward where Storm Cloud had been standing.

He wasn't there. Neither were the boys. God, she thought. She hadn't heard Storm Cloud *or* the boys leave!

"Well, well, well," Newton said as he approached her. "Here's Maisie, Coop. All by her little lonesome. Suppose she needs some company?"

Cooper unfastened the top button of his shirt. "She needs more than company, Newt. She looks awfully bored. How about if we give her something to do and teach her what it was her mother knew so well?" He tossed his rifle to the ground and quickly removed his shirt.

Maisie's fear turned into near hysteria. She knew if she called for Storm Cloud, he'd come instantly. But in coming to her aid, he'd be risking his life.

She lifted her chin. "What are you doin' here?" she demanded.

"Hunting," Newton replied. "Paw's got his mouth all set for fresh turkey, but there don't seem to be many around this year."

"To hell with the damn turkey, Newt," Cooper said, his eyes resting on the deep vee of Maisie's blouse. "We've bagged far prettier game right here."

Maisie raised a flaxen brow and forced a taunting tone into her voice. "Thought y'didn't have time to mess with me no more, Cooper Snickle. Thought y'was too busy trackin' that Indian."

He walked closer to her and curled his arm around her waist. "He's dead."

Her heart somersaulted. *"Dead?"*

"We never found him," Cooper admitted, his fingers sliding up to caress the side of her breast, "but he's got to be dead by now. He was wounded. He had no clothes, no food, no mount, and nowhere to go. Even if he didn't die all on his own, someone probably found and shot him. Nobody in their right mind would let an Apache savage live."

Newton moved behind her and placed his hands over her hips. "Paw's got us back to looking for that bank robber, Smokey Joe. We've also been trying to break Paw's demon stallion. We still haven't managed to ride him, but we will. There's nothing like taming and mounting a wild horse. Gives a man a good feeling. It's the same with a woman. You're going to give us that good feeling, aren't you, pretty girl?" He rubbed himself against her.

Her breath came shallowly as she tried to decide what to do. If she fled, they'd catch her. If she fought, they'd subdue her. God, even if she pretended to faint, they'd probably violate her anyway.

Her heartbeat thundered in her ears until she heard a loud and pitiful whine.

Cooper and Newton grabbed their rifles. "It's a bear cub, Coop," Newton whispered.

"And where baby is, mother is," Cooper added, his voice shaking with excitement. "They're probably looking for a place to spend the winter. Think Paw would like a big bear head to go along with the panther head we gave him last year, Newt?"

"Let's give him the cub head, too."

Though both men slunk into the forest, Maisie's fear continued to escalate. *Bears!* Did she dare call for Storm Cloud now? But what if Cooper and Newton heard her? Sweet Lord, had she escaped the Snickles' assault only to be attacked by a bear?

Her answer came when an arrow sang past her face and buried itself within the exact center of the straw target. She whirled toward the direction from which the arrow had come and saw Storm Cloud lower his bow.

"Bears," she tried to tell him, but heard no evidence of her voice. She trembled so violently, she began to sway. "Bears."

She watched him run toward her. In the next instant he enfolded her in his arms. "Storm Cloud! Cooper . . . Newton—"

"They are gone."

"But . . . Bears! We gotta run—"

"There are no bears," he said softly, losing his hands in the silken mass of her hair. "I made the sounds of the bear cub to lead those men away from you."

Blinking, she looked up at him, his explanation spawning a disconcerting question in her mind. "But—but what would you o' done if they hadn't left to find them bears they thought was out there?"

He moved his hands to her cheeks and traced her lips with his thumbs. "I would have killed them."

He spoke so softly, he touched her so gently, it was difficult for Maisie to believe him capable of killing. Only the lingering glint of brutal fury in his eyes proved the truth of his words.

"Tell me you are not hurt," he entreated, his deep voice brimming with concern.

His plea brought her a luxurious sense of tranquillity. His nearness created an unbearable need she yearned desperately for him to satisfy. "Storm Cloud . . ."

He watched her soft, pink lips part. Upon his bare chest, he could feel the crests of her breasts stiffen, and the mound of her femininity pushed sweetly at the center of his breechcloth. His body responded instantly, such violent desire exploding inside him, he could actually hear it roaring through his veins.

But in his heart whispered another sound. That of the vow he'd made. His promise never to give her a reason to fear him.

She'd only just discovered desire and was powerless against its potency, he knew. If he accepted her innocent surrender to him now, she would later regret everything that happened.

He would have to be strong for her.

So as not to jolt her into embarrassment, so as to ease her gently out of the strong grip of passion, he gave her a lazy grin and slowly turned his head toward the woods. "I left your brothers well hidden and ordered them to stay there. They will lose the little patience they have if I do not go for them soon. And I do not like to think about the trouble they find so easily. I have been called a savage many times, but when I am with your brothers, I wonder who is the savage and who is not."

Her bright giggle assured him that he'd successfully guarded her feelings. After gathering the boys, he led his three charges up a grassy knoll behind which lay the path to the cabin.

But before he could begin the descent, Dally grabbed his hand. "Look, Storm Cloud!" he shouted, pointing to the clearing in the distance. "There's the target you maked for us! And your arrow's sticked right in it!"

"We didn't get to see you shoot it!" Dilly wailed. "Can you shoot for us now?"

"Please?" Dilly begged.

Maisie could tell by the look on Storm Cloud's face that he had no intention of shooting another of his precious arrows at something as insignificant as a bundle of grass and pine straw—especially since it would only be for show. For the boys' sake, she decided to goad him into it. "Now, boys, cain't nobody aim good with this breeze blowin' like it is. 'Sides that, the target's at least seventy-five yards away. Storm Cloud pro'bly cain't shoot that far."

Storm Cloud saw the provocation in her brilliant blue eyes. She was challenging him, and Apache warrior that he was, he never backed down from a dare.

Slowly he slid an arrow from the quiver he wore on his back, smoothing the feathers that fletched the shaft before gently slipping the arrow's nock over the center of the bowstring. His midnight eyes never strayed from the faraway target as he extended his bow arm in front of himself and pulled the bowstring back to the top of his breastbone. The pulse in his neck and his windblown hair the only parts of him that moved, he sighted along the arrow shaft, calculating the speed and direction of the breeze and the distance to be shot.

Taken off guard by the virile and commanding sight of him, Maisie could barely take her next breath. Sunlight danced off his smooth copper skin and long raven hair while every lean stretch of muscle he possessed tightened with the strength he kept so carefully controlled. She'd never seen anything so beautiful as the masculine splendor he presented to her now.

And then he let the arrow fly. The slender shaft sliced through the air with a speed that defied the eye. Indeed, Maisie couldn't see the weapon at all until the sharp flint impaled the target, and even then she had to squint to find it.

The arrow had found its mark with staggering accuracy, splitting his first arrow in two.

She was stunned. "Well, sweet Lord in heaven, Storm Cloud. I reckon you could shoot the grease outta a biscuit without breakin' the crust."

She turned to face him, and was disarmed by his broad grin. Made all the more endearing by its crooked slant, his smile lured her toward him.

Two steps were all she needed to reach him. As his arms captured her waist, she laid her hand across the hollow beneath his cheekbone.

He was so strong and handsome and brave, she mused, her fingers caressing his temple. His finely honed skills were evident in all that he did, as was his intelligence, kindness, and generosity and tolerance. Lord, he was everything a woman could wish to have in a man.

And in that infinitesimal moment, the truth, like one of his arrows, struck her with devastating clarity.

She felt more than mere admiration for him. More than simple gratitude or sweet affection.

She was in love with Storm Cloud.

CHAPTER
6

Maisie tucked the blanket around Dilly and Dally, smiling when she noticed their bows sticking out from beneath their pillows. They rarely went anywhere without their weapons, and, after exhaustive practice sessions, the boys were now providing fresh meat for the dinner table.

Tomorrow they would compete in the Thanksgiving competitions. They'd shoot, and they'd race. And for the first time they had a real chance at winning.

Thanks to Storm Cloud.

"Woman," his deep, rich voice called softly. "What are you doing?"

She looked up and saw him standing in the threshold, his body silhouetted by the mellow firelight in the other room. One shoulder leaned against the door frame, he wore nothing but buckskin leggings and the sable cloak of his hair. His immunity to the cold fascinated her.

Drawn by his sheer magnetism, she crossed the room, stopping only when she was close enough to feel his warm breath ruffle the tendrils of hair at her temple. "The boys kicked their blankets off. I was just tuckin' 'em in." Tentatively she slid her hand into his. A melting heat spread through her.

God, she loved this man more with each flicker of her pulse.

"Your brothers will never become strong men if you do not stop treating them as babies."

Maisie noted that the sternness in his voice was tempered by the light of amusement in his dark gaze. Yet even so, a strange tension etched his features. "Storm Cloud?"

He saw her uneasiness and knew she'd sensed his mood. For both their sakes, he would keep his decision from her no longer. He led her to the front room, and, after draping her shawl around her slender shoulders, he escorted her to the splashing stream outside. Beneath the canopy of rustling pine branches that swayed over the bubbling creek, he circled his arms around her waist and held her gently to him. "To remember your eyes, I have only to look at the sky. And the sun will bring to me the image of your hair."

Wild apprehension shot through her. "Don't."

"I must. You knew the time would come."

She felt lost in the bottomless pools of his black eyes, the only eyes that had ever seen the secrets of her soul. "I knowed, but . . . but ever' time I thought on it, I made myself forget." Hot tears blurred her vision; a low moan of despair rumbled from her breast.

Her sorrow tortured Storm Cloud's very soul. His jaw working rhythmically, he bent to gather a handful of pebbles. One by one he tossed them into the creek, and wondered if there was any power on earth that would loosen the painful tightness in his heart. "I can never be a part of your world." He tried to make her understand. "I am hated here. And it is against the white man's laws for you to hide me. The longer I stay, the more risk there is to you and your brothers. I have paid my debt to you. The skills I have taught you will see you through the future. Your brothers will grow into fine men. Now I must leave."

"I'll go with you! Me and the boys—"

"No. *This* is your home, and you will stay here."

"But—but what about the boys?" she demanded, desperate to find some concrete reason why he shouldn't leave yet. "They been practicin' for weeks for them contests! It'll kill 'em if you don't watch 'em! You—you could hide in the woods. Nobody wouldn't see you there!"

He glanced toward the cabin, thinking of the two boys who had become like sons to him. "I will be with them."

"And then?" she pressed frantically. "After the contests . . . you're leavin'?"

He opened his hand and spread his fingers, watching as the remaining pebbles fell to the ground.

She knew his silence meant yes. "Just where the hell do y'think you're gonna go? Y'ain't got no more home back out west. And I cain't even *imagine* you livin' the rest o' your life on that damn reservation!"

"That is not your worry, woman."

She could find no more words to speak until those in her heart whispered to her lips. "It *is* my worry because . . . because I love you, Storm Cloud."

Her admission tore a groan from his chest. No longer able to remember his reasons for resisting her, he crushed her to him. Capturing her mouth with a kiss that held every shred of emotion he felt for her, he drank in her sweetness until he felt it flow through his senses like warm and precious honey.

His long, thick hair fell around her, hiding her from everything but him. She leaned into him, arched up to him, offering her entire self to him. "Storm Cloud."

He heard her plea in the sound of his own name, but knew she wasn't fully aware of what she was asking him for. Sliding his hands down to her bottom, he pushed her into his hips, urging her to feel his pulsing arousal, wanting her to realize how he would satisfy her longing.

At his action, the woman inside her came to life. A woman who not only understood the sensual mysteries that had remained so elusive, but one who wanted every hint of intimate pleasure the unveiling of those secrets would bring.

And she wanted to know such pleasure before Storm Cloud left her forever. "Yes," she breathed, circling her hips into the hollow of his. "I don't care about nothin' or nobody else, just you, only you."

He stiffened, the meaning behind her words knifing into him. She referred to the townspeople and sought to make him believe their judgment of her no longer mattered.

The realization killed his desire instantly. In passion's place rose a self-condemnation that sickened him.

With one powerful motion he forced her away from him. "No. We will not do this. It would dishonor both of us."

"But—"

"No," he repeated, shaking his head. "I am not your husband, and it is possible that the joining of our bodies will create a child. I must go, but I will not leave you to face the hatred of the people in the town. And do you forget the pain of having no father? I will not believe you would give the same pain to a child of your own."

She couldn't argue against anything he told her. Indeed, his foresight made her love him even more.

But a love that would never have the chance to be expressed gave her no pleasure. "Storm Cloud—"

"We have said what we had to say."

"You're really leavin'," Maisie whispered. "I ain't never gonna see you again. Won't never talk to you again."

He drew a bronzed finger across her pale cheek. "I will carry your memory with me always, woman."

"Woman," she repeated, searching the depths of his eyes. "Y'ain't never called me by name. I—I ain't special enough to you."

He stared at her for a very long time, painting her image in his mind. In this white man's world . . . in this strange land to which he'd come . . . through all the dark moments he'd suffered, she'd been the only light he'd found.

If only she knew how special she was to him.

But to voice his feelings would only cause her needless pain.

His silence hammered at her, shattering her last bit of rational thought. She felt as thought she were slipping into a mindless daze. "You—y'never even learned to use your napkin. I tried to teach you, but y'still use your hand."

He understood that her raw emotions led her to voice whatever odd notion entered her mind, and realized she would continue all night if he allowed it. "It is late, woman," he told her, forcing himself to sound harsh. "You must sleep now."

Her tears as silent as the anguish that crept through her heart, she fled to the cabin.

As Maisie led her brothers into Snickle's Corner Dilly pulled at the stiff white collar of his Pilgrim costume and scanned the crowd of people. The men, he noticed, were gathered around the paddock anticipating their turns to ride Burt Snickle's vicious stallion. The horse wore a bridle, but no saddle, prompting Dilly to decide no one could get a saddle on him. Those who had already had their turns riding the monster were nursing their resulting cuts and bruises.

The women were busy tending the meats that roasted over pits near the feasting tables, and the children played nearby. Dilly saw everyone he knew.

Except Storm Cloud. "Are y'sure Storm Cloud's here?"

"That's the thirty-eight-zillionth time you've asked Maisie that question, Dilly-Dumb-Dumb!" Dally snapped. "How many times does she gotta tell you that Storm Cloud cain't just walk into town like he owns it? Y'want them Snickles to get him?"

"I ain't dumb!" Dilly retorted. "I just wanna know where Storm Cloud is, Dally-Donkey-Dung!"

Dally rolled his eyes. "Dammit to hell, Dilly, he's pro'bly in a tree somewhere! All right? Satisfied now?"

"Boys, please." Maisie bent her head, lest they see her damp eyes. Lord, how was it possible for her to still have tears after having cried all night long?

And how on earth was she going to tell the boys the devastating news? Would Storm Cloud find a way to say good-bye to them before he left? Would any of them ever see him again?

The questions crashed through her mind. The answers to them left her sick with anxiety.

"Maisie!" a friendly voice boomed.

She saw Reverend Jenkins waddling toward her. "Mornin', Reverend."

He gave her cheek an affectionate pat and tousled the boys' hair. "We haven't seen much of the three of you in a while. I'm so glad you came today. My, what is that wonderful aroma I smell?"

She lifted her basket. "I brung some pumpkin bread."

"I'll be the first to sample it." He turned to the boys. "The contests are about to begin, and as usual I'm presiding over them. We're holding the footrace first. Are you boys going to run again this year?"

Dilly and Dally pressed their bags of weapons into Maisie's

hands and tore across the square to join the line of other boys who would be competing.

Reverend Jenkins beamed with approval and led Maisie to the starting line, where many of the townspeople were gathered to watch the contest.

Maisie watched Eula Birch and Les Winkler glare and then turn their backs. The rest of the crowd did likewise. But the familiar hurt their rejection usually caused her failed to come.

No further pain could be inflicted upon a heart already broken.

"All right, boys!" Reverend Jenkins shouted. "The race is a two-mile run that ends with a climb up Mount Snickle. Now you all know that Mount Snickle is no small hill, so whoever wins will be deemed a mighty champion!"

"Dilly and Dally are putting rocks in their mouths!" Wade Snickle hollered. "The Applejacks are nasty! The Applejacks are nasty! The Apple—"

"Wade, that's enough out of you," the reverend chided. He turned to Maisie. "The boys are eating pebbles."

She managed a sad smile. "Somebody told 'em that suckin' stones would keep 'em from gettin' thirsty."

"Ah, I see." The reverend winked at Dilly and Dally, then raised a revolver to the sky. "Follow the red-painted posts, boys! On your mark, get set, *go!*"

At the explosion of the gun, the group of boys sprang forward, leaving a cloud of dust in their wake.

For the next fifteen minutes Maisie not only endured the painful emptiness inside her, but the agony of intense apprehension as well. She'd twisted her curls into knots before catching sight of the two still-distant forms that appeared at the peak of the hill that rose in the field just outside town.

"I think one of them is my boy, Timmy!" Jed Nolly hollered.

Vaguely Maisie heard the excited shouts of the other spectators, but could only concentrate on the fact that something about the runners looked very familiar.

Side by side, the boys scrambled down the hill, dashed across the meadow, and raced into town.

Maisie's fingers trembled across her throat. The boys . . .

Dilly and Dally! Tears of pride welled in her eyes when they sped across the finish line and tied for first place. And a knowing smile touched her lips when the other contestants arrived and ran straight for the dippers of water their mothers held out to them. Dilly and Dally had barely worked up a sweat.

But then again, she mused, the other boys hadn't been trained by an Apache warrior.

"It's not fair!" Wade Snickle wailed, tears coursing down his dirty face as he staggered into town. "Them Applejacks *cheated*!" Before anyone could stop him, he raced back into the field.

Frowning furiously, Burt Snickle watched Wade run away, then grabbed hold of his other young son, Rudy. "Wade has shamed the Snickle family, Rudy," he whispered. "He's given up and will no doubt spend the rest of the afternoon pouting somewhere in the meadow. You've got to win the shooting contest, do you understand?"

Rudy nodded and strutted toward the shooting area.

Maisie and the boys followed. There, Maisie saw that the contestants were to shoot at a large white disk attached to the trunk of a pine. Whoever came closest to hitting the impossibly small black circle in the middle of the disk, would win.

"Too bad you can't ever enter the shooting contests," Rudy taunted Dilly and Dally. Glaring at the ribbons pinned to their shirts, he brandished his gleaming rifle.

"We're shootin' *this* year," Dally informed him.

Rudy sneered. "You don't have guns. You're too poor to buy any."

"We got these." Dilly held up his bag.

"What's in there?"

"None o' your beeswax, corn bread, shoe tacks," Dilly and Dally answered in unison.

Rudy glowered. "Even if you have cannons in those bags, you won't win. *I* will, just like Cooper and Newton already won the men's contest."

"They didn't hit the little black circle," Dilly pointed out.

"But they came the closest. No one shoots better than the Snickles."

Dilly and Dally exchanged a secret glance.

The contest began. Dilly and Dally chose to go last and watched as the other competitors shot. All the boys hit the target, but no one came as close to the black circle as Rudy.

"Your turn now, boys," Maisie whispered. "Make him proud."

They advanced to the place from where they were to shoot, a spot about twenty yards from the target, and removed their shirts. "We don't let nothin' but the wind betwixt us and our aim," Dilly explained, his chin jutting out as he looked at the shocked Reverend Jenkins.

"Uh . . . I see," the reverend replied. "Very well, boys, prepare your weapons." Curious over the secret weapons the boys carried in the sacks, he craned his neck to get a better view.

A hush fell over the throng of spectators as Dilly and Dally opened their bags, a quiet that was soon broken by a loud and collective gasp when everyone saw the unusual weapons the boys would use to shoot.

But no one in the gathering had a chance to protest. Swiftly the boys slid their arrows from their quivers, loaded their bows, and took aim.

Both arrows pierced the tiny black circle.

Maisie's cry of pride shattered the awed silence of the crowd. She rushed to hug her brothers. "Sweet Lord o' mercy, y'done it!"

"My goodness, those Applejacks won!" Naomi Potter exclaimed.

Burt Snickle stalked forward. "Unfair! Someone's been training those brats!"

Reverend Jenkins couldn't stop smiling. "You've trained your own sons, haven't you?"

"I . . . but . . . but they're supposed to use *guns*!"

The reverend rubbed his chin. "Well, now, Burt, I don't recall a single rule that specifies what sort of weapon must be used for this contest. All I know is that whoever comes the closest to the black spot wins. And Dilly and Dally Applejack outshot every boy and man here."

Infuriated, Burt spun toward the Applejack family. His eyes narrowed as he watched sunlight flash off the smoothly polished bows and arrows that had bested all the other weapons used in the contest.

Bows and arrows.

The words pounded through his brain, driving suspicion through his rage. "Just how is it that you possess such crude weapons?"

Cooper understood his father's insinuation immediately. "Paw, those are Indian weapons!"

"And only an Indian could have made them," Newton added, his voice crackling with anger.

"Have you been hiding that stinking Apache savage out at Applejack Shack?" Burt's gaze drilled into Maisie.

She didn't answer, but only concentrated on her mental image of Storm Cloud. Dear God, where was he? Had he heard the conversation and realized the Snickles would soon begin the hunt for him?

"Where is he?" Burt thundered. "You'd better tell me, or I'll—"

"Burt!" Les Winkler screamed as he raced across the street. "It's Smokey Joe! He hit the bank! He waited till the whole town got involved in Thanksgiving an' he robbed us!" Wildly he pointed to the rider galloping out of town.

Like an unexpected bolt of lightning, pandemonium struck the crowd. Women screamed; children cried. One terrified little girl knocked the rack of roasting turkeys into the fire pit. Men snatched up their rifles and dashed toward the stables.

"Dammit!" Burt roared. "It's going to take forever to get your mounts saddled! He's got my gold! All my precious gold!"

A sudden wind crashed through the trees, bowing branches and sweeping away Burt's hysterical shouting. As it blew through Maisie's curls, she shivered with a strange sense of awareness. That now-familiar sensation of being watched.

He was here. Near.

And every instinct she possessed shouted that he was about to reveal his whereabouts.

Her fear for his safety twisted into a knot of pure terror. "No," she whispered.

A bone-chilling howl rent the air, mastering the shrieking wind and Burt's wailing as well as every other sound. As the cry hit her ears Maisie spun toward the forest.

There in the rustling woods stood Storm Cloud, a buckskin

loincloth and a swath of shadows his only clothing.

Utter astonishment rippled through the crowd. Gone was the beaten and helpless captive they'd all seen huddled in the cage. Standing before them now was a man who manifested every danger imaginable . . .

A mighty Apache warrior.

CHAPTER
7

His steps as silent as whispers on velvet, Storm Cloud approached Maisie. "Once, you told me about money you had saved in this town," he began, his voice so low only Maisie and heaven could hear it. "This man who steals . . . He leaves with money that belongs to you?"

She understood his intentions instantly. Shaking so badly that she could barely stay standing, she clutched his thick upper arms and tried to push him back into the woods. "Forget about the damn money!" she demanded on a seething breath. "They're gonna catch you! *Go!*"

Storm Cloud pressed his hands against her cheeks. "You will answer my question, woman. And if you lie, I will know."

The hard edge in his voice and the stubborn glint in his eyes told her he would stand for no more of her hysterics. "Two dollars," she murmured. Dropping her hands from his arms, she took two steps away from him and waited for him to do what she knew he would.

His eyes mere slits, Storm Cloud watched the thief's horse gallop across the open field. Fury twisting his features, he threw back his head and let out a second bloodcurdling war cry. Then, with all the deadly speed of a hungry panther in pursuit of its prey, he bolted toward the paddock. One powerful leap took him sailing over the fence.

The wild stallion within the enclosure laid back his ears, pawed the ground, and charged.

But Storm Cloud stood as rigid as iced steel . . . until the frenzied stallion was almost upon him. Swift as a striking serpent, he grabbed the horse's flowing mane and swung himself onto its bare back.

The townspeople hurried to the paddock, dumbfounded by the warrior's deft handling of the horse. It was obvious that the savage stallion had met his match in the savage who'd mounted him. After only a moment of violent bucking and rearing, the animal shuddered in absolute surrender.

His long, muscular legs wrapped around the steed's body, Storm Cloud bent over the great stallion's neck, and took him soaring over the fence.

Black hair snapped in the wind like a long, silken banner . . .

Bronzed skin gleamed beneath the brilliant autumn sunshine . . .

And midnight eyes glittered. . . .

Bow in hand, Storm Cloud sent his mount galloping into the open pasture.

"He's going after Smokey Joe!" Jed Nolly cried.

"*Look* at him ride, Papa!" Abigail Nolly screamed. "He's just like the Indians in my picture books!"

At Abigail's words, the townspeople quieted, every person suddenly realizing they'd been given the rare opportunity to witness a true Apache warrior demonstrate the legendary skills that had made his people one of the most fearsome Indian tribes.

"God Almighty, nothing like this has ever happened here in little old Snickle's Corner!" Les Winkler shouted. "Let's go watch from the top of Mount Snickle!"

The throng of people rushed down the dirt road that led to nearby Mount Snickle, determined to behold the outcome of the chase.

But no one was more anxious than Maisie. Once she reached the hill, she, Dilly, and Dally were among the first to reach the peak. Together, they looked out over the wide-open field.

What Maisie saw almost sent her to her knees. Wade Snickle, who had found a place to sulk behind a cluster of large rocks in the field, was now racing through the meadow in an effort to escape the direct path of Smokey Joe's horse.

In the next instant, Smokey Joe leaned to the side, hauled Wade off the ground, and laid him across the horse's neck.

"He's taken Wade hostage!" Naomi Potter yelled.

"My son!" Horrified, Burt watched Wade try to wrap his small body around the horse's neck in a wild attempt to stay on.

Eula Birch nearly swooned. "Smokey Joe's pulled out his gun! Dear God, he's going to murder Wade!"

Dally began to cry. "Maisie, he's aimin' at Storm Cloud! He's gonna fire at Storm Cloud!"

Bone-melting fear seized Maisie as she watched Smokey Joe twist in the saddle and point a rifle at Storm Cloud.

"Storm Cloud!" His name burst straight from her heart, streaking over the meadow with all the speed and purpose of one of Storm Cloud's arrows.

The sound came to him on the wings of the wind. The terror it held struck his own heart, inciting him to put a swift end to her worry. Eyes riveted to his quarry, he set the stallion on a zigzag course. Thus, he became a target that was too difficult to hit. He then released the reins, reached over his shoulder, and slid two arrows from his quiver.

"Dammit, would you look at that!" Les Winkler screamed. "I've never seen such horsemanship in all my life! And look! He's going to shoot his arrows at Smokey Joe!"

"It's an impossible shot!" Jed Nolly hollered. "He's riding too fast!"

"Wade," Burt whispered, fear robbing him of his voice. "What if he hits my son?"

Every eye in the crowd watched as Storm Cloud prepared to shoot. Using only the incredible strength in his thighs to guide the thundering stallion, he clamped one arrow between his teeth, raised his bow, and shot the first arrow. The weapon had barely left the bow when he fitted the second arrow to the bowstring and took aim.

Not a breath could be heard as the citizens of Snickle's Corner watched the Apache arrows take flight. They skimmed through the air like two lethal birds of prey, ripping into the distance with awesome speed.

And with flawless precision, they brought down their victim.

Almost gracefully Smokey Joe fell from the saddle, one arrow impaled in his thigh, the other skewered through his trigger hand.

"My son!" Burt screamed. "Wade's still on the horse!" Instantly he moved to descend the hill.

"Burt, wait!" Jed Nolly grabbed Burt's arm. *"Look!"*

Oblivious to the multitude of stares, Storm Cloud directed the rugged stallion toward Smokey Joe's fleeing steed. When the two horses raced side by side, he leaned over, grabbed the waistband of Wade's pants, and yanked the boy onto his father's stallion. Holding the sobbing child close to his chest, he halted his horse. After gently lowering the lad to the ground, he sent the stallion chasing after Smokey's horse again. Once more he slid an arrow from his quiver and took aim.

In the breath of a second, the arrow cut loose the bag of gold from Smokey Joe's saddle. The satchel crashed into the tall grass.

Every shred of strength Storm Cloud possessed tensing with readiness, he waited until his mount was but a few feet away from the bulging sack before clutching the stallion's thick mane and pitching himself into the air. At the very moment his feet met earth, he snatched the pouch off the ground and was back on the stallion before the horse could break stride.

The crowd poured down the hill and raced into the field. Burt headed straight for his son while the rest of the throng surrounded Smokey Joe, who lay but a short distance away from Wade.

"The Indian's coming back!" Naomi Potter shouted, pointing across the meadow.

Storm Cloud slowed the stallion when he neared the gawking people. He stopped the huge horse beside Maisie, opened the money bag, and held it to her. "Take what is yours."

Numb with relief that he was unharmed, but frozen with the fear for his continued safety, she couldn't move.

"Do as I say, woman!"

His shout snapped her out of her icy daze. Her hands trembling so badly she could barely get them to work, Maisie withdrew two bills.

Storm Cloud closed the bag and urged the stallion toward

the man who had once beaten and imprisoned him. "Here is your precious gold." He tossed the heavy sack to the ground.

The blackest, most fierce eyes Burt had ever seen glared down at him. Petrified, he tightened his hold on Wade, bowed his head, and backed away.

With a lift of his chin, Storm Cloud accepted the cowardly man's surrender.

"Storm Cloud?" Maisie started toward him, but stopped when she heard a rumbling sound in the distance. Snapping her head toward the town, she saw two horses galloping into the meadow. In the next instant she realized the riders were Cooper and Newton.

Storm Cloud's hunters.

"Woman."

She looked up into his dark eyes, and in them she read his farewell. She tried to answer, but her all-consuming grief stole her voice.

Holding his bow high above his head, Storm Cloud released an ear-piercing cry and sent the stallion thundering across the field and into the surrounding forest.

In mere moments he'd disappeared from Maisie's view.

From her life.

The only two turkeys the town's hunters had been able to provide for the banquet had spilled into the roasting fire and burned beyond recognition. There remained plenty of venison and pheasant and a multitude of succulent side dishes, but the general consensus was that Thanksgiving wasn't Thanksgiving without freshly roasted turkeys.

The accident added yet more gloom to the uneasy mood of the community. The men attended to their duties of turning the meats over the spits, and the women stayed busy preparing the rest of the meal, but everyone went about their jobs in abject silence. Even Burt Snickle's usual blustering was suspiciously absent.

But no one was more dispirited than the Applejacks. Maisie and the boys sat beneath a pine tree, anxiously awaiting Cooper and Newton's return.

"Maisie," Reverend Jenkins said as he walked toward her and the boys. "They'll never catch him. Cooper and Newton chasing Storm Cloud . . . Well, that's like two whispers chasing the wind."

She wiped her eyes on the sleeve of her dress. "I—I gotta wait. Gotta see. Once I'm sure, me and the boys'll go on home. Don't nobody really want us here nohow."

The reverend looked up, the compassion in his eyes changing to hot anger as he watched his congregation tending to their tasks. He was well aware that many of them were plagued with guilt, and yet not a one of them had been able to swallow pride and comfort the Applejacks. "What they need is one of my loud and censorious sermons," he muttered. "A scathing lecture no one will ever forget. And by God, I'm going to give it to them right now!"

He stalked toward the crowd, but stopped abruptly when Cooper and Newton came riding out of the forest.

Maisie came off the ground as if some explosion inside the earth had thrown her. Wildly she searched for any sign of Storm Cloud.

"No, Maisie, we didn't get him," Cooper bit out at her. "We couldn't even find his damn trail." He dismounted and approached her.

Newton did likewise. "Your savage lover got away. But surely you won't have to wait long to have a piece of him back. There's no doubt in our minds that you've got his redskinned brat in your belly right now. He's been living with you, hasn't he? And you *are* your mother's daughter."

Every fiber of control Maisie possessed snapped. She covered her face with her hands and sobbed.

"Enough!" the reverend bellowed at the Snickle brothers. Quickly he went to Maisie and put his arm around her waist. "There now, my dear, don't cry."

He asked the impossible. "I ain't never knowed a man as good as Storm Cloud. I *loved* him! And—and if that makes me like Maw . . . then I'm *proud* to be like her!"

Dilly and Dally rushed to hug her, their tears dampening her black skirts.

Reverend Jenkins could contain his wrath no longer. "Two people!" he shouted at the crowd. "A man and a woman. One born without white skin, one born without a father. Though neither can be blamed for the circumstances of their births, both are shunned, both hated. Is it any wonder that God, in His infinite wisdom, chose to bring them together?"

Many of the townspeople bowed their heads and shuffled their feet on the ground.

Reverend Jenkins walked among them. "Braving bullets, Storm Cloud saved Wade Snickle, the son of the very man who captured and tortured him. Then he turned around and rescued the town's money. After having returned Maisie's to her, he could have left with the rest. But he didn't. Nor did he kill Smokey Joe, and there is not a man here who doubts that he could have. The courageous warrior showed profound mercy, a mercy he himself received from no one here but Maisie."

He stopped beside Maisie, but continued to scowl at the shamefaced people. "And what of this warmhearted girl?" he continued sternly. "Have none of you ever noticed that she shows not a shred of malice toward any of you? She certainly has just cause, but she's simply incapable of the poisonous emotion. Indeed, she returns your hostility with a smile. How many of us possess such powers of forgiveness? When will you open your eyes and see her true value to our community? It seems to me that instead of ostracizing her, you would seek to *imitate* her!"

He raised his arm and gestured toward the cooking food. "Today is Thanksgiving. In a short while we will partake of our bountiful harvest. While we prepare for the feast, let us ponder one who has nothing, one who has lost everything he was once so proud and thankful to have. And let us welcome and comfort the woman who loved him."

There were very few dry eyes in the crowd as everyone looked at Maisie. Embarrassed by all the attention and still aching over the loss of Storm Cloud, she lowered her head and tightened her hold on her brothers.

But Dilly jerked out of her embrace, his little chest heaving wildly. "Listen, Dally!" he shouted at his brother. "Do y'hear it?"

Dally nodded, a bright smile chasing away the sorrow in his features.

Maisie watched as her brothers ogled the dense forest. "What do y'hear?" she queried anxiously.

Dilly and Dally looked at each other, their eyes wide with joy. "A deer," Dilly answered.

"But not a *real* deer," Dally clarified. "A blade o' grass."

Maisie scowled with absolute bewilderment. "Grass? Boys, what—"

"If y'fold a blade o' grass a certain way and blow into it, y'can make the sound deers make," Dilly explained. "The deers come so close, y'can shoot 'em while lookin' into their eyes."

Maisie felt her heart slide to her feet.

Only one man could have taught her brothers that bit of knowledge.

He was back.

CHAPTER
8

His bearing as regal as that of a king, Storm Cloud urged the stallion out of the woods and into the parting of the crowd, his every instinct trained on the two armed men who'd tried to hunt him down.

He stopped the steed. "I have come to speak. You will listen?"

"Yes!" Reverend Jenkins shouted. "Yes, of course we will!"

Storm Cloud inclined his head in gratitude. "Many years ago," he began, his voice strong and steady as he spoke to the gathering, "the white men came to this land from across the sea. It was the time of Ghost Face, when the land was white with snow. They faced many hardships and wondered how they could survive without food. Some of them died."

He paused a long moment before continuing, allowing his words to root in the minds of his rapt audience. "With the coming of the spring, the Indians arrived to assist them in the planting of corn. The harvest was good, and the white men had a feast and thanked their God. The Indians came to this feast with gifts of meat. And the white men and the Indians sat together and shared the food and the friendship . . . and the peace."

He pulled a bulging sack off his shoulder. Upon opening it, he withdrew three fat turkeys. "I am Nubarrón. Storm Cloud. I am a Chiricahua Apache, and I come to your feast with this gift of meat. I wish to sit at your table and share the food, the friendship . . . and the peace."

Holding the turkeys out for the people to see, he waited for the welcome he wasn't totally certain he would receive, and remained ready to flee if the need arose.

One little girl tugged on her mother's skirts. "Mama, we always have Pilgrims at our feast, but we've never had any Indians. It would be just like the first Thanksgiving if Storm Cloud sat down and ate with us."

The child's declaration was all the crowd needed to hear. Someone cheered, and the people swarmed around the pawing stallion.

Storm Cloud laid the turkeys across the multitude of out-stretched hands, then dismounted. Once again the throng parted for him.

He walked straight for Maisie and her brothers. One dark look at Dilly and Dally kept the excited boys quiet and still as he took Maisie's hand and led her to the crowd. "I left this woman today," he announced, his fingers caressing hers. "I thought what I did was the only thing I could do. But I did not remember that when the people here saw me, they would know I had stayed with her, and that they would make her feel deep shame for taking me into her home. When I thought of this, I knew in my heart that I had to defend her."

He drew himself up to his full height, his midnight gaze searching out each face in the assemblage. "This woman has done nothing wrong. She shared her house with me, and her food. She gave her companionship, her caring, and her laughter. But she did not give what was wrong to give. I speak the truth. If there are any among you who would dishonor her, let those people face me now."

Cooper and Newton strode forward, rifles in hand. "We'll face you!" Cooper shouted. "Maisie Applejack's a whore!"

"Just like her mother!" Newton added.

His motions so fast they were blurred, Storm Cloud snatched two arrows from his quiver and raised his bow toward the two men who had dared to disgrace the woman at his side.

"*No!*" Reverend Jenkins roared.

Frantically Burt Snickle raced to stand before his sons. "Stop! For God's sake, please don't!"

In quick succession, Storm Cloud shot both arrows.

Wailing in horror, Burt spun around, sure he would see his sons die before his very eyes.

What he saw were two very shaken men with arrows in their Pilgrim hats. He hugged them, then slapped them. "Go home! Both of you, go home and *stay* there!"

Red-faced with humiliation, Cooper and Newton slunk out of sight.

Burt struggled with his own mortification. Slowly he turned to face the warrior who'd rescued his young son and shown clemency to his two older and foolish sons. His shoulders slouched, he crossed to where Storm Cloud stood. "It shames me to remember that I once believed you were less than a human being," he began softly. "I have learned today that you are a bigger man than I. I offer my most humble apologies to you, and as founder of this town, I'd like to be the first to welcome you to Snickle's Corner." He held out his hand for a shake of friendship.

Storm Cloud made no move to accept it. "And what of this woman? You have given her many reasons to weep. You will say nothing to her?"

Burt nodded and placed his hand on Maisie's shoulder. "I'm sorry. I was wrong about you, Miss Applejack, and I regret all the years of heartache I've caused you. If you would allow me, I would like to build a house for you and the boys here in town. Applejack Shack isn't the place for you."

"She will not live in the town," Storm Cloud declared. "Her place is with me. As her husband, I will rebuild her home and provide for all her needs." He held out his hand and shook Burt's.

Concentrating as she was on the startling image of Storm Cloud's dark hand locked with Burt's stark white one, it was a moment before Maisie realized what Storm Cloud had just said.

Her knees buckled; she braced herself for the fall.

It never came. Instead she found herself enfolded in Storm Cloud's strong arms. She peered up into his glistening black eyes. "You . . . you said *husband*."

"I will be your husband when I take you for my wife. This is not true, woman?"

At the name he'd called her, her happiness vanished. Rage screamed through her. "Y'think I'm gonna marry a man who don't think I'm special? You're so empty-headed that if I was to give you a penny for your thoughts, you'd owe me change! I'd *never* wed up with a man who didn't love me!" Twisting, she tried to escape his hold on her.

He merely brought her closer. "Who here is the one who must listen to the wedding vows?"

Reverend Jenkins watched Maisie's fight with Storm Cloud. "I am. But—but I'm not altogether sure Maisie wishes me to unite the two of you in holy matrimony."

"You're damn right I don't wish no unitin'!" she flared, still struggling to free herself from Storm Cloud's arms. "I'd as soon spend the rest o' my life tryin' to nail melted butter to a tree!"

"It will soon be her wish," Storm Cloud promised. "You will listen as I pledge my heart to her."

The reverend frowned. "Storm Cloud, there is a specific wedding ceremony I am required to perform. Perhaps you and Maisie can work out your differences while I go fetch my Bible?"

"I will wait no longer to make this woman my wife."

The reverend had never witnessed such bold obstinacy, and understood then why many years and scores of soldiers had yet to subdue the Apache nation. "But . . . I . . . you . . . Maisie . . ."

Dismissing the stammering man, Storm Cloud gazed down into Maisie's flashing blue eyes. "Stop fighting me, woman. I am trying to marry you. You will listen to the voice of my heart as I take you for my wife."

She hissed at him. "My name ain't *woman*! It's—"

"Take this, Maisie!" Dally interrupted as he grabbed an arrangement of golden chrysanthemums off one of the feasting tables.

Dilly grabbed the flowers away from his brother and quickly pressed them into Maisie's hand.

"Here, Dilly!" Wade and Rudy called, gathering yet more flowers.

Naomi Potter and Eula Birch rushed forward to place a

flowing lace tablecloth upon Maisie's flaxen curls. "There!" Naomi cried.

Eula beamed. "Oh, Maisie, you make a beautiful bride!"

Storm Cloud waited patiently for the women to finish. When they stepped away, he made another attempt to marry Maisie. "As I need air to breathe, I need you," he wooed her softly. "You are a song that sings through my veins and lifts my spirit. I would face a thousand arrows for you, and I would return the arrows many times over to see that no harm comes to you. I will father and love your sons and your daughters, and I swear to accept your brothers as my own children. Hear my vow, woman, and know that all that is precious to you will be precious to me."

He swept his long, dark fingers through the golden cloud of her hair. "Maisie," he murmured tenderly. "Maisie, my woman with eyes of sky and hair of sun, for as long as my feet walk this earth, I will love you with a passion deeper than the deepest seas."

Like a slender candle set too close to a fierce flame, she melted against him. Bright tears filled her eyes as his declaration of love rang endlessly through her. "Maisie," she whispered. "Y'called me Maisie. Oh, Storm Cloud . . ." She could find no more words to express the depths of her joy.

Reverend Jenkins sniffled and dabbed at his wet cheeks with a handkerchief. He'd beheld many weddings in his life, but never one more beautiful than the one he'd seen today. No ceremony written in any manual could have been more binding.

He held his hand over Storm Cloud and Maisie. "By the authority invested in me, I now pronounce you man and wife. Storm Cloud, you may kiss your bride."

Right before Storm Cloud's lips met hers, Maisie smiled up at him. "Y'gotta promise me one more thing."

He returned her smile. "Anything."

"Your napkin," she whispered, her lips grazing his. "I learned to skin a deer, and you can damn well learn to use a napkin. Promise?"

Storm Cloud threw back his head and laughed. "Promise." His strong, bronzed arms tightening around his wife, he lowered his mouth to hers in a kiss that held the very essence of love.

The citizens of Snickle's Corner cheered wildly, but no one more loudly than Dilly and Dally. Thrilled beyond measure, they wrapped their arms around the newlyweds. "Is Storm Cloud our paw, or our brother, Dally?" Dilly asked.

"What the hell kind o' difference does it make?" Dally replied. "Either way he's ours to keep! Ain't that right, Reverend?"

Nodding, Reverend Jenkins smiled broadly and continued to watch the physical proof of Storm Cloud's love for Maisie. Finally, at long last, he mused, there had come into Maisie's life a man who had seen through her rags and the stain she bore through no fault of her own.

The thought moved him to quote a passage from the book of Proverbs. "When one finds a worthy wife, her value is far beyond pearls. Her husband, entrusting his heart to her, has an unfailing prize. She brings him good, and not evil, all the days of her life."

At the reverend's words, Storm Cloud felt his heart swell with gladness and gratitude. He'd lost his entire world, but he'd found another with Maisie.

And her value was, indeed, far beyond pearls.

AUTUMN SONG

Jo Anne Cassity

Dear Reader,

I was a young bride when I first visited the little town of Spiceland, Indiana. It was, and still is, a small farming community that echoes of the past. It was also the home of my husband's grandparents, Clarence and Maude Cassity, who had a small farm outside of town.

Every year in late September my husband and I used to take our vacation and stop in Spiceland to see his grandmother, other relatives, and friends. I loved those visits and grew to love the people there.

So when I was given the opportunity to write "Autumn Song," Spiceland and its townsfolk immediately came to mind, along with the idea of making a lonely young widow the heroine. Not only would I have the chance to write my favorite kind of story, but I would be able to focus it on my favorite season and a setting very much like the friendly little town I remember so well.

I wrote "Autumn Song" in honor of Clarence and Maude and the warmhearted people of Spiceland. In memory of their neighborliness, I decided to change the name to Friendly, which is where my story takes place. My characters are fictional, but I believe they could very easily have existed.

My hero, Parker Reed, is a footloose drifter who finds Friendly anything but friendly. After all, being thrown in jail on trumped-up charges, then forced to work a cantan-

151

kerous young widow's farm until harvest, is hardly his idea of hospitality.

My heroine, Molly McPherson, is a tenderhearted but very stubborn woman. She truly appreciates her neighbors and eccentric father-in-law's efforts to provide her with a farmhand, but Parker, with his cocky grin and shiftless ways, does not fit her picture of a suitable candidate.

Josh, Molly's sweet adolescent stepson, thinks Parker is terrific and looks forward to the adventure of having a young, able-bodied man around to help him work the neglected farm.

As we all know, love is a powerful and strange emotion. It grows where it will, despite efforts to the contrary, despite differences in backgrounds and personalities. And I thought harvest, being the season of completion, would be a beautiful time of year for these two people to reap the wonder of their love for one another and, in doing so, give Josh all the love he needs and deserves.

I chose the year 1880 because I love the simplicity of that time period. I added a handful of quirky characters, like Grover Phillips, the town's bumbling sheriff, and Bull Garrett, a big, clumsy, faithful deputy. Then I stirred well and sprinkled liberally with plenty of star-dusted evenings, a big harvest moon, and a host of frosty mornings. Oh, and I added a pinch of humor, too, for fun and in tribute to the memorable people of Spiceland.

Writing "Autumn Song" was a very special treat for me. I enjoyed every minute I spent with Parker, Molly, Josh, and the people of Friendly, Indiana. It was like going home again. I sincerely hope you'll enjoy your visit in Friendly, too.

Jo Anne Cassity

CHAPTER
1

"They're comin', Molly!" Thirteen-year-old Joshua McPherson yelled, then turned and loped off toward the prisoner wagon that was making its way up the narrow dirt road.

"Hey, Bull!" the boy called out to a large man astride a huge horse. "Hey, Grover!" he hollered to the smaller man driving the wagon's team of horses.

"Hey, Josh!" Bull Garrett returned with a wave and a wide grin.

"Howdy, there, Josh!" Grover Phillips responded warmly.

Molly straightened and lifted the bucket of water from the well before turning to follow her stepson. Sweat trickled down her sides and melted into the waistband of her skirt. It was a hot day for May. Too hot. A white sun hovered over the yet-to-be-planted fields. A hawk rode across the hazy blue sky. She raised a hand to shield her eyes from the sun's glare and gazed out at the approaching wagon. She eyed it with distaste and, though few would have guessed it, a measure of compassion. The sight of its cagelike appearance seemed cruel somehow. Inhuman. She'd always thought it didn't seem quite civilized to cage a man in such a manner. Yet she knew such wagons were necessary and common enough to towns—even small towns like Friendly.

She sighed, hoping her father-in-law had found her a man worth feeding this year—a man young enough and able enough to actually plant a shovel into the ground, instead of one old enough to be planted himself.

When the prisoner wagon left the road and entered the barnyard, she lowered the heavy bucket to the ground, ignoring the water that slopped into the dust, and went out to meet her new work hand.

Parker Reed glared daggers through the bars.

He watched the tall, stiff-spined woman move toward his cell on wheels, then looked beyond her to the square, gray pile of sticks that masqueraded as her house.

His heart sank even further.

God, that house was ugly! Just about the ugliest thing he'd ever laid eyes upon.

Though it appeared to be sound enough, the roof sagged miserably, and the porch steps hung off one side at a weird crooked angle. The only redeeming element Parker could find within the entire depressing scene was the lovely old oak that stood a small distance away from the house.

And that was hardly enough to lift his spirits.

He looked at the woman again.

So! This was her! Hmmph! No wonder the town had to waylay innocent men to work her farm. She was plainer than a rock and far too thin, he decided, studying her intently. Her dark red hair was pulled back from her face into a coiled braid so severe it stretched the skin of her cheekbones taut. Her eyes, though large and dark, were expressionless and cold. Her complexion, unlike that of the soft, pale, protected skin of the Southern belles he'd known, was tinted gold and sprinkled with freckles.

Yessiree, he reaffirmed silently, this was one hard woman. Definitely not his type. Definitely not a woman he cared to spend the next several months with.

But then again, he admitted to himself, he'd yet to meet any woman he wanted to spend that amount of time with.

As he watched her approach he yearned for escape.

He lowered his sandy eyebrows and tried to look dangerous. Maybe she'd be so damned scared of him she'd refuse him, and having no other use for him, the demented locals would return his horse and belongings and send him packing. On to his destination, San Francisco.

God, how he needed a drink! And some decent food. And a woman, too—a soft one, a real one, once his temper cooled off a bit.

But right now he had to keep his head clear and figure a way out this mess.

He thought of the sign he'd passed on his way into town yesterday: WELCOME TO FRIENDLY, INDIANA, it had read. PLEASE CHECK ALL FIREARMS WITH THE LOCAL SHERIFF. THIS HERE IS A FRIENDLY TOWN.

And he'd done just that—checked his firearms, left his horse and belongings at the livery, then gone over to the saloon to quench his thirst. The next thing he knew it was morning, and he was in the town's jail, confused and angry, with a lump the size of Kansas on the back of his head.

Friendly! Hmmph! Parker snorted and lowered his brows even further.

"Here he is, Molly!" Bull called out pleasantly as he reined in his horse. "Just like the judge promised!"

Molly halted before the wagon. She widened her stance, plunked her hands on her hips, and stared at Bull silently for several lengthy seconds. Finally she turned her gaze on Parker and said, "Take him out. I can't get a good look at him scrunched up like he is in that cage."

"Sure thing, Molly," Grover said, and climbed down from his seat. He moved toward the door of the cage, glancing over his shoulder at her. "Judge said to say he was powerful sorry it took him so long this year. We thought we had you a fella last week, but the varmint lit out 'fore we could convince him working your land was in his best interest." He turned to Parker. His tone equally pleasant, he said, "Come on outta there, mister, so Molly can get a better look at ya." Then to Molly: "This one's a mite younger than the other fella was. Judge thought he'd suit you better anyhow, being as ya got so much as needs doin' around this place this year."

Awkwardly, with his cuffed hands held out before him, Parker dropped his legs over the side of the wagon and stood, unfolding his tall, lanky frame. He groaned inwardly, his cramped muscles complaining. His scowl deepened to where his eyebrows touched the golden tips of his eyelashes.

Her dark gaze sharp, Molly scrutinized Parker from the top of his sandy-blond head down to his fancy, once-shiny gentleman's boots. Her gaze grew skeptical. "He's kinda scrawny, isn't he?"

Parker bristled. Scrawny! In all his twenty-nine years, no woman had ever dared called him scrawny. In fact, back in Virginia, where his father was one of the wealthiest planters in the state, he'd once been considered quite a catch. Her disdain galled him. He ground his teeth together until they hurt.

Chuckling, Bull swung down from his horse. "Judge thought you'd say that. Also said if anyone could put meat on a man's bones, you could."

"Hmmph!" Molly said.

Hmmph! Parker thought.

Joshua moved to stand beside Bull. His blue eyes wide and curious, he studied the handcuffed man for several silent seconds, then glanced up at Bull. "He shore looks mean."

Bull dropped a meaty paw onto the boy's shoulder. "Naw, he ain't too awful mean. Kinda cranky, though. And he don't talk much. When he does, he's got this smooooth accent. Southern, I'd guess." Bull shook his head and gently cuffed the boy on the side of the head. "Can't say as he has the best of temperaments, but then what do ya expect outta his kind?"

"What'd he do?" Molly asked, her eyes locking with Parker's.

"Got drunk and disturbed the peace."

"The hell I did!" Parker exploded, and swung around toward the large man, his hands straining against the cuffs.

"Judge said you did, so you did," Bull announced quietly. "Judge McPherson's word is the law in our town." He shrugged. "And you had a trial."

"You call that a trial?" Parker said in disbelief. "I never even had a chance to defend myself!"

"Now, there ain't no need for you to take on so, Mr. Reed," Bull said patiently, kindly, shaking his head. "No one has anything against you personally."

"Well, praise God!" Parker snapped sarcastically, and swung back around to nail Molly with what he hoped was his hardest gaze.

Molly stared back, her gaze harder by far. "We don't blaspheme the Lord's name in any way around here, mister," she said softly, but the reprimand in her words echoed loudly.

Parker's gaze grew belligerent. In his most affected Southern accent he drawled, "Well, allow me to beg yer pardon, ma'aaaam."

Animosity rose between them like a field of spooked birds. A tense silence hung heavy for several seconds. Molly broke it by turning to Bull and asking, "What'd you say his name was?"

"He won't say, but he had papers in his belongings that say his name is Parker Reed."

Parker's face grew red, then purple. A vein popped out on his forehead and pulsed with his anger. He pivoted toward Bull, his eyes protruding. "You went through my papers?"

Grover stepped forward. His voice was most apologetic when he said, "Now just a minute. It ain't Bull's fault. It's standard procedure to impound a criminal's possessions. Being as I'm the sheriff and Bull's my deputy, we figured we had the right—"

"But I'm no goddamn criminal!" Parker yelled, taking malicious pleasure in ignoring Molly's warning about blasphemy. He gestured wildly with his bound arms. "I haven't done anything! I was just passing through—"

"But you disturbed the peace."

"The goddamn hell I did!"

"Judge said ya did," Grover insisted.

"Your judge is an eccentric old man!"

"He's still the judge," Grover said, not even bothering to deny Parker's charge. Judge McPherson's eccentricity was common knowledge among the residents of Friendly, but they loved and respected him just the same.

Joshua leaned over toward Molly. "He sure cusses a lot." The boy fought to keep the admiration out of his voice.

"Don't he, though?" Molly's mouth flattened into a thin line of disapproval.

His eyes still fixed on the stranger, Joshua idly pushed a stone around in the dirt with the toe of his scuffed boot. "He's younger than most we've had."

"That he is," Molly agreed.

"Tall, too . . ." Joshua offered.

"Skinny, though," Molly pointed out again while her eyes lit on his hands. They were large and wide and, she suspected, strong, but they were also pale and smooth, with no sign of calluses. She'd be willing to bet those hands had never even held a shovel, let alone done a hard day's work with one.

"We could feed him. That would make him stronger." Despite himself, hope crept into Joshua's voice. After all, it had been a long time since there had been a man around this farm. A real man, that is. Not one of the old, drunken miners that passed through on their way to other places. This man was not old, and despite his bedraggled appearance, he didn't have the look of a drunkard. He shore swore mighty fine, too. Yep, Joshua decided, this one was a keeper.

"Mm-mm . . ." Molly considered Joshua's words.

"We gonna keep him?" Joshua asked.

Molly sighed. She raised her gaze and stared off into the distance. The barren fields echoed silence and neglect. There was so much to do, and she was so tired. Far too tired for a woman of only twenty-six years.

"Molly?" Josh prompted, tugging on the sleeve of her blouse.

Molly's gaze came back to Parker. She sighed again. She didn't like him. Not one bit. She didn't like his handsome face, his arrogant attitude, or his smooooth Southern accent. There was something about the man that just screamed trouble. Not to mention the fact that she thought him a truly sorry specimen of a man. But he was young and able. She couldn't ignore that fact. The softness that was so evident in him could be worked out in time. And, she knew, if she turned down this one, her only alternative was to accept Silas Turner's offer of help. He'd been only too eager to offer to get her crops in for her. But after she'd spent one evening in his company last month, all of her instincts told her that acceptance of his help would not be wise. She was far more apprehensive about what Silas was hoping to gain in return for his kindness than she was apprehensive about this fancy, footloose stranger. After the harvest, the stranger would move on and leave her and Josh to themselves.

Silas would not.

He was looking for a wife to replace the one who'd died on him last fall, as well as a mother to care for his three young children. And the fact that his land connected with hers was the added incentive that had led him to seek her company several months ago.

But Molly McPherson was no fool. Not this time.

Common sense won out, and she sighed once again.

"Well, Molly," Grover prodded, anxious to be on his way, hoping she'd take the cantankerous prisoner off his hands.

Molly's eyes found Grover's, then Bull's. Her face relaxed in resignation. "I don't reckon we have much choice in the matter. The crops need to go in by next week—they're late already, and the barn's leaking bad. The fences have to be mended, or we're gonna lose the few cattle we have. There's so much that needs to be done around here I can't remember it all. . . . We're already behind. Josh and I can only do so much. . . ."

Bull took Parker's arm. "Then where do you want him, the milk house or the corncrib?"

Molly narrowed her gaze. "Think he'll run?"

"Sure as the sun's gonna rise tomorrow," Bull answered without pause.

Parker seethed. His blue eyes flared with indignation. *Damned right, I'll run. You just watch and see how fast, lady.*

"Then lock him up in the corncrib," Molly said without preamble, and turned on her heel and walked back to the well to retrieve her bucket.

CHAPTER
2

"Wake up, Mr. Reed," Joshua said, and stuck the barrel of his shotgun through the slats of the corncrib. Gently he nudged the sleeping man in the ribs.

Parker's eyelids parted into slits. The gray light of dawn stabbed at his pupils. He slammed his lids shut, groaned, and attempted to roll over onto his side, only to find himself hampered by several ears of corn. One lodged up against his nostrils, partially cutting off his air. He tried to ignore it, then something poked him in the ribs once again.

"Come on, mister," Joshua entreated. "Molly's waitin' breakfast."

Stubbornly Parker held his eyes closed. "Only fools and old folks get up this time of the morning, son." And Molly McPherson, he added to himself with disdain, remembering only too clearly where he was.

Joshua poked him again—this time a little harder.

Irritated, Parker parted one eyelid to gaze up into the barrel of the shotgun. He flinched, and both eyes flew open wide. He pushed the gun barrel aside with his cuffed hands. "Jesus, son!" he yelled. "Put that goddamn thing down!" Scowling, his back aching, he struggled to sit up, only to feel a thousand needles zing a painful path through his cramped legs.

"Molly said to keep it on ya, just in case you got it in mind to run."

"Where the hell am I gonna run to with these things on?" Parker motioned with his cuffed hands, his expression thunderous.

"Molly says ya never can tell 'bout a criminal—"

"I ain't no goddamn criminal!" Parker exploded. Then, seeing the boy wince at his harsh tone, he felt an uncomfortable twinge of shame. His glower deepened.

The boy took a key from his pocket. "Stick your hands out here. Molly said I could take 'em off till time to lock ya up tonight. She says if after a couple of weeks ya show ya intend to stick around, then ya can bunk in the milk house over yonder. We fixed it up for our help. It'd be more comfortable for ya. It has a bed and all. For now, Molly said to give you this." Joshua gestured to the blanket he'd laid at his feet. "At least you'll be warm enough bein' it's just about summer and all."

"Mighty kind of your ma," Parker snapped, sticking his arms through the slats.

"She ain't my ma," Joshua clarified easily, ignoring Parker's barb. "My real ma's dead. Molly's my stepma." The boy worked the key into the lock of the cuffs, unlocked them, then took them from Parker's wrists and hung them in his back pocket. Patiently he waited while Parker worked the stiffness out of his hands and arms.

Parker's eyes rose; their gazes locked. Out of curiosity Parker asked, "What about your pa?"

Joshua gave a careless shrug. "He lit outta here six months after he married Molly. That was nine years ago. Left us a note sayin' he was goin' off to build a new life for all of us out west so we wouldn't have to work this farm." Joshua paused, then added, "He never did have much use for the farm like the judge hoped he would when he gave it to him."

"The judge?" Parker questioned, confused as to what the old man had to do with this farm.

"My granddad. Judge Elias McPherson. He's my pa's pa. My pa was his only son. The judge kinda looks after me and Molly best he can. And me and Molly"—Josh shrugged—"we look after each other."

Parker's mind clicked. Clarity dawned. No wonder the old fool waylaid innocent men and sentenced them with trumped-up charges. Molly was his daughter-in-law.

"Me and Molly do, though," Joshua went on. Noting Parker's confused stare, he verified, "Like the farm, that is. Me and Molly like it fine. It's our home." The boy spoke the last words with a measure of pride, even while he glanced around at the barren fields, the small house that desperately needed a coat of whitewash, and the old barn whose roof sagged in sad need of repair. And as he so often did, Joshua McPherson found himself wishing he were older, stronger. . . .

"Your pa ever come back?" Parker asked, awkwardly making his way over the sparse layer of corncobs to the crib's hatch.

"Yep. 'Bout two years back."

Confused once more, Parker waited while Joshua untied the knots securing the latch of the door. "So where is he?"

Joshua turned and gestured to a small hill in the distance. On it stood two wooden crosses. "Up there. Buried beside my ma." His voice devoid of emotion, he explained, "He tried to cheat the wrong man in a card game and took a bullet in the belly." He shrugged again. "We weren't surprised when the pine box arrived with him in it. A little sad. But not surprised."

As Parker stared out at the hill in the distance, a queer knot tightened in the pit of his gut. He frowned, angered by its presence. The last thing in the world he wanted to feel for this boy, or the starchy, coldhearted woman who was his jailer, was compassion or pity. But there it was just the same. As sharp and real as the taste of a good swig of whiskey. God, how he needed a drink!

His gaze came back to Joshua's. The boy was thin, but well built. His face was handsome, but more than that, his eyes reflected intelligence and honesty. Bemused, Parker felt shamed by the integrity he read in the youngster's face.

They studied each other for the space of several seconds, until Joshua finally blushed and broke the silence by reiterating, "Molly's waiting breakfast."

Parker stepped down into the dew-dampened grass. He stretched long and tall, silently thankful to be able to do so. An old rooster strutted by, stopped before Parker, gave him a disinterested glance, then turned his attention to a partial ear of corn that had fallen through the slats of the crib. A large hound dog wandered by, lifted his leg on the side of the outbuilding, then moped off toward the slice of sun that had just slanted across the porch.

"Come on," Joshua prodded, gesturing with his gun toward the house. "Breakfast'll be cold 'fore we get there to eat it. And Molly says we got lots to do today."

Parker fell into step beside the boy. He slid him a sly, almost wicked glance. "You always do what Molly says, son?"

"Mostly."

"Mostly, huh?"

"Well . . ." A cautious grin caught at the corner of Joshua's mouth. " 'Cept when I skip school and head on down to the fishin' hole."

Despite himself, Parker found himself grinning. "I did that more than a few times myself when I was about your age."

Joshua's gaze met Parker's. Respect was born. "Yeah?"

"Yeah. Sure beat the hell outta school."

Joshua nodded and decided to live dangerously. "Sure as hell does."

From her place by the window, Molly watched the lanky stranger keep pace with Joshua. They seemed to be having a great time together, talking and laughing.

Their camaraderie irritated her.

She hoped Reed's shiftless ways wouldn't rub off on Joshua. She thought it odd that she'd never worried about such a thing with the other men Elias had sent her. But then, something told her this man was different. She sensed it sure as she could sense rain while it was still on the horizon.

And the reason was more than just his good looks, which in themselves were a crucial mark against him. Oh, he was handsome, all right. Too handsome. Even scowling like a scalded duck yesterday, he was still a looker. And you never could trust a handsome man, Molly acknowledged inwardly. Joshua's father had been a looker, too. Look what trusting him had gotten her.

She felt a twinge of guilt at having such bitter thoughts.

After all, trusting Frank McPherson had gotten her Joshua. And she truly loved the boy every bit as much as she would have loved a child of her own—had she ever been so blessed.

But Frank hadn't stayed around long enough to take care of that. In the few months they'd spent together, he'd barely touched her. The few times he had, well . . . it had been a hasty, frantic thing. Not at all the tender, joyful union she'd imagined in her girlish dreams. Not at all the joining she'd hoped for, ached for.

But she had found joy in Joshua. He'd been all of four years old when Frank had brought her here. He'd been barely five when Frank had left them.

She had been seventeen. Young, trusting, and in love with a man who'd never loved anyone but himself. A man who'd married her for no other reason than to palm off his responsibilities onto her youthful shoulders.

Her mother had warned her against him. Right up until the day she died, her mother had said, "I told you, Molly. Men as pretty as him don't marry girls like you,'less there's something else they want from them other than love."

The pain of that reminder brought her back to the present and made her think of Silas. He was not a particularly handsome man, but he was strong and responsible. But he, too, wanted something from her. Once again, it wasn't love. This time she knew the truth.

She swallowed her sadness and studied Parker's movements as he sauntered up to the porch. He walked with an easy, almost careless gait, as if he had all day stretching before him and nothing important to do with so much as a minute of it.

Her lips flattened into a thin straight line. Well, she'd show him! She was willing to bet he'd never done a serious day's work in all his life. He'd probably never had a responsibility of any kind, either. No wonder he could laugh. No wonder he could move as effortlessly as the wind.

Hearing his footsteps hit the porch, she spun and turned her attention to the stove, taking the last, rather crisp pancake out of the heavy iron skillet.

"Hope you made plenty, Molly! I'm hungry as a bear, and so is Parker!" Joshua called out as he came through the door.

Molly turned and placed the slightly burned cake onto Parker's plate, feeling a jolt of satisfaction at doing so. Her gaze locked with Parker's, but she addressed her words to

Joshua. "The man's name is Mr. Reed to you, Josh." Her voice was soft, but her tone spoke her disapproval of the familiarity that had arisen so swiftly between the boy and man.

"But he said I could call him Parker—"

Molly's expression was firm. "And I'm saying—"

"Beggin' your pardon, ma'am, but I did tell him I'd rather he use my first name," Parker put in respectfully, thinking of the boy who watched the confrontation. It wouldn't do for a boy to learn disrespect toward his stepmother at his knee. It just wasn't proper. But Parker's gaze was every bit as steady and direct as Molly's. Their eyes did battle. Parker refused to back down.

"Hmmph!" Molly huffed, surprised at the intensity of his stubbornness. Piqued, she swung back around to face the stove.

Hmmph! Parker repeated inwardly, surprised he had won. Winking his victory at Joshua, he sat down and attacked the almost black pancake as though he'd never eaten anything tastier.

The day wore on endlessly. Parker was exhausted and more than a little irritable. He stared at the matching rumps of the two huge mules in front of him, as he guided them down the field like Joshua had shown him. While he did, he imagined that hell must feel like this. Hot and merciless. One eternal moment stretching on into the next. Forever and ever and ever . . .

He glanced over his shoulder and saw Molly behind him, steadfastly planting her corn into the crooked rows he'd created. The sight of her unwavering resolution, despite the discomfort she must feel, infuriated him.

He hated her at that moment. After all, it was all her fault he was here. She might get satisfaction out of working this land, but he sure as hell didn't.

He hated farming!

He always had.

He'd run away from his own heritage because he detested the future his father and mother had mapped out for him. As Thaddeus Reed's youngest son he was expected to take an active part in the operation of his father's plantation, even though he didn't stand to inherit the big house. He did stand to inherit a certain amount of wealth and a good measure of land on which he could build his own house when the time came for him to settle down.

Bullshit! Parker thought, remembering. Maybe his two older brothers, Joseph and Owen, wanted to spend their lives stuck out on a plantation in the middle of nowhere. But he hadn't.

So at twenty he'd lit out. He'd wanted to see things, experience life, taste it, drink it up, get down and dirty and wallow in it if he wanted to. He knew he couldn't do that in Hatford, Virginia. So he'd left. And when he'd returned three years later for his mother's funeral, he learned his father had disowned and disinherited him.

Six years had passed since then, and Parker had never gone back. Somehow he knew he never would.

So where are you now, Reed? he asked himself, wiping away the sweat that trickled down his forehead into his eyes, burning them.

I'll tell you where, you damn fool! You're stuck out on a broken-down farm in the middle of nowhere, at the mercy of a prune-faced woman who would have stoked fear into the hearts of any of Father's overseers!

Yessiree, you've done mighty fine for yourself, Parker! he told himself.

He thought of San Francisco, of the saloon that waited for him, the saloon he'd swindled off his old friend, George, and wondered if maybe this was his punishment. Maybe God had finally zapped him a good one.

Damn! Surely God couldn't fault a man for doin' somethin' that came so natural! He thought of the women he'd find at his saloon, the whiskey, the card games. . . .

The thirst for escape became a living, breathing, tangible thing.

His resolve set, he tightened his jaw, wiped the sweat from his forehead with his forearm, and hollered to the mules, "Git up there now!"

CHAPTER
3

At the end of the third week of June, Parker got his chance to escape.

On Saturday night, exhausted from a full day's work, he leaned back into a corner of the corncrib, bent one knee, and watched the moon rise, full and bright, above him.

While dusk faded into darkness he thought over his weeks of captivity.

Oh, he'd been a model prisoner. Yes, indeed. He'd even surprised himself.

With Molly McPherson staring craters into his back, he'd plowed and helped plant all her fields, and although he was stiff and sore, he even felt a measure of pride when he thought about all they'd accomplished.

As for those blasted, ornery mules of hers—after nearly cursing them deaf, he'd finally developed a real talent for them, and Parker was almost sure they'd developed a twinge of respect for him in return. They no longer tried to nip his ass every time he bent over in their presence.

He considered that progress of a sort.

Then there was Joshua. Parker had to admit the boy had grown on him. And he had grown on the boy. He had no doubt about that. They'd gone fishing together that evening, and it was the gaining of Joshua's trust that would enable his escape tonight. He'd talked the boy into leaving the handcuffs off, promising him he'd be there in the morning.

As he remembered his promise guilt pricked him sharply. He knew, were he to stay, he would soon be moved out to the milk house. He'd been lucky so far. Even though the corncrib was far from comfortable, the weather had been mostly dry and mild, allowing him to rest with some measure of peace.

He looked out toward the house and watched the light fade in Joshua's window. The boy would be disappointed to find him gone.

In seconds, the sweet, mellow sound of the boy's harmonica floated out on the night wind and joined the other twilight sounds. Parker smiled a bit ruefully. The boy performed this ritual each night before falling asleep, and Parker had come to enjoy the simple melodies more than he ever would have imagined.

He shook his head, then dropped his chin to his chest, squeezing his eyes shut tight. Damn! He really hated to hurt that boy. He supposed, had he ever settled down, it would have been a fine thing to have had a son like Josh.

As for Molly—well, although he'd grown truly fond of the boy, he'd grown no fonder of the woman. In fact, he downright disliked her as much as ever.

Before he came to Friendly, he'd yet to meet a woman he couldn't melt with his charms. But he'd met one now. Despite his best efforts at befriending her and gaining her trust, Molly McPherson remained imperious and aloof.

She was, as he had first surmised, a coldhearted woman if ever there was one.

If she had a virtue at all, it was that she was a better cook than any woman his father had ever employed. Parker couldn't complain about the food. But as for her temperament—Molly McPherson had to be the iciest woman God had ever planted on His green earth. She didn't belong on a farm, she belonged in one of them so-called igloo huts up north, where the weather matched her frigid nature.

Not only was she cold, she was also suspicious and hostile as hell. He doubted any man would ever gain her trust.

Come morning, she might be angry to find him gone, but she wouldn't be surprised.

As he acknowledged that truth his head came up. His heart uncharacteristically heavy, he opened his eyes and gazed off into the distance, letting Joshua's music and the night sounds seep into him. Strange how he'd never noticed how lulling such sounds could be, how peaceful it was to sit in the stillness and just listen. He thought about where he would normally be on a night such as this, and for a moment he didn't miss the frantic activity, the banging of the piano keys, the loud voices, the clink of glasses, the forced feminine laughter. . . .

He looked at the house once again as Joshua's music faded into silence. Parker's eyes reluctantly focused on Molly's window. A soft light glowed within her room.

He would have to wait until she slept. He frowned. He was willing to bet she had eyes like an owl and could see in the dark. As he studied the flicker of the light she crossed in front of the window and stopped. Slowly she began to uncoil her hair, working her fingers through the thick braid to loosen it. Then, letting the loosened strands fall past her shoulders and down her back, she tipped her head to the side and began to work a brush through the heavy mass. She was dressed in a long white nightdress that the soft breeze, riding in through her partially open window, pressed against her body. The light shone behind her, outlining her tall, slender form in careful detail.

Parker's stomach muscles clenched. He'd never considered her this way before—as a woman, instead of his jailer. It jarred him, and he felt a swift, hot rush of desire.

Angry with himself, he tried to fight his reaction to her. *Dammit, Reed, you've been too long at this place!*

But the hunger remained, fueling his determination to make good his escape.

He wondered if she knew he could see her and doubted that she did. In fact, he was sure she would be mortified if she knew.

And yet he couldn't stop watching her. Not yet.

There was something about her that aroused his curiosity. Was there ever a time when she'd acted young? Josh had told him she had just turned twenty-six, but she seemed much older.

Observing her at different times in the past several days, he'd seen a glimpse of the girl she'd once been. When she looked at her stepson, her eyes softened, and the lines of her mouth became pliant and tipped upward. Once, when Joshua had teased her, she'd actually laughed, and her entire face had come alive. For a brief second Parker had thought her lovely. But the moment had passed as swiftly as it had come, and Parker was sure the sun must have baked his brain to oatmeal, for she was just as stiff and starchy as ever, her large, dark eyes just as cold and vague.

Still, Parker knew if anything made her happy, the boy did. She never wasted a chance to let him know she loved him, that he was special, important to her. Parker respected her for that.

But he couldn't help but wonder if she'd ever known true happiness.

He doubted it. And for some strange unfathomable reason, he felt a stab of pity for her.

As he watched she suddenly looked out toward the corncrib. She stiffened, as though she sensed he watched her, and quickly moved away from the window.

But while he waited for the light to dim in her room, the stab of pity remained. When the light finally faded into darkness and he let himself out of the corncrib, the compassion he felt for Molly joined forces with the guilt he felt about Josh, and together they gave Parker Reed's conscience a powerful working over.

It took him nearly two hours to get to town. He ran most of the way, thankful for the moonlight that lit the road so clearly.

When finally he reached Main Street, he halted and dove into the deserted doorway of O'Malley's General Store while he took inventory of the activity of the town. But all was still and quiet. He surmised that the folks of Friendly were a hardworking bunch and would be up bright and early for Sunday services, as the street was practically deserted, except for two old, practically unconscious drunks who wouldn't remember seeing him anyway.

Expelling a sigh of relief, Parker slunk his way through town until he reached the livery. He knew he would have to forgo collecting his firearms, but he hoped Grover Phillips had replaced his papers and any other possessions he'd taken from his saddlebag.

On silent feet, Parker entered the stable, and taking a chance that only the horses were waiting in the darkness, he whispered, "Hero. You in there, boy?"

The horse's answering whinny made Parker release a hefty sigh of relief. "Hot damn! We're gettin' outta here!" He reached into his pocket and found one of the matches he'd stolen from Molly's cupboard, then struck it against the sole of his boot. Darkness blazed into light. Parker stared straight into the barrel of Bull Garrett's rifle. Beside him stood Judge Elias McPherson, dressed in his ratty black frock and hat, grinning like a mindless fool.

"Hello, Mr. Reed," Bull greeted. "We been expectin' ya."

"Indeed we have," said the judge.

"Here he is, Molly," Bull said, helping Parker out of the caged wagon. "He's 'bout as predictable as my hound dog. Judge said he'd show up sooner or later if we waited long enough. It was sooner." Bull let loose with a loud hoot of laughter.

Parker furrowed his brows and glared at them all.

In the pink light of dawn, her long red hair hanging loose down her back, Molly pulled her robe around her, jerking her belt so tightly around her narrow waist, she almost cut herself in two. She faced him, her lips puckered tighter than any laced corset; her eyes were no longer cold and flat, but alive and sparking with indignant anger. "So this is how you repay our kindness!" she spat out.

"Kindness!" Parker nearly choked on the word. His eyes bugged. "Hell, lady, I've been your goddamn prisoner for almost a month! You've almost worked me into an early grave! Then at night you cage me up like some goddamn worthless animal!"

"Obviously that was a necessary precaution!" Her eyes told him she thought him as worthless as a man could be. She turned and glanced at Joshua, who blushed hotly and dropped his gaze to study his bare toes.

Noting Joshua's discomfort, Parker surprised himself by rushing to the boy's defense. "Leave the boy out of this. It's not his fault. I asked him not to cuff me. I promised him I wouldn't run."

She gave Parker a look that could have frozen water in the middle of an August afternoon. "He shouldn't have trusted you." Her voice was devoid of sympathy. "I told him he'd be sorry if he did."

Parker's jaw tightened. His blue eyes seemed to set off sparks. "Is that how you intend to raise that boy?" Parker gestured toward Joshua. "Teachin' him not to trust folks . . . just because you can't?"

Color flooded Molly's cheeks. She drew herself up so straight that Parker heard the bones in her back snap in protest. "How dare you question the way I raise my son?"

Sensing a full-fledged battle brewing, Bull stepped between the two. "Here, now, you two. Judge said you was to get on together, and this ain't gettin' on. Now, I can't be stayin' around here all day to protect ya from each other. Judge said I was to drop Mr. Reed off and get back to town."

Parker and Molly faced off, glaring venom at each other.

I could get on better with her mules, Parker thought.

I could get on better with one of those old, drunken miners, Molly thought.

At least he's back, Joshua thought.

The following week, with Molly and Joshua helping as well as instructing him, Parker began the countless other chores.

But the three worked together in strained silence.

Parker was indignant.

Molly was furious.

Joshua was hurt.

Although Parker had no intention of giving up his plan to escape, he realized he would have to bide his time. Joshua would not trust him again so easily. The boy's guarded eyes and stilted conversation told him that. And Molly . . . well, she watched him like a hawk all day long, and at night she made damn sure he was securely cuffed—not only cuffed, but cuffed to the slats of the corncrib. It galled the hell out of him! But even if he hadn't been locked up, he knew the odds of him collecting his horse and belongings and slipping out of Friendly were almost nonexistent. The whole goddamn town was in cahoots to hold on to him as Molly McPherson's personal slave. They were the craziest bunch of locals he'd ever met. So for the time being, until he hatched a new plan of escape, he knew he was stuck and might as well behave himself.

Besides, the shelter and comfort of the milk house were looking better to him with each passing day.

The days that followed were long and tiring. Parker mended fences, milked cows, cleaned barn stalls—the list went on and on and on. It was difficult, awkward, unfamiliar work. Of course, any work other than lifting and shuffling a deck of cards was difficult and unfamiliar to Parker.

Yet, surprisingly enough, he found himself learning to make the best of the situation. If nothing else, Molly McPherson fed him well and regularly.

One morning, when Josh came out to wake him for morning chores, he handed him a pair of sturdy trousers, a pair of wide, black suspenders, and a pile of old but clean work shirts. "Molly said to give you these. And you can sleep in the milk house from now on . . . without the handcuffs. Molly says you earned the right. She says she don't suppose you intend to run again, bein' as how everyone expects you to try."

Parker couldn't help but chuckle, acknowledging the truth of Molly's supposition. He took the clothes from the boy's outstretched arms, silently thankful for the offering. Although Bull had brought him out the rest of his clothing, a gambler's fancy duds were hardly appropriate apparel for a man working a farm—not to mention the fact that his shirts had grown snug and uncomfortable. His arms and chest had thickened considerably in the past several weeks.

"Thanks," Parker managed. He captured Joshua's gaze. "These your pa's?"

Joshua nodded. His eyes were dispassionate. "Yep."

"You don't mind me wearin' them?"

"I don't hardly remember him. If Molly don't mind, I don't either. Breakfast's waitin'." Joshua spun toward the house, dismissing him.

The boy had barely spoken more than ten words at a time to him since the day Bull had hauled him back from the livery. Parker felt an intense urge to mend the rift, to regain some of the respect he'd lost in the boy's eyes. "Josh, wait. . . ."

Joshua halted and slowly turned.

Parker closed the distance between them. For a moment he faced the boy, wordless and uncertain. Explanations and apologies had never come easy to him. "I'm sorry, son. I truly am."

"I'm not your son." The words were spoken softly, without anger or disrespect.

"No, you're not." Parker paused and chewed his lower lip thoughtfully. Then, very quietly, he said, "But I wouldn't be at all disappointed if you were." His chest felt uncomfortably tight as he watched the boy digest those words. Joshua swallowed, blinked, then swallowed again, turning his misty gaze to the green-tinged fields beyond.

For several moments they remained silent, listening to the morning come alive; then, very slowly, Joshua's blue eyes came back to Parker's. "Why'd you run?"

A small, wry smile tugged at one side of Parker's mouth. "I figured it was the only way to get the hell outta here," Parker answered honestly. "Farming . . ." He shook his head and looked off into the distance. "It's not for me, son. I got places to go."

"Where?"

"San Francisco. There's a saloon waitin' for me. The Silver Sail. I won it from an old friend." He winked, then amended with a twinge of conscience, "Sort of won it, I guess you might say."

"Yeah?" Joshua's eyes lit with interest. "What are ya gonna do with it?"

"I'm gonna work it." They started off toward the house. Parker slid the boy a curious glance. "You ever been in a saloon?"

Joshua shook his head. "No, Molly don't approve of such places."

"No. I imagine she doesn't." His expression turning solemn, Parker hurried to tell him, "And she's right, ya know. Those places can be nothin' but dens of iniquity. No place for a decent young fella like yourself." His grin returning, he asked, "You like girls?"

Joshua's cheeks blazed. Wordlessly he nodded, while his Adam's apple rode up and down the long column of his neck.

As they stepped onto the porch Parker chuckled and slapped him on the back. "You sure as hell do, whether Molly likes it or not."

CHAPTER
4

"I'm not goin' up there!" Parker told Molly, one warm July morning as they stood facing each other in front of the barn.

Surprised by his refusal, Molly anchored her hands on her hips and calmly asked, "Why not?"

Parker seamed his lips and refused to answer. He wasn't about to tell this woman, who so often regarded him with cold disdain and only lately had begun to treat him with a measure of respect, that he was afraid of heights. As far as he was concerned, the damned barn roof could cave in until next year's victim was delivered to her doorstep to fix it.

"Well?" Molly prodded.

Parker's stubborn silence was her only answer.

She narrowed her eyes in irritation. He narrowed his in defiance.

They glared at each other, while animosity vibrated between them.

But Parker remained adamant and silent. For all that it had galled him, in all the time of his captivity, he had never once refused to carry out Mrs. McPherson's orders. Part of the reason for his obedience was that he liked to eat, and she fed him well enough. Despite the unfairness of his situation, his "pain in the neck" conscience acknowledged the reality of her need for a work hand. The biggest part of the reason he'd done the work he had, however, was Joshua. Parker felt working a farm as neglected as this one was simply too damn much responsibility for any thirteen-year-old boy. He sensed Molly didn't expect or want the boy to work so hard. But Josh, being the boy he was, worked as hard as any full-grown man just the same.

But, regardless of Parker's desire to lighten the boy's load, he wasn't going up on any goddamn roof!

He was glad Josh had gone into town, so he didn't have to witness this confrontation. At least he wouldn't lose any respect in the boy's eyes over this matter.

"Well, Mr. Reed," Molly prodded again, her dark eyes daring him to respond to her question, "why not?"

Parker set his jaw. "I just won't, and that's all there is to it."

Puzzled more than angry, Molly stared up at the man. He had changed over the past six weeks. His face, no longer pale, was now a deep bronze from the many hours he'd spent in the sun. His hair, bleached as light as sun-soaked wheat, was a handsome contrast to his newly acquired complexion. Her gaze dropped to his hands. They, too, had changed. No longer soft and white, they were now brown and callused and gave evidence to the fact that she'd been correct in one of her first assessments: they were indeed strong. Strong enough to work her farm as no man had ever done before him. Her eyes returned to his. Despite the fact that she didn't like him much better than she had when he'd first arrived, she had to admit she'd been wrong about him in many ways. To her surprise, he'd turned out to be a fast learner. And he handled those practically worthless mules of hers better than she or Josh had ever been able to. As for Josh, well, she'd never seen him laugh so often and so easily. That alone lightened her heart, and though she had never told him, she was grateful to Parker for that.

But there was still a roof to mend, and he was wasting the morning while the hot Indiana sun rose relentlessly above them.

"All right, then," she said, and sighed heavily. "I'll do it myself." Resigned to the task, she turned and headed off toward the barn door.

Stunned by her reply, Parker let his jaw drop. He'd expected a fight from her, or at the very least her most venomous contempt. But he'd not expected her decision to do the job herself. He stared at her stiff back for several seconds, until finally he found his voice and bellowed, "Now, hold on a goddamn minute!"

Molly ignored him and kept walking, her head high, her back as straight as the handle on a hoe.

He caught up to her and took her arm, spinning her around to face him. "You're not going up on that roof!"

"Yes, Mr. Reed, I am," she stated calmly.

"No, Mrs. McPherson, you're not!"

She stared at him silently for a moment, then arched one well-shaped auburn brow in question. "And why aren't I?"

"Well . . . because . . ." He paused, trying to think of a valid answer without alerting her to his own weakness. "Because a barn roof is no place for a woman! You're not goin' up there!"

Her eyes sparking with indignation, she tilted her head back in challenge. "Yes, Mr. Reed, I am," she reiterated. "When it comes time to bring the crops in, I don't want to lose them to mildew. And I don't need sick animals. I need a sound barn roof. If you won't go up and fix it, then I will." She shook his hand off and spun, entering the barn. The smell of decay and rotting wood was pungent and only served to fuel her determination to carry out her threat.

"The hell you will!" he bellowed to her back, and stalked off after her.

"I'd appreciate it if you'd slop the pigs, Mr. Reed," she said blandly over her shoulder, and went over to a large wooden box set against the wall. "And please watch your language. It's so profane." She lifted the lid, withdrew a hammer, a belt to hang it in, and a heavy box of nails. Then she reached for several boards that were propped against the wall.

Parker felt his temperature rise. Slop the pigs! Hell! he thought, his pride stung. His language profane? Bullshit!

He tilted his head back and stared up at the huge, gaping hole above him. He imagined himself up there, belly flat on the roof, holding on for dear life. His stomach flipped over, and nausea threatened. The woman was going to be the death of him. He thought about San Francisco and wondered if he'd ever live through the summer to get there and see it. Probably not. He'd probably have a spot up on that hill right beside her footloose husband.

Furious, he stormed across the barn and yanked the hammer out of her hand, causing her eyes to widen in surprise. "All right, goddammit! I'll fix the roof!"

Without warning, Molly jerked the hammer back and faced him off. "No, thank you, Mr. Reed," she said calmly through clenched teeth. "I said I'd fix it myself and I will. Please go slop the pigs!"

Parker's face turned from bronze to a deep shade of purple. A vein pulsed in his forehead. He glowered down on her. She was a tall woman, taller than most. Yet he still towered over her by several inches. He glared his meanest. She narrowed her eyes in defiance. He reached for the hammer. Stubbornly she lifted both brows and held the tool out of his reach, behind her back, taking malicious pleasure in doing so. He swore and lunged for her; she sidestepped him. He lunged again; she sidestepped to the opposite direction. Another lunge, another step, but this time his foot caught on the hem of her skirt while her foot hooked behind his ankle, and together they fell to the dirty floor with a host of mingled grunts, into a heap of tangled arms and legs.

"Goddammit, woman!" Parker exploded, rolling her over onto her back. He covered her body with his own, pinned one arm above her head with one hand, and with his other hand yanked the hammer away from her while she struggled to catch her breath. He threw the tool into a corner. "I said I'll fix the damned roof, and I will!"

Winded, her lips parted, she stared up into his face wordlessly.

Angry, he stared down into hers.

Her heart beat a frantic rhythm, and she forgot about the roof, the hammer, everything except that he was a man, warm and alive and not wholly unkind. As she stared up into his clear blue eyes she wondered what he saw as he gazed down at her so intently. Did he see the same awkward, freckle-faced, redheaded girl her husband had seen? Thinking he surely must, her eyes slipped shut, and her cheeks grew pink.

But she was mistaken in her assumption. More so than she could ever have imagined. What Parker saw as he gazed down at her was a woman—slender, but soft beneath him, with thick, lush, red-gold lashes that hid her lovely dark eyes from him. He saw her as vulnerable, feminine, and warm, her lips full and compliant. And he felt an intense desire to kiss her.

He thought about his reaction for a fraction of a minute, quickly abandoned the idea as insanity, and began to lift himself off her. Then a surge of curiosity got the best of him, and before he could change his mind, he lowered himself once more and gently pressed his lips to hers.

He sank into her and felt the soft intake of her breath while his pulse began to throb throughout his body. He let his mouth move over hers slowly, deliberately, while she lay still and silent, neither aiding nor halting him. His tongue touched her bottom lip, and when she parted her lips in a soft gasp of surprise, his tongue pressed inward and tasted of her mouth.

Molly's breath caught in her throat. His free hand came up to cup her neck while his tongue, silken and wet, touched hers, stroking her mouth softly, gently. She felt a catch down deep in the lower region of her stomach, and she knew she should stop him, knew she was playing with fire, but she also knew she needed this—had needed this for so very long.

At last she was learning what she had never learned with her husband, with anyone—the wonder of a kiss, the magic of a gentle caress, the discovery of desire. It was a very heady thing, an adventure beyond compare. For a moment she allowed herself to abandon prudence while she tasted, accepted, and reveled in the experience.

Parker was baffled. He'd expected her to fight, at the very least he'd expected an immediate verbal thrashing. But when he lifted his head, and she finally opened her eyes, she remained silent and still beneath him. Instead of the cold hostility he'd thought to see reflected in her gaze, he read surprise and vulnerability. That touched him as nothing ever had. As he eased his weight from her he began to mumble an apology.

But she surprised him even more when she interrupted him and very simply said, "You can fix the roof now, Mr. Reed."

CHAPTER
5

Parker fixed the roof that day.

He climbed down in the middle of the morning and lost his breakfast, then climbed down again after lunch and lost that, too.

Yet despite all his discomfort, not only did he fix Molly McPherson's roof, but he did a damn good job of it.

That evening she came out of the house, plunked her hands on her hips, and gazed up at his handiwork. When she turned and smiled at him, Parker felt losing his breakfast and lunch was a small price to pay for the respect he'd finally won.

The next day he shoveled out the rest of the stalls in the barn, swept the hard-packed dirt floor clean, and organized the toolshed—to his own liking.

The following week, hoe in hand, with Joshua at his side, he cultivated between the quickly growing rows of corn. He found, to his surprise, that the tasks he performed were not such terrible chores. In fact, though the sun beat down on him with a vengeance and his back ached furiously, he gleaned a certain satisfaction in noting the growth of the crops—the crops he'd helped to plant.

And as July burned its way into August, so began a ritual. Every morning before he went up to the house for breakfast, he would stop, prop his hands on his hips, and look out toward the fields, marveling that as his father's son, he'd never taken time to notice the miracle of growth.

But he did now. And the fact that he did was a miracle in itself.

On this particular August morning, after he'd studied the fields and eaten a hearty breakfast, he stood near the well, peering into the mirror he'd rigged against the suspended bucket, while he shaved the dark-gold stubble from his jaw.

Today was Sunday, and another miracle was about to occur: he was going to church.

He arched an eyebrow in an exaggerated look of pretended piety and mumbled, "Hello, Brother James. And how's the missus this fiiiine Sunday mornin'?"

Parker chuckled.

Well, that oughta shake a hallelujah or two out of heaven's gates, he supposed. If only ol' George could see him now. He'd probably tell him he was getting exactly what he deserved for cheatin' him like he'd done—stuck out on a farm, miles from any real civilization, attending Sunday services, of all things. . . .

Straightening his expression, Parker peered into the mirror, stretched his neck upward, and ran the razor down his throat.

Grimacing, he forgot George. He wasn't particularly happy about the prospect of sitting in the McPherson family pew, or any other pew for that matter. But Josh had asked him to go, and Parker, though he'd tried hard to think up a viable excuse, could not. Besides, he really hated to disappoint the boy, since the rift he'd created by his attempted escape had almost completely healed. Up until today, Josh had asked very little of him. The Sundays he and Molly had trotted off to services, they had fed him, then left him to himself for a couple of hours. After they'd moved him out to the milk house, they hadn't even bothered to handcuff him while they were gone, figuring he couldn't go far without his horse and belongings.

They were right, of course.

So today, after he finished shaving and ran a brush through his hair, he dressed in his gentleman's best—ignoring the fact that his favorite dark coat was a bit snug across the shoulders and his trousers a little tight through the thighs.

Then he went out to hook up Mrs. McPherson's buggy, as he did every Sunday.

"Ready, Parker?" Joshua called out, running toward him, looking lankier and more awkward than ever in his pressed Sunday suit, his cheeks bright pink, his hair slicked straight back from his forehead like wet duck feathers.

Parker almost chuckled at the sight of the awkward adolescent. But he held himself in check and turned his attention to checking the horse's reins, noting as he did how easily he performed these now familiar tasks. "You bet," he answered Josh over his shoulder. He swung back toward the boy. "Where's Mrs. McPhers—" But the question died on his lips as Molly came out of the house and down the steps. His hands stilled, and his mouth gaped as he watched her move across the dew-stained grass to join him and her stepson.

She'd maintained a careful distance from him since that day in the barn, avoiding his eyes, yet always speaking in a controlled, polite tone. But she'd been less stiff with him than she had been in the past, and she seemed much more concerned about his comfort—even to the point of inquiring about his favorite foods, which, once she'd learned, she'd wasted no time in preparing.

He had been careful to keep a tight rein on his thoughts, which all too frequently returned to that day, reminding him that for all her staunchness, Molly McPherson was a woman, a soft, warm-blooded woman, after all.

He was never more aware of that fact than now.

His eyes practically left his head as he studied her. Her hair, freed from the prim restraints of the coiled braid, glistened in the early-morning sunshine, like the richest of autumn's red-gold leaves. It hung loose and full down her back and was caught up becomingly at both sides of her face by two small silver combs. Instead of her usual dark skirt and white shirtwaist, today she wore a pale green, high-necked dress that molded neatly to her breasts and narrow waist. The tapered, gathered skirt draped her hips gently in the front and met in folds in the back to fall gracefully over a small bustle.

"Looks pretty, don't she?" Josh whispered up at Parker. "The last time she wore her hair like that was when Silas Turner took her to the church social last spring."

Parker stared dumbfounded and wondered who the hell Silas Turner was and why he hadn't heard of him before now.

But while he watched her cross the damp lawn, thoughts of Silas Turner dissipated, and a strange uneasiness gripped his heart. His face felt hot, as though he'd been blasted by the last fierce wave of summer heat.

Well, I'll be damned! he thought, feeling his hands shake where they gripped the reins. Since when did the sight of a pretty woman shake him? he wondered. Since Molly McPherson became that pretty woman, that's when. He felt an imaginary noose tighten around his neck.

The feeling, whatever it was, was far more confining, far more binding, and a hell of a lot more threatening than any cage on wheels or handcuffs could ever have been.

He stared at her, unaware of the frown that marred his handsome face.

When she reached him and lifted soft brown eyes to his blue ones, however, the scowl disappeared from his face, and he stupidly muttered, "Mrs. McPherson . . ."

"Morning, Mr. Reed," she replied softly, completely unaware of his discomfort. "I'm glad to see you've decided to join us for services this morning. A little religion never hurt anyone."

"No, ma'am, I suppose it wouldn't," Parker mumbled, completely oblivious to the fact that he'd agreed with her.

She smiled a bit uncertainly, surprised at his words. She'd expected a caustic retort, or a sarcastic smile at the very least. But his expression was earnest, his blue eyes steady. She swallowed her bemusement, held out her hand, and waited.

His gaze dropped to her hand. He stared blankly at her fingers, as though he'd never seen a female hand before. Then, very slowly, his eyes rose to hers, and he smiled, took her hand, and helped her up into the buggy while he silently admired the sprinkling of freckles adorning her nose.

That very morning Parker learned who Silas Turner was, and he wasn't a bit happy with the revelation.

After the congregation had been properly chastened and blessed, everyone gathered in the churchyard to visit for a spell before heading on home to start Sunday dinner. There was little time for conversation during the morning services, since most folks in Friendly took their religion quite seriously. But once they were freed from the solemn severity of God's house, everyone launched into the latest gossip—whether the latest gossip concerned the size of young, unmarried Emma Logan's growing waistline or the state of the local crops.

From his place between Molly and Joshua, Parker watched the mingling crowd of parishioners. He felt more than a little out of place, an intruder within this little community, where everybody's business was anybody's business. Yet every now and then he caught a few sentences of conversation and had to chuckle at the familiarity with which they discussed each other. There was very little malice in the discussions—mostly people voiced concern and curiosity more than anything else.

"Howdy, there, Mr. Reed!" Bull called out, coming up behind the trio.

Parker turned and nodded. "Garrett," he greeted civilly, surprised that he could even do so, considering the big man was one of his original captors. But Bull had stopped by the McPherson farm frequently, and although he was loath to admit it, Parker had come to enjoy the big man's easy company and looked forward to his visits.

An elderly woman came up and captured Molly's attention, pulling her aside, while Joshua loped off toward a group of boys his own age.

"How are ya gettin' on, Mr. Reed?" Bull asked, his wide face friendly as ever. At his side stood Grover Phillips, looking every bit as sociable as his deputy.

Parker raised an eyebrow. "I'd say I'm gettin' on better than I expected."

Bull chuckled. "I'd say ya are."

Despite himself, Parker chuckled, too.

Bull leaned forward. "Ya know, Molly's farm ain't never looked so good. And that boy," he said, gesturing with his head toward Joshua. "Well, he thinks you're the best thing that came his way since Christmas."

Parker pocketed his hands and gazed out in Joshua's direction. His expression grew solemn, thoughtful. "He's a fine boy." He spoke the words quietly, more to himself than to anyone else.

"That he is," Bull agreed.

"And Molly," Grover added. "She's a fine woman. One of the best."

Parker's gaze found Molly. He watched her smile patiently down on the elderly woman as the woman loudly continued to lament her many aches and pains. "I can't argue that," he agreed. Each day he spent on her farm he became more aware of Molly McPherson—as a person, as a woman. He turned and nailed the two men with a curious stare, anxious to put thoughts of Molly's womanhood from his mind. "You know, I've always wondered who the hell hit me on the head that day I came into town."

Bull blushed crimson and fidgeted nervously for a couple of seconds. At his side Grover cleared his throat and elbowed the bigger man in the ribs. "Go on. You might as well tell 'im. After all, he's done a fine job for Molly."

If possible, Bull's cheeks grew even brighter. "Well . . . I guess you could say I did . . ."

Parker's brows flew upward. "You! But why?"

" 'Cause the judge said to catch the next drifter that came into town, and you was him!" Bull's face mirrored his apology.

"But that's insane!"

Grover nodded. "Yep. Suppose it is."

"Just like that?" Parker yelled, forgetting where he was. "You just pick out any innocent soul that happens to be passing through your town and ya bean him, pronounce him a criminal, and impound his possessions?"

"Yep." Grover nodded matter-of-factly, not bothering to lie. "That's pretty much the way we do it."

"How long have you been doin' this?"

Grover rolled his eyes upward, calculating thoughtfully. He tipped back his hat and pursed his lips. "Oh, probably nigh onto eight years now," he finally said. "Been doin' it ever since Frank ran off and left Molly on her own." His expression grew solemn. "We're mighty fond of Molly, ya know. 'Course, we try to be choosy and make sure the man we pick ain't dangerous or nothin' and we try to make sure he ain't got a wife and young'uns to care for. After all, we wouldn't want to leave Molly alone on that farm with a true criminal, and it wouldn't be proper stealin' a man away from his family."

The scheme was so strange, so ludicrous, so absurd, yet so unconditionally accepted by these two men and their fellow townsfolk, that Parker stared at the two in stunned disbelief. To his own surprise, a chuckle rose within his chest and eventually burst out. The chuckle grew, and before he knew it, he was hooting with loud laughter, accompanied by Bull and Grover.

The judge, who had been passing the time of day with Maribel Weathers, noticed the trio's condition and left her to join the three men. He slapped Parker on the shoulder, making his laughter die to a hoarse cough. "My, my, what has you so cheerful this mornin', son?"

Parker gazed down at the old man. He wanted to be angry, wanted to be filled with righteous indignation, but as he stared down into the old man's kindly gray eyes and realized the extent of his love for his daughter-in-law and grandson, somehow the last thing in the world Parker could summon was anger. Instead he felt an odd, burgeoning respect for the eccentric old fellow. At least he was sane enough to love his family. Who could fault a man for that?

Absentminded as he was, the judge forgot his question and launched into another. "My, wasn't that a rousin' sermon!" he commented to no one in particular. But to Parker he said, "It's good to see you in church, Mr. Reed."

Before Parker could voice a reply, the judge turned and waved to a short, stocky man, who was engaged in conversation with a group of men across the churchyard. "Silas! Silas Turner. Over here!"

The man lifted his head and turned toward the judge's voice. Within seconds, he'd joined Parker's small group. "Hello, Judge. Grover. Bull," Silas said, purposely ignoring Parker.

"Silas," the judge returned.

Bull and Grover nodded stiff greetings. Silas Turner was not one of their favorite neighbors. He was known for being a hard, compassionless man, who'd worked his first wife into an early grave.

An uncomfortable silence fell. The judge broke it by introducing Parker. "Silas, this here is Parker Reed—Molly's summer work hand. Mr. Reed, this is Silas Turner, Molly's closest neighbor."

Silas looked at Parker closely, his mind clicking. *So this is the man spendin' nights on Molly's farm*, he thought.

Parker almost choked on the mention of "work hand." It galled him, yet at the same time he was amused that this town continued to pretend he was anything but a kidnapped slave. First they labeled him a criminal, then a prisoner, now somehow he'd become Molly's willing worker. What a bunch of crazies! But while he was thinking that through, he was also sizing up Silas Turner in return: *So this is the man who escorted Molly to the church social*, he thought.

Antagonism rose like a wall between the two men.

"How're the crops, Silas?" the judge asked, gleefully enjoying the tension he sensed vibrating between the two men.

"Fine," Silas answered, his eyes never leaving Parker. "How 'bout you, Reed?" he asked, nailing him with a cold stare from his small dark eyes. "How're Molly's crops faring this year?"

"Fine," Parker answered without preamble, wondering what right the man had to ask. Exactly what was he to Molly? And while he held the man's challenging stare and thought about that question, for the first time in his life Parker, who had never known a true pang of jealousy, felt the full discomfort of its vicious sting.

CHAPTER
6

That evening, as the sky blushed scarlet and the sun slowly slipped into the horizon, Molly sat in her rocker on the porch and listened to Joshua play his mouth organ.

On the newly repaired and painted steps, the boy sat with knees splayed wide, his eyes closed, as he played through many familiar tunes and a few he had created himself.

Parker sat beside the boy. His long legs stretched out before him, his feet hooked at the ankles, he sat content, relaxing against the porch post, whittling on a piece of wood he held in his work-roughened hands. He'd taken up whittling in the past several weeks and found it a calming habit he truly enjoyed.

Evenings such as this one had become routine for the three of them. Sometimes they sat in silence, comfortable just to be in each other's company. Other times they would discuss the day's work or the state of the weather.

And sometimes, when Parker felt especially ornery, he'd entertain Joshua with stories of his adventures, noticing out of the corner of his eye that Molly listened, too. He supposed there were times she disapproved of some of his wilder tales, but she no longer voiced her disapproval. In fact, every once in a while he would hear her chuckle softly beneath her breath at something he'd said that was somewhat less than proper or conventional.

He grinned to himself now, noting that two months ago she would never have chuckled at anything he said.

He turned, his gaze seeking hers. Her eyes locked with his.

To Parker, she was beautiful. Still dressed in her pale green Sunday dress, she looked as pretty and fresh in the fading daylight as she had in the bright morning sunshine.

He dropped his gaze, musing.

She was not like any other woman he'd ever known. Molly was no pampered, protected, coy Southern belle who was out to snare herself a rich husband. Nor was she a painted, coarse, saloon tart, full of flattery and lewd remarks, whose sole purpose was to empty his pocket.

No, Molly McPherson, with her red-gold hair, huge brown eyes, and freckled nose, was something extra special all in herself. . . .

Still playing his harmonica, Joshua launched into a slow, familiar waltz.

Listening to the lovely bittersweet tune, Parker had an idea.

As the fireflies lit around them and dusk deepened, he laid aside the piece of wood he'd been carving and decided to take a chance. He rose to his feet, crossed the porch to stand before her, and held out his hand. His voice was soft with entreaty when he asked, "May I have this dance, Mrs. McPherson?"

Curious, Joshua turned to watch the exchange.

Molly's cheeks blazed her surprise. She stared up at Parker—flattered, flustered, terrified. Steeped in a gamut of turbulent emotions, she was unable to pull her eyes away from his.

Dance? Me? she thought, staring up at him.

Parker continued to gaze admiringly down at her.

Molly swallowed thickly. God only knew how long it had been since she'd danced. She'd probably fall flat on her face.

But that was the least of her apprehensions—Parker was her greatest fear.

After that one kiss—that one wonderful kiss, on that one wonderful day—she wasn't at all sure she should be that close to Parker Reed ever again. There was something about him that drew her, that called to her, something that would be a dangerous thing to tempt.

Because he would not stay. That she knew. Come the end

of harvest, he would be gone, and she and Josh would never see him again.

When she finally found her voice, she shook her head. "I'm afraid I'm not much of a dancer, Mr. Reed. I—"

"Then that makes two of us," Parker told her, and grinned lazily, the lines around his eyes crinkling with good humor. "I don't mind sore toes if you don't." He gestured with his head toward Joshua. "It would be a shame to waste all Josh's talent."

Molly looked at her stepson. In the meager evening light, she could not make out his expression, but she knew he would be pleased to have his music enjoyed in such a manner. And he had never seen her dance. That realization brought her a twinge of sadness. He'd never seen her do much of anything except work. She supposed it would be good for the boy to know she could laugh and dance. . . .

. . . And oh, despite all her apprehensions, despite all her fears, she truly did want to dance with Mr. Reed tonight.

Her heart won out, and she rose, accepting Parker's outstretched hand. As he led her down the steps his hand felt warm and firm and wonderfully masculine around hers. She felt the calluses that marked his palms and fingers, and tenderness for him grew. He'd earned those calluses, every one of them, here, on her farm. And other than the day Bull had recaptured him and the time he'd hedged at fixing the barn roof, he'd never complained about the work.

When he stopped in a sliver of moonlight, beneath the wide, protective branches of the ancient oak, she turned to him and experienced a second of deep uncertainty.

He sensed her hesitation and was careful not to draw her too close. She, in turn, was careful not to meet his eyes.

They began to sway to the haunting sounds of the lovely ballad.

He stepped on her toes twice; she stepped on his so many times she lost count. Once he groaned loudly, and alarmed, she studied his face. His grimace of pain was so comically exaggerated, she forgot herself and laughed.

He laughed, too, and drew her closer.

"You're a wonderful dancer, Mrs. McPherson," Parker remarked, smiling down into her eyes.

"And you, Mr. Reed, are a terrible liar," Molly returned, grinning.

They both laughed, knowing she spoke the truth, but they continued to dance just the same.

When at last Joshua ended the ballad, he immediately launched into another—not allowing the two a chance to part or rest.

As the soothing August breeze whispered of autumn and Joshua's harmonica sang out the melody to song after song, Molly McPherson and Parker Reed forgot about who they were and how they'd come to be sharing this evening. As their steps became smoother their smiles became easier, and they enjoyed a sweet, very magical moment together, twirling under the full Indiana moon, with the fireflies dancing circles along with them.

Later that night, Molly tossed restlessly in her bed. Her light blanket felt confining, like a smothering, weighted shield that held her imprisoned, pressed into the confines of her bed. She threw off the coverlet and rolled onto her back, pressing her palms to her breasts. She felt hot, feverish, achy.

In her mind she relived every moment she'd spent dancing in Parker's arms.

She rose from her bed and went to the window. She gazed through the shadows at the milk house, and the terrible longing within her gave way to a heated yearning that seemed to set every nerve in her body afire.

Oh, Molly, you fool, an inner voice berated her. *Don't you know he's just like Frank? As soon as the crops are in, as soon as harvest has past, he'll leave you. And then what will you have?*

She thought a moment, feeling bereaved and lonely, overwhelmed by the memory of Parker's beautiful blue eyes as they'd gazed down at her just hours ago. Even though no other man had ever looked at her thus, her instinct told her she'd read desire in Parker's eyes. And the fact that that desire was directed at her only intensified the longing she felt for him.

So, with a shaky sigh of resignation, she pushed aside convention, swallowed her trepidation, and whispered her answer into the darkness. "I'll have the memories. Which is far, far, more than Frank ever gave me."

Parker woke with a start. He sensed Molly's presence immediately. He propped himself up on one elbow, his gaze focusing on her where she stood in the open doorway.

She stood, silent and uncertain, bathed in a soft glow of silver moonlight, wearing only a thin, white nightdress. Her hair, unbound and glorious, hung almost to her waist. He had the distinct urge to touch it, to wrap his hands in it, to pull her face close.

He was aware that he was uncovered and clothed only in his drawers, but he thought it would be foolish to try to cover himself. At this late hour she would have come to him for only one reason.

He'd had trouble falling asleep, and when at last he had, he'd slept fitfully. Now he knew why. She filled his mind and disturbed his rest. And while he ached to have her, he was afraid to take what she offered because the end result would bring them both pain.

"Molly," he said softly, using her given name freely for the very first time. The sound of it on his lips made him realize what a sweet name it was—how well it suited her. How could he have been so blind to think her hard, cold?

Strong? Yes. Protective of Joshua and what was theirs? Most certainly.

During the time he'd spent with her, she'd acted many different ways, but never hard and cold.

Struggling against his desire for her, he tried to summon any shred of common decency he might possess, and told her quietly, earnestly, "You know I can't stay. Come the end of October, when the crops are laid by, and Grover returns my horse and belongin's, you know I'll be movin' on. . . ." He let the sentence trial off, hoping she'd turn around and go back to her house where she belonged—praying she wouldn't. . . .

She took two hesitant steps into the milk house, bringing her face into full view. "I know," she whispered. "I'm not asking you to stay."

"Then why, Molly?" he asked, puzzled, wondering why she would offer herself when she didn't stand to gain anything in return. "Why would you want to do this . . . ?"

"Because—" Her voice broke, and her eyes slipped shut. She swallowed and allowed herself a moment to steady her emotions.

Watching her, Parker felt an odd painful catch in his chest. She sounded so young, so vulnerable.

"Because," she finally continued, opening her eyes and looking directly into his, "I need this . . . with you. . . ."

The simple honesty of her answer touched him, making him want her all the more. Slowly he swung his legs over the side of the bed and went to her. Resting his hands on her shoulders, he felt her tremble beneath his touch. "I don't want to hurt you, Molly. . . ."

She nodded. "I know that."

His hand came up to her face, cupping her smooth cheek in his rough palm. "You're so damn pretty. . . ."

Tears swelled in her eyes, and she shook her head, as if to say he needn't tell her such foolish things.

Reading the disbelief in her eyes, he took her face in both of his hands and very tenderly tipped her chin upward, pressing his lips to hers in a soft, slow kiss. When finally he lifted his head, he tightened his brow and fervently whispered, "Listen to me, Molly girl. You're more than pretty. You're beautiful."

When he took her hand and led her to the bed, Molly almost believed him.

CHAPTER
7

They stood beside the narrow bed, facing one another.

Experienced man that he was, he studied her wordlessly for several long moments, wondering how to begin their lovemaking.

She studied her toes where they peeked out from beneath her gown, wondering if he had changed his mind.

Uncertain, she raised wide, dark eyes to him.

He sensed her worry and lifted his hand to her hair, touching it gently. "Are you sure about this, Molly?"

Her throat tight, she found she could not answer. She nodded.

He stroked her hair gently. "I've wondered many times what your hair felt like. Ever since that morning Bull brought me back, and you met us out by the barn." He gave a small chuckle, remembering her fury. "Your hair was loose like this that morning." He smiled down at her and admitted verbally what he had never even admitted to himself. "As waspish as you were, I thought you were beautiful."

Molly forgot to breathe. Her heart seemed to stop beating. She shut her eyes and put aside all shyness, all reluctance, and did at that moment what she truly desired to do. She took his hand from her hair, sought out the other one, then turned both palms up and brought them to her lips. Very slowly she kissed his calluses, treasuring the presence of every one of them. She heard him sigh and felt him press closer. When he took his hands from hers and pulled her to his chest, she went up against him most willingly.

"Molly," he whispered into her hair, "I want you so much."

His words stoked the fire within her. "Do you?" she asked, needing to believe him.

He pressed his lips to her brow, her eyelids, her cheeks, while very gently his hands rode her rib cage to find her breasts. "Oh yes, Molly. Ever since that day in the barn. There hasn't been a day that I haven't wanted this . . . with you. . . ."

Her eyes rife with doubt, she looked up at him. "Frank never really did, you know. . . ." There was a sadness in her voice that seemed to seep out of her.

"Then Frank McPherson was a fool." Parker lowered his head and kissed her hard. "A damn fool," he whispered vehemently into her mouth. His tongue was hot, probing, his breathing labored. His hands caressed her breasts through her nightdress, moving downward to rove over the slender curve of her hips, pulling her pelvis flush against his.

Molly felt desire rush through her. Their tongues touched, circled, twirled, and danced. Breathless, she broke the kiss and sighed his name.

Growing impatient, he eased her gown up, pulling it over her head. "It'll be good, Molly," he said softly. "I'll make it good for you." He prayed he could. He hadn't been with a woman in so long he hoped he could move slowly, give her what she needed—realizing now that he had never given much thought to the physical or emotional needs of any of his past bed partners.

He stripped off his drawers and stood before her, naked and unashamed.

Molly studied him—beautiful blond man that he was—and thought, *I'll remember this night forever. The way he touched me, the way he looked at me. The words he said to me. And even though I'll never see him again once he leaves Friendly, I'll be glad for this night when he loved me this one time.*

She reached up a hand to touch the golden hair on his chest. "Thank you, Parker." Her voice shook; her hand trembled where she pressed it to his heart. "For everything . . . I know you did not come here by your own choice. . . ."

Their eyes locked in silent communication.

"Molly . . ." he said, and covered her hand with his own, gazing down at her through the opalescent slivers of moon-light. "This is my choice." His gaze, hungry and hot, roved over her body. She was indeed beautiful. Her breasts were high and firm, her waist narrow, her stomach smooth and flat, her legs long and shapely. The sight of her made his pulse drum erratically.

Groaning deep within his throat, he took her into his arms and eased her down onto the bed, pressing her against him. She basked in the joy of having his body against hers, firm and hot, completely male. He reveled in the sensation of her body close to his, sweet and soft, totally female.

They lay with nothing between them except the bittersweet reminder that their time together was limited, that it would not last, that this joining they would so willingly share would happen only this one magical night.

He lowered his head and kissed the hollow of her throat, each breast, her rib cage, then the silky plane of her stomach. She threaded her fingers through the thick strands of silver-blond hair, smelling him, wanting him.

When at last he touched her softly, deeply within, he gave her what her husband had never given her: a lesson in desire, the promise of passion—as intense and powerful as the first, fierce summer storm of the season.

He moved over her then and pressed his body into hers, and she almost wept with the sweetness it brought to her heart. For the first time in her life she felt full, complete, wonderfully whole.

She savored the rhythmic rush of his breath on her cheek, the taut strength of his muscles beneath her hands, the glorious weight of his body on hers. She squeezed her eyes shut and whispered his name.

While Parker moved patiently, gently, within her, he learned a lesson of his own about this act they were sharing. It was no lust-driven, emotionless coupling, like most others he'd known. No . . . this was a glorious thing, a burgeoning, blossoming, billowing thing that awed them both, leaving them breathless, taking them to a place neither one had ever known could exist.

When at last she arched and tensed around him, he gave one last powerful lunge and shuddered over her, and they both found completion and knew a deep satisfaction—a keen sense of oneness.

For a small golden speck of time, yesterday ceased to matter, tomorrow cast no shadows, and they lay sated and replete in the haven of each other's arms.

The next morning Parker woke to find Molly gone. Somehow he'd known he would. He turned onto his side, closed his eyes, and inhaled the lingering sweetness of her scent. He lay abed feeling a wonderful sense of joy, mingled with an odd sense of loss. He knew she would not come to him again. He forced himself to put aside the sadness that thought brought, and rose. When he'd finished his morning chores, he went up to the house.

Joshua met him at the door. "I'm goin' into town for supplies this mornin'. Wanna come?" he asked, his smile eager and bright.

Parker grinned. "Sure." His gaze left the boy and sought out Molly.

He spotted her standing near the stove. She was dressed in a crisp white blouse and pale blue skirt, covered by a spotless white apron. But her hair captured Parker's attention most. Instead of the usual tightly wound coil, the shiny red mass was caught up at the sides by tiny combs and hung loose and full down her back. When she turned and met his gaze, he smiled his appreciation.

Her own smile was a bit uncertain, but her cheeks were flushed with pleasure at his approval, and her eyes glowed with a new tenderness that was meant for him alone. And he knew it.

After breakfast he and Josh hitched the team of horses to the wagon and headed for town. The late-August air was pungent and ripe with the promise of September.

Holding the reins loosely, Parker let the horses set their own pace. "School should be startin' up soon," he said to Josh.

The boy shrugged, disinterested. "I ain't plannin' to go back this year."

Parker frowned his disapproval. "Why the hell not?"

Joshua turned his attention to the blotch of mud stuck on the tip of his left boot. "There ain't much need for a farmer to be educated. Besides, there's too much that needs doin' at home for me to be runnin' off to school every mornin'."

Parker waved a persistent fly out of his face. "What does Molly have to say about this?"

"She don't like it none," the boy answered honestly. "She says there ain't no reason a farmer has to be ignorant."

Parker nodded his agreement. "She's right. A boy needs an education whether he wants one or not."

Josh threw Parker a challenging glance. "Did you go to school?"

"Hell, yes!"

"Did ya like it?"

"Hell, no!"

They eyed each other seriously for the space of about three seconds, then Parker cracked a grin, and they both chuckled and turned their attention to the swaying rumps of the horses before them.

But Parker was not finished with Joshua yet. The fondness he felt for Josh spurred a certain sense of responsibility for the boy's welfare. So when they pulled into town, Parker turned and nailed him with a look that said he expected his next words to be heeded. "You do like Molly says, Josh. You go to school. You need to be around youngsters your own age, and there are things you need to learn you can't learn stuck out on that farm all day. Besides, what you learn in school will only make you better at what you do, whatever that is." He laid his hand on the boy's shoulder and gave it a little shake. "You mind what I say, now, you hear?"

His expression solemn, Josh was silent for a long moment, then finally he smiled and said, "I hear ya, Parker."

While Josh went into O'Malley's General Store with the list Molly had given him, Parker checked each horse's bridle, then gave each a carrot he'd hidden in his pocket. He was just about ready to follow the youngster into the store when he heard a familiar voice bellow out behind him, "Parker Reed! Is that you, you cheatin' sonovabitch?"

Parker spun around just in time to catch a deft right to his jaw. He stumbled back, righted his footing, then quickly ducked, avoiding the next well-aimed blow. He held up his hands, affecting his most charming grin. "Now, George. Hold on there. Is that any way to greet your best pal?"

George Hoffer narrowed his shaggy dark brows in anger. "Best pal! A pal doesn't cheat a friend like you done me!"

Parker's eyes grew innocently large. His voice took on an offended tone. "I didn't cheat ya, George. Holy hell! I won that saloon fair and square."

"Yeah, just like we won that card game in Savannah three years back."

Parker grinned and wiggled his eyebrows wickedly. "Didn't that beat all, though?" he asked his former cardplaying partner. "I can still see the look on that Englishman's face when we cleaned him out." Parker hooked his hands on his hips and threw back his head and laughed.

George straightened and dropped his fists to his side, his anger quickly diminishing. "Hmmph!" he huffed, disgusted with himself as much as he was with Parker. He never could stay mad at Parker long enough for it to do any good. He turned his attention to a cloud of dust stirred up by a passing wagon.

Watching George's temper stabilize, Parker closed the distance between them and threw an arm over the smaller man's shoulder in a gesture of easy camaraderie. "Dammit, George, it's good to see you! What the hell are you doing here in Friendly?"

Relieved to see his friend alive and whole, George relinquished the last shreds of his anger. "Looking for you, goddammit!"

"Me?" Parker said, incredulous.

"Hell, yes!" George snapped bad-naturedly. "I've been waitin' since the end of June for you to show up in San Francisco so I could teach you how to run the Silver Sail. I didn't want you coming in all wet behind the ears and ruining everything I spent the last year of my life putting together. When you didn't show by the end of July, I figured something must have happened to you." George gave Parker a disgruntled glare and tried to hide his concern for his friend behind a wall of feigned gruffness. "Bein' the no-good polecat that ya are, it's not like you to forget to collect your winnings."

Parker chuckled. Good old George. Steal his saloon right out from under him, and he still remained a faithful friend. The thought humbled Parker. "Well, that's mighty kind of you to worry about me like that, George." Parker's expression turned solemn and earnest. "Thank you," he said. "You're a good friend."

Unused to sincerity of any kind from his friend, George grew red in the face. "Aw, shit," he blustered, and shook off Parker's arm. "Don't be getting all mushy and sentimental on me now. I couldn't care less if you fell in a hole and broke your worthless goddamn neck. I just didn't want my saloon sitting there waitin' for some fool, is all." Taking a step back, George finally got a good look at Parker and paused a moment, awed by what he saw. Gone were the fancy duds his friend usually sported, and in their place were plain brown trousers, a red-checkered shirt, and wide black suspenders. His shirt sleeves were rolled up to his biceps, revealing thick, hard muscle. "Christ Almighty! Where the hell did you get those arms?"

Parker flexed his arms proudly and grinned. "I grew 'em. Don't that beat all?"

"Shit! Shit! Shit!" George muttered, shaking his head in amazement as he looked into his friend's tanned face. "What in hell are you doing here?"

On a dusty planked walkway, amid the easy bustle of an ordinary day in Friendly, Parker told him the whole story.

CHAPTER
8

George stared at Parker in blatant disbelief. "You're making this up, aren't you? You just want me to feel sorry for you!"

Parker threw back his head and laughed. "Hell, no!" he insisted. "You can ask Grover and Bull. They'll tell you I'm not lyin'."

"Grover and Bull?" George frowned, puzzled.

"Friendly's sheriff and deputy," Parker explained. "You don't need to feel sorry for me. Stayin' here hasn't been so bad."

George snorted, still skeptical, and cocked an eyebrow. "Since when have you done—let alone enjoyed doing—an honest day's work?"

Parker sobered, considering his friend's question. "Can't say as I ever have until now."

Bemused, George studied Parker's expression.

Around them, several of the passing locals waved and called out cordial greetings to Parker, as if he were, and always had been, one of their own.

George's confusion intensified. Not only was he puzzled by the bizarre circumstances of his friend's situation, but he was even further baffled by his friend's and the local people's total acceptance of such an outlandish arrangement. Despite Parker's orneriness, despite the fact that he had literally swindled the Silver Sail right out from under him, George still held a strange sort of affection for the man who had been his friend for so many years. In pensive silence, he pocketed his hands. Finally he said, "One of us, or both of us, needs to get back to San Francisco. I left Mike in charge. But he can't run things for long. Accounts need to be paid. Things need to be done." George grew silent again for the space of several seconds, then made an instant decision. "I'll help you get out of here."

"What do you mean?" Parker asked, feeling a prickle of apprehension.

"Tonight!" George's face grew animated. "I'll come out to the farm and get you. I can get an extra horse. And you don't need the lease if I'm with you to prove you own the saloon. As for Hero . . . well, I know how fond you are of that horse, but if you like the McPherson boy so much, leave Hero here for him."

Parker listened silently, carefully masking the increasing heaviness in his chest.

"The only thing I ask in return . . . is to be your partner," George stated. "Instead of sole ownership of the Silver Sail, you'll share ownership with me." He smiled, pleased with his cleverness at manipulating the return of at least partial ownership of his beloved establishment.

Parker sighed and dropped his gaze. He could leave. He could actually have his freedom once again if he wanted it. But instead of the heady rush of elation he'd expected to feel at making that desire become a reality, he felt a strange sort of emptiness.

He thought of Joshua, of how the boy would feel to find him gone, and he closed his eyes in self-disgust. Then he thought of Molly, and his heart actually ached.

But whether he left now or waited until the crops were harvested, abandoning Molly would be hard.

Still, his departure was inevitable. He knew he was not the staying kind.

Leaving now would be easier, he supposed, than later. He thought of the yet-to-be-harvested fields and felt saddened by the fact that he would not be able to bring in the crops he'd helped to plant.

He acknowledged that it would be dishonorable of him to leave when there was still so much work to be done. But then, he had never claimed to be an honorable man.

He knew Silas Turner was gnawing at the bit, waiting for the opportunity to come to Molly's aid.

Parker had sensed that immediately. Silas wanted Molly. And though it galled him to admit it, Parker truly believed Silas would be the better man for her. But the thought of Silas touching her, as he had touched her the night before, made Parker feel physically ill.

"Well?" George prodded, breaking into Parker's thoughts, anxious for a response.

Parker looked up just as Joshua came through the door, carrying a sack of flour draped over his shoulder. A smiling, barrel-shaped Mr. O'Malley followed behind. "Hey, Parker. What you been doin'?" Joshua asked.

Parker smiled, but his smile was strained, forced. "Just passing the time of day, waiting for you." Resigned to what he would do, he sighed and met his friend's gaze. "Come for me at midnight," he said under his breath. "I'll meet you out on the road."

Alone with her thoughts, Molly sat on the porch, listening to the wind rustle the treetops and the crickets sing around her. She laid her head back against the curved head of the rocker and deeply inhaled the waning scents of summer.

The harvest would start soon. Before long, Parker would be gone.

She had no regrets, no pangs of repentance. What he had given her had been good and right and beautiful. And it was hers forever. She found comfort in that thought.

She smiled into the darkness, comfortable with her memories, and gazed out at the milk house, grateful to the man who slept within.

Through the meager light afforded by the cloud-shrouded moon, Parker watched George make his way up the narrow road. He hefted the small bundle of his belongings up onto his shoulder and trotted off to meet him. But when he reached the oak tree in front of the house, he stopped, turned, and gazed at the porch in a web of confusion and longing.

Then he saw Molly.

She stood very slowly. Although he couldn't see her eyes through the midnight shadows, he felt her disappointment as keenly as if it were his own. He wanted to speak out, to give her an explanation, to ease the pain of his abrupt abandonment, but the words locked tight within his throat, refusing to be uttered. Before he could manage to force them out, she silently turned, went into the house, and set him free.

"What the hell took you so long?" George asked, irritated.

Parker stopped before him, his mind clicking furiously. Clouds scudded across the moon, leaving it brilliant and free to light the land around them. Parker looked out across the ripe fields and felt a deep sense of loss.

"Well, come on!" George hollered, holding out the reins of the horse he'd bought from a local farmer. "Get on."

Sighing, Parker silently accepted the reins and threw his bundle over the horse's rump.

Molly woke later than usual the next morning. She felt tired and listless, having rested poorly throughout the night.

Knowing Joshua had most likely finished his morning chores and was probably awaiting breakfast, she rose, crossed the room, then bent over the washbasin and splashed tepid water up onto her face.

From outside her window she heard Joshua's voice and figured he must be talking to one of the animals.

Her throat tightened, and her eyes drifted shut. Josh. *Oh, God help me.* Parker's leaving would be so hard on him. He would feel so hurt and disappointed. She blinked back the swift hot rush of tears, aching for her son. Though she had not thought it possible, she hurt for him even more than she did for herself.

She was not angry with Parker, just confused and disappointed. She had always known this time would come, but she had thought, as she'd watched him change in the past months, that he would stay to see the season through.

Again, she had been a poor judge of character.

She dressed quickly, brushed her hair thoroughly, then reached her arms up to braid and coil it as she so often had in the past. But something broke within her, and blinking back another rush of tears, she caught up her hair on the sides of her head and let the back hang free. If Parker Reed had taught her anything, it was that she had every right to enjoy her femininity.

A loud hoot of Joshua's laughter came from the kitchen.

Molly wondered what he could find so amusing. Obviously he'd yet to learn Parker had gone. She left her room, making her way down the narrow hall to the kitchen. But as soon as she stepped inside the kitchen door, her footsteps died. Her heart leaped; her eyes misted. Parker and Joshua stood at the stove, flipping pancakes and arguing over who had mastered the proper technique.

Sensing her presence, the two cooks turned to greet her.

Joshua's smile grew wide. "Sit down, Molly. We're cookin' for you today."

"Mrs. McPherson," Parker said quietly in greeting, his eyes locking with hers.

You stayed, she said to herself, wanting to believe this wasn't temporary.

He crossed the floor to the table, pulling out her chair for her. "Allow me, ma'am."

As though in a trance, she crossed the room to the chair, accepting his offer. Once seated, she looked up at him. She studied his face, her eyes speaking an eloquent question.

He smiled down at her and softly said, "My sentence was until harvest, Molly."

Her throat felt tight, her chest heavy. "There isn't a sentence anymore," she whispered, aggrieved there had ever been one.

"But the crops still have to be harvested."

"Yes," she agreed, assuming he'd stayed only out of kindness, and even for that she was thankful. "But the crops are my responsibility," she added, "mine and Josh's."

"But we planted them together." His expression was earnest, his voice soft.

"Yes," she whispered.

"Then we'll bring them in together."

And so they did.

August exploded into the richness of September.

It was barely into the third week of the new month when Indiana was blessed with its first frost. The leaves on the trees took nature's cue and blazed into a rhapsody of color. While October beckoned, the hours of daylight shortened, and the workday lengthened.

The days passed swiftly. Parker, with Molly and Joshua at his side, worked the fields from dawn till dusk each day. On the second Sunday of October, after church, the three headed over to a neighboring farm for a husking bee. Everyone who could spare the time and who planned to hold such an event of their own attended.

Parker found this, too, was a tradition he enjoyed. The gatherings were as much fun as they were tiring.

During the third week of October, Molly and Parker held a husking bee of their own. Most of the neighbors—excluding Silas, who stayed home and stewed over the fact that Parker was still staying in Molly's milk house—attended.

By the end of the fourth week of October, as the land grew lush in burnt colors of gold and scarlet, and the air grew ripe with the scent of decaying leaves, Molly McPherson's fields were harvested and plowed.

Early one brisk morning, she stood alone in the autumn sunshine, her heart heavy, full of a host of conflicting emotions. The chill bite of November rushed in on the wind, stinging her nose and cheeks. She gazed out at her harvested fields and grew humble with thanksgiving. They'd had a good year— the best they'd ever had. That thought brought with it the bittersweet reminder that she had Parker to thank for her bounty.

Without him, she and Josh would not have fared nearly so well. Without Parker, she might even have had to accept Silas' offer of help. That would not have come without a price.

She pivoted slightly and turned her attention to her house. It still needed a coat of whitewash, but Parker had fixed the sagging porch, her steps, her barn—which was now sound and dry. Not only had he fixed the roof, but he'd mended and filled every crack, every small crevice he could find within the building. Her stock and her crops would pass the winter well, thanks to him.

By tacit agreement, neither had mentioned the one special night they'd shared, yet it remained a sweet, evocative memory.

She swallowed back her pain and vowed she would not dishonor the time she'd had with him by crying.

Now was the time to honor that vow.

Last Sunday, after their husking bee, the judge had promised to stop by with Parker's horse and belongings today. Harvest was over; Parker's sentence was complete.

He would leave her today.

She looked toward the milk house. The heaviness in her chest became an oppressive thing. She would miss him terribly. There was no use denying that.

She had fallen hopelessly, desperately in love with him.

Who would have thought it? she asked herself, smiling sadly, remembering their first, tense, antagonistic meeting, remembering how she'd thought him a truly sorry specimen of a man. But he'd proved her wrong. Parker Reed was a fine man—strong and gentle, kind and loving. . . . She closed her eyes, remembering his hands on her body. He was passionate, too. Oh, he was indeed a very passionate man. And he'd made her laugh. She smiled to herself. No man had ever made her laugh.

Who would have thought it? the voice within echoed back to her.

"Yes, who indeed?" Molly whispered to the wind.

Parker gathered his few belongings into the bundle he'd carried with him the night he'd intended to escape with George.

He left the milk house, closing the door, refusing to look back, not wanting to remember the night he'd spent with Molly within the confines of the small snug building.

He stepped out into the coolness of the morning air, squinted against the sunshine, and took a deep breath.

He was free.

And yet he'd never felt so completely desolate in his entire life.

Slowly he crossed the yard, his gaze rising to the road beyond. A wagon and a rider on a horse moved toward him. Judge McPherson sat on the wagon seat beside Grover, who steered the horses. Bull rode beside the wagon, leading Parker's horse behind.

"Hey, Bull!" Joshua yelled out. "Hey, Grandpa! Grover!" But his voice, though loud enough in its youthfulness, lacked the enthusiasm it had held that long-ago May morning when Parker had been delivered to Molly's doorstep as her summer prisoner.

Parker's gaze sought out Molly. She stood beside the well, holding a bucket of water, concentrating on the approaching wagon. The morning sun shone down on her hair, so like the deep, beautiful autumn colors that surrounded her. Seeing her thus, he felt a poignant rush of nostalgia.

"Hey, Parker!" Bull called out, pulling Parker's attention away.

Parker raised a hand in greeting to the three men.

When the wagon stopped before him, Grover climbed down, then helped the judge to the ground.

Elias McPherson closed the space between them, holding his hand out to Parker. "You've done a fine job here, son." He glanced at Molly, who remained by the well, then at Joshua, who studied the dirt at his feet with intense interest. "We're sorry to see you go." The very eccentric, very wise old judge knew he spoke for everyone present.

Parker's grin was a bit sardonic. "It seems strange to say it was my pleasure . . . but it was." He turned to Josh and placed a hand on his shoulder. "You do like Molly tells you."

Josh nodded, refusing to meet the older man's eyes. "I will, Parker," he murmured.

"And you stay in school, you hear?"

Swallowing thickly, the boy nodded again.

His own throat uncomfortably tight, Parker patted Joshua's shoulder and said hoarsely, "You're a fine young man, Josh. The best I've ever known. You remember that."

Wordlessly, Joshua pressed against Parker's chest, wrapping his arms tight around the man's waist.

His throat burning, Parker hugged the boy close for several long minutes, then took a deep breath and looked at Molly. Her eyes locked with his. She offered him a small smile and crossed the yard to join the small group. As he watched her Parker's heart caught in his chest, while Joshua silently moved back out of the way to allow Molly and Parker a moment to themselves.

They'd said their good-byes the night before. She'd thanked him for everything, and for the first time since the night they'd made love, he kissed her softly under the full harvest moon, desperately wanting to tell her what he felt for her, afraid that if he did, he would only make their parting more difficult.

So he'd kept his feelings safely locked within his heart.

When he left her, he'd gone to sleep trying to convince himself that once he'd joined George in San Francisco, once he'd resumed the frantic, exciting, pleasurable, pointless life he'd lost, he'd forget about this farm, about Josh, about Molly McPherson.

But deep inside he knew he couldn't forget, he knew he wouldn't.

Because he loved them. He loved her. God, how he loved her.

Ever since the night they'd danced together in the moonlight, he'd known what he felt for her was something special—something different from anything he'd felt for any other woman.

Now, as he stood before her in the sundrenched splendor of the last day of October, he knew he'd never be happy without her. So being the gambler he was, he decided to cast one last wager. He spun, nailed the judge with a calculated stare, and said, "I was in town last week, you know?"

The judge eyed him quizzically.

Parker nodded, puffed out his chest, and widened his stance. "Yessiree. In fact I had a whiskey over at the saloon."

Baffled, the judge remained silent, curious.

"I really hate to admit such a thing," Parker went on in a matter-of-fact tone, "but I have to say I got a bit rowdy." He turned to Bull and winked. "Wouldn't you say I got a bit rowdy that day?"

For several seconds Bull looked at Parker as if he had mush for brains; then, finally catching on, he nodded. "Yep! I'd say he got a mite outta hand." He turned to Grover, his eyes communicating a silent message. "Wouldn't you say he got outta hand, Grover?"

Grover's expression went dead serious. He hooked his thumbs in his waistband and turned to face the judge. "I'd say he did a helluva job of disturbin' the peace! Worst I've ever seen!"

For a long time the judge stared at the three men. Then he narrowed his eyes. "Is that a fact?" he asked.

Parker nodded, pursed his lips, and gazed up at the blue sky. "Yep. I'd say the least I deserve for bein' the hellion I am is to have my sentence extended for a spell." He gave Grover and Bull a meaningful glance. "What do you boys think?"

Bull coughed; Grover cleared his throat. Joshua's eyes widened, and Molly quit breathing.

"Yes, sir, Judge," Grover said. Beside him, Bull nodded emphatically. His expression stern, Grover went on, "We can't let this varmint get away with committin' such a crime in our town."

Amused, the judge smiled and chuckled. In time, he sobered and eyed Parker slyly. "How long a spell are you talking, Mr. Reed?"

Parker turned and faced Molly. "For as long as Molly will have me." He took a step closer. "Until death do us part." He watched the emotions play over her face, took her hand, and quietly asked, "Will you, Molly? Will you have me?"

Abashed, Molly dropped her gaze. Her heart seemed to spin within her chest, while her mind struggled to capture the reality of what he was asking.

"But, Parker," Joshua said, his face suddenly animated by what he'd heard, "what about your saloon?"

Parker grinned and looked down at the boy. "I told George that if I didn't show up by Christmas, it's his." He shrugged, chuckled, then admitted, "By rights, it belongs to him anyway."

"Well, Molly," Joshua said eagerly, "are we gonna keep him?"

Molly raised misty eyes to her stepson, then to her father-in-law, who beamed his approval at her. Finally her gaze found Parker's. When she spoke, her words echoed the very ones she'd spoken at their first meeting. "I don't reckon we have much choice." Then, her eyes reflecting love, her expression soft with joy and hope, she added, "There's so much that needs to be done around here—I can't remember it all. Besides . . ." She paused a moment, then smiled. "I love him. Even if he is afraid to climb up on a barn roof."

"Hmmph!" Parker grunted, his face breaking into a sheepish grin. He dropped his bundle to the ground and reached for her, pulling her into his arms. Pointing his chin to the sky, he howled out his joy, then kissed her soundly, caring little that the onlookers hooted and clapped their approval.

When he lifted his head and looked down into Molly's face, he thought about all he'd missed while imprisoned on this shabby little farm, and he smiled to himself, realizing he'd missed nothing at all; instead he had found himself, had found friends and a home, had found a reason for existing.

Parker Reed had found everything a man could ever want or need, right here on fiery Molly McPherson's farm, outside of a quirky little town called Friendly.

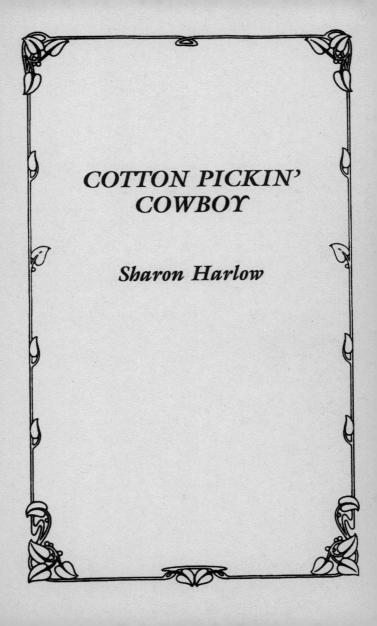

COTTON PICKIN' COWBOY

Sharon Harlow

Dear Reader,

I grew up on Thompson's Ranch in West Texas, near the town of Colorado City, in cotton and cattle country. My parents started out leasing land on the ranch almost fifty years ago for farming cotton, then somewhere along the way Dad became ranch foreman and bought a farm of his own.

Sometimes the only thing the cooler autumn days brought was relief from the stifling summer heat. But in good years, the changing season brought the anticipation of harvest, the satisfaction of success, the security of paying off the bills and maybe having a little left over.

In early fall, puffs of white began to dot the green cotton fields as the maturing bolls burst open. Soon the whole field became a striped tapestry of white cotton and reddish-brown earth. Today the cotton is harvested by mechanical strippers, but in my childhood it was done by hand. The cotton pickers— men, women, and sometimes children—would arrive early in the morning, swarming over the field with long sacks dragging along the ground behind them as they pulled the cotton from the plants. It was hard, tedious work—toil both my parents well remembered from their younger days. I tried it once, for about five minutes, and gained a deep respect for anyone who stuck to the job.

Then there were the cattle. To a bovine eye, the grass is always greener on the other side of a fence, and for some reason a cotton patch holds a special appeal. I've chased my share of cows out of the field, praying all the while that they wouldn't turn around and chase me in the other direction! And I never, ever took on a bull. A braver soul was needed to order those beasts around, preferably someone on horseback or in a pickup.

Many of our neighbors were much like my dad, both farmer and cowboy, depending on which job needed doing—and maybe which hat he was wearing. But there were cowboys around who wouldn't set foot in a cotton field. And from the stories the old-timers tell, it was a lot worse back in the early days. Only a man in love would break with that tradition.

Although my love for my husband took me clear across the country to live, the land and the history of West Texas live in my heart. The town of Crooked Creek is imaginary, but it is typical of the area at that time. Nate and Sarah are typical, too. Strong women were needed to help settle that rugged land. I suspect that after they got there, many of them found greater inner strength than they had ever imagined. As for Nate, a sweet talkin' cowboy had a way all his own, and once he set his sights on a woman, he didn't let up until she was carrying his brand.

I hope "Cotton Pickin' Cowboy" leaves you with a smile, and that your life is filled with love and happiness.

—*Sharon Harlow*

I'd enjoy hearing from you. You can write to me at:
4910 S. 287th Street,
Auburn, WA 98001

CHAPTER
1

Nate Kendrick curled his hands around the hot mug of coffee and stepped out onto the front porch of the Silver Spur ranch house. His warm breath mingled with the steam from the cup, forming a tiny white cloud that curled up in front of his face before it drifted away in the unseasonably crisp morning air. His gaze moved along the smooth line of the horizon to Lonesome Butte, standing dark and ghostly blue against the pale gray sky, a silent sentinel guarding the far corner of his land.

Bold strokes of pink, purple, and gold chased away the lingering shadows in the sky, revealing the grassland before him. It sloped away from the house to a narrow valley, gradually rising on the other side to gently rolling pasture. Low-lying mesquite trees dotted the landscape, forming bright patches of green against the tawny blanket of fall grass.

Nate sighed to himself, soaking up the beauty before him like a thirsty man drinking a dipper of cold, sweet well water after a long, hot ride. He never grew tired of it. Each morning he looked at it as if for the first time.

He found strength in the quiet of dawn, yet lately these moments were not as peaceful, not as satisfying as they once had been. Over the years loneliness had occasionally come calling, but it seldom stayed for long. This time, seemed like it had burrowed in for the winter.

Down in the barnyard, the rooster announced the day. Nate smiled slightly. That tough old bird would keep crowing until someone opened the door to the chicken coop so he could strut around in front of the hens. In the corral, one of the stallions nickered to his mares, and they replied with soft praise. Long fingers of glistening light stretched to the sky, and the red curve of the sun broke the horizon. High overhead, two hawks soared in a lazy circle, riding a golden trail of light.

"Must be something about turnin' twenty-eight that makes a man take particular notice of nature pairin' up," Nate muttered.

He saw his foreman, Frank Jones, heading toward the house. Frank had spent most of his life on horseback and had the bow legged gait to prove it. Since he was trying to hurry, that might explain his pained expression, but Nate doubted it.

"Trouble?"

"More'n likely. Jeb and Shorty went into town last night."

"Jeb get drunk?"

"You didn't hear him? He was singin' hymns until he passed out. The real mournful kind about wayfarin' strangers and such. If I'd heard one more tale of woe, I might have put him out of his misery."

Nate leaned one hand against the porch post and took a sip of coffee. "What saloon did he shoot up?"

"None that I heard about." The foreman looked down, spat a squirt of tobacco juice at the ground, and watched it puddle in a dark brown ball on the dry dirt. "Shorty says he thinks Jeb cut some bob wire on their way home. He was pretty lit himself, so he can't be sure."

"He what?" Nate jerked up straight, sloshing coffee over the side of the cup. It had been over ten years since the arrival of barbed wire in West Texas, and generally speaking, most of the troubles that came with it had settled down. He well remembered the bitterness and hardship, even bloodshed. "That ol' coot! Doesn't he know the days of open range are gone for good?"

"Now, Nate, you know he does—when he's sober. But when he gets to drinkin', he starts thinkin' about the good ol' days. Starts actin' like it, too."

"My granddaddy never abided fence cutting, and Jeb knows it. He would have fired him in a minute." Nate looked out across the prairie. "Maybe I should, too."

"Where would he go?"

That was the problem. There was no place for old, washed-up cowboys. Nate thought there should be a big ranch for the old-timers somewhere, one with miles of open space and few fences, where the horses rode easy and the winters were mild. He didn't know of such a place, so he kept Jeb and a couple of others on the payroll. They caused a few problems now and then by drowning their sorrows and trying to relive their youth, but he figured their knowledge of cattle and horses was worth something even if they couldn't move as fast or work as hard as they once did. If it hadn't been for men like Jeb, his granddaddy and the other ranchers never would have settled West Texas. And he wouldn't have ten thousand acres of good grazing land and three thousand head of cattle.

"Which fence?"

"Shorty wasn't sure, but he thinks it was over by the Dawson place."

Nate smacked the heel of his hand against the porch post in disgust. He wasn't a swearing man, but if he had been, it would have been a good time to test his proficiency. "Tom Dawson doesn't need any more trouble. You pour a bucket of water over that old man's head and a pot of coffee down his throat. When he can sit on the wagon seat, send him and Shorty over to fix the fence." He sighed. "Better send a couple of other men with them so it's done right. I'll ride over and see if the cows are in Tom's cotton patch yet. Dock Jeb and Shorty a week's pay—Jeb for doing the cuttin' and Shorty for not stopping him. Maybe that'll make them think next time."

Frank grinned. "Shorty will blame Jeb for losin' his pay and bellyache about it for a good six months. That ought to get it through the old man's thick head."

Nate downed the rest of his coffee, then went inside the house and set the cup on the kitchen counter. His stomach rumbled, reminding him of the fluffy buttermilk biscuits and the chicken-fried steak and gravy the cook was rustling up down in the cook house. Breakfast would have to wait. His cattle could do a lot of damage in the time it took to chow down. By the time he reached the corrals, one of the cowboys had his horse saddled.

Nate mounted and glanced toward the bunkhouse. Two men dragged a still-sleeping Jeb out the door and across the bare dirt yard to the horse trough, dutifully dunking his head under the water. The gray-haired man came up sputtering and cussing a blue streak. They dunked him once more for good measure. As Nate rode away the laughing cowboys escorted Jeb back toward the bunkhouse, where Frank stood in the doorway with a pot of coffee and a grim expression.

He raced across the pasture, the sure legs of his cow pony, Whiskey, eating up the miles between his house and Tom Dawson's. He slowed for a stretch of hilly terrain, carefully crossing the gullies carved deeper every year by occasional downpours, then nudged the animal back to a gallop as the land flattened out into undulating prairie.

He knew Tom better than he did the other farmers whose smaller places surrounded his spread. He considered him a friend, which was not something he could say about all his neighbors. Tom was only a few years older than Nate. He was married, had three boys, a new baby girl, and a wife who had not regained her strength after her daughter's birth.

Tom also had a broken leg, courtesy of a greenhorn's ignorance. Or foolishness. Nate wasn't sure which. Tom had been helping a new neighbor clear some land of brush and rocks two weeks earlier. When the wagon was partially loaded, the man decided to move it, not taking care where he placed it or how well he set the brake. A few minutes later the brake gave way, and the wagon rolled down the incline. Tom jumped out of the way, but at the last second the wagon hit a bump and veered in his direction, one wheel rolling over the calf of his leg. The doctor said it wasn't a bad break, but he would be hobbling around on crutches for some time.

Neat rows of fluffy white cotton came into view as Nate neared the Dawson place. The thick clusters of green leaves on the knee-high plants made a picturesque backdrop for the large, white bolls. From what little he knew about cotton, it looked as if Tom would have a good crop. At least he would if Nate's cows didn't trample it first. Five were already in the field, and several more were moseying toward the gaping hole in the fence. They wouldn't eat the cotton, but they could do plenty of damage in their quest for the occasional weed or blade of grass—or what was left of the garden.

He groaned as one old lop-horned cow lifted her nose in the air and started toward the garden patch in a determined line, disregarding the fact that she was wreaking havoc on the rows of cotton in her path. Curious, the other cows meandered along behind her. Nate slowed his horse, not wanting to spook the cattle into doing worse damage before he even reached the downed fence.

Andy, the youngest boy, came running out of the house in his bare feet and long johns. The five-year-old ran across the yard and into the field toward the cows, waving his arms and yelling. The old lop-horn stopped and stared at the boy. Andy skidded to a halt and stared back.

Fear clenched Nate's gut. If that stubborn old cow decided to challenge the youngster, Andy might be trampled. There was no way Nate could reach him in time.

CHAPTER
2

A movement at the house caught Nate's eye. A woman jumped off the porch and raced toward the boy, her white nightgown and brown robe drawn up to her knees with one hand, a broom in the other. She practically flew across the tiny hills and valleys of the furrows, trampling a few cotton plants herself in the process. Nate couldn't even tell if she had nice legs because they were pumping up and down so fast—not that he would be inclined to notice something like that at such a tense moment.

She didn't slow down until she was between the boy and the cow, then she dropped her skirts, grabbed the broom with both hands, and soundly whacked the bewildered animal right between the eyes. The old heifer snorted, backed up two steps, and shook her head, then turned and ran toward the hole in the fence with her tail high in the air, scattering the other cows in her wake. They regrouped, trotting behind the leader.

Nate drew Whiskey to a halt well away from the fence. Any movement until the cattle were past it was liable to send them off in every direction but the right one. The woman chased after them, swinging the broom and yelling for all she was worth. When the animals were back on his property, Nate nudged Whiskey to a walk, figuring he would give the lady a few minutes to catch her breath. Approaching her slowly would also allow him time to look her over without being too obvious.

Must be Tom's old-maid sister, Sarah, he thought. Tom had mentioned a few days earlier that she was coming out from Dallas to help until he got back on his feet. He had described her as sweet, shy, and rather plain. Nate thought his friend, and every other man Sarah Dawson had met, needed spectacles.

The belt on the faded brown calico wrapper had obviously been tied in haste, an expedient means of keeping the middle of the robe closed. One button at the bodice and three below the belt were fastened, leaving a tantalizing strip of muslin nightgown exposed from bosom to throat and from midthigh to her ankles. She was no raving beauty, but the figure draped by the soft material was anything but plain—generous curves in all the right places accented a naturally slim waist. The simple square neckline of the gown was trimmed with a narrow edging of embroidery. Nate's fingers twitched as his gaze followed a line of tiny, primly fastened buttons that marched down the front of it, disappearing behind the closed lapels of the wrapper.

Sunlight danced on her shoulder-length brown hair, capturing glistening strands of gold and threads of burnished copper. Her flashing eyes were like coffee mellowed with a touch of rich cream—just the way he liked it—and her cheeks were as rosy as the mountain pinks that covered the rocky hillsides in late summer.

Nate opened his mouth to apologize, but clamped it shut again when a bellow sounded off to the right. He looked quickly in that direction. One of his prize bulls, a giant roan Durham named Gladiator, had decided to show off and play lord protector for his harem.

"Get behind the fence, ma'am," he shouted, kicking Whiskey into motion and grabbing his coiled lariat from the saddle horn. Gladiator pawed the ground, then thundered in their direction. Nate galloped around in a wide half circle so he could approach the bull from the side. Forming a loop with the end of the rope, he rode up beside the animal, yelling and slapping it on the shoulder and across the side of the head with the lariat. Gradually he turned the angry beast away from the fence and drove it farther back into the pasture to rejoin the herd.

When Nate cantered back to the fence, the woman and boy were waiting for him, huddled behind a section of barbed wire that remained attached to the rough cedar posts. "Wow, Mr. Kendrick! You sure can ride." Andy wiggled from his aunt's protective embrace. "Can you learn me to be a cowboy?"

"Maybe someday, son. For now, you'd better run on back up to the house and get warm. You mama is out on the porch looking for you, and you wouldn't want to scare her."

"Yes, sir," said Andy with a grin, his excitement fully intact. He started toward the house, but then stopped and spun around. "You sure whacked that old cow, Aunt Sarah. You done good for a city gal."

"Go to the house, Andrew."

The saddle creaked as Nate shifted his weight and turned his gaze to Sarah Dawson. The color had faded from her face, leaving pale white cheeks where wildflowers had bloomed only moments before. He suspected that now that she had considered her morning's activities, she was probably scared spitless. He briefly considered sliding down from the horse and offering her a comforting shoulder and warm embrace. Women liked that sort of gallantry, and he knew he wouldn't mind it a bit.

She moved the broom, raising the bristled end up in the air, resting the top of the handle on the ground in front of her. When she curled both hands around it, he decided he'd better stay put and be prepared to ride out of harm's way.

He touched the brim of his hat with his forefinger and thumb and dipped his head slightly. "Good mornin', ma'am."

"Good morning, my foot! It's a terrible morning. My nephew could have been killed! Trampled or gored by your stupid cows. You should take better care of your property, Mr. Kendrick, especially when someone else's property and lives are at stake."

Nate knew he should explain or maybe defend himself, but when she paused for a deep breath, he was momentarily distracted. His gaze wandered just a bit, but he quickly brought it back to her face. Captivated by the fire in her eyes, he only half listened as she ranted about the ruined cotton. Would a man's touch—his touch—ignite that same flame? He was surprised by how badly he wanted to find out.

Tom not only needed eyeglasses, he needed his head examined. Nate suspected Sarah could be sweet when she had a mind to. The fact that she was so upset about the danger to her nephew and the damage done to Tom's cotton showed she cared. But shy? That was stretching it.

"And that bull. That monster is a menace. I've a good mind to get Tom's gun and shoot it," she said, pounding the end of the broom handle into the ground for emphasis.

That got his full attention.

He stiffened. She wouldn't dare, he thought, then decided he couldn't be certain. She was as riled up as a mountain lion guarding her cubs. He protected what was his, too, especially something as important as a prize bull. "Anyone who harms that animal will owe me a small fortune."

Her chin went up a notch, but a couple of fingers fluttered nervously on the broom handle.

He stared at her, his expression stern and unrelenting. "I know Tom doesn't have that kind of money. Do you?"

"No." She swallowed hard.

He'd already had enough trouble to last him a whole day, maybe even a week. He'd skipped breakfast and his second cup of coffee, and had thoughts running through his head and feelings running through his body that no gentleman ought to have for a friend's sister. "Well, ma'am, it would take a long time for you to work it out in trade. A lot of days." His gaze slid over her, and he couldn't seem to keep it from lingering here and there. Irritation made him reckless. "And a lot of nights."

"Oh!" She blinked and took a step backward. A hot flush traveled up her neck and filled her face. She reached up to clutch the ruffled lapels of the wrapper against her throat, but touched soft muslin and bare skin instead. Her eyes widened, and she looked down, discovering the partially open robe and improper display of nightgown. A strangled little sound came from her throat as she spun around and started for the house.

Nate felt like a first-class heel.

"Ouch!" She stopped and, leaning against the broom for balance, plucked a grass burr from the bottom of her bare foot. With a sniff, she limped on toward the house.

Nate felt even worse. He swung down from the horse and hurried after her, his high boot heels sinking in the soft dirt, slowing him down. "Miss Dawson, wait."

She speeded up her pace, only to stop with a yelp. This time she had picked up two grass burrs. She angrily jerked the first sticker from her foot, but it stuck in her finger. Nate caught up with her, grabbing her arm when she lost her balance and almost toppled over.

"Don't touch me," she whispered, but it might as well have been a shriek.

He leaned down and cradled her foot in his hand, removing the grass burr, then gently took her hand in his and carefully pulled the sticker from her finger. A little drop of blood beaded on her skin, and he had a strong urge to lift her hand to his lips and suck the sting away. He slowly uncoiled his fingers from around hers but remained in her path.

"Miss Dawson, I apologize. There was no call for what I said." His heart twisted when she kept her gaze directed at the ground. Instead of fire, pain and humiliation shimmered in her misty eyes.

"You are the rudest man I've ever met," she said hoarsely. He wasn't quite, but Sarah prayed he wouldn't catch the lie. Most men simply treated her as a servant, or worse yet, as part of the furniture.

No other man, not even her fiancé, seemed to realize she was a flesh-and-blood woman. That was the problem. Seeing admiration and desire in his eyes had thrown her for a loop. There she was, half out of her mind with fright and anger, railing at him like a shrew, and he had given her that look. The look that said he was attracted to her, the one that said he wanted to touch her, to kiss her . . . and with her standing there in a nightgown and wrapper, her hair all a mess, and her feet bare.

She had seen that kind of interest in a man's eyes before, but it had never been directed at her. She was too mousy, too plain, too dull. It had rattled her, dislodging the tenuous hold she'd had on her emotions, filling her with longings that were new and foolish.

Lord have mercy, she didn't want to think about the heat that flashed through her when he wrapped his big, callused hand around her cold, dirty foot. It had felt so different from her fiancé's soft hand. Of course, Wendell's hand was always cold, and he had never ever touched her foot. *Men must get terribly desperate out here. And I'm a very silly woman.*

"Ma'am, please forgive me," said Nate, hating himself for embarrassing her and for acting so crass. "I paid an arm and a leg for that bull and have a lot of dreams ridin' on him. I guess it gets my dander up when he's threatened." He sighed heavily. "I know that's no excuse for acting like a ja—uh, donkey, but it's the only one I've got."

"I wouldn't really have shot him."

"I realize that now."

She glanced up, meeting his gaze. She wanted to look away, but found herself trapped by the intensity of his clear blue eyes. He pulled off his dark brown hat and plowed his fingers through sun-bleached, light brown hair. Holding the hat carefully by the crown, he placed it between them, almost like a shield.

"Sarah, let's start over," he said quietly. "So far this hasn't been the best morning for either of us." A slow smile spread across his face. "I'm a whole lot nicer after breakfast."

She felt a smile tug at her lips. "Me, too. I haven't even had a cup of coffee."

"I had one, but it takes at least two to make me tolerable."

"Then by all means, Mr. Kendrick—"

"Nate."

"Nate. Let's get you another cup." She smiled shyly and dropped her gaze.

"Yes, ma'am," he said with a grin. He eased the hat on his head, then holding the brim carefully front and back, adjusted it properly. "You'd better ride Whiskey, or you're liable to get your feet full of grass burs."

"I don't know how I missed them on the way out."

"You were going so fast, I doubt if your feet touched the ground." He took the broom from her hand and tossed it aside.

She managed not to gasp when he quickly stepped behind her, settling his hands around her waist. He effortlessly lifted her so she could put one foot in the stirrup and grab hold of the saddle horn. He released her, but kept his hands out, ready to assist as she rather ungracefully hoisted herself up, threw one leg over the horse, and settled into the saddle. Her feet dangled against the horse's sides, far above the stirrups. The nightgown and wrapper did not cover her legs from midcalf down, and her face grew warm at such an unseemly display.

"All set?" He looked up at her, his hand resting on Whiskey's reddish-brown neck.

"Yes, thank you."

Nate picked up the broom, took the reins, and stepped in front of the horse, leading him at a slow walk. He checked out the damage his cattle had done, estimating an amount he thought would be more than a fair settlement, and turned his gaze toward the house.

He might as well have been blind for all he saw of it.

During the past three or four years, farmers had come into the area in droves, buying up every available section of school land for a dollar or two an acre. The cattlemen and cowboys had not seen much good in this invasion of their territory except for one thing—many farmers brought along a daughter or sister of marrying age. Most of them, especially the ones who were reasonably pretty, were wooed and wed before their menfolk harvested the first crop.

Nate had looked over the remaining women—even secretly scouting out the ones who would be ready for marriage in a year or two—and concluded that he would have to widen his territory. There wasn't a woman within twenty miles that he could see spending his life with.

The image of a graceful feminine leg burned in his mind's eye, a gently curved calf with smooth, milky-white skin and a delicately turned ankle, contrasting vividly with Whiskey's chestnut coat. He had never considered feet to be enticing, but the one that had rested in the palm of his hand was, with its creamy softness and delicately curved arch.

A tiny smile lifted the corner of his lips. Maybe he'd give Jeb and Shorty a bonus.

CHAPTER
3

"You been chasin' any more cows, pardner?"

Sarah looked up from her grocery list, her gaze flying across the general store in Crooked Creek to the tall cowboy smiling down at her nephew. Well, there's one wish that didn't come true, she thought ruefully. Nate Kendrick hadn't turned into an ugly troll in the week since she met him, which was probably good for him but bad for her peace of mind.

If anything, he was even more handsome than before. His Levi's were just as faded and comfortable looking, but the polished boots weren't as worn and had a slightly lower heel to make walking easier. The blue Western-style shirt beneath his unbuttoned leather vest was a little fancier, a little newer.

As if sensing her gaze, Nate looked at her, his eyes warm and friendly, a pleasant smile lighting his face. "Mornin', Miss Dawson," he said politely, touching the brim of his charcoal-gray Stetson with the tips of his fingers.

"Good morning, Mr. Kendrick." Sarah smiled nervously, then quickly looked away, trying in vain to focus on the shelves of canned goods in front of her. She needed to keep her mind on the task at hand, not on a man she had no business thinking about in the first place.

Her brother's larder was appallingly empty. It was no wonder his wife had not regained her strength after little Janey's birth, and Tom was thinner than she had ever seen him. They made sure their boys had enough food, although it was mostly beans and corn bread, but she could easily see where the parents had gone without in order to spread the provisions a little further.

Tom had quietly explained that he did have money, but every cent had to go to the bank for a mortgage payment. He had planned on working for Nate and another rancher, mending fences and doing other jobs that the cowboys hated, to earn what was left of the payment and to see his family through until the cotton was picked and sold. But his broken leg put an end to those well-made plans.

Unfortunately Sarah was not in much of a position to help. Her job as a salesclerk in a large mercantile in Dallas provided the basic expenses for herself and her widowed mother, leaving only a tiny amount each month to save for emergencies. Her mother took in sewing, alterations mainly, which gave them a little cushion and a few comforts. Sarah's employer had granted her a leave of absence, but since she would not be earning any income during her time away, she had left most of her last wages with her mother. The train ticket had taken the rest and almost all of her rainy-day fund.

She could not sit by and let her family practically starve. Upon arriving in town that morning, she had gone to the train depot and turned in her ticket home. The refund was not a great deal of money, but it would help feed the family until the cotton was harvested. If she was careful, she would even have a little left to give Tom toward the mortgage payment. She had never had any dealings with bankers, but thought surely the man would give Tom extra time to make the payment since he was unable to work.

Distracted by Nate's presence, she set three cans of pears, three of peaches, and two of apricots on the counter before she thought about checking on the price. "Excuse me, sir, can you tell me the prices of your fruit?"

"Yes, ma'am. The pears are twenty-five cents, peaches are twenty-three, and the apricots are twenty."

"Oh, my," she said softly. That was considerably more than she was used to paying, and it was at least ten cents more per can than the price in the Sears, Roebuck and Company catalog. She hesitated, then put back one can of peaches and one of the pears. Out of the corner of her eye she saw Nate purchase a pound of gumdrops, instructing the clerk to divide it into four small bags. He handed each of the boys a bag of candy and stuck the other one in his coat pocket. She shuddered to think what he paid for the candy, considering the high price of the fruit, but greatly appreciated his thoughtfulness.

She moved on to the canned vegetables, relieved and yet disappointed when he was no longer in sight. *Stop thinking about him. You're engaged to be married, for heaven's sake, and shouldn't even be noticing another man, much less thinking about him half the time.*

With determination and a surprising amount of effort, she brought to mind the image of her betrothed, Wendell Tidwell. Instantly her rebellious brain began comparing him with Nate, then decided it was a lesson in futility. Both men were tall, but where Nate was muscular and strong, Wendell was as thin as a pencil. He probably couldn't lift a twenty-five-pound sack of flour if he had to. Nate was ruggedly handsome, his skin browned by the sun. Wendell was nondescript and pale as a ghost from sitting at a desk and working with ledgers all day.

"You must like a lot of string beans."

She jumped. Wendell was ice. Nate was fire.

She looked down at her basket in dismay, trying to ignore the heat emanating from the man next to her. "Well, for pity's sake."

"How many do you want?" Nate asked, amusement tinting his voice.

"Three." They both reached into the basket at the same time. His fingers brushed hers as they picked up different cans. Sarah held her breath, not looking at him as he set the can on the shelf. She replaced the second one, picking up a can of corn instead and putting it in the basket. "I guess I wasn't paying close enough attention. I wanted some corn and peas, too."

When he made no comment, she looked up. He was glaring at the small pearl-and-gold ring on the third finger of her right hand.

"Are you engaged, Sarah?" His low voice held a hint of disbelief. She wasn't sure if he didn't want to believe it, or if he was surprised because she had actually trapped a man.

"Yes," she said, her tone defensive.

"I see." He shifted slightly away from her, his bearing stiff, a frown marring his brow.

No, you don't see, she wanted to shout. She could tell him that Wendell had a good job and was frugal and often congenial. But how could she admit that she was twenty-six years old and he was the only man who had ever come calling? How could she tell him they had been engaged for eighteen months, and that Wendell had postponed the wedding twice?

"Aunt Sarah, can we go watch the train come in?"

Sarah blinked and looked down at her brother's oldest boy, Brad, who was ten. "I have to finish the shopping, and I don't think your father would want you to go down there alone."

"It would be okay if we walked down this side of the street. The saloon's on the other side." John, the eight-year-old, looked up at her with pleading eyes.

"When I finish here, we'll go down."

"But it'll be here in a few minutes. We heard the whistle already."

"I'll go with them," Nate said gruffly.

She looked up at him, feeling a twinge of disappointment because the warmth had disappeared from his eyes. They weren't cold, but whatever emotion he felt was carefully hidden. "Thank you. I hate to disappoint them. They get to town so seldom."

Nate nodded curtly. "You boys wait outside by the front door. I'll be out in just a minute." Without another word to her, he walked across the store, stopping to talk to the storekeeper. The man nodded, glancing at her once before riveting his attention on Nate.

She turned away, watching the boys through the store window. In a few minutes Nate joined them, and they started off down the street. As Sarah added more corn and peas to her basket, she remembered her mother's warning, one that had been oft repeated over the years.

Don't set your sights on a good-looking man, child. Handsome men don't take plain wives, and if they do, they're always looking for someone prettier. You're a good, sweet girl, Sarah, but all you can hope for is a good, plain man.

Then, after Wendell came courting, her mother reminded her that she was already twenty-four and considered by many to be on the shelf. When Wendell postponed the wedding for the second time, her mother reminded her that he had sensible reasons for asking her to wait. *You will not break your engagement because you're in a snit. We don't have much money, but we're honorable people. We follow through with our obligations. Besides, Wendell has promised to provide for me, too. Not every man would support his mother-in-law.*

She glanced down at the ring on her finger, wishing her mother had kept her admonitions to herself, and that Wendell would embezzle company funds and go off to the wilds of Africa.

"Your aunt going to get married soon?" Nate asked casually as he and the boys strolled toward the train station. He fished a gumdrop out of the bag in his pocket and popped it into his mouth.

"Supposed to in about four months, but it don't seem likely," said Brad.

"Why's that?"

"Because they been engaged nigh onto two years. Every time they set a weddin' date, Wendell postpones it."

"Pa says he's just usin' her," added John.

"What?" Nate scowled down at the boys.

"He eats at their place every night."

"Their place?"

"Aunt Sarah lives with Grandma Dawson. Pa says all Wendell is interested in is a good home-cooked meal. Pa don't think too much of him," said Brad.

Nate didn't either. There was no reason for her to put up with such treatment. Unless she loved him. Maybe this Wendell character was some fancy ladies' man, the kind women fell for and couldn't get over. He had to be handsome as sin and rich as a cattle baron.

"What does he do for a livin'?"

"He's an accountant," said Brad. "But I don't think he makes a lot of money,'cause he lives in this little house next door to Grandma and Aunt Sarah. He doesn't have a buggy or horse. Says they cost too much to keep."

Skinflint. "I guess he rents one when he wants to take your aunt someplace."

"I guess so," said John thoughtfully. "But I don't think he takes her too many places. They walk to church on Sunday and sometimes go for a walk in the park when the weather's nice."

"Must be good-lookin'."

Andy giggled and the other boys grinned. "Ma said he was about as plain as an old faded pair of long johns."

CHAPTER
4

The train rolled in with screeching wheels and bellows of steam, capturing the boys' complete attention. They stood on the wooden platform, delighting in the rumbling beneath their feet while the big engine huffed and puffed as if anxious to be on its way. With the imagination of the young, they hoped and prayed for the arrival of some dark, dirty desperado, silver six-guns slung low on his hips, handlebar mustache waxed to perfection, and glinting eyes hardened by his dastardly deeds.

Nate let them have their fun, glad for a few moments to think about what he had learned. She must be in love with him, he thought, although he didn't see why. She deserved better. He remembered the way she had protected Andy, risking her own safety. And how, after they had returned to the farmhouse that morning, she had quickly changed clothes and flew around the kitchen whipping up a good breakfast out of next to nothing. She wouldn't let Amanda lift a finger, insisting she relax in her rocking chair. She was loving and considerate, and he suspected she could be one mighty passionate woman—with the right man. She deserved a man who appreciated all of her good qualities, not just her cooking.

The boys' disappointed groans brought him back to the present. The only person who stepped off the train was a small man with a bowler hat and a heavy bag, obviously a display case of some kind. No one got on the train. Folks around Crooked Creek didn't do too much traveling.

They waited until the train pulled out of the station, one last shrill whistle lingering in the air as it disappeared around a small hill. As they started back toward town the boys watched the salesman heft his heavy bag down the street.

"Well, at least he had a handlebar mustache," said John, not wanting to be disappointed. Suddenly he grinned. "Maybe he's a Pinkerton agent in disguise."

"And on the trail of some outlaw. His case is loaded with guns. That's why it's so heavy. What do you think, Mr. Kendrick?" Brad looked up at Nate with a sparkle in his eyes.

"Reckon he could be a Pinkerton man posing as a whiskey salesman. That mustache was something to behold, wasn't it?"

"Yep," the three boys said in unison.

"It was a lot more funner goin' to the train station this time," said Andy.

"This time?" Nate knew the family had not met Sarah upon her arrival. She had arranged for a man from the livery stable to drive her out to the farm.

"We were here this morning."

"Hush, Andy. You know we're not supposed to say anything about that," warned Brad.

Nate drew to a halt, looking down at the boys with a frown. "Did you sneak off from your aunt Sarah this morning?"

"No, sir." Brad shifted uneasily and glanced at his brothers. When they nodded, he explained. "Aunt Sarah brought us down here to the station first thing. She got her money back for her return ticket."

The grocery money, thought Nate.

"She said she didn't bring much with her, and well, with Pa laid up and all, he can't work, so things are a little tight right now."

"How does she plan to get back home?"

"She said she'd find some work and earn the money." Brad frowned, looking far older than his ten years. "I tried to tell her there weren't any jobs around here, Mr. Kendrick, but she wouldn't listen. She said right now she was more concerned with gettin' Ma and Pa healthy again, and that they wouldn't ever get their strength back if they didn't eat good. She said she'd worry about getting home when the time came."

Nate felt like kicking himself because he hadn't been more insistent on helping Tom. He had asked if they needed anything and had been reassured that they didn't. Remembering the stack of supplies Sarah had placed on the counter, including such everyday staples as flour, baking powder, and cornmeal, he realized he should have ignored his friend's pride and searched the kitchen cupboards.

At the same time he experienced a surge of hope and elation. Sarah wasn't anxious to go home. And if he worked it right, she might be persuaded to stay—if he wanted her to. He reckoned he needed to be sure his interest would last a lifetime before he started trying to win her heart.

With a flash of insight, startling in its clarity, Nate realized he didn't simply want someone to warm his bed, cook his meals, and bear his children. He wanted the kind of love his grandparents had shared, the kind that made life richer and the hardships easier. He wanted someone who would love the country as much as he did, a woman who could appreciate the glory of dawn over Lonesome Butte.

"We'd better get back and see how Sarah's doing." He hustled the boys along, intent on righting a wrong. When they arrived at the general store, a clerk had just begun loading the supplies in the wagon. They walked into the store to find the storekeeper patiently explaining to Sarah why there was an extra box of canned fruit and vegetables.

"Mr. Kendrick told me to add those things, ma'am."

Sarah turned to Nate. "That's very kind, Mr. Kendrick, but there is no need."

"I think there is." Nate studied her face for a moment. She obviously knew the need but didn't want to accept charity. "These three sprouts will empty that larder faster than a pack of coyotes. Besides, Tom's my friend, and I want to help. I'll be mighty disappointed if I don't get to."

Sarah hesitated, knowing Tom wouldn't like it. But when she thought of Amanda and how thin and tired she was, she quickly made up her mind. "Very well. I wouldn't want to disappoint you, Mr. Kendrick," she said with a shy smile. A tender warmth sprang to life in his eyes, holding her captive, sending a flutter through her heart.

"I'm glad to hear that, ma'am." He wanted to pursue that line of thinking, but mindful of three young boys examining a row of cookie boxes and a middle-aged shopkeeper industriously polishing the counter at his elbow, Nate glanced away.

Suspecting that he had read far more into her words than she had intended, Sarah felt her cheeks grow warm. She looked over at the boys, thankful to have a distraction. "Did anyone interesting get off the train?"

Brad glanced at Nate, then looked at his aunt, his expression serious. "Yes, ma'am. He looked like a salesman, but we all decided he's a Pinkerton man in disguise."

"A Pinkerton man?" Sarah worked hard to hide her smile, but she couldn't quite keep the twinkle out of her eyes. "My goodness, what do you think he is doing here?"

John looked from side to side, scouting for suspicious eavesdroppers. When he found no one else in the store besides the owner, he said in hushed tones, "He's on the trail of a gang of outlaws."

"Really?" Sarah glanced at Nate. He grinned and winked at her, sending the color back into her cheeks.

"He's after Purple Pete," said Andy.

"Purple Pete, huh? Sounds like a bad hombre." Sarah couldn't hide her grin any longer, especially when the older boys and Nate looked at Andy in disbelief. "And how did he earn that name?"

"Because all he wears is purple, from his boots all the way up to his hat." Andy grinned. "Know what they call his gang?"

"No, what?"

"The Plum Gang, 'cause he won't let 'em eat nothin' but plum jam on their biscuits."

They all laughed.

"And 'cause when they ride out of town, they're plumb gone," added John, which brought more laughter.

"You boys are as funny as a vaudeville show." Nate smiled and ruffled Andy's hair. "We'd better keep an eye on you, or you'll be headin' out of town with the next road company.

How about some dinner over at the Rusty Gate? It's not fancy, but the food's not half-bad."

Sarah hesitated, surprised by how much the invitation pleased her. Wendell had never taken her out to eat, always saying she could cook better than anyone else. She was a good cook, but she was also very aware that he didn't want to part with his money. She looked at her nephews' hopeful expressions. There was no telling how long it had been since they had eaten in a restaurant or even had a decent meal.

Then she looked at Nate. The challenge in his eyes was unmistakable. By midafternoon everyone in town would know he had taken her out to dinner, and the storekeeper was certain to elaborate on every look or word the two had exchanged while on his premises. It wouldn't matter that three youngsters tagged along, they would still provide a juicy bit of gossip for some very bored people.

All of her life Sarah had done what was expected of her. By disposition, she was a peacemaker, often stifling her own wishes or needs to keep harmony in her world, and because of her compliance, others had always controlled her actions. Some, like her mother and Wendell, had even tried to dictate her thoughts.

Nate was asking her to risk a little gossip, to do what she wanted to do. She had never done anything to raise an eyebrow, but she sensed that if she refused, she would always regret it. "That would be nice," she murmured. "Thank you."

"Good." A pleased smile spread across his face. "Let me put in my order with the storekeeper, and I'll be right with you." He turned and talked to the owner, while they walked to the door. He rejoined them a few minutes later. "Are you boys hungry?"

"Yes, sir." Brad grinned. "Ma says we're always hungry."

"Growing boys usually are. I've been thinking about Hank's fried chicken all morning. My stomach's been complaining about the wait for the last half hour. Let's go."

The boys scampered on ahead. As Nate and Sarah walked through the doorway he touched her back, directing her toward the left with the gentle pressure of his hand. Wendell had done the same thing innumerable times, but it had never caused her heartbeat to quicken. She felt very foolish to react so to such a simple, polite gesture, yet when he dropped his hand, she instantly missed his touch. *Oh, dear, Sarah. Don't make a fool of yourself.*

The small restaurant was not too crowded when they first arrived, but all the tables soon filled up. Nate was well known and well liked. He politely introduced Sarah to those who stopped by their table, which was just about everyone who came in. The food was excellent, and the boys polished off their plates of fried chicken, mashed potatoes and cream gravy, and green beans without any problem. They attacked their slices of peach pie with the same enthusiasm.

When a small man with a handlebar mustache took a seat nearby and removed his bowler hat, Nate shifted slightly toward Sarah. "That's our Pinkerton man," he said quietly, moving his head minutely in the man's direction.

She peeked around him to see the infamous detective, then ducked back, pressing her lips tightly together. Her mistake was in slanting a glance at Nate.

"A fearless lawman," he said with a straight face and twinkling eyes, "always gets his man. Purple Pete hasn't got a chance." She giggled, then laughed outright before clamping her hand firmly over her mouth. The boys heard his low comments and grinned.

"He won't have any trouble catchin' the Plum Gang either," he said in a slow, deliberate drawl. "They spilled the jam and are all stuck together." She laughed again. "In one big lump with the biscuits." She shook her head, desperately trying not to laugh out loud. The boys giggled, caught up as much in her laughter as in Nate's silly words.

He watched the merriment dance in her eyes and wondered again how anyone could consider her plain. She grew prettier every time he saw her. The creamy muslin shirtwaist, with its wide leg-of-mutton sleeves and high collar, was tailored, yet soft and flattering. With her hair tucked up under a no-nonsense rust-colored hat, she looked very prim and proper, and utterly enticing. He wondered if he was the only man who noticed the graceful line of her neck and her delicate chin.

His gaze dropped to her lips, curved upward in a smile. Her laughter reached inside of him, wrapping his heart in gentleness and warmth. He leaned closer, lowering his voice for her ears alone. "You have a beautiful smile, Sarah. If you were my woman, I'd do everything I could to see it often."

CHAPTER
5

Mortified, Sarah broke away from his penetrating gaze and folded her napkin precisely into a rectangle, placing it on the table. She should have known better, but she had never expected him to make fun of her, at least not in a public place. She fought against the sense of betrayal, against the shame. "Are you finished, boys? We need to get back to the farm." She cursed the tiny tremor in her voice.

"Sarah?" Nate stared at her, as if puzzled by her reaction.

"Thank you for dinner, Mr. Kendrick. It was delicious."

As she pushed out her chair he jumped up to assist her, wondering if it was his compliment or his implied interest that had offended her. "I'll walk you back to the store."

"There's no need. We can find our way without any trouble."

"It's no trouble." He wanted to grab her arm and make her look at him, but since everyone else in the restaurant was doing the looking, he kept his hands to himself. "I'll just pay the bill, and we can be on our way."

Sarah felt the curious stares of the other patrons. She managed a weak smile and looked up at him, focusing her gaze on his left earlobe. "We'll meet you by the door."

When they left the Rusty Gate, he sent the boys on ahead to see if the buckboard had been loaded with the groceries. "I'd like to know how I offended you." Nate nodded to a woman passing by. At her wary glance, he decided his irritation showed.

"Don't patronize me, Mr. Kendrick."

"I'm not patronizing you. And the name's Nate."

He cupped her elbow as they walked down a couple of steps to the street, then curled his fingers securely around her arm, detaining her as a buggy rolled by.

"I'm quite capable of crossing the street on my own," she snapped.

"Of course you are. That's why you almost stepped in front of the mayor's buggy." He didn't release her, even after they crossed the street and were safely on the boardwalk. "Sarah, I meant every word I said back there."

"Don't mock me, Nate Kendrick." Suddenly she was propelled through an open doorway into a shell of a building. Sunlight poured through gaping holes in the charred roof. The back wall of the building had burned, and the three remaining walls were partially blackened from a long-ago fire. "Let me go!"

"Yes, ma'am." Nate released her, only to swing around and plant his hands on either side of her against the front wall. They were sheltered from the eyes of those passing by, yet a single cry would bring her help should she need it. "Sarah, I said something that hurt you. I want to know what it was."

She couldn't meet his gaze. The faint, pleasant scent of Yankee Shaving Soap teased her nostrils, and a shaft of sunlight warmed her face. On the other side of the wall, two men walked by, discussing cattle prices, their voices fading as they stepped down and crossed the street. A wagon lumbered past, its wheels crunching against the scattered rocks in the street, the team's harness creaking with each step. In spite of her hurt and anger, his nearness and the sheer power radiating from him played havoc with her senses.

"You said I had a beautiful smile," she whispered, unable to keep the hurt from her voice.

"You do."

"No, I don't," she cried softly. "My mouth's too wide, and my teeth are too big. I look silly when I smile, like a horse."

"Who told you that?" he demanded.

"My mother. And . . ." Her voice trailed off.

"And?"

"And Wendell," she whispered, feeling the shame of it all over again.

"Your fiancé?" Contempt filled Nate's voice. When she nodded, he muttered an appropriate description of Wendell under his breath. "He told you that?"

"No. Mother was the one who said it. He just agreed with her."

"Oh, Sarah." Nate gently cupped her face in one hand, nudging it upward until she looked at him. "They're wrong. When you smile, your eyes sparkle like the stars on a clear fall night. Your whole face lights up, and it makes a man happy just to watch it." He could see the doubt in her eyes and the need to believe him.

"Your teeth aren't big, and your mouth sure isn't wide." His gaze dropped to her lips. "It's just right. Just right for smiling . . . and for kissing." He traced the hardened edge of his thumb across her lips, feeling the whisper of air as she inhaled sharply. "If we weren't right in the middle of town in broad daylight, I'd prove it to you."

He reluctantly dropped his hand and stepped into the doorway so he would be visible from the street. "Yes, ma'am, Miss Dawson, it was quite a fire. For a little bit, folks were afraid the whole town might go up in flames. But the bucket brigade did a fine job." He moved onto the boardwalk and looked back at her, a twinkle of mischief in his eyes.

"Good for them," muttered Sarah, warily stepping through the doorway. To her relief, no one was close by, and the people across the street were engrossed in their own business. Her nerves were so shattered, she was afraid that if anyone spoke to her, she would either scream or answer incoherently. Her heart pounded, and her hands shook. Amazingly he had not lied about wanting to kiss her. His eyes had been filled with passion and tenderness when he touched her lips in that disturbing, wonderful caress. Could it be that he hadn't lied about her smile, either?

Neither of them said a word until they reached the general store. The boys were in the back of the buckboard, peeking into the boxes of supplies. "Holy Moses, Aunt Sarah, you sure bought a lot of good stuff," said Brad, his eyes glowing.

"I didn't buy all of this." Sarah looked into the wagon bed, resting her hand on the top edge of the sideboard. There were at least twice as many boxes as there should have been. "Oh, dear. I'll have to speak to the storekeeper," she said, clearly dreading it. "I can't pay for all of this."

"You don't have to." Nate leaned his forearms on the sideboard next to her. "I added a few things."

"A few things! Nate, you're being very nice, but I can't let you do this."

"I can afford it. It's what I should have done when Tom got hurt. I would have, too, if I'd known how bad the situation was. He didn't let me pay him near enough for the damage my cattle did to the cotton, so this is my way of settling it. Let me help, Sarah. It's important to me."

She looked up at him. "You're a kind man, Nate Kendrick."

He shrugged uncomfortably. "Don't let it get out."

"And I think you have a soft spot for children." In the wooden crate in front of her were three boxes of cookies— vanilla wafers, lemon snaps, and ginger snaps. Other sweets were tucked in with the rest of the supplies. "How many boxes of cookies did you buy?"

"One of every kind in the store. There's a box of marshmallow bananas in there somewhere, too." He grinned when she made a face. "Maybe I should have bought chocolate bars instead."

She smiled slightly. "Maybe." She looked at the contents of the boxes packed securely in the wagon—five pounds of cheddar cheese; soda, butter, and graham crackers; several kinds of nuts and a bag of popcorn; ham and bacon; cans of clams, sardines, and Columbia River salmon; oatmeal and farina; pickles and a box of Bakers Cocoa. There were also three times as many cans of fruit and vegetables as she had purchased. "Did you leave anything in the store?"

"Not much. Oysters, I think."

Sarah looked at him again, hesitated, then smiled.

He smiled back, his eyes glowing happily. He slid his hand across the wagon and covered hers. "Yes, ma'am, I do like your smile," he murmured.

A sweet warmth unfurled in her heart, healing a hurt she had been unable to mend on her own. With it came a deep and poignant longing for a future better than her past, for something she could not have. "Thank you, Nate. For the groceries . . . for everything."

"It's my pleasure." He squeezed her hand gently, then moved his away before anyone noticed.

"I'm worried about Amanda. She's so down. The doctor brought out some cod liver oil. He said it should build up her strength. I'm hoping my visit will perk her up, too. I think she gets terribly lonely, and with Tom laid up, she hasn't been able to go anywhere since the baby came."

Nate thoughtfully glanced around. Since it was Saturday, the normally quiet little town bustled with life and excitement. "Let's have a dance."

"What?" Sarah had never been to a dance in her life, but she felt a little thrill when he included her. She knew the steps, but she had never danced with anyone other than her father, and that had been years ago.

"Let's have a dance next Saturday night. We can have it at my place. One of my cowboys is pretty handy with a fiddle, good enough to keep feet stompin' and bodies movin'. I'll invite all the neighbors, and they can bring the kids."

"How will we get Tom over there? He's hobbling around on crutches a little, but it would be impossible for Amanda and me to get him into the wagon."

"I'll pick you and your family up personally. Tom's lost so much weight, I can probably throw him in the wagon by myself. It'll do them both good to get out of the house and visit with folks, and give you a chance to meet the neighbors." He leaned down a little closer to her ear. "And it'll give me a fine excuse to put my arm around you and hold you close. Yes, ma'am. I'm going to enjoy this party."

"Nate!" Sarah smiled shyly and ducked her head. "You're embarrassing me."

"Just speakin' the truth, darlin'."

"I'm going in to pay my bill." She gave him a prudish old-maid glance but didn't realize the soft pink in her cheeks ruined the haughty expression. "Keep your sweet talk to yourself."

"Yes, ma'am." He grinned wickedly. "I'll save it for the party."

She rolled her eyes and bustled into the store. After she settled her bill, the storekeeper held out three letters.

"These came in on the train, Miss Dawson. They were a little slow getting the mail down here from the station this time." He squinted at the letters, glanced behind her at Nate, then shifted his gaze back to her. "Feller must miss you, sending two letters so soon and all."

Sarah took the envelopes. One was from her mother. Reading Wendell's meticulous handwriting on the other two, she felt a jab of shame. "Then it's a good thing I wrote him this morning, isn't it?"

She turned and almost ran into Nate. He stepped aside, his angry gaze clashing with hers when she looked up at him. Shame stabbed her again. Engaging in even a minor flirtation with this handsome rancher was outrageous. Not only had she wronged Wendell, she had wronged Nate as well, and made a fool of herself in the process. But she was too inexperienced to know how to rectify the situation.

Now he won't have the party. She told herself her disappointment was for Tom and Amanda. *I won't get to dance with him or feel his arm around me.* Not knowing what to say, she walked past him, wishing she could take away the hurt and anger she saw in his eyes.

"Sarah." His commanding tone stopped her two steps from the door. "I'll pick y'all up next Saturday at three o'clock. That way Tom and Amanda can rest awhile before the other folks arrive."

She nodded, but afraid her face would reveal the joy she felt, she did not look back.

CHAPTER
6

As the fiddler struck up a new tune Nate dropped into a chair beside Tom Dawson in one corner of the bunkhouse. The room had been cleared of beds and all the accompanying cowboy paraphernalia to make a ranch-styled ballroom. He had claimed Sarah for the first four dances, but when the caller teased them after the last one, he decided he'd better give some of the other men a turn and not embarrass her.

Shorty, the cowboy who had been with Jeb when he cut Tom's fence, had jumped at the opportunity. The young man, who was just Sarah's height with his boots on, grabbed her hand and pulled her into the circle for the Paul Jones.

Nate's gaze went to the dance floor, settling with undisguised warmth on Sarah's flushed, laughing face. Delicate tendrils of hair had escaped from the puffy knot at the top of her head and curled down beside her ears and across the nape of her neck. The hairstyle was soft and feminine and almost as enticing as the morning he first met her when her hair had been flowing freely around her shoulders. He glanced at his friend, then back at Sarah. "You look a mite puzzled."

"My little sister has changed from a caterpillar to a butterfly. Granted, it's been a year since I've seen her, but she was always such a quiet, shy little thing. I'm having a hard time believin' she's the same woman."

"I thought she was pretty the first time I saw her. And she's got more spirit than you give her credit for." Nate's gaze never left her as the caller ordered the dancers to form a double circle, ladies on the inside facing out, gents on the outside facing in. At the next call, the ladies joined hands and so did the men, each circle going in opposite directions.

"It's never showed before. I reckon it's because she's out from under Mother's thumb. I'd forgotten how hard that woman can be. I never took much guff off her, but Sarah never wanted to stir up trouble." Tom frowned. "I married young and moved out when Sarah was twelve. Guess I didn't pay as much attention as I should have, especially after Pa died. I might have made things easier for her. I've never seen her smile or laugh so much. I have an awful feeling the real Sarah has been hidden away all these years."

The caller cried "Paul Jones," and each man on the dance floor took the woman in front of him in his arms and danced the two-step. Nate felt a twinge of jealousy as Sarah smiled up at her new partner, a robust young man from one of the neighboring farms.

"She's not going to hide away again. Not if I can help it."

At the determination in Nate's tone, Tom studied his friend's face. With his good looks and charming manner, Nate was always a hit with the ladies. He treated each one with respect and gentleness, whether she was a beauty or homely as a roadrunner. Tom thought he had detected something more in the looks Nate gave Sarah. Now, as he saw the hunger burning in his friend's eyes, he was certain of it.

"She's engaged."

"To the wrong man. I intend to do something about it."

"That may be harder to do than you think. Sarah's been raised to honor her commitments, above all else. And to be honest, I suspect Mother had a hand in getting Wendell to come courting in the first place. She won't take kindly to her plans being thwarted. She'd make Sarah's life miserable if she broke off with Wendell and then nothing happened between you two."

The caller declared, "Heifers in the middle, strays outside." The two circles formed again. A few measures later he proclaimed, "Swing your partners, swing 'em wide." As a tall cowboy slid his arm around Sarah's waist and swung her around exuberantly, lifting her a foot off the floor, the full skirt of her olive-green dress swished around his legs. Nate almost came up out of his chair when she wrapped her arm around the man's neck in surprise. "Swing them again, lift 'em high." Once more she flew around in the air, and her eyes held a hint of fear.

Nate stood up, glaring at his employee, but the man didn't notice. The song ended, and the cowboy swung her around again, a little easier this time.

"Whoo-ee, Miss Sarah, you're as light as a feather." The cowboy grinned down at Sarah, her face flushed more from embarrassment than from exertion. "Can I have the next dance?"

"The next dance is mine." *And every one after it.*

"Aw, boss, you've already danced with her more than anybody." The cowboy's grin faded as he turned and met Nate's implacable stare. "But guess you know a good thing when you see one," he mumbled, nodding to Sarah and taking his leave.

"Yes, I do." Nate rested his hand at Sarah's waist. "Come get something to drink." The full sleeve of her dress brushed against his chest.

"Nate, you weren't very nice to that man." Intensely aware of his touch, she glanced up at him as they walked toward the refreshment table. His face was calm, but his eyes glittered as if he was angry.

"I suppose you like flying through the air like that." He poured her a cup of punch and thrust it into her hand.

"Well, it was a little scary, but I have to admit it was fun, too." She looked over to where Amanda sat holding little Janey. Two other women sat with her, and they all appeared to be having a grand time catching up on the news and gossip. Amanda's pale face glowed with happiness, and her eyes sparkled as she laughed out loud at something one of her friends said. *Thank you, Nate, for tonight.*

"I guess having his arm so tight around you and being pressed up against him was fun, too."

Sarah didn't miss the sarcasm in his voice. *Why, he almost sounds jealous. But that couldn't be.* Giddy from dancing and from having the time of her life, Sarah decided to tease him a little. "Well, it wasn't terribly unpleasant," she said with a tiny smile.

When Nate made a low noise in his throat that sounded suspiciously like a growl, she looked up at him. He was staring across the room at the hapless cowboy, who wiggled uncomfortably under his boss's angry frown. *Oh, dear, he is jealous.* The revelation almost took her breath away and made her heart soar.

Far too many times in the past week she had discovered that a woman did not need to be young to have girlish dreams. She had spent way too much time thinking about Nate and imagining how the dance would be. Both the man and the party had far exceeded her expectations. How could this handsome, wonderful man be jealous over her? She found it hard to believe, but when she glanced across the room at the misery on the cowboy's face, she knew she had to make amends, or the poor man would suffer the consequences.

"But it wasn't particularly pleasant, either. He had to squeeze too tight to keep me from flying across the room and bouncing off the wall." The thundercloud slowly faded from Nate's face, but he still looked unhappy. When the fiddler began the lilting notes of a slow waltz, the first one of the evening, Sarah placed her cup on the table with deliberate care.

Feeling more daring than she had ever dreamed herself capable of, she gently put her hand on Nate's arm. When he looked down at her in surprise, she met his gaze with more calm than she actually felt. "Dance with me, Nate."

A slow smile spread across his face, filling his eyes with tender warmth. "Yes, ma'am." He took her hand and guided her onto the dance floor. Drawing her into his arms, he held her a tiny bit closer than was acceptable, but not close enough to cause a scandal. He felt her stiffen. "Don't be afraid, darlin'. It's all right."

It was heaven. "I just remembered that I've never waltzed before."

"Just relax and follow my lead. You'll do fine." He drew away slightly to make it easier on her and began to move his feet. She caught on to the steps quickly, and he pulled her closer again, even closer than before. Her eyes widened as she looked up at him.

He met her gaze with a look that sent shivers scampering across her skin.

"That's it, sugar. Lose yourself to the music." A light flamed in his eyes. "Lose yourself to me," he murmured.

Sarah knew she should look away, knew she should force him to put more space between them, but she couldn't. She couldn't tear her gaze from his, couldn't help it as her body leaned a whisper closer. Everything took on the semblance of a dream. The others in the room faded to the fringes of her consciousness. Her world consisted of the haunting strains of the music and the man in her arms, this cowboy prince who, for a small space in time, turned her into a princess. She drew the moments into her heart, weaving them into the fabric of her soul so they could never be taken from her.

Nate watched her face as they moved to the music, gazing in wonder as she became beautiful before his eyes. Lost in the magic, he kept silent, fearful of breaking the spell, and wondered if his face revealed all the things he was feeling. Her closeness stirred his desire, but even more, it kindled the yearning in his heart, the longing for someone to share his life, the need for a woman to love, one who would love him in return.

The song ended and Nate saw his disappointment mirrored in her eyes. "Be mine for tonight, Sarah," he whispered. "Let all the dances be mine." When she nodded slowly, he thought his heart might fly right out of his chest. "Do you want to rest a bit?"

"Yes." Sarah desperately needed to sit down, amazed that her wobbly legs had carried her through the whole dance. If anyone had ever told her how a man could make her feel, she would never have believed the truth. No, not just any man, she thought. Only this one.

Nate found her a chair and fetched them each a glass of punch and a piece of cake to share. He sat down beside her, introducing her to the farmer and his wife who sat nearby. They chatted through two songs, then walked around the room visiting with the neighbors while the fiddler and caller took a break. Sarah's nephews raced by, excited about a game they were playing in the corner with their friends.

"Would you like to step outside for some air?" Nate knew they would probably not be alone, but he wanted to see her face in the moonlight.

"Yes. It's getting warm in here."

They walked out onto the bunkhouse porch. On one end, several of the cowboys were enjoying a smoke. On the other, a group of men carried on an easy conversation about the perils of farming. Several couples, mostly those who were courting or newly married, wandered off the porch into the shadows around the bunkhouse.

"How's Whiskey?"

"He's fine."

"Survived the indignity of carrying a barefoot lady, huh?"

Nate chuckled. "Yeah. He figured it was a little beneath him until I explained how noble it was to rescue damsels in distress. Then he got a swelled head." Sarah laughed softly as they stepped off the porch. He slid his arm around her shoulders. "Want to go say hello?"

She hesitated, relishing his warmth, the weight of his arm across her shoulders, and the gentle pressure of his fingers on her upper arm. Knowing full well that greeting the horse was not the only thing Nate had in mind, she whispered, "Yes."

They walked across the yard and past the corrals where most of the horses were kept. There was a large, three-sided covered shed at the end of each one where the animals could find shelter when needed. Whiskey and a couple of other prized horses resided in a private stable. Nate pulled back the door, leaving it open so they could see their way by moonlight. They walked down the wide aisle, stopping at Whiskey's stall.

"Hello, pretty boy." Sarah rubbed the horse's nose when he stuck his head over the gate. "How's my friend tonight? Are we keeping you up with all the music?"

Whiskey nickered softly, nuzzling her hand. They both petted him for a few minutes until Nate said, "I guess we'd better go back. I don't want folks to talk about you."

"I suspect they're already talking." She gave Whiskey one last pat on the head and turned toward the door.

"Probably. But I doubt if the talk is malicious. Most of these folks are pretty tolerant." He caught her hand and walked a few steps with her, then drew to a halt. She stopped, too, looking up at him uncertainly.

Moonlight from a high window bathed her face in ethereal light. He stepped closer, curling his fingers around the back of her head. "Sarah, you're so beautiful," he whispered, caressing her cheek with his thumb.

She shook her head in denial.

"Yes, you are. And I've been wanting to kiss you all night." He chuckled wryly. "I've wanted to kiss you since the first time I saw you."

"Nate, we shouldn't." But, oh, how she wanted him to.

"No, we probably shouldn't, but I'm going to anyway." He lowered his head and feathered a kiss at one corner of her mouth. When she didn't pull away, he brushed his lips across hers—once, twice, three times. He felt her shiver and drew back, lowering his hand, his heart pounding like a young buck kissing his first girl. Her eyelids were closed, the long lashes dark and thick. She raised them slowly, revealing the wonder in her rich brown eyes, and sent a wave of desire exploding through him.

Before she could say anything, he picked up her hand and placed it on his pounding heart. Her eyes widened, and she said the first thing that popped into her head. "You must have been stuck out here a long time."

He blinked in surprise, then chuckled as her face turned beet red. He could see the hot color rise even in the near darkness. "My, my, such unladylike thoughts." She tried to pull her hand away, but he held it captive against his chest. Her heat burned through his shirt and undershirt like a brand. He welcomed it, for with that kiss, she had stolen his heart completely. "I've stayed away from ladies of the evening for a long time now, but no woman ever made me feel the way you do, sugar."

"Don't," she whispered, tears of despair pricking her eyes.

The distant strains of a lively tune reached their ears. Nate knew he had to get her back to the party, or there would be talk for sure. He released her hand, and she jerked it away from his chest, curling her fingers into a tight fist beside her leg.

"This isn't the right time or place to talk about this, Sarah. I don't want to spoil the party for you." He brushed her cheek with his fingers and smiled gently when she slowly raised her gaze to his. "Let's go enjoy all those dances you promised me."

CHAPTER
7

Sarah knew she should have told Nate that she didn't want to dance every dance with him, even though it would have been a lie. She knew she was being selfish, but for once in her life she allowed herself that privilege. There would never be another night like this for her, never be another man in her life like Nate. And, she soothed her conscience, it wasn't as if she had him to herself every minute. Many of the dances were square or circle dances, where exchanging partners was a matter of course.

Taking a break to catch her breath after a rousing polka, she glanced over at Tom and Amanda. Tom's head was against the wall, and Amanda's rested on his shoulder. Both of them were dozing. Little Janey slept in her arms. The boys had curled up in a corner long ago and fallen asleep. Sarah touched Nate's arm, pointing her finger toward her brother. "Can you take them home in the dark?"

Nate wanted to tell her it was impossible because he didn't want her to leave, but the road between his place and theirs was a good one. With a bright, full moon, it would be easy to see the way. "We can. If you want to stay here, I could take them on home. The party will probably last until dawn. Some of the roads aren't as good. It's dangerous for folks to travel on them at night, so they just keep on dancing."

"No, I should go, too. Amanda will need help getting the boys to bed."

"One last dance." When she nodded, Nate crossed the room and asked the fiddler to play something slow. He returned and when the music began, he drew her into his arms, leading her in a double-shuffle two-step. They danced almost in one spot, shifting slightly to alternating sides.

Because he wanted so badly to pull her against him, Nate kept a good space between them. "Have you enjoyed tonight, darlin'?"

"Yes. I've never been to a dance like this before."

Nate smiled. "I don't reckon it's like parties in the city. We do get a little rowdy sometimes."

"I meant I've never been to a party before."

He frowned. "Never?"

"Well, I've been to teas and church socials, but never to a party where there was dancing. My father taught me how, but there's never been the opportunity to try it until tonight."

"Wendell doesn't dance."

"No. He says it's foolishness."

Nate pulled her closer, but not as close as he wanted. "He's the fool."

Sarah let the comment pass. "I suspect he never learned, so he doesn't know what he's missing."

"I think I'm glad for that."

"Dancing with him wouldn't be the same," she murmured, not realizing she had been thinking out loud until she looked up and caught Nate's smug grin.

"I'll wait until later for you to explain."

"You may have to wait a long time."

"We'll see."

They danced in silence until the song ended. Sarah went to wake Amanda and Tom and collected their coats. Nate told his foreman, Frank, where he was going. He spoke to a few of the neighbors and told them to stay as long as they liked and that he would be back after he took the Dawsons home. While he harnessed the team to the buckboard and drove it up to the bunkhouse, Tom and Amanda said good night to their friends. Frank and Nate carried Tom out to the wagon. After he and Amanda were comfortably settled and covered with a blanket, Nate and Sarah gathered up the kids. She herded the older boys as they practically sleepwalked to the wagon, and Nate carried Andy out.

"Do you want to sit with me or snooze with the rest of them?"

"I'll sit with you. Wouldn't want you falling asleep and driving us off into a gully somewhere."

Nate grinned and lifted her up onto the seat. He spread a blanket over her legs, then walked around and climbed up beside her, his upper arm resting against hers as he sat down. He picked up the reins, released the brake, and tapped the horses' backs gently with the leather straps. After placing his feet in a comfortable position, he rested his thigh firmly against hers, separated by the thin barrier of the blanket. "It might get a bit breezy up here, so if you get cold, feel free to snuggle up."

Sarah didn't see how she could get much closer, but half an hour later she slipped her arm beneath his and pressed it to her side.

"Cold?"

"A little." Mostly she wanted to touch him, to recapture the feeling of dancing with him, of being in his arms.

He reached down and pulled the blanket over his legs. "Scoot a little closer."

She obeyed and tucked the blanket tighter around her outside leg. Within moments his heat began to warm her chilled bones.

"Better?"

"Yes." In more ways than one. She gazed out across the prairie, surprised at the brightness of the moonlight. A jackrabbit raced across the road in front of them, and in the distance a coyote howled. His call was quickly answered by another mournful cry from the other direction. She could make out clumps of mesquite here and there and the dark cattle stretched out asleep beneath them. Even Lonesome Butte was visible, rising above the prairie like some mystical altar. "It's so beautiful out here. So quiet and peaceful. I get up early every morning just so I can see the sunrise."

Nate's heart swelled with love.

"Do you miss Dallas?" he asked, his quiet voice barely audible above the creak of the wagon.

"No, not yet. I thought I would, but I haven't. It's so nice to be with Tom and Amanda and the children." Without thinking, she rested her head on his broad shoulder. "Thank you for the party. It did them both a world of good. Did you see how happy she was?"

"Yep. Tom looked cheered up, too."

"He was. It's always good to get together with the neighbors. He does love to talk farming," she said with a smile. "It's funny, him being a farmer. We were both raised in the city, but he always wanted to be out in the country. Father ran a grain-and-feed store, and Tom helped out there when he was younger. But after he got big enough, he went to work for a farmer near town. Even Father saw he was happiest there, so he didn't complain."

"Your father sounds like a fine man."

"He was. I miss him a lot, even though he's been gone a long time."

"What about your mother? What's she like?" Nate already had a good idea, but he wanted to hear what Sarah would say.

She hesitated. Being away from her mother had opened her eyes to many things, especially the fact that her mother had controlled every aspect of her life. Sarah had discovered many things about herself in the last two weeks, and Nate had shown her several more. "She's very domineering," she said at last. "But I think her intentions are good."

Nate made a sound of disagreement. "I can't see any good in saying that you had an ugly smile."

"I think she really believes it, and that she thought she was somehow protecting me, trying to keep me from looking foolish."

"Do you still believe it?"

"No." She absently caressed his arm through his heavy coat. "You convinced me otherwise."

"Good. Maybe you need to reconsider some of the other things she's told you."

"I am."

"Like what?"

"I'm not the timid little mouse I always thought I was. Standing up to those cows showed me that. And . . ."

"And, what, sugar?"

She raised her head, gazing up at him. "You've made me feel better about my looks. I'm no beauty, I know, but at least now I don't feel plain and ugly. I'll always thank you for that."

"I doubt if you were ever plain and ugly," he said tightly, angry that anyone had led her to believe such a thing. He wanted to say more, but he heard Amanda stir and sleepily murmur to her husband. "We're almost home, folks. Be there in about five minutes."

When they got home, Nate carried Tom inside. Amanda put the baby in the crib as Sarah guided the sleepy boys through the door and into their bedroom.

"Pull your boots off, boys, and crawl on into bed. You can sleep in your clothes this time," said Amanda. She and Sarah helped the boys with their boots and pulled the quilts up over the youngsters as they collapsed on the mattresses. When they returned to the front room, which served both as parlor and kitchen, Nate was adding some mesquite logs to the stove.

"I just put a little in so it would take off the chill. You'll probably want to sleep awhile before morning." He stood up, brushing a bit of bark from his fingers.

"Thank you for a wonderful time, Nate. It was so good to see the neighbors." Amanda's smile was warm and happy.

Tom caught her hand in his. "Sometimes it's good to hear how others have come through hard times." He looked up at her. "We're going to make it, Mandy gal. Jim Anderson and his boy will get started on our cotton on Monday. He planted a couple of weeks later than I did, so theirs won't be ready for a while."

Nate glanced at Sarah. She appeared puzzled. "Does cotton go bad if it's not picked at a certain time?" he asked, looking back at Tom.

"No. Normally there isn't any great rush, but I've got a loan payment due in two weeks. I hadn't thought I'd have to depend on the cotton money, but this dang leg messed everything up."

"I'll give you what you need. You can pay me back later."

"No. Can't do that. I've already taken too much from you." Tom's expression declared his determination. "I won't be beholden to a friend for money. I made that mistake once, and when I couldn't pay it back on time, it cost me the best friend I ever had. I won't do it again. We'll make it."

Nate cursed his friend's pride, but understood it just the same. "Well, if things don't work out, let me know. I won't let you lose this farm, even if I have to hurt your stubborn pride." He grinned. "I could always charge you sky-high interest, if that would make you feel better."

"Thanks, but I'll pass." Tom's smile softened the firmness of his words. "Thanks for the party. You put the roses back in both my girls' cheeks."

Nate bowed slightly. "My pleasure. Well, I'd better be headin' back. Those cowpokes are liable to start spikin' the punch if I'm not around." He looked at Sarah. "Could I talk to you for a minute?"

She glanced nervously at Tom and Amanda.

"Go ahead." Tom yawned and stretched his arms above his head. "Us old folks are headed off to bed."

"All right." She hadn't removed her coat, only unbuttoned it. She fastened a couple of buttons as she walked to the door. "I won't be long."

"Take your time." Tom grinned at her look of surprise and told Nate good night.

Sarah and Nate stepped out onto the porch, closing the door behind them. A chilly breeze had sprung up while they were inside. He grabbed her hand and led her around to the side of the house out of the wind. He took off his hat and tossed it on the top of a covered wooden cistern nearby, then leaned against the house and gently pulled her toward him. When she was close enough, he slid his arms loosely around her.

"Nate—"

"Shh. Don't talk. Not yet." He lowered his head, touching her lips with heartbreaking gentleness. With a tiny whimper, she swayed toward him, and he deepened the kiss ever so slightly.

Sarah felt his hand slide between them and his fingers fumble on the buttons of her coat. A breath of cold air whisked across her bodice as the buttons came undone, then his big, strong hands slipped beneath the coat, curving around her waist. Deepening the kiss even more, he pulled her toward him. Smoothing his hands up and down her back, he molded her body against his, the heavy folds of their open coats draping around them in a warm cocoon.

She ran her fingers over the hard muscles of his upper chest and slid her hands up around his neck, threading her fingers through his hair. Weakness swept over her, and along with it came a need far greater than anything she could have imagined. She leaned against him for support, instinctively seeking fulfillment.

Nate groaned deep in his chest. He had meant to be a gentleman, had intended to go slow, but her wonderful, eager response sent his good intentions flying. He kissed her again and again, pausing only for air. She was his woman, no matter how much she tried to deny it. And if it took moving mountains to convince her, he'd do it.

Sarah was lost to the wild sensations spiraling through her, lost to his touch and his kiss. Wendell had kissed her before, a few quick pecks on the mouth, but nothing in her existence had prepared her for such passion, not in a man, not in herself.

Wendell.

She twisted her head to the side and shoved on Nate's chest. "Stop. Please, stop."

He lifted his head and eased his hold, refusing to let her go. "It's all right, sugar."

"No, it's not," she cried, her throat thick with despair and guilt, her body aching for his touch, her heart breaking. "I'm promised to another man."

"Does he make you feel the way I do? Do you go up in flames like dry kindling when he touches you?"

She shook her head. "It doesn't matter. I'm promised to him. I can't break that promise."

"Not even for love?"

She looked up at him in astonishment and shook her head. "You can't love me." *No one can.* "You're just lonely. Some beautiful, interesting woman will come along any day, and you'll see that I'm only a temporary amusement."

"A temporary amusement! Good Lord, woman, who's been putting those words into your head?"

"Men like you don't fall in love with women like me."

Nate sighed in exasperation. "That sounds like more of your mother's brand of wisdom." He cupped her face in his hands, nudging it upward until he could gaze into her eyes. "I don't know about other men, but I know this one is falling in love with you. You're a beautiful, brave, and caring woman, Sarah Dawson, and I'm going to make you my wife."

"Nate, I've made a commitment to Wendell. I can't go back on it."

He dropped his hands to his sides. When hers remained resting on his chest, no longer pushing him away, he felt like cutting loose with a good ol' Rebel yell. Curling his hands lightly around her waist, he asked, "Do you love him?"

"No." The answer was so swift and sure, it surprised them both. She stared at his chest, unconsciously playing with the second button on his shirt with her index finger. "I like him, most of the time. He's the only man who's ever come courting—"

"Until now."

"—and he has been faithful in that regard. I owe him my loyalty. Judging from his letters, he really misses me. He's frugal and has a good, steady job. And he is dependable."

"Except when it comes to getting married. I hear he postponed the wedding twice."

She looked up in surprise. "He had good reasons."

"Such as?"

"The first time his mother was sick, and he had to go to St. Louis to see about her. The last time he wanted to wait until he had more money put away. He's saving for a house."

He pulled her a little nearer. "Sarah, I have a house already. And about ten thousand acres of good Texas grassland."

Her eyes widened.

"My job is steady. Sometimes more steady than I'd like." He smiled, then his expression sobered. "Right now things are good. Cattle prices are high, and I'm doing well. Things don't always stay that way. There may be some hard times ahead, but I'm pretty good at managing my money. I'm frugal, but not a skinflint like someone else I've heard about." He ran the tip of his finger down her cheek. "I can't give you every luxury, but I'd do the best I could to see you comfortable and happy."

"I know you would." She rested her cheek against his chest, tucking her forehead against his chin. If only she could find a way to break off the engagement without hurting Wendell.

"I know you want to do the honorable thing, Sarah. I respect you for that." He squeezed her gently. "But it would be far worse to marry him and be miserable the rest of your life. Now, go inside before I start kissing you again, and we freeze to death."

He released her and she stepped back, pulling her coat closed. They walked around to the front of the house, stopping by the buckboard.

"Thank you for a lovely night, Nate. It's been wonderful."

"We've got a lifetime of wonderful nights ahead of us, darlin'." When she shook her head sadly, he curled his hand around the side of the buckboard, his face contorted with anger. "He doesn't have any idea what a treasure he has in you."

Suddenly he reached out, sliding his hand around to the small of her back and hauled her toward him. Curving his other hand around the back of her head, he held her still and slanted his mouth over hers in a hard, possessive kiss. "You break off the engagement, Sarah, or I'll run that fool clear out of Texas."

CHAPTER
8

Rain fell all day Sunday, a slow gentle rain that was greatly welcomed on the grassland. For the farmers whose cotton was ready to pick, the rain came at an inopportune time. Sarah could tell Tom was worried, although he tried to reassure them.

"One good sunny day will be enough to dry out the cotton. The fields might still be a little muddy, but Jim and Ed will do all right." When she questioned him about it, he educated her as to the ways of many bankers—there would be no extra time to make the payment.

Sarah knew without his mentioning it that starting late would make it more difficult to get enough picked, hauled to town, sold, and ginned by the mortgage deadline. She said nothing, but quietly determined to help in any way she could.

The family spent Sunday dozing, reading, or playing quiet games. Sarah spent most of her time thinking about Nate. She loved him. She couldn't deny it and wanted with all her heart to believe he was falling in love with her.

All afternoon she tried to come up with some plan to end her engagement without feeling like a louse, something that would satisfy her mother. She wasn't exactly afraid of her mother. It was just that she had a way of harping on things forever. She still nagged Sarah about breaking her favorite teapot, the one she had knocked off the table when she was ten years old. It was difficult to concentrate on the problem, especially when memories of Nate's kisses kept teasing her.

When she awoke Monday to another gray, drippy morning, the solution seemed so simple that she wondered why she hadn't thought of it before. As soon as the breakfast dishes were done, she sat down and wrote to Wendell, explaining about cashing in the return train ticket. She asked him to send her the money to replace it. It was a test to see how much he cared about her, and whether he would truly provide for her as promised. It was a test she sincerely believed—and hoped—he would fail.

When the rain stopped and the sun came out in the afternoon, she wanted to take the letter to Crooked Creek right away. Tom tried to persuade her to wait until the next day because the roads were still muddy and slick. She didn't capitulate until he pointed out that she had already missed the eastbound train.

That same afternoon a neighbor dropped by on his way home from town, bringing another letter from Wendell. The previous ones had been newsy and affectionate—at least as affectionate as he ever got. He had surprised her with the almost romantic manner in which he described how much he missed her and the way he kept encouraging her to hurry home.

The tone of this letter, however, exhibited his annoyance with her continued absence. He was obviously out of patience and tired of playing the romantic suitor. He couldn't understand why she remained in West Texas, believing that surely by this time Amanda had regained her health enough to care for her own family.

The whole letter irritated her, but when he complained about having to cook his own meals and ordered her home immediately, Sarah understood what he missed the most. She took the buckboard into town on Tuesday, leaving right after breakfast, and mailed her letter requesting the train fare. It took only a day for mail to get to Dallas by train, so she did not think it would be more than a week before she heard from him. Unless he had trouble making up his mind.

She prayed he would not surprise her by sending the money. If he did, she would feel bound to honor her pledge to marry him, even if, in his eyes, her best attribute was her cooking. If he proved to be as selfish as she thought he was and refused to send the money, even her mother would not be able to fault her for ending the engagement.

Nate came by the farm while she was in town, but according to Tom, he only stayed a few minutes. He apologized for not coming over sooner or being able to stay until she got home. They were moving a thousand head of cattle to other pastures, and he had to act as wagon boss for one outfit. He promised to be back to see her by Saturday night.

"It sure must be something herdin' all those cows," said John at supper. "All that danger and excitement."

"What danger?" Sarah almost dropped the bowl of mashed potatoes.

"Oh, fightin' off mountain lions and wolves and stuff."

"And rattlers. They gotta watch out for rattlers up in the rocks," added Andy around a mouthful of salmon croquette.

"And stampedes," said Brad. "That many cows can be real dangerous if spooked. Sometimes cowboys are trampled to death during a stampede."

"That's enough." Tom studied Sarah's white face. "The boys are exaggerating, Sarah. We don't have much problem with mountain lions and wolves anymore. And the rattlers are tucked up nice and warm in their dens."

"What about stampedes?" she asked, her voice strained.

"I reckon they have 'em on occasion, but from what I hear, they're usually caused by a storm. Thunder and lightning and such. We won't be having that this time of year."

"Oh." Sarah had not given any thought to the potential danger of Nate's work. She realized she had little idea what happened on a ranch. She had believed it was pretty much like Tom's farm, only on a larger scale. But Tom had two milk cows and a couple of horses. He didn't own thousands of cantankerous cattle and bulls like Gladiator. Would she spend every day worrying about what tragedy might befall him? Would she become a harridan like her mother because of her fear for him?

Lost in thought, she barely heard the rest of the conversation during the meal and only toyed with her food. She absently helped Amanda clear the table and do the dishes, alternately conjuring up all sorts of problems that Nate might have and silently praying fervently for his safety.

"He's good at what he does." Amanda put her arm around Sarah's shoulders and hugged her. "From what I hear, Nate Kendrick is one of the best cattlemen around. He grew up on that ranch and has been working cattle since he was a little boy. He'll be even more careful because he'll have you to come home to."

Sarah looked at her sister-in-law. "I haven't told him I'd marry him."

"But you want to, don't you?"

"Yes. But now I'm afraid. Maybe I'd be better off marrying someone I don't have to worry so much about."

"Women always worry, no matter where we are. Guess it's just the way we're made. I know what you're feeling. After Tom got hurt, I kept thinking about all the dangers out here and worrying about him and the children. But I know this, I'd rather be married to a man I love and see him risk getting hurt every day than spend one minute married to a man I couldn't love."

As Sarah lay in bed around midnight, listening to the rain once again drip off the roof, she knew that in spite of the danger, she wanted to spend her life with Nate in this rugged land he loved so much.

Wednesday dawned bright and clear, but the cotton was too wet to pick. By that evening it had dried out sufficiently to begin the harvest the next morning. Unfortunately they had barely more than a week to get the money for the loan payment.

"Boys, I'm counting on you to work hard the next few weeks." Tom put down his fork and looked solemnly at his youngsters. "John, you'll have to stay home from school this year, too, and pick cotton. You're big enough to help."

"Yes, sir." John sat up a little straighter in his chair.

"Brad, you'll have to show your brother how to do it. No ordering him around, though, you hear?"

"Yes, sir. We'll do our best, Pa," said Brad.

"I know you will." Tom smiled at them, a hint of sadness in his eyes. "It's a heavy load to put on you so young, and I'm sorry for it. Next year I'll be able to help, and you won't have to miss so much school."

"That's okay, Pa. Most everybody misses durin' harvest. Only the little kids showed up last year." John smiled, pleased not to be included in that number again.

"I'll help." Sarah met her brother's surprised look with one of determination. "Brad can show me how to pick the cotton, too."

Tom shook his head. "Sarah, it's hard, backbreaking work."

"Tom Dawson, I refuse to sit by while your sons try to save this farm. If these boys can work that hard, so can I. I'm sure I won't be as good as an experienced picker, but every little bit will help. Amanda's feeling better now. She can take care of the cooking for a few days without me underfoot." She grinned at his don't-argue-with-your-big-brother expression. "I'm not sayin' I'll do the whole field. Just enough to help you with the loan payment."

"You're gettin' downright sassy, Miss Priss." Tom shrugged. "All right, but I'm warning you, you don't know what you're getting into. Just remember that you can quit anytime." It was his turn to grin. "After all, I ain't paying you any wages."

"Didn't expect any from you, you ol' penny-pincher." Sarah stood up and began clearing off the table. She winked at Amanda. "At least it will get me out of washing dishes for a while."

"You'll be glad to go back to washin' dishes. I'll give you a pair of my cotton gloves, but you'll still get cuts from the cotton burrs." Amanda put her hand on Sarah's shoulder. "I hate for you to do this, but I know I'm not up to working in the field. I appreciate what you're doing to help us. This farm means the world to Tom, and truth be known, I love it here myself."

"So do I." Sarah smiled, suddenly realizing how much she meant it.

Jim and Ed Anderson arrived shortly after sunup. Sarah and the boys were waiting for them and quickly climbed

into the wagon to ride to the field. Even Andy went along
to help. Jim drove the horse and wagon partway down one
of the rows of cotton and stopped. Everyone climbed out of
the wagon, picked up a cotton sack, and walked back to the
edge of the field.

"We'll each take a row, ma'am. When your sack starts
gettin' heavy, take it on down to the wagon and dump it.
You'll be better off to take it down pretty often. Hauling
around too heavy a load will tire you out quicker. And it's
nice on your back to get a break from being bent over."

Jim slipped the wide strap of the cotton sack over his head,
resting it on one shoulder. The strap draped across his chest
and back, allowing the long, narrow bag to hang at his side.
The bottom half dragged along the ground behind him as he
started down the row.

Like the ones the men were using, Sarah and the boys' sacks
were made of heavy ducking but were half the size. Andy's
bag, which his mother had stitched up for him the night before,
was even smaller. Sarah watched Brad and slipped the strap
over her head just as he and the Andersons had done. When
the other boys did the same, she took a deep breath and looked
at her oldest nephew. "Okay, teacher, show us how this is
done."

"Well, you walk down the row, picking each plant clean.
You pull the cotton out like this." He reached down and pulled
four puffs of cotton from an open boll. "You have to watch it
'cause the burr is sharp and can cut the dickens out of your
fingers. And you have to look around under the leaves good,
or you might miss a boll."

"That don't look too hard." John stepped over a row and
carefully set to work.

"Once you get the hang of it, try to move a little faster, or
we'll never get done."

"Pa said you weren't supposed to boss."

"I'm not. Just tellin' you how it is." Brad looked out at
the wide expanse of brown and white in front of them. "Pa
said we'd need at least two bales to make enough money.
Maybe three, dependin' on how much they pay him for the
cotton."

"How much does it take for a bale?" Sarah glanced down the

row at the wagon. The added sideboards extended the capacity of the big wagon to twice what it normally was. It would take a lot of puffy cotton to fill it up.

"A wagon load if we pack it tight."

"Oh." Sarah's heart dipped at the hard task before them. She studied the first plant in her row, which appeared to hold about ten fat clumps of white, fluffy cotton. The top of the plant came up to the middle of her thigh, so she would have to bend over to reach most of it.

She leaned down, examining the bolls carefully. The big puffs were divided into four or five fairly equal segments, separated and supported from each other by the hard burr. Sometimes there was another wad of cotton in the middle, sometimes not. She touched the cotton gingerly, discovering that inside all that fluff were hard kernels, which she supposed were seeds. From the bottom, the brown burr on a four-sectioned boll was in the shape of a cross, five sections looked like a five-pointed star. Each prong on the hard burr was sharply pointed.

She began, gingerly pulling the cotton from the boll. Once comfortable with the process, she picked up the pace and promptly jabbed the end of a burr through the cloth glove, slicing her finger. Gasping, she looked down at the bloodstain forming on the brown material.

"Ouch!" Andy's sharp cry drew her gaze. The little boy blinked back a tear as he stared at his finger, then pressed his lips together in determination and went back to work.

Sarah could do no less.

She thought her back would break before she got enough cotton in the sack to justify a trip to the wagon. She straightened slowly, calling out to Andy, "Let's go dump our cotton." He trudged down the next row, stopping by her side. His little bag was almost full. "My goodness, look at all the cotton you've picked. You're doing so good."

Andy studied her bag, which was two thirds full. "You got more."

"Yes, but I've got bigger hands. I can pull it out quicker." She rotated her neck and rubbed the small of her back.

"I'm glad I'm not a big people yet. I don't have to bend over."

"You're lucky. Are you tired?"

Andy nodded. "Maybe I'll rest a little while."

"That's a good idea. After you sit a few minutes, why don't you take some water over to Mr. Anderson and his son?" Andy nodded in agreement as they carried their sacks to the wagon. They dumped the cotton in the wagon bed and stared forlornly at the tiny pile.

"Oh, dear. It seemed like a lot in my sack." Sarah dropped the sack over the tailgate of the wagon and walked over to where the covered crock of water sat in the shade of the cotton plants. She scooped out a dipperful of water, giving Andy a drink before she quenched her own thirst. The boy dropped down beside the wagon, leaning against the wheel. Sarah peeled off her sunbonnet, letting the breeze blow across her damp forehead for a few minutes. Although it was only midmorning, the sun had already begun beating down on them.

John and Brad joined them, adding their load of cotton to that in the wagon. They each took a drink and stretched a bit, then headed back to where they left off. Sarah plopped the sunbonnet back on her head. "Andy, why don't you take a dipper of water down to Mr. Anderson and Ed," she said, retying the bonnet strings. "Then you can take a longer rest if you need it."

"Okay." The boy dipped out the water and walked slowly down the furrow so he wouldn't spill it. Sarah went back to work and found that daydreaming about Nate made it a little easier.

At lunchtime they went to the house, riding on the layer of cotton that covered the bottom of the wagon. The men fed and watered the horses, then joined the family for dinner. Sarah ached with fatigue, but she tried to hide it from Tom and Amanda, knowing they would stop her from going back to the field. They rested for about half an hour before returning to work, leaving Andy sound asleep in his mother's lap.

When they quit at sundown, Sarah and the boys could do little more than eat and drop into bed. The wagon wasn't even a quarter full. They repeated the routine on Friday and Saturday, but by Saturday evening, Sarah didn't even bother with supper. She simply staggered into the house and fell across her bed, instantly asleep.

That's where Nate found her when he came courting a few hours later.

CHAPTER
9

"Sarah, wake up." Nate gently squeezed her shoulder. She didn't move. Light from the coal-oil lamp in the front room shone through the open bedroom door, draping the room in a soft, intimate glow. Nate sat quietly for several minutes, watching her. She lay on her back, with a Texas Star quilt drawn up to her waist, the toes of her shoes peeking out from beneath it at the foot of the bed. He noted the lines of weariness around her eyes and the dark smudges beneath them, the exhausted stillness of her slumber.

Her hands lay on top of the quilt, resting at her waist. Her fingers were swollen and cut. He carefully picked up one hand, counting nine cuts on it alone. Two of them looked fresh and needed doctoring.

Being away from her all week had been enlightening and a new lesson in frustration. He had been distracted while working and mournfully lonesome at night. The stars made him think of her eyes when she smiled, and the sunrise reminded him of light glinting off the gold and copper in her hair. The pink of the sunset brought to mind the flush in her cheeks when they danced and her soft blush when they kissed.

Earlier in the week, during the cold, wet nights, he dreamed—both sleeping and awake—of sharing a quilt with her in front of blazing mesquite logs in the fireplace. When the days turned warm and bright, he thought of the sunny laughter that brought a smile to his soul.

He hated to wake her, but Amanda said she hadn't eaten any supper. Selfishly he wanted to hear her voice, wanted her to know he had kept his promise and come to see her. He needed her to know how much he had missed her—and wondered if she had missed him.

"Sugar, you should wake up now." Nate lightly smoothed his fingers across her cheeks, smiling when she wiggled her nose and shifted slightly. "Sarah," he murmured in a singsong voice. "Oh, sweet, pretty Sarah, you need to get up and eat supper." She sighed softly, a tiny smile lighting her face, and murmured his name. Nate leaned down and kissed her cheek, then brushed her lips with his. "Sugar, if you don't wake up, I'm liable to crawl in bed with you, and your brother will be after me with a shotgun." He smiled against her lips, then drew back a bit. "Come to think of it, that's not such a bad idea."

Her eyelids flew open. "Nate, you're safe!" She threw her arms around his neck and raised up, closing the distance between them, kissing him with all the joy and thanksgiving in her heart. He wrapped his arms around her, supporting the back of her head with one hand and her torso with the other, and took all she offered, wanting more. He deepened the kiss, drawing her firmly against his chest, losing himself in her sweetness.

Slowly the sound of Tom talking to Amanda in the other room reached him. He eased upright, bringing her up with him, and reluctantly ended the kiss. Pressing his cheek against hers, he held her close. "Sugar, I was only kiddin' about the shotgun wedding. But if we keep this up, it'll be happenin' directly."

She didn't particularly care. It would certainly solve her problems. In that moment she realized she could never marry anyone but Nate Kendrick. She didn't give a hoot about Wendell's feelings or what her mother thought. All she wanted was to stay in Nate's arms forever. But she didn't want him forced into marriage, nor did she want to do anything that would cause him embarrassment or shame. She slowly dropped her hands back to her sides, leaning away from him when he did the same.

"Guess I don't have to ask if you missed me." His smile held a gleam of pure satisfaction.

"Conceited man." She smiled back. "I guess it's safe to say you thought about me a few times, too."

"More than a few." He touched her cheek in a tender caress. "Just about every minute. I let more stragglers wander off than I did when I was a kid."

Her smile faded. "The boys told me some of the things that could happen when you're driving cattle. I was so worried about you."

Surprise flickered across his face. "There wasn't any need to be afraid." An unexpected warmth blossomed in his heart. It had been a long time since a woman had been concerned for his safety. And that had been his grandmother. Sarah's worrying touched him in a whole new way. "It was all pretty much routine."

"Did you see any mountain lions or wolves?"

"No mountain lions. We spotted a few wolves, but they kept their distance. Didn't give us any trouble." He could only imagine what the boys had told her.

"What about rattlesnakes?"

"Didn't see a one."

"No stampedes?"

"No, ma'am." He smiled. "The herd was too tired from sloggin' through the mud to stampede. We don't have too much problem with that anyway since the pastures are fenced. The cattle know they don't have much room to run. They don't like hittin' barbed wire." He picked up her hand, cradling it gently. "Looks to me like you were in more danger than me. I don't want you going back out in that field, Sarah."

"I have to. They'll never get it picked in time if I don't help."

"I'll hire some men to do it. I don't want you working so hard."

She shook her head. "Tom would never allow it. You know how proud and stubborn he is. He's adamant about not accepting money from a friend."

"What about Jim Anderson? He's helping."

"He owed Tom for cutting his hay back in August. And by the time Jim's cotton is ready, Tom should be back on his feet. They help each other out every year."

"Guess I'll have to find something to barter. I had planned on hiring him to cut new fence posts before he got hurt."

"I'm afraid it would take an awful lot of posts. We must need half a dozen men to pick enough cotton to make that loan payment. The boys and I do our best, but we're dreadfully slow compared to the Andersons."

"Well, I'll think on it a spell. Maybe I can come up with something." He stood, gently gripping her arm. "Now, come eat some supper. Amanda kept it warm for you." He helped her out of bed, a dark frown creasing his brow as she winced and moaned with every movement. "This is dumber than a stump."

"What is?"

"You working so hard. It's not right." *No woman of mine is going to be a slave.*

"I won't be doing it past next week, that's for sure." Sarah stretched her back carefully. "But please don't say anything to Tom. He feels bad enough already."

"Bad enough to let me do something about it?"

Sarah laid a hand on his arm in supplication. "Let it be, Nate. This is difficult for him as it is. I don't mind working hard for my brother. Taking care of each other is all part of being a family."

"I still don't like it."

"You don't have to. Just put up with it." Impulsively she stood on tiptoe and planted a quick kiss on his lips.

"You're not playing fair, woman. You ain't supposed to kiss until the argument is over."

"I thought it was over." She looked up at him with wide, innocent eyes and a tiny smile.

"Brazen hussy." He smiled and tweaked a curl over her ear. "I'll drop it for now."

They joined the others in the kitchen. Nate sat at the table, nibbling on peanuts while she ate. He visited with Tom and, though it was hard, said barely a word about Sarah working in the field. "You going to give your hands tomorrow off?" He smiled at Tom, masking his true feelings.

"Yep. I ain't a slave driver, although it probably looks like it." Tom sighed. "Jim is going to try to round up a few more of the neighbors to help. Trouble is, most of them have payments due, too."

"Would you like to go to church in the morning, Sarah? Or are you too tired?"

"I'd like to go." She was too tired, but she would never admit it. Amanda had told her about the small community church Nate had built on one corner of his ranch. One of the neighbors was a minister as well as a farmer and tended his little human flock most every Sunday. She had hoped to go at least once while she was visiting. Now, given the possibility that she might be making her home in the area, it seemed very important.

"Good. Amanda, would you and the boys like to go?" He glanced at Tom. "I'd offer to take you, but I don't think you'd be very comfortable in the pews."

Tom nodded in agreement. "Little hard to put my leg up there."

"I think I'll let the boys rest this time," said Amanda thoughtfully. "I don't like for them to miss church, but they're so tired, they'd probably sleep through the service anyway. Maybe we could try again next week?"

"Sure thing." Nate visited for a while, then rose to go, stifling a yawn. "I'm pretty frazzled out myself, so I think I'll mosey on home." Sarah had been sitting beside him on the sofa, a good two feet of space between them. He stepped over near her and bent down. Before she realized what he intended, he grazed her lips with a sweet, tender kiss. "Good night, sugar. I'll see you in the morning."

"Good night," croaked Sarah. She glanced at Tom's smile and tried to keep her face from turning scarlet. She failed completely. With a wink and a grin, Nate settled his hat on his head and sauntered out the door.

CHAPTER
10

"You look mighty fine this morning, Miss Sarah," said Nate as he handed her into the buggy after church. Mimicking a not-so-young farmer who had spent more time watching Sarah than he had the preacher, he added with an exaggerated drawl and a twinkle in his eye, "Pretty enough to make a man walk into a porch post."

Sarah giggled as Nate strolled around the back of the buggy to his side and climbed in. "Oh, dear, I thought I was going to burst out laughing right in that poor man's face."

"Now, Sarah, that would have been unfriendly, seeing as how he was trying to court you right under my nose." Nate flicked the reins, and the horse started up, quickly hitting a steady trot.

"I'm not that hard up," she said with a chuckle.

"And I never took that old man to be so dense." He glanced at her, relieved to see she was still smiling. "I'm sorry if I embarrassed you when I put my arm around you."

"I suppose I should have been embarrassed." She paused, remembering the way he had silently proclaimed his territory to the insistent farmer—and everyone else. His action had surprised her and left her inordinately pleased. "But I wasn't," she added softly.

"Good. I just couldn't stand the thought of him tryin' to kiss you with that scruffy old beard."

Sarah burst out laughing. "Oh, dear, that would have been distasteful."

"Scratchy, too."

She laughed again, and since they were well away from the church and the neighbors, she slipped her hand around his arm.

They rode in contented silence until they neared the edge of Tom's farm. Nate glanced at her, his gaze running over the tailored chocolate-brown full skirt and bolero-style jacket with the fashionably wide upper sleeves. It was a very flattering style, particularly with her slim waist.

"He was right, sugar." He cleared his throat, glancing at the feather-bedecked hat perched on top of her head. "You do look mighty fine. Except for that hat."

"What's wrong with my hat?" She released his arm, pinning him with her gaze.

"The brim's too wide." He gave her his most lost-hound-dog look. "I can't get underneath it to kiss you."

"It's no wider than your Stetson. Besides, it's broad daylight." She glanced at the road so he wouldn't see the sparkle in her eye.

"What's that got to do with it?"

"Kissing is for nighttime," she said primly.

"It's for any dad-blamed time I feel like it."

"Oh." She paused, then smiled. "Well, I suppose that's all right as long as it is in private."

"I'll concede to that." He slanted her a lazy, tempting look. "Don't suppose this is private enough."

"Don't suppose so." Sarah simply let herself enjoy their banter and the feelings he stirred in her. "Especially with two cowboys coming to meet us."

"Them? That's just Shorty and Jeb. They don't count." He chuckled at her miffed expression. "Reckon they do." Nate slowed the buggy to a halt as the men drew up beside them and nodded in greeting to Sarah. When they looked at Nate, he smiled. "Afternoon. How was town?"

"Same as always." Jeb grinned. "Left it like we found it."

"Glory be! Those poor city folk won't know what to think."

"Couldn't afford to bust up anything," grumbled Shorty, glaring at Jeb. He nudged his cohort every chance he got about the week's pay he lost when Jeb cut Tom's fence.

"Yep, things are getting expensive these days." Nate kept a straight face with effort. "Well, I'd better get Miss Sarah on home. Take it easy."

"Yes, sir. Nice to see you again, ma'am. We dropped a couple of letters off at Tom's for you. Came in on yesterday's train."

"Thank you." *Wendell's answer.* Lost in thought, Sarah barely noticed when Nate flicked the reins, and the buggy started moving again. *Oh, Lord, please let him be the miser I think he is.*

Nate sensed her tension and decided not to pry. As much as he wanted his ring on her finger instead of that confounded accountant's, he needed to let her work out things with Wendell herself. They finished their journey in silence.

When they arrived back at the farm, Amanda had dinner waiting for them. Sarah helped her put the food on the table while Nate visited with Tom and the boys.

"There are two letters on your dresser," said Amanda quietly as she handed Sarah a bowl of green beans. "One from Wendell and one from your mother."

"I know. We met Jeb and Shorty." Sarah put the serving spoon in the beans and took a deep breath. "I think I'll wait until after Nate leaves before I read them."

Amanda nodded, studying her sister-in-law's pale face. "Did you tell Wendell you wanted to break the engagement?" she asked quietly.

"No. I asked him to send me the money for the train ticket home."

Amanda grinned. "That's the same thing."

"I hope so." Sarah's smile was fleeting. "But even if he surprises me and sends the money, I'm not going to marry him," she whispered to Amanda. "I can't." She glanced at Nate, who was holding little Janey and making faces at the baby, trying to get her to laugh. "Not now."

"Good for you." Amanda caught Sarah's hand and squeezed it. "Everything will work out. And even if your mother gets her dander up, you'll be living way out here." She smiled. "Living so far from Dallas has some definite advantages."

Sarah's eyes widened. "Oh, dear. I never thought about how to provide for Mother."

"That shouldn't be any problem. After all, she has the money your father left her."

Sarah's heart plummeted to her knees. "What money?"

Amanda's hands paused in midair as she reached for the platter of baked ham. She slowly turned back from the stove. "The life insurance. Didn't you know?"

Sarah shook her head as a swell of anger rose from the depths of her soul. For almost ten years, since she was seventeen, she had worked at a job she detested, afraid to quit because she didn't know how she would provide for her mother. She had paid all the bills and done without many things that would have made life much more pleasant because she was a dutiful daughter. She was obligated. *No more.*

"Sarah, are you all right?"

Amanda's worried voice penetrated the anger and seething resentment. Sarah took a deep breath. "Yes. No. But I will be as soon as I calm down. I suspect I'll soon be better than I've ever been."

"I'm sorry. I thought you knew. You've always been so sweet and never complained about staying with your mother. We just assumed you wanted to be there. I'm really sorry we didn't say anything."

"It's not your fault. Do you know how much she has?"

"No. I think he left her about five thousand dollars, but Tom said she has made some good investments, so there should be more." Amanda frowned. "What have y'all been living on?"

"My income. Practically every cent of it went for bills."

"Oh, no! She told us she was helping support you."

"She did help some with her sewing, but that money seldom went for bills. It provided a few extras now and then." *Mostly for Mother.* "But it won't do any good to cry over spilt milk. At least now I have more freedom to make the choices I want." She looked at Nate. Sensing her gaze, he glanced up and raised a questioning brow. She turned away, afraid her face revealed too much. "We'd better get the rest of dinner on the table before everything gets cold."

Nate covertly watched Sarah during the meal. She tried too hard to be cheerful. Something had upset her, but he had no idea what it had been. As far as he knew, she had not read her mail, so it must have been something Amanda said while they were fixing dinner.

He finished his last bite of apple cake and smiled. "That was a fine meal, Amanda. It's good to see you feeling better again." She smiled her thanks. "I hate to leave so soon after dinner, but I need to go into town for a while. Got some business to attend to."

"I'll walk you out." Sarah pushed back her chair and jumped to her feet.

Taken aback, Nate rose more slowly. He glanced at Tom and grinned wryly. "Get the feeling she's in a hurry to get rid of me?"

"Looks like." Tom shrugged as if to say, *Who understands women?*

Sarah looked a little sheepish as she handed Nate his hat. "Sorry. I just need a little time to myself."

"I can understand that. Just don't lock the door the next time I come callin'."

"I won't." Sarah walked with him out to the buggy, standing beside it as he climbed into the seat.

"You all right, darlin'?"

She nodded. "I need to think through some things."

"And read your mail."

"Yes, that, too."

He caught her hand, brought it to his lips, and dropped a lingering, tender kiss on her palm. "I'll be home before dark. I'll be there if you need me." He searched her eyes, then kissed her hand again. "I'll always be there if you need me, Sarah."

"Thank you," she whispered, knowing her love shone in her eyes. "Come by tomorrow. I should have everything worked out by then."

Nate grinned. "Yes, ma'am."

After he drove away, Sarah changed into an everyday work dress and helped Amanda with the dishes. Then she picked up the letters and walked out the door.

"Where you goin', Aunt Sarah?" called Andy. The boys were playing baseball in the open space between the house and the barn. John had a bat. Brad was the pitcher, and Andy was the outfielder. "We could use a catcher."

"Not this time, boys. I'm going for a walk."

"Want some company?"

"Not this time." She smiled at her nephews. "Maybe later."

"Okay." Andy smiled and went back to the game.

Sarah walked out to the pasture and found a big rock to sit on. The wind blew softly, rustling the dry grass, and a mockingbird serenaded her from a distant hill. The sunshine warmed her but not uncomfortably so. She sat quietly for a long while, soaking up the serenity of the countryside, occasionally glancing down at the letters on her lap.

Slowly, peace filled her soul. It no longer mattered how Wendell responded to her request for train fare. In fact, Wendell no longer mattered at all. She loved Nate, and, incredibly, she believed he loved her. She smiled, gazing out across the pasture to where it connected with Nate's ranch. He was not a man her mother could manipulate, so she probably would not like him. Sarah didn't care.

She tore open Wendell's letter, her smile growing broader by the second. Not only did he refuse to send her the money, but he was aghast that she had dared ask for it in the first place. He tersely ordered her to get a job to earn the train fare home. That was all. No indication that he missed her. Not even an affectionate closing, only his name written in an irritated scrawl.

"Ah, Wendell, you came through for me." Sarah laughed in delight.

After a bit she opened her mother's letter, which contained a few surprises. Wendell was seeing someone else, a thirty-year-old widow of more than modest means. Mrs. Dawson was greatly annoyed at his ungentlemanly behavior and irritated beyond endurance because he had been seen on several occasions dining in expensive restaurants with the woman. She indignantly reminded Sarah that he had not once taken her out to eat and ordered her to end the engagement immediately.

Sarah was too relieved to be more than mildly irritated with Wendell. She would simply send back his ring with the advice that he'd better spend a little more on the next one. With a chuckle at the thought, she turned back to the letter and gasped when she read the next line.

A gentleman from their church, who owned a small but profitable men's clothing store, had been calling regularly on her mother during Sarah's absence. He had proposed, and she had accepted. Since they would soon be married, it would not be appropriate for Sarah to return to Dallas expecting to live with her mother. She would just have to stay with Tom and Amanda.

Mrs. Dawson had heard that there was a shortage of females in West Texas, so men weren't too particular. She couldn't expect anyone handsome or rich to be interested in Sarah, of course, but as long as she kept her smile subdued and showed him what a good cook she was, she might find a farmer who would be willing to take her as a wife. She might have to settle for an older man, a widower who needed someone to care for his children. Yes, that would probably be a good match, reasoned Mrs. Dawson, since Sarah was not plagued by an unladylike, passionate nature.

Thinking of Nate—handsome, rich, passionate Nate—Sarah let the letter fall to her lap. "Ah, Mother, if you only knew."

Her peals of joyful laughter could be heard clear back at the house.

CHAPTER
11

"You hire some more pickers?" Jim Anderson looked at Tom with a bemused smile and a sparkle in his eyes.

"No." Tom frowned. "Why?"

"Well, your field is crawling with 'em, and I sure didn't come up with any. I think you'd better ride out with us and see what's going on." He grinned. "I ain't never seen field hands like these."

Tom maneuvered out to the porch on his crutches, then Jim and his son carried him over to the back of their buckboard. Sarah, Amanda, and the children hurried out, climbing in after him. Within a few minutes they neared the field.

"Holy Moses, will you look at that," breathed Andy in awe.

Their mouths hanging open, the whole family stared at the spectacle in the cotton patch. Twenty cowboys, with cotton sacks slung over their shoulders, trudged down the rows in their high-heeled boots, gingerly plucking the cotton from the bolls. With their Western shirts, wide-brimmed Stetsons, and colorful bandannas tied at their throats, they made quite a sight. Generally speaking, each man worked slower than young Andy, but there were so many of them that a large swath of plants had already been picked clean. Nate worked right along with them, in the row nearest the road. The men's horses were tied along the fence. Nate's buggy sat at one end of the line of animals.

"Well, I'll be." Tom grinned, then frowned. "I can't let him do this."

"Yes, you can." Sarah had a sneaky suspicion what he was doing. "Just see what he has to say."

Tom looked at his sister's beaming face and nodded. "All right." Turning back toward the field, he called, "Hey, Kendrick, what in tarnation are you up to?"

Nate straightened with a wince and grinned. "Killin' myself and most of my men." He lifted the cotton sack strap over his head, knocking his hat topsy-turvy. Laying the sack on the ground between the rows, he straightened his hat and walked over to the wagon. "I thought maybe we could work a trade."

Tom smiled. "What kind of trade?"

"Well, you need to get the cotton in and make that mortgage payment. Since you're running out of time, I figured I could provide the workers."

Tom raised an eyebrow. "They're pretty slow. And they don't look real happy about it."

"For the bonus I'm payin' them, they don't have to be happy," said Nate with a grin.

"You know it'll be a while before I can do much work." Tom frowned, but it was feigned this time. "I'm not sure I want to do enough work to pay all these fellers."

"Well, if you go along with my bargain, you won't have to do a lick of work."

Tom chuckled. "Sounds like my kind of deal. Now, I just wonder what I've got to barter that would be worth all that much." He glanced at Sarah with affection.

Nate stepped closer, his expression growing serious, his gaze fixed on his love. "The most important thing in my world." His gaze shifted to Tom. "Sir, I'd like permission to marry your sister."

"You've got my permission and my blessing. But I reckon we ought to see what the lady has to say about it." Both men looked at Sarah.

"The lady says yes." Sarah's face glowed with love as she smiled down at Nate, her eyes glistening with unshed tears of happiness. "A thousand times yes."

"Yee-ha!"

Sarah jumped as Jeb broke loose with a bloodcurdling yell, waving his hat in the air. The other cowboys followed suit. After a noisy thirty-second celebration, they headed for the cotton wagon.

"Quittin' so soon?" Tom scratched the back of his ear and looked at Nate.

"I didn't figure they'd stick to this kind of work too long. They don't know how to act if they ain't sittin' on a horse. So I dragged the banker down to his place of business yesterday afternoon and paid the mortgage payment. You can pay me back when the crop is in. This way you won't have to worry about a deadline." When Tom started to protest, Nate held up his hand, silencing him. "I know you won't take money from a friend, but I figured you might not mind too much since Sarah and I are getting married." His gaze met Sarah's. "After all, taking care of each other is all part of being a family."

"Oh, Nate, I love you." Sarah stood up and leaned over the side of the wagon so he could lift her down. She kissed him before he could set her on the ground.

"Yuck! Do grown-ups really like all that mushy stuff?" Andy looked up at his brother in disgust.

"Yeah, squirt. I guess they do." Brad ruffled Andy's hair.

"I thought you wanted your kisses in private," murmured Nate as he eased away from her.

"I couldn't wait," she whispered, a soft blush staining her cheeks. "But I'll take some in private, too, if you're offering them."

"Yes, ma'am." He grinned wickedly. "That's why I brought the buggy."

"You two go on and get out of here," said Tom gruffly. "I suspect you've got some talkin' to do."

Amanda giggled, and Nate grinned. Sarah's face turned bright red.

"Come on, sugar. I'm gonna show you one of the prettiest places in all of Texas." Draping his arm across her shoulders, Nate guided Sarah toward the buggy.

"Don't forget that's my baby sister you're hangin' on to, Kendrick. Mind your manners."

"Yes, sir." Nate tossed him a wave without looking back. "I love you, Sarah Dawson," he murmured against her ear, squeezing her shoulder gently. He hustled her into the buggy, practically running around to his side of the vehicle.

When they were on their way at a fast trot and with the upraised hood of the buggy shielding them from those in the field, Nate tore off his hat and bent down, kissing her. When they finally broke apart, she smiled up into his eyes.

"Don't you think you'd better watch where we're going?"

"Naw. Brownie knows how to follow the road." He glanced at her hair. "You forgot your sunbonnet."

"I left it at the house. We were in such a hurry to get to the field that I went off without it." She couldn't quit smiling. "But it doesn't look like I need it."

"Nope. I'd just take it off anyway." Nate turned back to the road and slowed the horse, guiding it off into the prairie. "This may get a little bumpy, but it shouldn't be too bad."

Ten minutes later he stopped the buggy at the top of a small hill. "There you are, ma'am. This is the southwest section of the ranch."

Sarah gazed out across the wide vista before her. As far as she could see, thick knee-high golden grass waved in the breeze. A little creek meandered across the stretch of land, bordered here and there with wild plum thickets and weeping willows. Fat, healthy cattle grazed on the extra hay that had been spread out for them, and little calves scampered around in a game of chase. In the background, Lonesome Butte stood majestically. "It's beautiful."

"There's only one place prettier, and that's the view from our front porch." He slid his arm around her, pulling her against his side. She rested her head on his shoulder. "I can't wait to show you the sunrise from your new home."

"I don't want a long engagement."

He grinned from ear to ear. "Neither do I. Maybe we could send a telegram to your mother, and she could come out on the next train."

"I don't think so. She's getting married, too."

"What?" He looked down at her. "When did this come about?"

"Since I've been gone." She briefly explained about her mother's courtship and marriage and also about Wendell seeing another woman.

"That snake. I knew you were too good for him."

"I can't be angry with him." She shifted slightly, looking up at him. Tracing his lips with her finger, she smiled. "After all, I've been seeing another man."

"True."

"Besides, it gives me a wonderful excuse to end the engagement without having to worry about hurting him."

"You aren't hurt by his unfaithfulness?"

"Nope." She grinned. "Terribly relieved. I realized Saturday night that I could never marry him. You're the only man I want to belong to."

Nate lowered his head, kissing her slowly. After several delightful minutes, he kissed the tip of her nose and sighed in contentment.

"Me, too." Sarah snuggled in his arms, looking out across the land that would be her new home. The afternoon of the party they had been guests at his house, and she had liked it immediately. It wasn't fancy, but it was warm and comfortable and had plenty of room for a family. A warm glow filled her heart at the thought of holding Nate's child.

There would be room for her mother and new stepfather to visit on occasion if they wanted to, although Sarah couldn't imagine her mother setting foot on a ranch. She had never once visited Tom's farm. Her anger and bitterness about the way her mother had treated her vanished in the light of her happiness. As she remembered the scene in the field that morning, her joy bubbled up in a giggle.

"What's so funny?"

"I can't wait to see my mother's face when she meets you for the first time."

"Why?"

She turned around and kissed him soundly. "Because she thinks I'll be lucky to catch some old widower, a dirt-poor farmer who needs someone to watch over his kids." She silenced his protest with the tip of her finger. "She'll never expect such a handsome man. And a rich one to boot."

"What are you going to say when you tell her about us gettin' hitched?"

"That we're passionately—no, I don't want to shock her too much. I'll just tell her that we're in love."

He grinned devilishly. "I liked the passionate part. You can tell her that it's the forever kind of love." At her tender smile and nod of agreement, he asked, "But aren't you goin' to tell her what I do? What kind of home you'll have?"

"Got the itch to brag a little?"

"Yep."

"I'm only going to tell her one thing."

"What?" he asked, tilting his head slightly.

She plucked a wisp of cotton from his shirt front and tickled his chin. "That you're the best cotton pickin' cowboy in West Texas."

If you enjoyed this book, take advantage of this special offer. Subscribe now and get a

FREE
Historical
Romance

No Obligation (a $4.50 value)

Each month the editors of True Value select the four *very best* novels from America's leading publishers of romantic fiction. Preview them in your home *Free* for 10 days. With the first four books you receive, we'll send you a FREE book as our introductory gift. No Obligation!

If for any reason you decide not to keep them, just return them and owe nothing. If you like them as much as we think you will, you'll pay just $4.00 each and save at *least* $.50 each off the cover price. (Your savings are *guaranteed* to be at least $2.00 each month.) There is NO postage and handling – or other hidden charges. There are no minimum number of books to buy and you may cancel at any time.

Send in the Coupon Below

To get your FREE historical romance fill out the coupon below and mail it today. As soon as we receive it we'll send you your FREE Book along with your first month's selections.
